D0947420

SWEETEST SORROW

Forbidden Series
Book Two

J.M. DARHOWER

ISBN-10: 1-942206-18-6
ISBN-13: 978-1-942206-18-7

"Parting is such sweet sorrow
That I shall say good night till it be morrow."
Romeo and Juliet, Act 2 Scene 2

PROLOGUE

The air was damp, thick with filth, overpowering with the stench of dirt and mildew. Despite it being summer, coldness had settled between the solid concrete walls, the windowless chamber offering no ventilation.

A basement.

The moment Dante Galante regained consciousness, he sensed he was underground. The dense air invaded his lungs and coated the inside of his tattered chest, making every breath strained, like he was slowly suffocating.

Buried alive.

That was how it felt.

Darkness surrounded him, the kind of darkness that felt like a void, like one wrong move and he might get lost in it, never to be found again.

He blinked and saw nothing.

Blinked again. Nothing still.

How long had he been there? An hour? A day? A week? Maybe more. He'd been tormented mercilessly, beaten until he could no longer stand, strangled before being brought back to life again.

Again and again, they pushed him to the edge, but he'd yet to tip over. They could break his body, but they weren't going to break *him*.

He wouldn't let them.

So they tortured him until he lost consciousness, taunting him all along, waiting for him to crack. *'We'll put you out of your misery,'* they promised. *'All you have to do is ask.'*

Dante said nothing.

He barely made a noise.

He endured it in silence, passing out before waking up to suffer even more.

Pain was nothing to a man who had been burned alive at five years old. Nothing they could do to him would ever surpass the feeling of his body on fire, the sensation of his shirt melting right into his skin, fabric dripping like candle wax, charring him.

Compared to *that*?

This was a piece of fucking cake.

Hours. Days. Weeks. Who knew?

Time passed, and his body grew weaker, but his resolve remained strong. He was going to die. He'd come to accept that. There would be no crying, no begging, and not a stitch of fear. That was what they wanted from him.

He wouldn't give them the satisfaction.

So he lay there, listening to the world above him, a world that wouldn't try to rescue him if he screamed, waiting for them to finish him off. He was deep in the heart of Barsanti territory. He had no friends there.

It happened unexpectedly, the basement door thrusting open, bright light filtering through. Dante winced from the harshness, too drained to move, unable to shield his eyes as someone descended the stairs. He blinked as they approached, trying to make out his surroundings, his gaze meeting his captor's.

Roberto Barsanti.

The man stopped in front of Dante, his shadowy figure blocking out the blinding glare. Fury swirled through Dante, strengthening him. He considered lunging, attacking, making a break for it even though he wouldn't make it far.

He thought about it.

He almost did it.

Until the man spoke.

"Your sister's dead."

Those words, in that impassive voice, stalled Dante's heart for a long beat. *No. No. No.* It couldn't be. He didn't want to believe it. *Couldn't* believe it. Dead? *No fucking way.* Not his sister. Not Genevieve. It was just another form of torture. They'd broken his body but he hadn't caved. They were going to try to break his spirit, and he couldn't let them.

So he just glared at the man, trying to control his strained breathing, hoping like hell the sudden spike of fear he felt didn't show.

He didn't want them to see.

God, no, don't let it be...

"She's dead," Barsanti said again, his vacant stare fixed on the grimy wall before he turned back to Dante. Tears swam in his usually callous eyes. Intense fear swarmed the room, mixed with a sense of devastation, but it wasn't radiating from Dante. No. The man in front of him was cracking, even more than Dante ever had. "Your sister is dead, and my son..." A long pause, so long Dante's mind raced for a way to finish that thought, realizing the truth a fraction of a second before the words left Barsanti's lips. "He's dead, too."

Dante let out a shaky breath, words on the tip of his tongue, the first ones he would utter since they'd snatched him. *Just kill me now.* He swallowed the thought back, resolved to stay strong, but something forced itself from his busted lips, a whisper in a gritty voice. "Fuck you."

In a blink, Barsanti drew back his arm, his fist connecting with Dante's face, pain exploding through his skull.

This is it, he thought, as the blackness took him.

I'm dying alone in the dark.

CHAPTER 1

Primo Galante hadn't driven a car in over sixteen years.

He missed it sometimes... the feel of the wheel beneath his hands, the revving of the engine, his foot pressing on the gas pedal as the car weaved through the city streets, offering the kind of freedom he'd always yearned for.

The freedom to just *go*.

Wherever. Whenever.

Ah, how he loved having that kind of control.

It wasn't the same, watching the world fly by from the backseat of a chauffeured black sedan. You see, the city looks different through thick, tinted windows. Less freeing. No longer the brave eagle soaring through the sky, he'd become a caged animal, shielded behind shatterproof glass, separating him from the rest of the wildlife that swarmed the concrete jungle. Harsh reality had put a leash around his neck, strangling him to the point where mere precaution twisted into irrational panic.

He'd gripped so tightly to his family after the explosion that had killed his Joey that what had been left of them slipped between the fingers of his clenched fists. His wife, dead, her car slamming into an overpass years ago. Dante, presumed dead, his car abandoned in an alley, blood splattered all over the driver's seat. And his daughter, his little girl, his beautiful Genevieve...

Primo couldn't yet bring himself to admit what might've come of her.

But as he stood out on Pier 76 at one o'clock in the morning, his gaze glued to the charred, twisted remains of a blood red Lotus Evora on the back of an NYPD flatbed tow truck tucked inside an open garage, police tape surrounding it as a forensics team scoured it for clues, he couldn't discount the truth.

Genevieve was gone now, too.

Maybe dead, maybe not, but regardless, he'd lost her.

There was no coming back from what happened.

The electronic gate to the right of Primo buzzed before shifting open. He tore his eyes from the crushed metal mess that had belonged to the Barsanti boy, instead turning toward the impound lot. He was there for one reason and one reason alone, and dwelling wouldn't do anybody any good.

Night clung to everything around him, casting shadows along the rows of seized vehicles. Primo shoved his hands in the pockets of his black slacks as he took a deep breath to conceal his nerves. He kept his chin up, his shoulders squared as a uniformed officer approached.

"Mr. Galante, thanks for coming out." The officer offered his hand. Primo's gaze darted to it before he looked the man in the eyes again, making no move to shake it. Not out of some sort of code of conduct, keeping him from being respectful to law enforcement.

His palms were sweaty.

He didn't want anyone to know.

"I appreciate the call," Primo said. "And the discretion."

"Of course," the officer said, dropping his hand. "Follow me."

They strode through the gated lot, to where the black BMW was parked in the back, a sunshine-yellow tassel hanging from the rearview mirror. Genevieve had graduated high school mere months ago.

Still so damn young.

A life wasted, and why?

Primo approached his daughter's car and glanced through the windows, his eyes skimming along the leather seats. Although it was dark, his vision obscured, the inside appeared pristine with not a hint of blood to be found. He stepped back, surveying the outside of the car. Besides a dent on the front end, some of the paint swiped off, it seemed unharmed.

"Minor fender bender," the officer said. "I ran the tag at the scene and it came back to you, so I figured you'd want to take care of it."

Primo nodded. "Off the record?"

"Always," the officer said. "Wasn't hard slipping it in under the

11

radar. Everyone has been preoccupied with what happened in Little Italy tonight."

Primo's eyes drifted past his daughter's car, again seeking out the hunk of twisted metal tucked into the garage. "I bet."

"You wouldn't know anything about that, would you?"

"What makes you think I would?"

"Call it a hunch."

Silence permeated the air as the men stared at each other. Yeah, Primo knew all about it. He'd felt the ground quake beneath his shoes. He *still* felt the devastation, his world imploding as the car exploded, because it had taken with it more than just a good-for-nothing Barsanti boy.

It had taken something precious to him.

Hope.

After a moment, Primo lowered his head, his shoulders hunching just a bit. He didn't humor the officer with a response.

"Do you have the keys?" he asked, staring out through the shadowy lot, his gaze sweeping along the cloudy sky, a gray haze blocking the moon, like thick smoke after a fire is doused.

"Right here." The officer pulled them out of his pocket, the keys jingling together in his hand. "I can get one of the tow guys to drop it off at your place."

Primo considered that for a second—a brief second, where he almost agreed. Instead, he turned to the man and shook his head. "That won't be necessary. I can get it there myself."

The man's eyes widened. "You?"

"Don't look so shocked," Primo said, stepping around the car, pulling his sweaty hand from his pocket and holding it out. "I remember how to drive."

The officer dropped the keys into his palm, not saying a word as Primo unlocked the driver's side door. The man took a step back, watching with skepticism, as Primo climbed in behind the wheel. He would've been offended by the officer's reaction, by the blatant disrespect doubting him portrayed, but his nerves were too frazzled to feel anything beyond his unease. He took a moment to adjust everything, to try to get comfortable in the cramped front seat, but it was useless. There was nothing comforting about what he was doing.

"Do you even have a driver's license anymore?" the officer asked.

"Does it matter?" Primo quipped, because no, he didn't. His expired years before and he'd never found reason to renew it. "What are you going to do, ticket me?"

"No, I'm just worried—"

"Worry about yourself," Primo said. "That's who you ought to be worrying about, since you seem to want to stick your nose in my business and ask questions you ought not be asking."

The officer held up his hands defensively as he took a step back. "You have a good night, Mr. Galante."

A good night? *Impossible.*

Those nights were all behind him. They were memories, ones he would never relive, because everything good had disappeared, leaving him there... behind the wheel for the first time in sixteen years. A long chunk of time to most, but it had been the blink of an eye to him. The freeing feeling was gone, though. No more soaring. Somebody had clipped his wings. *Time for a crash landing.*

Primo shut the door, clutching the keys so hard in his fist the grooves dug into his damp skin, leaving marks. He took five seconds to pull himself together before he stuck the key in the ignition.

Another five seconds before he had the courage to turn the damn thing.

There was a click, and Primo held his breath, his stomach churning and chest aching. Suddenly, he was almost two decades younger, standing in that pizzeria parking lot, his eyes glued to his eldest son through the windows of his car. His heart battered his rib cage. He knew right then. He *knew.* Five more seconds and his son would disappear.

He was sick and tired of his children *disappearing.*

Primo always savored those seconds, but he couldn't do it anymore. He had to stop dwelling. He turned the key the rest of the way and the engine awoke. No explosion. No chaos. Just him behind the wheel again—only so much older now.

He put the car in 'drive' and pulled through the lot, toward the open gate. As he passed the mangled sports car, he averted his gaze.

Traffic was light at one in the morning. For that, Primo was grateful, because driving a car was nothing like riding a bike. Back when he'd driven, cars had been monsters made of rigid metal, not these light fiberglass masses stacked with electronics. So many lights and beeps coming from the dashboard. Back in his day, a dashboard was only good for propping up your feet.

It took him almost forty-five minutes to make it home. He pulled the BMW into the driveway, hesitating before he cut the engine.

Silence surrounded him.

Pulling the key from the ignition, he stepped out of the car. Lights shone from the house, hastily left on when he ran out of the place hours earlier.

Before he made his way inside, noise rang out behind him in the street, squealing tires shattering the peace. His eyes cut that way, a black sedan approaching.

Primo was unarmed and alone. For the first time in years, he'd allowed himself to be vulnerable. *Never again.* The car skidded to a stop in front of his property, the back passenger door flinging open. He waited for the ambush. He waited for the bullets. He waited for gunfire to light up the darkness, but instead, the car sped off.

Something flew out of the backseat, slamming the asphalt hard before rolling, the wheels of the barreling car almost running over it. Primo crept closer, curiosity fueling him, as his gaze trailed along the shadowy mass they had discarded.

Filthy bare feet.

Ripped, bloody clothing.

Black-and-blue skin.

Before the car had even vanished, recognition struck Primo.

Dante.

* * *

Scorching, dry air blew through the open windows, rustling the crinkled map on Genna's lap. She clutched both sides of it, trying to keep it in place, as she tucked her foot beneath her, relaxing on the long, dirty bench of the old blue Chevy truck. The engine roared, the truck shuddering whenever Matty pressed harder on the gas pedal.

Genna let out a breath, blowing some tendrils of dark hair that fell from her sloppy bun into her flushed face. "It's hot as balls, Matty."

He laughed, the sound barely registering above the rumble of the engine. "Hot as *balls*?"

"Yes. Balls."

"Well, you know, balls aren't actually *that* hot."

Genna turned her focus from the outdated map to Matty. He glistened with sweat, beads of it running down his tanned face. Long gone were the sweaters and button-downs, abandoned for a plain white undershirt. The temperature outside had to be well above a hundred that late summer day. *August.* "What?"

"They aren't that hot," he said again, casting her a sideways look. "They're a few degrees cooler than the rest of the body, anyway. That's why they hang down like they do and why they move, you know… they're self-regulating."

Was he seriously talking to her about the intricacies of testicles?

The fucking swinging *testes*?

"Ugh, thanks for the science lesson." Genna grimaced. Functional? Absolutely. But they were far from attractive. "Doesn't negate the fact that I feel like a sweaty ball sac over here."

"Well, that's what happens when you head south," he said. "It gets hotter."

Genna was certain there was a sexual innuendo in there somewhere, but she was too frustrated to play along.

"No, it's what happens when you steal a truck made in the 1840s," she countered. "Jesus Christ, was air conditioning even invented back then? No wonder Cleopatra hired people to fan her."

Matty laughed again, this time louder, more genuine. "Genna, there's so much wrong with what you just said that I don't even know where to start."

She rolled her eyes, turning back to the map. "You're frying my brain in this furnace-on-wheels."

Matty let go of the steering wheel with his right hand and reached over, brushing his knuckles along her warm cheek. As annoyed as she was, as *hot* as she was, his light touch still managed to make her shiver. "We'll stop soon and get a room for the night."

"You promise?"

"Yes."

"Somewhere with air conditioning?"

"Are there places without it?"

15

Genna glanced out the window, seeing nothing but endless wilderness as they weaved through the dense mountains of Virginia. She felt like she had slipped into an alternate universe where civilization no longer existed. Genna was a city girl, through and through, and this? Well, this was a nightmare. "Considering the fact that it feels like we're filming *Wrong Turn 6* right now? I'm gonna have to say yes."

They drove for a little over an hour longer, until they reached the North Carolina border, and found a motel just outside the city of Greensboro. Genna stepped into the small room and threw herself down on the bed. Lying back, she spread her arms out and kicked her shoes off as Matty tinkered with the air conditioner and cranked it the whole way up.

Cold air blasted out as it rattled as loud as the damn truck, cooling Genna's sticky skin. From the corner of her eye, she watched Matty pull off his shirt and toss it to the floor before unbuttoning his jeans. "I'm taking a shower, if you want to join me."

"No, it's okay," she muttered, fighting back the voice in her mind chastising her. *What the fuck is wrong with you? Look at him! Go forth, and get soapy wet with that motherfucker!* "I'm just gonna lay here and cool off and you know... probably never move again."

Matty finished stripping, leaving a trail of clothes leading to the bathroom. Moments later, the soothing sound of rushing water met Genna's ears, nearly lulling her to sleep. *No rest for the wicked.* Sighing, she pushed herself up and rubbed her tired eyes.

It hadn't even been a full day yet. The alarm clock on the nightstand beside the bed read a quarter till two in the afternoon. Almost seventeen hours had passed since she stood on the street corner in the darkness and watched her life incinerate. She still felt the explosion in the tension in her muscles, a vibration in her bones as her body trembled. A flurry of emotions battled for control—lingering sadness, sheer terror, and a sense of uneasiness—twisting her insides and leaving her a tangled mess.

She felt like she didn't know herself anymore, much less the guy naked in the bathroom. For all intents and purposes, Genevieve Galante and Matteo Barsanti had died in Little Italy... so who were *they*?

Her gaze turned to the bathroom door as it stood cracked open.

16

Matty was all she had now, the only thing keeping her grounded, keeping her feet planted on the shaky ground. Well, him and... little him.

Genna's hands drifted to her stomach.

Or her. Whatever.

It was much too soon to tell, given the baby resembled a lima bean at that point, but the doctor had assured them everything seemed fine. They'd stopped at a small hospital in New Jersey, where Matty had assured her they'd be safe, but Genna wasn't a fool to think *anywhere* was beyond her father's reach. They'd lingered in the area just long enough to catch their breath, long enough for Matty to get his hands on a couple burner phones for them to use in case of an emergency.

Genna sighed, grabbing the map she'd found in the glove box of the stolen truck—or *borrowed* truck, as Matty had called it. *We'll leave it somewhere for them to find, just as soon as we're out of the area.* She spread the map out in front of her, smoothing out the creases as her fingers scanned the area around their current location.

The water in the bathroom shut off, the only noise the drone of the air conditioner. Matty strode back out, a white towel loosely wrapped around his slim waist. Heat rushed through Genna. Her face flushed as she impulsively scanned his chest, her gaze lingering along the trail of hair running down his toned stomach. She averted her eyes, so not to be caught gawking, but his amused chuckle told her he'd noticed the attention.

"Any luck?" he asked, plopping down on the bed beside her without bothering to get dressed. Genna fought to keep her eyes to herself, but all of that glorious bare skin was much too tempting to ignore.

"Any luck with what?" she mumbled.

"With finding somewhere to go."

"Oh, no." *Focus on the map, Genna, not the man.* "Not yet."

"You've got the entire country in front of you," Matty said. "We can go anywhere you want. Just take your pick."

Easier said than done. She scanned the area, tracing her fingertips along the highways. "It's just... I can see it all, and I know what it is, but that doesn't tell me anything about what it's like. All these red and blue roads, weaving together, going here and there... they're kind of like veins, you know? You can tell me where they go and what they do, but it says nothing about the person they make up." She groaned before he even had a chance to respond. "That probably makes no fucking sense."

"It makes perfect sense," he replied, reaching over and grasping her hand to still it. "Kind of profound, actually. Must not have fried your brain, after all."

"Damn near."

"And I get it. It's not easy deciding the future."

"So how do I choose? How do I *know*?"

He gazed at her. "How did you know about me?"

"I didn't," she said. "I still don't. I don't *know* anything. But it was a feeling I got. You know, it... *you*... well, it just felt right."

"Then that's how you choose," he said. "We settle down when something feels right."

"What if it never does?"

"It will," he assured her. "Besides, silver linings, Genna. If we don't know where we're going, we'll never really be lost, right? Wherever we end up will be where we're supposed to be."

He made it sound so simple. Genna glanced back down at the map, reading the neighboring city names. "You know there's a town called Climax near here?"

"There's also a High Point."

"No shit?"

"Saw a sign for it earlier. Climax and High Point."

"Huh." She scanned the area again, finding it. "That's kind of redundant, don't you think?"

"Redundant, maybe, but there's nothing wrong with that," he said, running his hand up her inner thigh. "You can never have too many, well, you know..."

She shivered as his fingers grazed her through her jeans. Clenching her thighs closed, she smacked his hand away. "Ugh, not now."

"Why? Need to brush your teeth?"

"As a matter of fact, yes."

"Don't worry about it," he said. "I just won't kiss you."

"Yeah, because *that's* romantic. Besides, I'm all dirty and sweaty and yucky."

"So?" He leaned over to kiss her neck. "I'm just gonna get you sticky, anyway."

Laughing, Genna pushed him away. "How can you even think about sex right now?"

"I'm a guy," he said, shrugging as he stood up. "It controls me more than I control it."

Matty dropped his towel, his naked body emphasizing his point. He was *hard*. Before Genna could say anything, her cheeks flushing at his obvious arousal, Matty snatched up his discarded filthy clothes and put them back on.

She watched him incredulously. "What are you doing?"

"Getting dressed."

"Those clothes are disgusting."

"Yeah, but they're all I have."

"So?"

"So I can't go out naked, Genna."

"What? Why?"

He laughed. "Pretty sure that would warrant an indecent exposure charge."

"No, I mean why are you going out?"

"Maslow's hierarchy of needs." He glanced at her as if that explanation should clear up her confusion. "We have to fulfill the bottom before we can work our way toward the top."

"Okay, Mr. Ivy League... drop the Confucius and put it in *my* terms."

Matty pressed his palms against the bed as he leaned over to kiss her, not at all bothered when she kept her lips clamped shut. She *did* need to brush her teeth, after all. "We need things from the store."

Ah. "Why didn't you just say that?"

"I did."

She stared him in the eyes, drinking in the devotion shining out at her. Past it, though, she sensed the sadness. He was putting on a brave front, but she knew him well enough to see he was torn up inside and barely holding it together. Something had clawed its way under his skin, piercing his strong armor.

Climbing to her feet, Genna sighed. "Let's go."

"Stay here." Matty held his hand out to stop her when she started toward the door. "It's hot, and you should just relax. I'll grab whatever you need."

"Really?"

"Yes."

"But I—"

"Just tell me what to get, Genna."

"Munchies," she said. "Cheetos, and cookies, and maybe some beef jerky."

"Okay."

"Oh! And some chocolate! A Kit-Kat! No, wait, a Snickers bar! Or better yet, one of those ice cream Snickers bars. Hell, *two* of them. One for now, one for later." She paused. "Oh, Now & Laters. You should grab some of those, too."

He chuckled. "Candy. Got it."

"And some Coke."

"The soda?"

"No, Matty, the fucking powder." She rolled her eyes. "Of course the soda."

"Should you have that? You know, since you're pregnant? It's got caffeine in it."

"Are you really going to deny me? *Me*, the mother of your child?"

She'd been teasing him, but her words sparked something in his expression—something she too felt churning in her gut. It was a twisting, a slap of sobering reality. She was the *mother of his child*.

Holy Hell.

"Of course not," he said. "What else?"

She rambled on and on, blurting out everything she thought of, from clothes to toiletries. He balked at a few of her requests, like razors and underwear, his slight discomfort amusing Genna.

"I'll probably need some other girly things," she said, quirking an eyebrow. "So maybe I should just, you know… go along."

Matty pulled the truck key from his pocket as he motioned toward the door. "Come on, let's go to the store."

Smiling as he conceded, Genna followed him, the heat blasting her as soon as she stepped outside. *Ugh, I wanted to go why?* Matty started the truck, hesitation in his movements when he stuck the key in the ignition. The ancient vehicle rumbled, lurching when he put it in gear and pulled away from the motel. He drove onto the highway, finding a department store not too far away.

Once inside, Matty grabbed a cart, and Genna strolled beside him through the brightly lit store.

"We do have money, right?" she asked, grabbing a bag of chips and tossing it in the cart. "We're not shoplifting this shit, right?"

"Right." He eyed her peculiarly. "Why are you asking?"

"Well, for one, because it's way too hot outside to be running from *theft prevention*," she pointed out. "And because we haven't really talked about things like money. I know I don't have any. I don't have anything, except maybe my charm at this point, so I wasn't sure..."

Matty stopped the cart in the middle of an aisle. "I told you if you stayed with me that I'd take care of you, and I meant that, so don't worry about things. Let *me* worry. You just keep being *you*."

"I wanna help, though. I wanna do my part."

"You already are," he said, pulling her to him, his hand pressing against her stomach. "You're doing your part, Genna."

"Don't try that sexist shit out on me," she said, poking him in the chest. "I won't be one of those barefoot, pregnant, and in the kitchen kind of women."

"Thank God for that," he said, his expression serious. "The kitchen is the *last* place you ought to be hanging out in."

Genna rolled her eyes, pushing away from him, and strolled down the aisle. Nothing else was said about it as they went through the rest of the store, covering every base, the cart close to overflowing. When they reached the register, Matty tossed everything up on the conveyer belt as Genna grabbed a soda from the small, refrigerated case. She unscrewed the cap, sipping on the Coke and watching their bill mount.

Matty glanced at her, raising his eyebrows. "Your soda."

She held it out toward him. "You want some?"

"I want to pay for it."

"Oh."

She let the cashier scan it before taking another sip. Matty paid their total with a thick stack of cash and led her from the store, to the truck baking in the blistering sun out in the parking lot. Genna tried to help with the bags but Matty waved her away.

Sighing, Genna climbed into the cab of the truck and kicked off her shoes, propping her feet up on the cracked dashboard. The heat made breathing painful, the air hazy, her clothes sticking to her skin. After loading the bags onto the rusty truck bed, Matty climbed in beside her.

The engine rumbled when he started it, the truck violently shaking before shutting right off. He had to turn the key three times to get it to stay cranked.

"I don't think this truck is going to last very long," she warned.

"It'll be fine," he said, a hint of aggravation in his tone as he raised his voice. "Just stop worrying."

Genna stayed quiet as they drove back to the motel. She didn't offer to help then, knowing he would refuse her again. Instead, she went straight to the bathroom and tore off her grubby clothes before climbing into the shower. The icy cold spray stung her skin, making her shiver as it pelted her full-blast. *No hot water. Awesome.*

Closing her eyes, Genna leaned back against the shower wall and slid down into the tub. She bent her legs, wrapping her arms around them, as she rested her cheek against her knee. Tears stung her eyes, streaming down her cheeks, the lump in her throat making it hard to breathe.

Genna's entire world had been turned around and she didn't know which way was up anymore. Where was she going? What was she doing? She had left it all behind, everything she had ever known gone, and there was no going back. Her life, gone forever, leaving her a semblance of a person she only vaguely recognized.

And that terrified her.

The swell of emotion overwhelmed her, swallowing her in darkness, as she sat in the tub and sobbed. She got so lost in the moment that she didn't hear the door open, didn't hear the heavy footsteps through the bathroom.

The shower curtain yanking open startled her. Alarmed, she sat up with her back straight, her eyes meeting Matty's as she shivered. He gazed down at her, the vibrant blue shadowed by exhaustion. Genna hoped the water washed away evidence of her tears but his sorrowful sigh and the deepening of his frown suggested otherwise.

Reaching over, Matty turned off the water and grabbed a white threadbare towel. Wordlessly, he wrapped it around her as he helped her to her feet. He pulled her into his arms and carried her back into the room, laying her down in the bed.

Matty held her as her tears came out full-force again. She cried herself way past exhausted, falling into a deep, torturous sleep, her mind refusing to shut down even though her body had long ago threw in the towel on consciousness.

Images flashed in her mind, brutal memories pelting her, ripping her right back to that moment, back to the city. Blood red paint glistened under the streetlight, sparkling like a stunning ruby. The neighborhood was still—*too* still, in fact. It was as if someone had pressed pause on the universe.

Unnatural.

Genna stood on the corner in Little Italy, her heart beating so hard she felt it in her throat. The thumping echoed in her ears in harmony with the footsteps along the pavement behind her. Slowly, Genna turned, her breath catching.

Matty.

He swaggered past, brushing against her, his cologne swarming her like a cloud. Closing her eyes, she breathed him in. Something about his scent relaxed her, a subtle spicy aphrodisiac that was uniquely him. It was *home.*

When Genna reopened her eyes, she stared at his back, watching him walk away. It was like he hadn't even seen her standing there, waiting. He swung his car keys around a finger, the sight making the hair on her arms prickle from alarm. Something was wrong... so very wrong. What was happening? Where was he going?

She opened her mouth to call his name but no sound came out. Matty continued on, unlocking the driver's side door of the Lotus with his key.

No. This wasn't right. What was he doing?

Genna tried to go after him, to warn him, to *stop* him, but it was as if a wall stood in front of her, blocking her, locking her in place.

An invisible boundary separating them.

Matty climbed in the car and shut the door. As if in slow motion, Genna stared through the back window, watching his shadowy figure as he stuck the key in the ignition. Frantically shaking her head, she screamed until her throat felt raw, her lungs scorching, but the neighborhood remained deathly silent, abnormally still.

One second... two seconds... three seconds passed, counted by the beats of her frenzied heart, as Matty turned the key. Silence reigned for what felt like an eternity.

In the blink of an eye, it was all gone.

BOOM

Gasping, trying to catch her breath, Genna sat straight up, blinking rapidly to adjust to the darkness. *No. No. No.* Her hands pawed at the bed, feeling only sheets.

No warmth. No body. No Matty.

"Matty?" she yelled, panicked, as she climbed out of the bed.

The door to the motel room opened, a burst of warm air rushing through. Matty stepped inside, clutching a cell phone.

Matty.

Genna ran right at him, leaping up, jumping into his arms. Legs wrapping around his waist, she buried her face into his neck, trying to ward off tears as her body shook.

"What's the matter, baby?" he asked, kicking the door closed behind him before carrying her over to the bed. "What's wrong?"

"I woke up and you were gone. I thought... I mean..."

Matty dropped his phone down onto the mattress as he hugged her, rubbing her back. "Reception in here was shit so I stepped outside, trying to get a better signal."

"Who were you calling?"

"A friend," he said. "The one who helped us with everything. I was seeing if he knew of anywhere safe, you know... if he knew a place where we could settle for a while, get us out of these motels."

"Did he?"

"He's going to get back to me."

She wanted to ask more but the words wouldn't form as he pulled her back into the bed, holding her.

"I'm here," he whispered, kissing the top of her head. "I'm not going anywhere. I *promise.*"

CHAPTER 2

"Did you hear? Can you *believe* it? They said he's up in surgery right now."

"Is he going to make it?"

"Maybe... who knows? Does it even matter? I just can't believe the guy's not dead yet."

"Oh my God, you're *so* bad!"

Gabriella Russo glanced up from where she sat at the information desk in the Presbyterian Surgical ICU, glaring daggers at the back of the pair of nurses: Cindy Lou Who and her spiteful old friend, the Grinch. Cindy's blonde hair was French braided into pigtails, while the Grinch wore hers incredibly short, a sandy-colored mop balanced on top of her head. Both wore bright blue scrubs, the usual around there... a fact that Cindy often whined about. *Why can't we wear patterns? I've got these kitty-cat scrubs I'm dying to show off!*

Oblivious to the attention, the nurses continued with their gossip as Cindy giggled.

She *giggled.*

"I'm just being honest. Who cares if he lives? They're going to send him over here to us, and for what? He's just going to take up a bed. And I don't care what they say... *I'm* not taking care of him. I want nothing to do with that. I'm not busting my ass saving his life when we're all probably better off if the guy dies, anyway."

"I feel the same way."

Gabriella cleared her throat, loud enough to make both nurses look at her. Cindy was thirty, while the Grinch—real name Geraldine—had to be pushing fifty. Both had seniority over Gabriella, at barely twenty-six, but neither seemed to have a lick of *compassion.*

Cindy, at least, had the sense to appear ashamed at being overheard, but the Grinch just rolled her eyes, like Gabriella's intrusion was a mere annoyance to her.

Before Gabriella could say anything, chaos erupted in the ICU, security rushing onto the floor, escorting a tall, thick-built man wearing a black suit. Gabriella recognized him, shock running through her.

Primo Galante.

Oh my God. It can't be.

Security showed him to the waiting lounge across from the information desk, trailing him. Whether they did it for his protection or everyone else's safety, Gabriella wasn't quite sure.

Probably a bit of both.

"I've got other things to take care of," the Grinch said, keeping her head down as she scurried away. Cindy, on the other hand, couldn't stop staring as the man feverishly paced. It wasn't until the elevator doors opened again, the patient wheeled in, that Cindy sprinted from the hallway, ducking out of sight. *Friggin scaredy-cat.*

At once, Primo was back out in the hallway, barking orders at everyone. *Do this. Do that. Don't just stand there. Do something!* Security intervened, to calm him, but the man was determined... Gabriella had to give him that.

"Nurse?" the attending on duty shouted. *Dr. Michael Crabtree.* He was a frigid little man, one Gabriella was never particularly fond of working with, but he was at least good at what he did. The doctor looked around, his face scrunching from annoyance. "Where did the nurse go?"

Gabriella sighed. The Grinch was on point. She'd been assigned that room and whatever patient ended up in it. But it was obvious from the disappearing act that she hadn't been kidding about not treating him.

"I can take this one," Gabriella said before the charge nurse had to intervene and go hunt down the Grinch, who clearly wouldn't be any help to the patient. "I'll switch rooms with Gr—uh, Nurse Geraldine. Not a problem."

Monica Burns, the charge nurse, eyed her warily before shrugging it off and switching their rooms on the board, giving Gabriella the patient.

"What is she, a *teenager*?" Primo bellowed, glaring at her as she approached. "I want a *real* nurse, not some girl playing dress up!"

Gabriella let him have that one. She *did* look young.

"Nurse Russo is exceptional at her job," Crabtree said, shooting her a look that said he might not believe his own words. There was panic in his eyes, something that wasn't good coming from the guy in charge. "She's fully capable of looking after Mr. Galante, as capable as every other nurse on staff."

"Maybe you're *all* incompetent!"

Gabriella ignored their back-and-forth, sliding past the men into the room. It cleared out as staff got the patient hooked up to all of the machines. The ICU worked like an assembly line in a factory. Everyone had a specific job and they did it efficiently. *In, out, away.* Until a problem arose, it mostly all fell on the nurse. Her job was to make sure he stayed alive. To make sure his heart kept beating. To make sure he kept *breathing*.

No big deal, right?

"If you mess up, so help me God, you're going to regret it," Primo growled. "Every single one of you will pay. I'll see to it. I'll have your jobs. I'll have your *lives*!"

Worried glances were exchanged between some of the staff as security again stepped in, attempting to calm the man down. Gabriella tried to shut it all out, focusing her attention on the patient. She paused when she looked down at him, her stomach clenching at the sight of his battered body.

Dante Galante.

Crabtree joined them, clutching a chart, the glass door to the small room sliding closed behind the doctor as Primo grudgingly stayed out in the hall.

Right away, they went through his diagnosis, listing a host of problems, a laundry list of wounds that had been inflicted. Gabriella listened, taking it all in as her eyes stayed glued to his face.

What in the world happened to him?

He was intubated, not breathing on his own, the whole gauntlet of intervention done. While alive, yes, she wasn't sure he would stay that way. Death knocked on his door, begging to be let in, and judging from the look of him, it wouldn't be hard for Death to pull off some *breaking & entering*, robbing him of his last breath.

He lay there, not moving, his eyes closed. For someone with such a big reputation, she thought, he sure seemed... *small.*

"I want to be clear here that complications are *not* allowed," Crabtree said. "I'd rather we do too much than not enough. So we're going to monitor him closely and get him the hell out of here as soon as possible. Understand?"

A murmur of agreement flowed through the room.

Once Dante was stable, the room cleared out, all except for Gabriella and the doctor. She continued to stare down at him, not moving, watching as a tear slid from the corner of his eye, running down the side of his face, the pillow beneath his head absorbing all evidence of it.

"Are you okay, Nurse Russo?" Crabtree asked. "I need you on the same page with us here."

"I'm fine," she said quietly. "He's, uh... crying."

Crabtree scribbled something in the chart before closing it, not even looking at the patient. "It's a natural defense. All it means are his tear ducts are working. A miracle, really, considering everything else on him seems to be broken. Someone worked him over good."

Good. That word felt so wrong in that context.

There was nothing good about the condition he was in.

"I know you were taking your break when you got pulled into this, so go ahead and grab a few minutes to yourself," Crabtree suggested. "Catch your breath."

"Yes, sir."

"Oh, and the patient's father is his decision-maker, so make sure you introduce yourself properly, you know, since everything will have to flow through him."

Gabriella scowled. Being a critical care nurse meant that a good chunk of her job was spent dealing with families. No matter how distraught, Gabriella had to help them see what was best for the patient. Just as she occasionally offered hope, more often than not, she was in the business of crushing dreams with realism. Often people clung to every miniscule sign of life, ignoring the blatant signs of an inevitable death, causing more suffering than what would've been natural.

But how do you explain that to someone without sounding like the worst person in the world?

Stepping out of the room, she hesitated, coming face to face with Primo. "Mr. Galante, I'm—"

"I don't care." His voice was sharp. "Who you are means nothing to me. Just... *fix him*."

Despite the harshness of his tone, Gabriella sensed the fear in those words.

"We'll do everything we can," she said. "They're going to be running some tests soon, but you're welcome to visit with him for a few minutes, if you'd like."

Primo looked past her, into the room. "I would."

"And I know he's unconscious, and he looks like he's sleeping, but it's widely believed that people in his condition are capable of hearing what everyone is saying. Talking to him may help him wake up sooner."

Primo simply nodded before stepping into the room, passing the doctor on his way out. Gabriella watched as Primo stalled at the end of the bed, just staring at his son in silence.

He didn't utter a single word.

Sighing, Gabriella walked away, giving the man some privacy. She headed to the elevator, taking it down to the first floor, and steered toward the cafeteria, desperate for some coffee. *Strong* coffee. The blackest, bitterest coffee ever produced, with obscene amounts of caffeine in it, the kind with enough of a jolt to jumpstart a racecar.

Still a few hours left in her shift before she could even think of going home.

"Oh my God, it's *so* crazy, right?" a young girl whisper-shouted into her cell phone, sitting alone at a small table inside the little on-site coffee shop. She wore a set of scrubs, a nursing assistant badge clipped to her. "Cindy that works up there texted me a minute ago and said he is *all* fucked up."

Gabriella shook her head before ordering a large coffee. *Unfriggin-believable*. The folks at the hospital would figure out how to cure cancer before they ever came up with a solution to eradicate the infectious gossip.

"It just makes me wonder, you know, about the other one," the girl continued, her voice no quieter. "You know, that thing that happened last night? The explosion? I heard that guy was one of

29

them, too. I mean, maybe not *as* bad." She paused, laughing. "Don't you think it's all kind of... I don't know... *exciting?*"

Walking by the table, Gabriella snatched the girl's phone right out of her hand, pressing the button on the screen to hang it up. She dropped the phone back down in front of her, letting it hit the table with a thud.

"Hey!" the girl exclaimed. "What's your *damage,* lady?"

"They're people," Gabriella said, her voice shaking as she tried to hold it together. "Real people, with real lives, and people who love them. You want to talk about someone's death? Want some misfortune to find exciting? Go watch *Grey's Anatomy.*"

* * *

Thick black smoke rolled out from beneath the hood of the truck, tainting the early morning sky. The stench singed Matty's nose, making him grimace when he inhaled. The sun was just starting to peek up over the horizon and already the day was off to a terrible start.

"So, uh... can I start worrying now or what?"

Matty cut his eyes at Genna as he turned the truck key for probably the tenth time, listening as the starter stuttered, but the engine refused to come to life. Cursing, he gave up and slammed his hands against the steering wheel.

Worry?

Yeah, it was time to start worrying.

Exasperated, he leaned back in the seat and stared through the grubby windshield at the long stretch of highway in front of them. Genna's gaze burned through him as perspiration rolled down the side of his face.

Matty was sweating, literally *and* figuratively.

He was so in over his head he was surprised he could still even breathe. It felt like the world was on his shoulders, pressing upon his chest, trying to suffocate him. It was a burden he willingly took on, a weight he was happy to carry if it meant Genna had less to worry about, but he could only do so much. He only *knew* so much. He had the best intentions, but he was nothing more than a guy—a guy with flaws and limitations, and little more than a fucking broken down truck.

"I don't know what to do," he admitted, offering the quiet concession as smoke surrounded them like an ominous black cloud.

"Well," Genna said, "lucky for you, I *do*."

Before he could ask what, Genna hopped out of the truck, slamming the door behind her. Matty climbed out and walked around to the back when she started that direction.

"There were some houses about a quarter of a mile back," she said, digging through the things they'd bought at the store. "They were right off the highway."

"You think we should go for help?"

"Something like that."

"I'll go—"

"Oh no, you won't," she said, cutting him off as she shoved something in her pocket, a smile touching her lips. "*I* will."

"But—"

"You heard me," she said, jabbing him in the chest with her pointer finger. "We've done it your way, Matty, and that's cool, but I'm not useless. And I swear to God, if you don't stop treating me with kid gloves, I'm going to punch you so hard you see stars for a week. I mean it. I'm *not* fragile. If I were, I would've already shattered by now."

Matty stood there, stunned by her outburst. Maybe she wasn't fragile, but she wasn't indestructible either. As much as she tried to conceal it, there was vulnerability beneath her hard exterior. He had seen as much the night before when she cracked, pent-up grief and fear shining through.

But he believed she meant it… he didn't doubt that she would hit him if he didn't take a step back, if he didn't give her space. So as hard as it was, as much as he hated it, he waved her away. "Go on then, Princess."

Grinning, Genna reached up on her tiptoes and planted a quick peck on his lips before turning away. Matty let down the truck's tailgate and plopped down on it, watching her strut down the highway.

Thirty minutes.

She had half an hour before he went after her. Instinctively, he glanced at his wrist, groaning when he came up empty. He never replaced his watch after Genna hustled it from him in their game of pool. Sighing, he leaned back on his elbows, not yet letting her leave his line of sight, his chest aching more the further away she got.

Maybe he'd make it twenty minutes instead.

She disappeared from the highway, cutting through some trees back toward the houses. Matty drummed his fingers on the rusty truck bed, impatiently counting in his head. How long had it been? Five minutes… ten… maybe fifteen?

It felt like hours to him.

Jumping to his feet, he wiped the sweat from his face with his shirt as he walked away from the truck. He'd made it a few steps when an older-model black Honda Accord sped toward him, swerving off the side of the road and skidding to a stop in the grass in front of Matty. Alarmed, he took a step back, eyes wide when the driver's side door flung open and Genna popped out.

He gaped at her. "What the hell did you do?"

"Got us some help," she said, leaving the door open as she rounded the front and banged on the hood.

"You stole another car?"

She cut her eyes at him, amused. "Come on, you're not *really* surprised, are you? I mean, this is sort of what I do, isn't it?"

"Not surprised," he said, shaking his head. "More like impressed."

Genna stepped to him, fisting the front of his sweat-streaked plain white t-shirt as she smirked, pulling him down for another kiss. "Told you I wasn't useless."

Matty transferred their things to the backseat of the Honda before climbing behind the wheel. He took a quick stock of the car as Genna settled into the passenger seat, cold air blasting out of the vents in the dashboard. He scanned the interior, noticing a small screwdriver jammed into the ignition.

Leave it to Genna to consider thievery tools a *bare necessity*.

Shrugging it off, he put the car in gear and pulled out onto the highway, giving a quick glance at the broken down truck in the rearview mirror as he sped past it. "So a Honda, huh?"

"Yeah, you got a problem with that?"

"No." He let out a laugh at her defensive tone. "Why would I?"

She shrugged, relaxing back into the seat. "Some people do. But mid-90s Accords are probably the most commonly stolen cars.

They're also one of the most *popular* cars. So that means there's a lot of them out there, and they go missing all the time, and well... it's easier to stay inconspicuous when you blend in."

"You put a lot of thought into that."

Genna turned to watch out the side window. "You might prefer to live in the moment, but I like having a plan. The easiest way to keep out of trouble is to always stay a few steps ahead."

* * *

They drove for about an hour until the gas light in the car lit up, flickering a dull orange, the needle hovering near empty. Matty pulled off the highway to the first store they came upon. Genna went inside, snatching a pack of Twizzlers from the candy aisle and tearing it open, gnawing on a rope of licorice as she strolled through the store. After fixing herself a cherry slushie, she grabbed a bag of cheese puffs and a honey bun before heading to the front. Matty stood by the register, paying for their gas, when Genna plopped her stuff down on the counter. He glanced at it, his eyes lingering on the open pack of licorice, and smiled as he pushed it toward the cashier. "All of this, too."

Glancing around, Genna's eyes drifted toward a rack of newspapers. She stepped that way, freezing when she caught sight of one. Right on the front page, big and bold, bore the headline:

Explosion Rocks Manhattan Neighborhood

She felt like she couldn't breathe when she saw the photo below it of the charred remains of Matty's gorgeous Lotus Evora. *So cruel.* Grabbing the newspaper, she stared at it, her hands trembling.

Front page of the fucking national news.

"That, too," Matty said behind her. "The newspaper."

Once their stuff was rung up, they collected it and headed out to the Honda. Genna's snacks were already forgotten, her abandoned slushie melting, as she fixated on the paper. After pumping gas, Matty climbed in the car, but he didn't drive away yet.

"What's it say?" he asked.

Genna scanned the article, struggling to absorb the words.

"You're presumed dead," she whispered. "They haven't found a body, obviously, but they're combing through the wreckage."

"What does it say about the explosion?"

"They suspect a mob hit. They, uh…" Genna faltered as she stumbled over the name *Joseph Galante*. "They compare it to the explosion that killed Joey, saying they haven't seen this level of violence in organized crime since that summer."

Matty said nothing else, starting the car up and pulling back onto the highway. Genna read the article twice more before discarding the newspaper in the backseat. She felt sick to her stomach and couldn't handle much more of it. *No more reading newspapers, ugh.*

"Did it mention you?" he asked after a while.

Genna shook her head as she grabbed another piece of licorice. "Not a single word about me."

What did they think happened to her? Was her father scouring the streets, searching for some sign, some way to bring her back home? Or did he simply write her off?

Neither would surprise Genna.

CHAPTER 3

Dante was dead.

He was sure of it.

Death was a son of a bitch, but it came mercifully quick. There one second, gone the next. He'd been awake, and suffering, and then nothing. *Nothing*. It was almost like being put to sleep.

It had all been taken from him in a blink.

Yeah, Dante was dead.

But somehow, someway, he was still fucking breathing.

He inhaled sharply, but it was like sucking air through a straw. He was suffocating, drowning in the bitter darkness, while loud shrieks pierced his ears. Confusion clouded his thoughts. He couldn't see a damn thing. Fiery red splotches melding with pitch black, like blood drops in a void.

He couldn't get a grip. Nothing he did made a difference. His body no longer worked. He couldn't move a fucking muscle. His voice was lost.

Heaven wasn't meant for him.

He was in *Hell*.

But goddammit, some way, some how, his lungs kept inflating.

"You need to hold on, okay? Can you do that for me? Try to relax. We'll get you through this."

The soft-spoken voice, serene and feminine, broke through the haze. It felt like déjà vu, like he'd heard it before. Like maybe this wasn't the first time he'd been told those words. Like maybe, somewhere, somehow, she'd already called to him. They washed through him until he could almost *feel* them, a strange sensation rushing through his comatose veins.

It took every ounce of strength he had to break through the

darkness. Bright white light blasted him, blinding him, as he forced his eyes open. Blinking, his vision cleared just enough for him to make out a blurry face. It was just a flash of creamy skin, dark hair and dark eyes, but there was something kind about them, something kind about *her*. It was something that warmed him from the inside when a soft smile touched the corners of her pink lips.

He was looking at an angel.

He was sure of it.

The piercing shrieks continued, so loud he almost didn't hear it when she spoke to him again.

"That's it," she whispered. "Just keep holding on."

The bright light surrounded her like a halo.

She was an angel of mercy.

She'd almost rescued him from the pit.

The sight of her nearly brought him back to life, but the world faded black again, and he could do nothing to stop it.

Dead.

Days. Months. Years. It still didn't matter. Dante had figured they would kill him, and he could've sworn they did. But that voice just kept calling to him, urging him to hold on, pulling him to the surface, again and again.

The first thing Dante saw, when regaining consciousness, was the face again.

That face.

It was still blurry, and he struggled making everything out, but he saw her standing by his side. While her presence should've brought Dante relief, panic bubbled in his chest. He couldn't move. *Literally.* He inhaled sharply, shrieking shattering the air when he did. He tried to turn his head to see where the noise was coming from and caught a glimpse of his surroundings.

Wires and tubes ran from his body in all directions, hooked to machines all around the room. Alarms went off as a heart monitor raced, the obnoxious blaring and beeping grating his skin.

A hospital.

The worst Hell there is.

"Try to relax," she said as she reached over to quiet the machine. "You may not like it, but the ventilator's helping."

It took Dante a moment to understand. The ventilator.

He might've still been dead, but now he realized he wasn't going to stop breathing... not as long as a machine did it for him.

It took some effort, but Dante managed to lift one of his arms as the woman tinkered with a machine beside him. He felt around on his face, his fingertips faintly grazing over bandages, before he found the piece sticking out of his mouth, the tube shoved down his throat. He wrapped a hand around it and pulled, panicking, and gagged when it started to budge. More alarms sounded, and the woman jumped into action, shouting for help. Others descended upon the room, crowding around him. It was a blink to him, flashes of people moving, as wooziness set in, a strange sensation rushing through his veins after a man shouted, "Sedate him!"

The woman appeared again then, looking down at him, another smile on her lips, but this one was different. This was a smile of sadness, not one of relief, as she shook her head, a peculiar twinkle in her dark eyes, like maybe he amused her. "What are we going to do with you, Mr. Galante?"

He tried to respond, his lips parting, but no sound came out. Not a breath. Not a whisper. *Nothing.*

"It's okay," the woman said, leaning closer. "Whatever it is can wait."

Not long after those words registered, darkness crept in, swaddling Dante like a blanket. As the world faded black around him, all he could think was, *if I have to die, please... please... don't let it be alone in the dark again.*

He fell into a deep, dreamless sleep, drugs running through his system so intense that he felt not a damn thing. And when he awoke later, he couldn't move. *Again.* This time, though, he couldn't even raise his arm. He managed to cut his eyes to the side, unnerved, his gaze settling on his hand. Thick cloth bands secured him to the bed like handcuffs. He struggled against them, trying to pull away, but they were too strong, or maybe he was just too weak. Exhaustion crept in a minute later, and he just lay there, gaze flickering to the ceiling, feeling defeated. Helplessness wasn't something Dante was accustomed to, and it wasn't a feeling he liked. A fucking machine was doing most of his breathing. Could he even say he was alive if his lungs wouldn't work without help?

The glass door across the room slid open. Dante didn't bother to try to look. Whatever drugs flowed through his veins faded more and more as the seconds ticked away. He flexed his fingers, the tips of them tingling, but he did little else in the way of trying to move. With consciousness came pain, a dull ache echoing through him, growing stronger.

He preferred it, though… preferred it to the numbness.

Someone approached, pausing beside the bed. Dante noticed them from his peripheral but didn't turn his head, instead closing his eyes to block out whoever it was.

"I know you're awake." Her voice was borderline playful, so close her words ghosted across his battered skin. "Your vitals give you away."

Dante opened his eyes again, his gaze meeting hers. His vision was clearer than it had been, clear enough to get a better look. She wore a pair of blue scrubs, a white badge clipped to the pocket. Try as he might, he couldn't make out any of the words written on it.

Even in dim lighting, though, Dante could tell she was beautiful. She was young, probably fresh out of nursing school, with a smile he suspected lit up a room, even one his presence darkened. Exotic, maybe even Italian, the kind of girl he could've brought home without any objections. In another life, he might've pursued her. In another world, he could've seen himself with a girl like her.

But in reality, she was probably much too sweet, much too kind for her own good.

The only angel he was destined to know was the fallen one.

He looked away again and stared at the ceiling. How long was this going to last? He had no idea how much time had passed. He didn't even know where he was. There were dozens of hospitals in the city. He could've been at any one of them. Last thing he remembered was a basement. How the hell had he gotten out of there? He couldn't wrap his mind around it.

He should've been dead.

He *should* be dead.

Why wasn't he?

"You're the most strong-willed person I've ever encountered," the woman said, pressing a few buttons on some machines beside him. "You're just laying there, not in distress at all, not fighting the ventilator."

Without looking at her, Dante struggled against the restraints to make a point. There wasn't shit he could do strapped down like a prisoner.

She laughed lightly. "Oh, no... I *know* you'd try to rip it out if your hands were free. You've done it a few times this past week."

Week.

He'd been there a week?

"That's not what I'm talking about," she continued. "Most patients, they find it excruciating. We have to keep them so sedated they're comatose or else they choke on the ventilator. And I get it, you know... it's uncomfortable. Unnatural. I understand why they fight. But you're just lying there, silent and still, biding your time. I've never seen someone so stubbornly calm before."

Dante glanced at her again. Her curiosity seemed genuine, but any explanation he offered wouldn't be what she'd want to hear. The truth was something he knew someone like her couldn't handle... not without it altering her view of the world.

Some people were fueled by hope.

Others, like him, long ago realized there was no hope for the future. There was only the present until your luck ran out.

His was damn near a dry well at that point.

So he didn't fight, he didn't struggle, because death wasn't something he feared. His last breath wasn't something he'd dread. The time would come, sooner or later, when he'd close his eyes for the last time, never to open them again, but that didn't leave him terrified of falling asleep. He'd accepted death at five years old, when his parents called in a priest to pray over him. Lying in a hospital bed not much different than the one he was in then, his chest ravished by fire, he silently prayed he'd die so he'd stop *burning*.

Since then, he'd just been waiting.

Waiting for that prayer to be answered.

Waiting for the fire to finally be put out.

Not that he looked forward to dying, because he didn't. Some battles were just a lost cause. And if he had to die, he was going to die with some goddamn dignity, not crying like a bitch over a machine pumping air into his lungs.

A moment later, a doctor walked in, flipping through a chart as he approached the bed. Dante eyed him not nearly as kindly as he eyed the nurse. The doctor was a small man, wiry with thick-rimmed glasses and thin gray hair. He paused at the edge of the bed, not an ounce of compassion in his eyes and certainly none in his voice as he spoke. "Mr. Galante, I'm Dr. Crabtree, I've been taking care of you since you were brought in. We'll be weaning you off of the ventilator soon. I'll have the restraints removed as long as you're cooperative, but we'll have to reassess that if you act out. We won't tolerate any of that roughneck behavior here. Do you understand? Nod if you do."

Dante just stared at the man. He'd raised his voice, like he was afraid he wouldn't be heard. The condescending tone grated Dante's nerves. He figured a lack of reaction should be answer enough, but the doctor waited, eyebrows raised, like he expected some acknowledgement.

Dante nodded once.

Whatever it takes to get the hell out of this bed.

"Good, good..." Dr. Crabtree looked quite pleased with himself. "I'm glad you're choosing to cooperate."

The doctor nodded toward the nurse, giving her permission to free him. She untied the restraints, getting rid of them. As soon as Dante was free, he reached up, feeling around on his face, fingertips grazing along the ventilator.

He almost did it.

He almost pulled the son of a bitch out just to spite the man.

The nurse shot him a look, though, that stopped him right away. It was a warning, daring him that he wouldn't like what happened if he went through with it. Dante wasn't one to take orders from just anybody, but he didn't push it, not this time. Instead, he held his hand up, pressing his thumb and pointer finger together and wiggling them, making the motion like he was holding a pen. The doctor's brow furrowed, terrible at *Charades*, but the nurse smiled.

"He wants something to write with," she said. "I guess he has something to say."

Dr. Crabtree hesitated, like he was debating whether or not to allow that, but obliged. "Go ahead and get him something... something that isn't sharp, you know, that he can't hurt anyone with."

The nurse seemed a little put off by the request, her face twisting as if the insinuation was absurd. Dante would've laughed, well... if he *could've*. It was obvious the doctor knew who he was. She, on the other hand, probably had no idea what kind of man she was dealing with.

She returned with a yellow legal pad and a bright red crayon, looking like she'd taken it straight from a fresh pack. She held it up as she walked past the doctor. "This too pointy for you?"

The doctor glanced at it and seemed to consider it for a second. "That'll be fine."

The moment the nurse turned, out of the doctor's line of sight, she rolled her eyes. Approaching the bed, she slipped the crayon into Dante's hand, her fingertips brushing across his skin as she let go. She adjusted the bed, sitting him up a bit further, before holding the pad up to him so he could scribble on it. It took a hell of a lot more effort than he thought it would, the crayon slipping out of his hand, his grip weak, his fingers trembling, but he managed to spell out a single sloppy word. *When.*

"When?" the nurse read aloud.

"When, what?" the doctor asked, his face buried in a chart.

Reaching up, Dante again grasped the ventilator. Before he could do anything more, the nurse yanked his hand away.

"He wants to know when you're going to wean him off the ventilator," she said.

Dante cut his eyes at her. *Huh.* Intuitive.

"Soon," the doctor said again.

Dante took the crayon and beat the tip of it against the paper, leaving sharp red marks all over the word '*when*'.

"He wants to know how soon," the nurse said. "He wants a time-frame."

The doctor sighed dramatically. "Within the next twenty-four hours."

Dante glared at him. Not good enough.

He used the crayon and tried to write again, blindly scribbling on the pad, right over the first word he wrote. The nurse watched him, her eyes narrowed as she riddled it out. "No— concert? Constant? Concept? Consent?" Her eyes widened as she looked at him. "Oh, consent!"

Dante nodded.

"He says you have no consent," she said, turning to the doctor.

"No consent for what?"

"To keep him intubated. He's saying you don't have his permission, therefore you have to remove it right away."

"Yeah, well, nowhere in Mr. Galante's *extensive* dossier did I read that he had a degree in medicine, so I hardly see how he knows the best course of treatment. Besides, he's in no condition to be making medical decisions. He's barely lucid."

Dante reached toward the pad with the crayon, having a hell of a lot to say to that, and scribbled jumbled words that barely resembled anything from the English language, but it didn't matter, because the nurse chimed back in without bothering to decipher what he wrote.

"He's lucid enough to communicate his wishes," she said. "He seems of sound mind to me, which means he has the right to refuse care that he doesn't consent to."

"We received consent from the next of kin when he was brought in," the doctor said. "We didn't need his permission."

"But you do now."

The doctor cut his eyes their way. "Pardon me, Nurse Russo, but when exactly did *you* become a doctor?"

"I don't need a Ph.D. to spot an ethical issue," she responded. "All that takes is a bit of common sense, sir."

The doctor glared at her. *Pissed.* Dante could tell he had something he wanted to say, something that would probably drive Dante to rip the ventilator right out and throw it at the guy, but he seemed to think better of it, shaking his head as he turned back to the chart. "I'll contact the respiratory therapist and we'll start the process of weaning him." He paused before mumbling under his breath, "If the patient doesn't give a shit about his own life, why should we care, right?"

Dante scribbled on the pad again, right on top of everything else he'd written, big, fat red letters, the lines bold: FUCK YOU.

The nurse glanced at the pad, cocking an eyebrow as she cut her eyes at Dante, before she turned back to the doctor, smiling sweetly. "He's expressed his gratitude."

The doctor had no response for that, waving them off as he walked away, the sliding glass door automatically opening so he could exit. Dante gripped hold of the crayon as he closed his eyes, his pain escalating. Just that little bit had taken it *all* out of him. He had a brief moment where he wondered if maybe he was making a mistake, if he were fucking up, but he didn't dwell on it long. The nurse chimed in before he got lost in his head, her voice chipper as she asked, "How about a visitor, huh? You haven't really had any of them. Might do you some good to see a familiar face."

Visitor.

Dante's eyes again opened at the same time the glass door to his room shifted open. He glanced that way, a swell of emotion hitting him, so intense his vision blurred. His heartbeat picked up in anticipation, the beep-beep-beeping of the machine chaotic, when his eyes fell upon his father. Primo Galante stood there, all stocky six-foot-four of him, dressed in a dark suit.

It had been weeks since he'd last seen his father's face. He'd left the house with his sister in tow, never to make it back home again. Never to see his father again. Never to see his sister.

His sister.

Oh God, Genevieve. He still saw that innocent little girl every time he looked at her, the one he had done everything in his power to protect. The one who had inadvertently saved his life sixteen years earlier as she toddled through the gravel lot of the pizzeria, forcing him to linger so he couldn't run after Joey like he so wanted to. The blast had just barely hit him that night. He'd been far enough away because of her that he'd remained somewhat intact. He owed his life to her, and it was a debt he'd never feel like he adequately paid back. He would've done anything for her. He *had* done everything for her. He compromised who he was, who he thought he needed to be, because she'd asked him to that night when he found out her dirty little secret, when he'd discovered the skeleton in her closet came in the form of a walking, talking Barsanti. It went against everything he believed, everything he thought… he ignored his gut and chose to give her a chance to figure it out herself.

Because at the end of the day, he believed in her a hell of a lot more than he believed in anybody else, even himself.

But it had been his job to keep her safe.

"Dante?" Primo's voice was hesitant as he stepped into the small room. "You don't even know how much it means to me to see you again, to see you... *awake.*"

The man looked like he hadn't slept since the last time they saw each other. Dark bags lined his bloodshot eyes, fresh wrinkles marring his face. Primo always seemed ten-feet-tall and bulletproof to Dante. His father, made of the toughest material known to man, was untouchable, impenetrable, and infallible. Despite all he'd suffered, the man had never shown a single crack. But standing in front of Dante at that moment was somebody else.

Standing in front of Dante was a broken man.

Turning his head, Dante eyed the nurse, raising his hand and waving his red crayon. When he caught her attention, she grabbed the yellow pad and flipped the page to a fresh one, holding it up in front of Dante.

He pressed the tip of the crayon to the paper and hesitated.

He hesitated, almost like he forgot how to write.

Like he wasn't sure how to spell.

He knew, of course. He knew exactly what he needed to write. But something stalled him, something that felt a hell of a lot like dread. The only time he ever felt fear anymore was when it came to his sister. When it came to her, he feared *a lot*, but mostly that someday, the time would come when he would let her down, when he'd fail at his most important job, when he wouldn't be there to pay her back.

After a moment, he spelled out her name, the letters wobbly, the red crayon faintly marking the paper, leaving gaps between the lines. The nurse raised the pad up when he finished, reading what he'd written out loud. "Genna?"

The name hit Primo like a ton of bricks. Usually calm, collected Primo Galante flinched. It was a brief reaction before he pulled himself back together, a second where he'd let his guard down, not expecting to be hit with it all so quick. He cleared his throat, straightening his expression, as he stepped closer to the bed. "She's not here."

That was all he said.

She's not here.

No explanation.

Not that one was needed.

Because Dante knew.

He knew it as soon as the man flinched. That was confirmation. Her not being there was just a cyanide cherry on top of an already poisonous sundae. Nothing would've kept Genna away from there... nothing short of her being *nowhere*.

Devastation rocked Dante. His stomach lurched, his chest burning, as bile tried to force itself up his blocked throat. He squeezed the red crayon so hard it snapped in half. He tried to remain calm, to hold it in, as his fingertips tingled. *No. No. No.* He chanted the word in his mind, willing himself to listen, but it was pointless.

The ache was just too strong.

His father spoke again, oblivious to Dante's reaction, rambling on and on about how elated he was, but it went in one ear and out the other, lost somewhere in the haze of hurt consuming Dante.

Thirty seconds passed before the first alarm went off. The ventilator detected he was struggling and put out an alert that his breathing was wrong. Nurse Russo, halfway to the door, swung back around. Concerned eyes glossed over him as she darted for the machine. By the time she made it there, the heart rate monitor followed suit, acting erratic.

Blinking rapidly, Dante felt the building tears. He tried to suck it up. He didn't want to cry. He wouldn't let himself do it. He'd survived torture without cracking. He couldn't have this be what broke him. He was stronger than that.

Anger surged through his veins to the point that fighting was impossible. His body shook as the machines screamed, his chest on fire when he started hyperventilating.

It was like sucking through a straw with a hole in it, getting nothing.

"Dante?" Primo called out. "What's happening?"

"You need to leave, Mr. Galante!" the nurse shouted at him.

"Dante?" he said, ignoring her. "It's going to be okay, son."

"Get out!" she barked as the glass door slid open, others rushing into the room. They surrounded Dante, and he wasn't sure if his father listened to the woman's order, because all at once, the world blurred.

The haze swaddled him, numbing him, dulling the burn and sweeping him away.

"They're sedating you," Nurse Russo whispered, gazing down at him. "Just until you stop fighting the ventilator."

* * *

The trip went much smoother once Matty and Genna had a car with air conditioning. Music from the radio filled the silence as Genna relaxed in the passenger seat, watching the world fly by outside the tinted window.

South Carolina

Georgia

Alabama

Mississippi

They traveled through the south, driving for hours before stopping to get a motel for the night. Bright and early the next morning, they would hit the road again, never looking back, never staying more than a few hours in one location. It was steady, even a bit tedious, the constant traveling with no destination, with nowhere to be, making the days all blur together.

"Are we heading west?" Genna asked, glancing up from the map in her lap to the road before them, spotting the sign declaring they were going west. "Never mind."

Matty chuckled, looking at her. Sunshine streamed through the car windows, making him squint. He had bought himself a pair of sunglasses back in North Carolina, but they'd disappeared somewhere between Mississippi and Louisiana, along with Genna's flip-flops and all of her hair ties.

It was hard to keep up with things when they were constantly on the move.

Genna scanned the map, locating the highway right outside of Paris, Texas. They'd been driving for about two hours, crossing over from Arkansas, but she was already growing tired of being in the car. Queasiness stirred in the pit of her stomach that she tried to ignore, but her morning sickness was starting to *really* kick in.

Just breathing nauseated her.

What she wouldn't give for a nice bubble bath and a nap long enough to put her in the *Guiness Book of World Records*. The motel they'd stayed in the night before had been a run down piece of shit, the bathroom grungy and the bed uncomfortable.

"Why?" Matty asked. "You want to go a different direction?"

"No, I was just..." She closed her eyes and took a deep breath, warding off a flare of sickness. "I was just wondering."

Genna reopened her eyes, seeing the scenery fly by the side window. *Big mistake.* Dizziness blurred her vision, bile burning her throat. She barely had enough time to smack Matty's arm in warning, making the car swerve, before she reached for the door handle. "Gonna be—"

Sick.

Matty slammed the brakes, the car screeching to a stop along the side of the highway as she flung the passenger door open and leaned out, purging everything from her stomach. He put the car in park, turning on the hazard lights, the tick-tick-ticking grating Genna's frazzled nerves.

Matty rubbed her back as he whispered, "It's going to be okay."

Laughing dryly, she relaxed back in the seat once the sickness passed. "Talk about déjà vu."

They'd done that before, her hanging out of a car and puking her guts out while he tried to pacify her. Hadn't worked before, and it wasn't working then.

Could we be more cliché?

Matty slipped his arm around her and pulled her to him, pressing a kiss to the top of her head. Her eyes closed as she took a moment to savor his embrace, knowing just a moment was all they had to spare, but it was a moment interrupted way too fast when Matty tensed. "Shit."

Genna opened her eyes, catching a reflection in the side mirror, red and blue lights flashing behind them. Adrenaline spiked her system, her stomach churning again. She tried to fight it, to take deep breaths and stay calm, but it was pointless. She was leaning back out of the car, heaving, before anyone said another word.

"Oh God," she gasped as she struggled to pull herself together. "I'm Jackson now. I'm *worse* than Jackson."

Matty shot her a look of confusion. "Who?"

"My car thieving ex-boyfriend. We stole a Honda and he puked on himself." Tears stung her eyes, breaking free and running down her cheeks as her emotions went from zero to sixty. "He got away with it and I didn't, and oh God, I'm screwed! We're *screwed!* I'm going to go to prison, real prison... ass-pounding prison! I'm going to have a fucking baby in prison!"

Matty grabbed her, his hands cradling her face. His expression remained calm as he stared into her eyes.

"Pull yourself together. You Galantes are stubborn, and resilient, and unrelenting, real pains in the ass, but you're not *this*. You don't fall apart when you see the police." His eyes flickered to the rearview mirror as a cop got out of the car behind them. "Maybe you Galantes don't trust us Barsantis, but you need to trust *me*, Genna. Please."

"I do," she whispered.

"Then calm down and let me handle it," he said, a slight smile touching his lips. "I got this."

Genna didn't believe he had it for a second, but she didn't object as he pulled away and pushed the driver's side door open to step out.

"Y'all all right?" the officer asked, approaching Matty, his accent so thick Genna struggled to understand the words. "Car ain't leave you stranded, has it? Need me to call you some help?"

"No, sir," Matty said, mimicking the officer's voice, a fake southern accent framing the words. "My wife's just got a bit of morning sickness, that's all. We were about to be on our way again."

"Ah, okay, just checking on y'all." The officer peeked into the car at Genna, tipping his hat. "Ma'am."

"Officer."

Matty exchanged some more pleasantries with the man before the officer walked away, heading back to his police cruiser. Matty climbed back in the car, his expression serious as he motioned her way. "Let's get out of here."

She barely got the door closed and her seatbelt on before Matty pulled back out onto the highway, leaving the cop along the side of the road. Genna watched in the side mirror, heart beating rapidly, not calming down until the officer took off in the opposite direction.

"So your wife's pregnant, huh? Tough break."

"Would you have preferred *baby mama*?"

"Probably would've made more sense with the Larry the Cable Guy accent you were rocking."

"The *who*?"

"Larry the Cable Guy," she repeated. "You know, the 'get 'er done' dude?"

"The *what*?"

Genna waved him off. "The point is, you sounded ridiculous."

"Yeah, well, considering the North Carolina license plate on the car, I figured it best to try to blend in. You know, so not to raise any suspicion and give the man a reason to run the tag."

Genna gazed at him, surprised by how much thought he put into that, although she shouldn't have been. He'd always seemed in control of situations, even way back in the defunct elevator that first day. Maybe he *did* have it handled, after all.

Sighing, Genna snatched up the map again, smoothing the crinkles out of it. "Paris, Texas. You think it's anything like the real Paris?"

"Maybe," Matty said. "I wouldn't put any money on it, though."

"Shame," she said. "I've always wanted to see Paris."

"You've never gone?"

She cut her eyes at him. "This is furthest away from home I've ever been."

That seemed to surprise Matty. "Your whole life you've had the world at your fingertips, but you've never seen any of it?"

"I wouldn't exactly say I had the world at my fingertips, you know, since my father had me under his thumb. I was only supposed to go where he had eyes, where he could watch me, just in case, and even when I went there, he sent Dante."

Her voice cracked as she whispered his name. *Dante*. Man, it hurt. Would it ever not hurt? She doubted it. Even knowing he wasn't waiting for her back in Manhattan, it almost felt like a betrayal, her being on the road like this. Her pseudo-bodyguard brother... what would he think?

"I'm sorry."

Matty's voice was quiet, genuine, as he reached over to grab her hand, squeezing it. Genna gave him a soft smile, whispering, "Thank you."

She appreciated his words, even though he didn't owe her an apology. He'd been just as innocent as her in all of it. She wasn't the only one who lost somebody. He'd lost a brother, too.

"We should do something," Matty said. "Whenever we stop, we

should do something for him. I know it won't be the same as having a funeral, but you deserve to be able to say goodbye to your brother."

"What, like tip a forty for the homies or something?"

Matty laughed. "Sure, why not?"

"Dante would find that funny," Genna said. "Well, I mean, he *would've*, you know..."

"I know."

Paris, Texas, it turned out, wasn't like the city in France. It was a quaint little town with not too many people and pretty much nothing to do. In less than an hour, they'd seen all there was to see. Genna stood in a parking lot beside the Honda, in front of the small replica Eiffel Tower, and stared up at the massive red cowboy hat on top of it. She hadn't expected glitz and glamor, but she was less than impressed.

She felt Matty's eyes on her. He stood just a few feet away, watching her as she stared at the tower. Slowly, her gaze shifted his direction.

"Do you think the real one is as underwhelming?" she asked.

He shook his head, not breaking eye contact. "I think it's impossible not to be in awe of something so magnificent. From the top, everything looks so small, like any problems you might have are trivial, because *you're* trivial, compared to what's around you. That's beautiful, I think... even almost a thousand feet in the air, it has a way of making you feel grounded."

"You speak like you've seen it."

"I've seen most of the world. It kept me out of the way, out of New York."

Sighing, Genna once more surveyed the fake Eiffel tower.

"I'll take you someday," he said, "if you want to see the real thing."

She did, but she didn't want him to make promises she wasn't sure he could keep. He was trying, though. He was *really* trying. And that, to her, meant everything.

"Okay, let's do this," she said, waving at Matty.

"*Here?*"

"Sure, why not?" she said. "I mean, come on... can you think of a better makeshift headstone than a tower wearing a cowboy hat?

That's some Billy the Kid *Regulators* type shit."

"Uh, okay."

He grabbed her hand as they approached the tower, walking along the brick path, and stopping a few feet away.

"Oh, Dante," Genna said, staring up at the thing. "I don't even know what to say."

"You tell him how you feel," Matty suggested. "You tell him how much he means to you."

"He was my best friend." She paused before laughing lightly. "He is my best friend, I mean. You *are* my best friend. You always will be. I don't know what happened to you... I don't know where you went after you dropped me off that day, what happened those hours before you didn't show back up. I just... I don't know. I wish I did, though. No matter what it was, no matter what happened or what you went through, I just really wish I knew."

Tears stung her eyes, and she tried to hold them in, but they streamed down her cheeks.

"I wish I knew. I wish I could've done something. I wish I could *still* do something. I wish you were here, so I could tell you how sorry I am for everything that's happened to you. You spent your whole life taking care of me, but who was taking care of you? Who made sure you were okay? Who was making *you* happy? Somebody should've been, because you deserved it. You deserved so much you didn't get. And I know you did bad stuff, and I know you hurt people, but you were a good person. You were the *best* person. You spent every minute of every day trying to make things okay, and maybe you just made it all worse, but the point is you tried to make the world better for us. So thank you, for that, because I don't know if I ever thanked you. I don't know if anyone ever thanked you, but they should've. I should've. *Thank you.*"

Matty grabbed ahold of her, pulling her to him as she sobbed, choking on those words. *Thank you.* God, how she wished she could've thanked him in person.

"I'm not supposed to give some eulogy for my brother," she said. "This is... *bullshit*. This isn't supposed to happen. And I know you'd say it was stupid and tell me to suck it up, but I miss you, okay? I really, really miss you, and I have no idea where you went. I have no idea where you might be. So here I am... here's *me*... accepting that I'll probably never know, but telling you that wherever you are, it's okay. You can be in peace. You deserve peace. Nobody ever gave it to you, so I really want you to take it anyway."

Genna felt stupid, standing there, doing that, but what the hell? What else could she do? It wasn't as if she could bury him.

She leaned her head against Matty. "Your turn."

He tensed. "*My* turn?"

"Say something."

Matty hesitated. "What can I say? You were, uh... I heard you were good at pool. Sucks we never got to play."

"That was weak."

"That's all I got."

"Come on, I'm sure you can think of something else."

"Uh, Dante Galante... your name kind of rhymes. Always thought that was neat."

Genna laughed. "Seriously?"

Before either could say another word, a faint ringing sound interrupted them. Genna tensed while Matty reached into his pocket and pulled out the cell phone he'd bought and shook it at her. "Sorry, gotta take this, baby."

He walked over, strolling a few steps away as he answered the phone. Genna watched him before glancing back at the tower, scanning it in silence.

"So, uh..." Matty hesitated as he returned, slipping the phone back into his pocket. "How do you feel about Nevada?"

"Nevada?"

"Yeah, there's a place there... somewhere we can go. Maybe somewhere we can call home."

Home. Genna liked the sound of that word.

"Isn't there an Eiffel Tower there?" she asked. "In Las Vegas?"

"Actually, yeah... it's about half the size of the real one. A lot bigger than this one."

"Well then, I'd say Nevada feels like it just might be right."

CHAPTER 4

The bumpy dirt path cut through the overgrown land, barely wide enough for a vehicle to pass. Not far off the deserted highway stood an old two-story house. Genna stared at it in the darkness, taking in the chipped paint and splintered wood, railings torn apart and missing, leaving jagged spikes along the massive porch. Her stomach twisted in knots. She'd seen enough horror movies in her life to know when a place just wasn't right.

And this place seemed about as wrong as it got.

"I know we're not exactly on vacation here," Genna said, "but do we really have to reenact *Cabin in The Woods?*"

Matty laughed quietly, although it wasn't exactly a happy sound. Exhaustion weighed down every part of him. Genna noticed it in his face and heard it in his voice. They'd been traveling for days, having to stop frequently thanks to Genna's morning sickness and incessant need to pee. *Pregnancy, whee!*

"We're in the desert, so I wouldn't call this the woods," Matty said. "Besides, it's more of a ranch."

"A ranch."

"Yeah, or you know..." He waved toward it. "A plantation home or something."

"Plantation home."

"Yeah, so I wouldn't call it a cabin."

Definitely not in Manhattan anymore.

"Well, then, my mistake." Genna eyed the house in the dim moonlight. "Nothing horror movie-esque about a ranch, huh? Should've invested in some cattle when we were in Texas. Maybe get some horses. You know, you might look good in skin-tight Wranglers."

Matty laughed again, this time lighter, as he reached over and cupped the back of her neck with his hand. His thumb stroked the skin absent-mindedly as he shook his head. "I don't think it's *that* kind of ranch."

"What kind of ranch is it?"

"The kind that keeps you isolated," he explained. "The kind that people hide out on."

"It's kind of sounding like *Cabin in The Woods* again."

He smiled in her direction. "We'll be safe here."

"Are you sure about that?"

"Safer than we would be back in New York."

It wasn't a 'yes', but it was close enough to it. She motioned toward the shabby house. "Well, then, what are we waiting for? Our ranch awaits."

The place was already unlocked. Matty shoved against the wooden door, forcing it open, a blast of stuffy air hitting Genna right away. Her nose twitched at the stale odor, dust tickling her nostrils. She reached along the wall for a light switch, her stomach dropping when she found one and flicked it up.

Nothing.

She wasn't surprised by the lack of electricity, but damn if it wasn't disheartening. All she wanted was a long bath and some kind of air conditioning, but the odds of either option happening were slim to none.

"Tomorrow," Matty said, lingering in the foyer of the house beside her, moonlight peeking in the open door behind them. "I'll make sure the power gets running then, I promise. I just have to make a few calls."

"What even is this place?" Genna asked, looking around at what little she could decipher in the darkness. A clunky rotary phone sat on a wooden stand not far from her.

"A safe house, I guess."

She tensed. "One of the Barsantis?"

"No," he said. "Not the Galantes, either."

"So... neutral ground."

He nodded. "Neutral ground."

She didn't press him on that. He'd kept her safe before on neutral ground, and she had no choice but to trust him again. Besides, they were twenty-five hundred miles away from New York City, in the stifling desert in the middle of nowhere. Primo's reach was undoubtedly long, but Genna wasn't sure it was *that* long.

"I'm going to look around," she said. "See what's here, you know... if there's anything."

"I'll unload the car," Matty responded, lingering as he stared at her. "Make yourself at home."

Once he finally turned, walking back out the front door, Genna set off through the house. Her footsteps were hesitant in the darkness, not wanting to trip over anything lying around. Old belongings were strewn throughout the place, hastily discarded, broken glass shoved along the sides of the hallways. No one had bothered cleaning up, but they'd cleared a path, which Genna was grateful for.

In the kitchen, she opened a few drawers, shifting through the leftover contents. She found a heavy black-handled flashlight shoved in a cabinet and clicked the button to turn it on.

Nothing happened.

Scowling, she unscrewed the bottom of it, grimacing when a set of corroded batteries dropped out, hitting the floor by her feet. *Gross.*

"Jesus, how old is this shit?" she grumbled, continuing her search. She found a matchbook in a drawer and snatched it up, squinting to make out the logo in the dim moonlight. *The Flamingo Hotel & Casino.* She held her breath, ripping a match out and striking it against the worn out strip on the back. It ignited, the flame sparking. "Ha!"

"Ah, she discovered fire," Matty said, stepping into the kitchen and dropping their bags on the floor. "Taking it back to the Stone-Age."

She shook the match out before it burned down too far, not wanting to singe her fingers. "Help me find some candles, Fred Flintstone. Maybe they don't have electricity, but even damn *Buddhists* have candles."

"Amish," he corrected her.

"What?"

"I'm pretty sure you mean the Amish," he said. "Buddhists aren't opposed to candles, but a lot of monasteries use electricity and technology, so..."

"Buddhist... Amish... really, what's the difference?"

"Not touching that one."

Genna scoured the kitchen some more as Matty disappeared, returning with a tall white candle in a glass jar, a religious votive with some faded Catholic painting on the front of it.

"Mother Mary to the rescue," he said, playfully shaking it in her direction.

Genna took it from him, blowing inside of it, gagging at the amount of dust that flew back out at her. She lit another match, holding it down into the candle, grateful it was just long enough to touch the wick, igniting it. The spark snap, crackle, and popped around the lingering dust, but the thing stayed lit, giving off enough light for her to see.

"We should stick to the downstairs for tonight," Matty suggested.

Genna had no plans to argue with him on that.

Carrying the candle, she made her way through the downstairs. A dining room was adjacent to the kitchen, a splintered wooden table in the center of it, reminiscent of the one Genna's family sat at every night for dinner. Past that was the living room, more furniture there—a couch and two chairs, an old television that looked like it might've been black and white. *Unbelievable.* Knick-knacks sat around, also collecting dust, long ago abandoned, left behind like everything else.

Genna had been to a few safe houses in her lifetime, places in the city her father secretly owned in obscure names, with little more than mattresses on the floor and a refrigerator in the corner, whatever they'd need to survive if they went into hiding for a few days. But this wasn't like any safe house Genna had ever encountered. Someone had once *lived* there. Someone had once called the place home.

What happened to them? Where did they go?

Who the hell were they?

Matty plopped down on the end of the couch, sending dust flying that had settled into the cushions. Genna laughed as the cloud of it lingered around him. Smiling, Matty opened his arms to her as he stretched out, motioning for her to join him.

She set the candle down on a small end table beside him before tucking in at his side. The couch wasn't the most comfortable, springs poking her as she sunk into it, but she felt content as she settle into his embrace, her head against his chest. Even though it was sweltering, the air stuffy, her skin covered in sweat, she found comfort in Matty's warm.

"We'll make the best of it," Matty said, kissing the top of her head. "You'll see... it'll all be okay."

She wanted to believe that. She wanted to believe that as long as she had Matty, as long as they were together, they'd be happy. The world wouldn't be perfect, but they'd make the best of it, and it would be okay.

Okay, because they had each other.

Okay, because of the baby.

Genna's hand drifted, resting against her stomach.

No matter how terrified she was, she had to hold it together. She'd lost her family. Her brother was gone, but even without him, she had to go on. As painful as each breath was, as agonizing as each what-if seemed in her mind, she had to keep taking steps forward, one foot after the other. She couldn't stumble and fall. Because soon, there would be another little Galante in the world, one that would need her the way she always needed her brother. One that would depend on her for protection; one that would need her to keep them from harm. And protection was vital, just as harm was possible, because this new little Galante wouldn't be like the others. No, this new little Galante would be mixed with Barsanti, and nothing was more dangerous than *that*.

"It'll be okay," she agreed, closing her eyes. "We'll be just fine."

* * *

The moment Dante's ventilator was removed days later, the questions started, pelting him like machine gun fire. *Rat-ta-tat-tat.*

Do you know where you are? Do you know your name? Do you know what day it is?

Do you know where the hell you've been?

Dante remained silent in the uncomfortable hospital bed, not answering a single thing thrown at him. He was groggy, in pain, and just plain annoyed by all of the damn questions. Tests were run. Drugs were pumped into his body before being taken back away. Just in case it was causing some reaction, some kind of dissociated response, in case it was making him mute, when they couldn't have that. No, not when they wanted their questions answered. Not when they needed something from him.

First, it was the slew of medical doctors before finally, they sent a psychiatrist. A fucking *shrink*. He'd been off the ventilator for forty-eight hours, breathing steadily on his own, his vitals strong, when the guy in the white lab coat took up residence across the room, tossing out a brand new question: *how are you feeling?*

How was he feeling? *Dead.*

Inside of him was rotting, decomposing, every second that passed making rigor mortis set into his chest, seizing whatever had been left. Despite his head riddling out the truth, his heart had held on, waiting for a miracle. Every time the sliding door to his hospital room opened, hope flooded him. Maybe it was Genna. Maybe she'd shown up. Maybe she'd survived whatever had happened.

What the hell *had* happened?

He hadn't been brave enough to ask that question, not when everyone around him was pressuring him for their own answers. So many faces popping up in front of him, not a single one pleasant.

No friends. No family.

Even Nurse Russo had been off-duty.

Or maybe she begged to be reassigned to get away from me.

So he endured the interrogations in silence, not uttering a word, staring down at his hands folded in his lap.

His eyes rose toward the psychiatrist, who sat there with a pen and a pad, ready to jot down whatever Dante said and assess whether or not he was out of his fucking mind.

"How are you feeling?" the man repeated, eye contact making him think some sort of progress was being had, but it would be a cold day in Hell when Dante played this game with those people.

Besides, it wouldn't have been smart to answer that.

He felt like ripping someone apart, piece-by-piece.

His gaze drifted back down to his hands.

"If you don't want to start there, we can start elsewhere," the psychiatrist said. "How about you acknowledge you at least understand what I'm saying? All I need is a nod of the head."

Dirt and dried blood was still caked beneath some of Dante's nails. He picked at it, wishing he could get out of that bed and shower, to wash off the filth, to purge some of the memories of what they'd done to him. Yeah, the doctors had let him breathe on his own, but everything else? Out of the question.

He couldn't even get up to go take a piss.

Fucking catheter rammed up his dick.

Granted, getting up in itself seemed impossible, considering he couldn't feel his legs. They still worked, though. He knew, because he could wiggle his toes.

Groaning, the shrink stood and stomped off. "This is pointless."

Dante closed his eyes, relief washing over him once the door slid open. Peace surrounded him for a moment. He relished being alone—alone to wallow in grief—until a soft sigh echoed from nearby, startling him. His heart stalled a beat. He heard the hesitation on the machine. That ignorant hope flowed through him again.

When he opened his eyes, it wasn't his sister's icy blue gaze that greeted him, though. It was Nurse Russo.

She didn't stare at him like everyone else, with the revulsion he'd gotten from so many since waking up. No, her eyes were kind, albeit a little hesitant as they regarded him for the first time in two days. Last time she'd stepped in his room, he'd been indisposed, intubated. Now, he was just a stubborn asshole.

He didn't sense fear in her, although she had to have riddled out by then what kind of man she was dealing with. Even stuck in that bed, Dante had heard the whispers, the staff out in the hallway talking about the thug in room twenty-two, tortured and almost killed by God-knows-who. But *whatever*, because he deserved it, right? Deserved it for being the kind of man who did the kind of things that invited those kinds of people into his life.

Nurse Russo, though, treated him like he was any other guy.

It felt almost like seeing a friend.

Dante looked away from her as the hope faded, his heart hardening just a little bit more. He tried to shift position in bed, to get comfortable, but nothing he did made much of a difference.

"It's the medication," the nurse said softly, watching him as he glared down at his feet, the sheet twitching as he willed the sons of bitches to move.

Dante's eyes shifted to her. "I don't like it."

His voice was scratchy and strained, the words painful. Side effect of having a tube crammed down your throat, he gathered. It was the first time he'd spoken in around her, and he could sense her surprise. Her dark eyes twinkled.

"Ah, so you're *not* mute."

Dante shook his head. "Just got nothing to say."

The nurse went back to doing whatever she'd come to do, pressing buttons on the machines, but she wasn't done with the conversation. "I can understand why you don't like the numbness, but it's better than the alternative."

"Which is?"

"Pain."

At the sound of that word, Dante laughed bitterly. He *laughed.* It didn't feel good, but he did it anyway. "A little pain never hurt anybody."

A soft smile played on the nurse's lips. "You seem to be accustomed to it."

Instinctively, Dante's hand drifted to his chest, the flimsy hospital gown covering the scars from his burns. He didn't make a habit of showing them off to people, but he knew the nurse had seen them. Everyone there probably had.

He evaded mentioning it, brushing off her assumption. Pain, he was used to, but the numbness had to go. "So, what do I have to do to get out of this place? Pay someone? Sign something? Petition a fucking court?"

This time, the nurse laughed. There was no humor in it, either. "Get out of here? I don't think you understand the severity of your injuries."

"Oh, I understand," he said. "I was there when it happened."

Before she could react, another voice cut through the room. "And what, exactly, would '*it*' be, Mr. Galante?"

The sound was like sharp claws ripping away at Dante's calm. He knew that nagging voice, the grating, mousy tone, the sarcastic edge that screamed '*look at me, I'm an asshole!*' His gaze turned to the doorway, to man clad in a cheap gray suit. He was a small guy, five and a half feet, a hundred pounds soaking wet, middle-aged with deep red hair and a thick moustache covering his lip. The guy, this squeaky little son of a bitch, reminded Dante of a hamster.

Practically a fucking rat, as it was.

Detective Bryan Tracey, with NYPD's Organized Crime Investigations Division. *Detective Dick.*

They'd had their fair share of run-ins over the years, a few useless conversations, where the detective hammered him with questions that he knew damn well Dante had no intention of answering.

Nurse Russo mumbled, "I can give you some privacy."

"Don't bother," Dante said. "I have nothing to say to him."

"It's fine," the detective said. "Continue what you were doing."

The nurse hesitated before going back to her work.

Detective Tracey lingered near the doorway, not coming any closer. "I've got to say, Galante, I honestly thought I'd never see you again."

"Hate to disappoint."

"Ah, I'd hardly say I'm disappointed," the detective said. "Multiple broken ribs, lacerated spleen, punctured lung, bruised kidney... not to mention the stab wounds. They say you were beaten from head-to-toe, severely dehydrated, practically *starved.* So instead of disappointed, let's go with surprised... surprised you're alive when someone wanted you dead."

"They wanted me to suffer," Dante corrected him. "There's a difference."

"Is there?"

Dante didn't humor him with a response to that question. *Of course* there was a difference. Sometimes surviving was the worst thing that could happen to someone.

The detective strolled closer. "Who did this to you?"

"I don't know."

"Where'd they keep you?"

"I don't know."

"Why'd they do it?"

"I don't know."

"Cut the bullshit, Galante... just tell me the truth."

Dante remained silent.

That was his right, after all.

"Look, I know what you're thinking, but this isn't the time for it," the detective continued. "You can't go back out onto those streets looking for revenge. I'm not a fool. I can make an educated guess about who's to blame, and I know you'll want them to pay for it. But at some point you have to break the cycle, and I suggest you do it now, before it's too late."

"It's already too late."

"So that's how this is going to be?"

"That's how it's always been."

The man glared, although he didn't appear surprised. He'd been playing the game longer than Dante. He knew the rules. He knew how things went.

"If this is how you want to play it, so be it, but mark my words: this war is *over*. Enough people have been hurt. Too many lives have been lost. So I suggest you take a step back and let me do my job, or you just might go down also. You got me, Galante?"

"I got you, Detective, but get me," Dante said. "I've spent my entire life protecting certain people, and no *threat* from you is going to stop me from doing that."

His expression shifted, the smugness he'd walked in wearing fading. The man had a family, a wife and a daughter, so maybe he knew all about protecting the ones he loved. But he didn't know what it was like to lose them. He didn't know what it was like to give your all but still *fail*.

"It wasn't a threat. It was a warning. Don't get in my way." The detective turned to walk out but paused in the doorway. "I'm sure your father's elated about your survival. Must have been torture, not knowing. I'm hoping we get to bring the Barsanti family the same kind of news, but so far it hasn't happened."

The detective walked out, leaving behind an unsettling tension that coated Dante's skin. He felt eyes on him, a curious gaze. He glanced at the nurse, seeing a flicker of something in her eyes.

Concern.

"What happened to you?" she whispered.

He stared at her as a strange sensation stirred inside of him, compelling him to tell her, to confide in her, but he shook it off before any of the truth spilled from his lips.

"It doesn't matter what happened," he said. "What matters is that I survived it."

She didn't press the issue, pushing some buttons on some machines, before stepping away. Pausing beside the bed, she looked down at him. "Some advice, Mr. Galante?"

He raised his eyebrows.

"This is their game here, not yours... meaning while you're playing, they make the rules," she said. "So you've got two options: either you play along or you forfeit. Because standing on the field, trying to make up your own rules, won't work for anybody."

She smiled, placing a hand on his shoulder and squeezing, before walking out of the room, leaving him to his isolating peace.

* * *

When Genna awoke on the grubby couch, bright sunlight streamed through the nearby windows, the glare blinding. *Holy shit*. Squinting, she pulled herself up to a sit, shielding her eyes. No curtains. No blinds. Who the hell lived in the desert and didn't block out the sunlight?

Masochists. That's who.

Her entire body ached, spots of her sore from the springs poking her all night long. Grimacing, she looked around, realizing she was alone.

"Matty?" she called out, her voice loud in the old house, bouncing off the vacant walls.

No answer.

In the light, the house appeared ransacked. Nails stuck out of the walls where pictures used to hang, broken frames sitting around, a layer of grime coating everything. Reaching over to the end table, she picked up a small picture frame than had been face down. The glass was smashed, inside of it a faded photograph—a man, a woman, and two kids: a boy and girl. *Twins*?

"It's like *The Shining* up in here," she muttered, standing up and stretching, before setting the frame back down. She strolled through the downstairs, peeking into the same rooms she'd seen the night before. There was no sign of Matty, so she headed for the stairs, skimming her hand along the thick banister. The wood was rough, and she jerked her hand back when a massive splinter jabbed her, stabbing right into her skin.

Groaning, she yanked it out, keeping her hands to herself as she made the trek upstairs, the wooden steps squeaking beneath her. The second floor was even more eerie, ruts dug all along the floor leading down the hallway. She peeked in rooms as she went, finding a master bedroom with the bed frame still set up, the mattress half-pulled off of it, annihilated like someone had torn into it, ripping it apart. The rest of the room was intact, empty wine bottles scattered all around the floor.

"Oh-kay," she mumbled as she moved on, heading further down the hall. She encountered a girl's bedroom next, judging by the belongings still hanging in the closet, old makeup scattered along a small vanity. Right across the hall, she opened another door, knowing right away it had belonged to the boy. An old comforter lay on the small bed, the logo faded but still obvious. *Batman.* Chicago Cubs memorabilia was scattered throughout the room, a small bookcase along the side of the room with old children's books stacked up on it. Genna stepped over to it, scanning the titles before pulling one out. *Where the Wild Things Are.* The copy was old and faded, the pages yellowing, the binding loose, but it held together when she opened it.

"What are you doing?" Matty's voice called out from the doorway behind her. Genna turned, seeing him standing there in nothing but jeans, sweat pouring down his bare chest, making his tattoos gleam in the sprawling sunlight, his tanned skin already sun-kissed, a hint of pink to it. He was filthy.

"Being nosey," she admitted, holding up the book. "What are you doing?"

"Trying to get the air conditioner running," he said, stepping into the room, his brow furrowing at the Batman comforter. He didn't comment on it, though. "There's a piece broken, so I'll need to find a store before I can fix it."

"Hate to break it to you, Matty, but A.C. requires electricity."

Matty stared at her as he reached over beside him, flicking the switch on the wall. The overhead light came on, flickering, before going right back out with a loud pop. Genna flinched, as Matty glowered at it. "Probably should grab some new light bulbs, too."

"You got the power turned on? How?"

He shrugged the question off. "Got the water running, too."

Genna stared at him, eyes wide. "No shit?"

"No shit."

"Oh God, does that mean I can take a bath?"

64

"Well..." He hesitated. "The hot water heater is busted, but otherwise..."

Genna launched herself right at him, wrapping her arms around him. He laughed, nearly falling, and hugged her back. Nuzzling into his neck, Genna inhaled the scent of him, oddly comforted by the stale odor of dirt and sweat. *Okay, that's totally gross.* But he'd been hard at work while she'd been asleep, busting his ass, trying to make things okay like he's said they'd be.

Tears stung her eyes, tears she couldn't hold back, as emotion consumed her. He was so good. *So, so good.* A Barsanti boy, one of the ones she'd been raised to see as the enemy, was doing everything in his power to make the world okay for her. Despite trying to swallow it back, she let out a sob, holding him as the tears fell.

"Whoa," he said, rubbing her back. "What's wrong?"

"Nothing," she cried. "Nothing's wrong."

"Come on, Genna, baby, don't lie to me." He pulled back to look at her. "Why are you crying? Tell me."

"I just..." Her voice cracked. "I love you *so much.*"

Confusion took over Matty's expression before a smile touched his lips. Pulling her back to him, he wrapped his arms around her, kissing the top of her head. "You're pretty okay yourself, you know... for a Galante."

All at once, the spell was broken. Genna let out a sharp laugh as she pushed him, the last few wayward tears streaming down her cheeks as she rolled her eyes. "Okay, *Barsanti.*"

He stared at her. "Guess that's not us anymore, huh?"

"It'll always be us... just nobody will know."

Jen Gallivant. That was her name on the fake documents Matty had gotten, while his said *Matthew Barton.* Close enough to their real names for them to remember but a big enough difference that nobody would make the connection. Genna *hated* it. She hated everything about it. As much as she'd once despised him being a Barsanti, that was who she'd given her heart to. Matthew Barton was a fraud.

She got it, though, as much as she hated it. Being them almost got them killed. They couldn't risk it.

"Well, then, Matthew." She scowled as she said that name. "Since the water is working, I'm totally going to take a bath."

"It'll be cold," he warned, "until the hot water heater gets fixed."

"Pfft, as hot as it is in this place? It'll barely be room temperature."

"Whatever you say." He kissed her forehead before stepping away. "You enjoy your bath while I find a store. You need anything else while I'm out?"

"Cake."

He cut his eyes at her. "Cake?"

"Yeah, chocolate cake with strawberry icing."

"Chocolate cake with strawberry icing."

"Yeah, and like... sprinkles on it. I love sprinkles. Oh, some chocolate sprinkles. A fuckton of them."

He ran his hands down his face. "Chocolate sprinkles."

"Some kind of ice cream would be nice, too, to go with it, if you love me."

"If I love you," he muttered, walking out before she could say anything else. She laughed to herself, stepping out of the room behind him, watching as he disappeared downstairs. Genna waited until he was gone, until the car started up outside, before she made her way to the bathroom.

She almost hadn't believed him.

It felt too good to be true.

But the moment she turned the squeaky knob and water shot out of the faucet into the bathtub, Genna let out an excited squeal. It filled as Genna stripped out of her dingy clothes, discarding them on the floor. She stepped into the water, yelping as the bitter cold nipped at her skin. She didn't hesitate, her teeth chattering as she sunk down into it. It would warm up quick enough. There was *no way* she was waiting.

No soap. No washcloth. Hell, she hadn't even sought out a towel. But that mattered not to Genna. It was the best goddamn bath she'd ever taken in her almost nineteen years on Earth. The water soothed her achy muscles, washing the grime from her skin. She lay in silence, staring up at the ceiling, as the water warmed.

"It's going to be okay," she whispered.

For the first time since leaving New York, she actually believed it.

It's going to be okay.

SWEETEST SORROW

* * *

An old Lincoln Continental.

1963? 1964?

Genna wasn't sure about the year, but the car was recognizable. Even broken down, the black paint faded and chipped, part of the body rusted out, she knew what it was as soon as she spotted it.

It was parked behind the house, visible through the living room window. The car had been through hell and back, ransacked just like the house, but still, she found it beautiful. The thing had charm.

Opening the back door, Genna stepped out into the hot summer afternoon, grimacing as the dry heat slapped her. Matty looked up when he heard her, smiling from where he was hunkered down beside the archaic air conditioning system, still trying to get it running. Probably a lost cause, but she said nothing, letting him do whatever he needed to do, whatever would make him feel better.

After all, it wasn't always about the ending. Sometimes it was more about what you did to get there.

She returned his smile as she stepped over to the car, surveying it. She ran her hand along the beat up front end, stepping around the driver's side as she glanced in. The vinyl seats were cracked, but otherwise, the interior appeared in decent shape.

"I wonder what happened to the people who lived here," she said. "They left a lot of stuff behind."

"So did we," Matty pointed out.

"We were running."

"Maybe they ran, too."

"Maybe," she said. "Do you think they'll ever come back for any of it?"

"I doubt it," he said. "Are we ever going back for our stuff?"

"We have no reason to go back. There's nothing there for us."

"Then what makes you think there's something here for them?"

"I didn't mean there was. I was just wondering if they still wanted any of it."

"Why?"

"Because I kind of want to keep this car for myself."

Matty laughed, setting down a wrench and plopping his ass

down in the hard dirt, stretching his legs out. He was filthy, drenched in sweat. "Whether or not the owner wants it has always been irrelevant to you, hasn't it?"

"Funny."

"If they wanted the car, Genna, I'm pretty sure it wouldn't be rusting out behind an abandoned house in the desert. But I don't really see what use it is to you. It doesn't run."

"I could fix it."

"Do you know how to fix it?"

"Not really, but I could learn."

"Is that smart? Fixing up a car in your condition?"

"Don't." She pointed at him. "I swear to God, I will suffocate you in your sleep if you pull that delicate pregnant woman bullshit on me one more time. I'm fully capable of doing stuff."

Matty shoved up from the ground, wiping his dirty hands on his pants, but it did little to clean them. Stepping over to her, she reached up, cupping her chin, smearing dirt along her jawline. "I know you're capable. I'm just saying…"

"You're saying blah blah blah sexist Barsanti shit, but I'm not going to listen to it. My father treated me like a fragile ice sculpture my entire life. Everyone acted like I was breakable, but I'm not. I'm not going to break. I don't need coddled. Don't *coddle* me."

"I promise not to coddle you," Matty said, pressing a chaste kiss to her lips. "Unfortunately, I think this air conditioner is fucked… unless you want to give fixing it a try?"

She scowled at him. *Smartass.* "I could've told you that. You need, like, a serious repairman."

"It probably needs an entirely new system. We'll have to make do. Maybe get some fans. Make it tolerable until I figure it out."

Tolerable seemed to be the name of the game. Genna glanced back at the house, studying the dirty outside. "How long are we going to be here?"

"Until we have somewhere else to go."

"And if we never have anywhere else to go?"

"Then we stay right here."

"So we've got an open invitation? The place is ours for as long as we want it?"

"Something like that." He eyed her. "Why?"

"I was just thinking, you know, maybe we should fix it up, too."

"The house?"

"If we're going to be living in it for who the hell knows how long, we should at least make it livable... a step up from tolerable."

He gazed at her, smiling. "Two months pregnant and you're already nesting."

"I'm what?"

"Nesting," he said. "Like how a mother bird builds a nest to lay her eggs in... when a woman's having a baby, she gets the instinct to make sure a place is all together for the baby to come home."

"Are you...?" She gaped at him. "Did you seriously just compare me to a bird?"

He laughed. "It's a real thing mothers do."

"How do you know?"

He leaned toward her for another kiss. "Because I know everything."

Groaning, Genna shoved away from him as she rolled her eyes. "I'll probably learn to tolerate this house of horrors before I tolerate that ego of yours."

"You love me."

"I do," she said. "But that doesn't mean I like you."

"Oh, but you do. You like everything about me. That Galante stubbornness just won't let you admit it." Smirking, he stepped past her. "I'm going to go take a shower now."

"I hope you freeze your balls off."

He laughed as he opened the back door. "Love you, too, Princess. Don't you ever forget it."

She watched him as he strolled into the house, trailing dirt with him. After he was gone, she turned back to the car, nodding to herself as she admired it.

Yep, totally fucking fixing it.

CHAPTER 5

The hospital inevitably evicted Dante from the ICU.

He was put into another room, on another floor, in another ward. A private deluxe suite, they'd called it. It was the size of a fucking closet. His medicine decreased and the catheter was removed as they called in a physical therapist and let him move around on his own.

But still, he didn't speak.

He had nothing to say.

The doctors seldom showed their faces, the psychiatrist wrote him off, and the nurses? Well, leaving the ICU also meant leaving Nurse Russo.

His nurse on the general medical ward resisted looking at him, much less engaging in conversation. He preferred it that way. He was grateful. It gave him time to stew without interruption.

But still, he had to admit he missed Nurse Russo.

He kept replaying the moment she'd kicked his father out of the room, the look of determination on her face when she demanded he leave. Worked, too, because he hadn't returned as far as Dante knew. He'd had no more visitors. He was sure his father would be keeping tabs, like always, but he hadn't shown his face.

Dante wasn't sure how to feel about that.

A few times he considered calling him, ready to ask his questions, ready to hear the answers he feared, but every time he stopped himself for some reason.

Maybe he liked living with his head in the clouds. Maybe he liked the false sense of hope.

He couldn't shake it.

The hope had settled in his bones. Every second of every minute of every hour, a part of him refused to accept that something had happened to Genna.

Sitting up in the bed, Dante leaned over the side of it, his head down and hands covering his face, when a light rapt of knuckles echoed through the room from the door. Dante's heart did its bullshit hesitation as the hope flared. He raised his head, seeing the last person he expected to see.

Gavin Amaro.

Even Genna showing up wouldn't have surprised Dante as much.

"Man," Gavin said. "You look like shit."

Dante laughed dryly, the motion hurting his ribs. He clutched his side, grimacing. "Yeah, well, you should see the other guys."

"I have," Gavin said, taking a step into the room. "They look like they normally do."

"Exactly." Dante motioned toward himself. "All of *this* will heal, but there's no helping those assholes."

Gavin smirked, crossing his arms over his chest as he leaned against the wall not far from the bed. He eyed Dante in silence, studying him for so long that it got under Dante's skin. While Dante wouldn't have called the two of them *close*, they got along well enough, more than he got along with most people.

A miracle, considering Gavin was as related to *them* as it got without being pure blood.

"Why are you here?" Dante asked quietly.

"Heard a rumor you were alive," Gavin said. "Couldn't believe it. Had to see it with my own eyes."

"Well, here I am. Nobody's killed me yet."

"Yet," Gavin repeated.

Dante nodded. "Yet."

"I'm glad," Gavin said.

"You? Glad I'm not dead?"

"If you can believe it."

"I don't know if I can," Dante said. "Never really took you for a sentimental bitch."

Gavin laughed at that, his laughter loud and infectious. "That's me. Sentimental bitch."

"Don't know why I'm surprised, considering I heard you had a kitten. That true?"

Gavin shrugged. "It's more of a cat now."

"That's just one step away from a fucking Chihuahua in a purse."

Again, Gavin laughed. "You don't know what you're talking about. Vito Corleone had a cat."

"No, he didn't. Marlon Brando picked up a stray cat on the set of *The Godfather* and it turned up in the movie. There's a difference."

"Brando was a cool guy."

"Brando was the kind of guy who would carry a Chihuahua in a purse."

"He was not."

"Dude had a pet raccoon. Who does that?"

"An artistic genius?"

"A sentimental bitch."

Another laugh, but no argument about that. Silence again overtook the room. Dante picked at his fingernails, finally clean from incessant showering, as Gavin's gaze bounced around at the horrendous flower garden that had popped up in the hospital room. He had something more to say. Dante sensed it. The unspoken words were so suffocating Dante damn near choked on the insinuations.

"You don't need to pity me," Dante said. "I don't want your pity."

"It's not pity."

"Then what is it?"

"Sympathy."

"You know, if you pick up a thesaurus, those words are synonyms."

Gavin sighed. "Yeah, well, it is what it is."

"And what exactly is it?"

Dante looked at Gavin, raising his eyebrows. Gavin stared back at him in silence before his expression softened, his lips tilting down into a slight frown. It was obvious he understood it then, that Dante didn't know specifics.

"It went down in Little Italy" Gavin said quietly. "Another car bomb."

Dante's stomach dropped. He closed his eyes, taking a deep breath, pain tightening his chest. Fucking car bombs. Even to that day, he sensed the violent tremble of the ground, felt the flames lapping at his skin as he inhaled the suffocating smoke. It was a moment he'd never forget. It was something he wouldn't have wished on anyone. "Genna's BMW?"

Kidnapping him hadn't been enough. They had to attack his sister on top of it, the only innocent one out of them all.

"Oh… no," Gavin said. "Matty's Lotus."

Son of a bitch.

Dante's eyes opened. "Barsanti blew up his own kid?"

"No," Gavin said, hesitating before adding, "It wasn't him."

Maybe the medication was leaving a haze over Dante's brain, because it took a full minute for him to grasp the true meaning of Gavin's words. If a bomb had been planted in the Lotus, chances were someone else would've been responsible.

Someone else, being the Galantes.

Someone else, being Dante's family.

"No." Dante shook his head as he clenched his hands into fists. *No.* It didn't make any sense. "My father wouldn't have done it. He loves his kids. He does. He loves us."

"She wasn't supposed to be there," Gavin explained. "And she wasn't… at first. She showed up right before the car blew up. Guess she found out what was happening and wanted to stop it."

"How do you know?"

Gavin didn't answer, but he didn't have to. Dante saw the agony in his steel-colored eyes. It was the look of helpless remorse… the look of someone who had witnessed the kind of devastation that only something like a car bomb could cause.

Sighing, Dante's gaze flickered to the ceiling as his eyes started to burn. *Don't fucking cry. Don't cry in front of him. Don't cry in front of anybody. Don't fucking do it.* "This is my fault."

"You can't blame yourself."

"The hell if I can't. I should've been there. I should've done more to protect her. She shouldn't have been left alone to fend for herself."

"She wasn't alone," Gavin said. "She had Matty."

"And a lot of good *that* did her."

"He tried. After you… you know… Matty did everything he could for her. He wanted to get her out. Wanted to get her away from it all." Gavin paused, like he was considering what to say next, and finished with a whisper. "They were planning to make a run for it, before the car went..."

Boom.

Once silence took over again, Gavin pushed away from the wall. "I should get going. If you need anything, look me up."

"I'll keep that in mind."

Gavin nodded, turning to leave. "And I meant it, you know... I'm glad you're not dead."

Dante waited until Gavin was gone before muttering, "Me, too, man. Me, too."

* * *

Gabriella stood in the doorway of the cramped hospital room down on the general medical floor. Seven in the morning and her shift up in the ICU just ended. Two new patients had come in, one of which occupied the recently vacated bed in room twenty-two. More often than not, when patients left, it was because they lost their fight. But sometimes, *happy endings* happened, landing them on this floor on their way out the door, their last stop before being released back out into the wild.

She seldom saw people again once they made it there.

She tried to separate herself from her work.

But sometimes, she couldn't help it.

Sometimes, she had a hard time letting go.

Dante lay propped up in the small bed, his arm draped over his eyes. He'd gained a few pounds since she first laid eyes on him, but the hospital gown was still too big for his body, loose around the neckline, exposing some of the scars on his chest. The lighting was dim, even the television off, but the room still managed to feel lively, courtesy of the vast array of flower arrangements and balloons shoved in the corners and along the counters.

Those things weren't allowed up in the ICU.

"So, I heard you're really digging the red Jell-O... true?"

Dante's arm shifted, resting across his forehead, as his eyes drifted toward her in the doorway. "False."

"Oh, well, that sucks," she said, stepping into the room as she pulled the container of Jell-O from behind her back, along with a flimsy plastic spoon. "Because I happened to have some with me, but I guess since you don't like it..."

He held his hand out. "Give it to me."

"But I thought—"

"Hand it over," he said, "and nobody gets hurt."

Laughing, she approached, handing him the Jell-O. Shifting in the bed to sit up, he tore the foil top off of the plastic container and took a bite.

He wasn't eating. Gabriella had heard the complaints, the frustrated whispers passed along between nurses, ones that violated a dozen hospital rules (and even a few laws, for that matter). An intolerable patient. Uncooperative. Bad-mannered. A full-blown *a-hole*, quite frankly. He accepted nothing anybody offered and he certainly wouldn't thank you for anything forced upon him. A nurse's *nightmare*. The only thing he seemed to touch was the red Jell-O off of his food tray.

"You know, you can't live off of that alone. No fat, no carbs, no cholesterol, no vitamins… just mostly a crap-ton of sugar."

He nodded, continuing to eat it. "You moonlighting as a dietician now?"

"Maybe," she said, "or maybe I'm just concerned about why you're not eating."

"Ah, moonlighting as a *shrink*." He motioned toward the door with his spoon. "They make you come talk to me?"

"Nobody made me do anything. I shouldn't even be here. It's kind of a gray area, morally."

"I'm a gray area, huh?"

"Basically."

"That's good to know."

"They'll tube you again," she said, sitting down in the stiff cloth chair near the bed. "If you don't get enough nutrition, if you keep refusing to eat, they'll revert back to a feeding tube."

"And if I refuse that?"

"Then you'll be refusing medical care and there won't be much else they can do for you."

"That's also good to know."

She watched him as he ate the Jell-O. The container was nearly empty, the spoon scraping the bottom of it, when he said, "It doesn't taste right."

"The Jell-O?"

"Everything else," he said. "It all tastes like shit."

"It's not uncommon for your taste buds to have changed," she explained. "It's just temporary."

"I don't like it."

She wasn't surprised. He didn't seem to like most things. He'd been complaining since he woke up.

"Maybe someone can bring you something from outside," she suggested. "Like a family member or a friend or a girlfriend..."

He finished the rest of the Jell-O, tossing the empty container onto the small table between them but keeping the spoon to chew on. "You took care of me for weeks. Did you ever *once* see any of those around?"

"Your father."

"I'd rather starve."

"They said you had a visitor last night."

"I'm not asking him for anything."

"There's no one else you can call?"

"Depends. You offering to give me your phone number?"

"I, uh..." Crap, was he *flirting* with her? "No."

"Then no," he said. "No one."

She found that hard to believe, knowing what she did. Maybe visitors had been scarce, but *somebody* out there was thinking about him. Reaching over onto the table, she plucked the small card from a massive bouquet of lilies. "Do you like flowers?"

"Fucking *hate* them," he muttered, lying back in the bed again.

Gabriella read the card.

Pleased to hear of your survival.
-Marco Valleni

Huh. Sticking it back in the bouquet, she moved on to the next one, and the next one, and the next one, finding the same general message written on each, amounting to '*good for you for not dying*' from an Italian dude with a newsworthy last name. She should've minded her own business. Heck, she shouldn't even haven been in his hospital room. But curiosity got the best of her, and he didn't object to her nosiness, his gaze trailing her as she explored.

Had he been bothered, he would've complained, considering

he complained about *everything*.

She squeezed around the other side of the bed, just enough space for her to move, plucking the card off of a vase of light blue hydrangeas. She pulled the card out of the little envelope, glancing at it. No specific name signed to it, simply, '*The Brazzi family sends their regards.*'

Frowning, she stuck the card back in the envelope, returning it to the flowers. *What a friggin cop-out.*

"You find someone I can call?" Dante asked, so close those words grazed across the back of her neck. She shook her head, not sure what to say. "Didn't think so."

"It'll get better," she said. "Maybe ask for some pizza when they order your lunch."

"Tried it," he said. "The pizza here is *shit*."

She scowled. It wasn't *that* bad. She ate it often.

"I should go," she said, turning to him in the bed. "Take care of yourself, Dante."

She grasped his shoulder, squeezing. He didn't react. He didn't say anything. Instead, he closed his eyes, once again draping his arm across them, blocking out the world.

Gabriella left the hospital and took the subway home to her small one-bedroom apartment in Little Italy, on the fifth floor of a rustic brick walk-up with an Italian market below. Exhausted, she made the trek up the narrow staircase leading to her door. She unlocked it once she got there, stepping inside.

Straight ahead was a small kitchen, cut off from the rest of the place by a thin wall. Beyond that, an open living room, little more than a black couch and an old coffee table with a television across from it, affixed to the white-painted wall. Behind a sliding door with frosted glass was her bedroom, the full bed taking up most of the space, leaving just enough room for her dresser and well, her *mess*.

Cleaning wasn't exactly her biggest priority. Clothes were strewn everywhere. Gabriella hated doing laundry, especially since the washing machines were in the basement of the building.

Down a short hall, beside the bedroom, was the lone bathroom, the size of a closet, one you could barely walk in. It wasn't much. By her parents' account, it wasn't *enough*. They worried about her living in the city, but Gabriella loved it.

She loved being self-sufficient.

Stripping out of her clothes, flinging them on the floor, Gabriella fell into her bed, face-planting her pillow, desperate for sleep.

After tossing and turning for a few hours, dozing off to inexplicably find herself awake again, Gabriella forced herself back out of bed to shower. Time moved fast while she shuffled slow, putting on a fresh pair of scrubs before making her way back to the hospital.

Another night.

Another shift.

Twelve more hours in the ICU.

On the way, she stopped at Como's Pizzeria, grabbing a small pepperoni pie to go. She detoured in the lobby of the hospital, heading to the information desk, approaching the woman sitting there, answering phones.

"Can you have a volunteer take this up to the general ward?" she asked, handing over the red and white pizza box. "Room 245... patient's name is Dante Galante."

"Uh, sure." She eyed Gabriella with suspicion, the morally gray area beginning to turn dark. "Is this from *you*?"

"I'm just delivering it," she said. "Nothing more."

Gabriella started to walk away when the woman called out, "Who's it from?"

She considered that before answering, "Tell him it's from a friend who thinks red Jell-O sucks."

Gabriella headed to a bank of elevators just as one opened. She stepped in with a few others, someone strolling in right behind her. A throat cleared as the doors closed, and Gabriella came face-to-face with Crabtree. "Doctor."

"Nurse." He nodded tersely. "Nice night for pizza, huh?"

"It's always a nice night for pizza," she said. "There's nothing better."

* * *

"Have I told you lately that I love you?" Genna mumbled with her mouth full. "Because I totally do."

Smiling to himself, Matty tore the plastic off the top of the tub of ice cream. She'd told him she loved him a moment earlier and a few minutes before that, too. In fact, she'd been repeating it non-stop since he'd carried groceries inside. "It's always nice to hear."

"Good, because I seriously love you."

Glancing over his shoulder, Matty watched as she shoveled a bite in her mouth with a plastic spoon, eating straight from the pan.

Chocolate cake with strawberry icing. Who knew how hard it would be to find? Every bakery had chocolate cake covered with vanilla or buttercream or even more chocolate but no damn strawberry to be found. So after searching for over a week, he gave up, buying the ingredients and a damn pan, baking one in the ancient oven.

It looked like shit. He was almost ashamed. He hadn't waited for it to cool before icing it, so crumbles of chocolate cake coated the top. He covered it with a container of chocolate sprinkles, giving up, hoping it would suffice.

It was the thought that counted, right?

The cake looked dry, like he'd baked it too long, and it came out of a box courtesy of Betty Crocker, but Genna devoured it like Martha Stewart herself had whipped it up in her kitchen.

"For the record: I love you, too," he said, pulling the top off of the ice cream tub. Half of it had melted in the heat, the freezer in the house worthless. Chocolate, vanilla, and strawberry converged, creating a discolored mess. Grabbing a plastic spoon, he dug it in, watching as liquid ran off the sides. "So, you want some soup to go with your cake?"

Genna took a few steps over, pausing behind him, and glanced at the ice cream. She shrugged and dug her cake spoon straight into the carton. "I like it better this way."

Matty leaned back against the counter, regarding her. "You're kidding."

"Nope," she said, giving up pretense and grabbing the entire carton, hugging it to her chest. She stuck her spoon in and stirred, mixing the flavors together. "My brother and I used to eat all of our ice cream like this."

Matty eyed her curiously as she said that. He knew she was talking about Dante, considering she'd been too young to ever remember Joey being alive. Matty remembered him, though. And one thing he never forgot about him was that if you gave Joey ice cream to eat, he'd mix it up until he could drink it. "Really?"

A small, wistful smile ghosted across Genna's lips. "Yeah, we'd wait until it was all melted and just slurp it from the bowl. It drove my parents crazy. I still do it sometimes, but he doesn't..." She paused, her smile falling. "I mean, he *didn't*. After my mom died, he stopped. He grew up too quick after that."

Genna stared down at the ice cream in silence, lost in a memory. Matty stayed quiet, giving her that, and didn't chime in until she took another bite. "Joey used to eat his ice cream that way."

Her eyes widened. "He did?"

"Galante family trait, I guess. Can't even eat ice cream right. Gotta make things messy."

Genna laughed, her expression brightening just a bit. "I am pretty good at making things messy."

"That you are," Matty agreed. "Might even go so far as to call it your specialty."

CHAPTER 6

Manhattan found itself in a late summer heat wave.

Dante could feel the passing of time as he sat on the small metal bench along the sidewalk, in front of the hospital, the muggy heat sticking to his sweaty skin. It had barely been August the last time he remembered, but there it was, already September, fall just a few weeks away. Blinked, and he missed it, the days ticking by. It was like sleeping through a month of your life... a month where everything you knew vanished.

It was like waking up in a new world, a different world, a world Dante didn't fucking like.

This world was stifling.

"I see you've been sprung."

The familiar female voice ghosted across Dante's warm skin, so close he damn near shivered. Nurse Russo stood just a few feet beside him, clad in her blue scrubs.

"More like I escaped."

"With the doctor's blessing?"

Dante shrugged. "Figured he was tired of looking at me."

Laughing, Nurse Russo took a step forward, motioning to the metal bench. "Mind if I join you?"

Dante slid over, giving her some room. "By all means, plop your ass on down."

She sat down, not leaving much space between them. A hint of her perfume wafted toward him, subtle but sweet, barely strong enough to be detected yet it was enough to make his head swim. *Vanilla.* He'd been lightheaded since he signed the release forms, leaving against medical advice. They wanted to keep him a few more days, out of precaution, but he'd denied that request.

But as he sat there, he wasn't sure why he'd insisted on leaving. It wasn't as if he had anywhere to go.

"I'm Gabriella, by the way." She held her hand out to him. "Friends call me Gabby."

Dante hardly touched her hand before pulling away. "Dante, but you already knew that."

"I did," she said, "but it's nice to hear *you* say it, seeing as how you were refusing to say much at all."

"Yeah, well, you never know who you can trust," he said. "Besides, they didn't care about anything I had to say, so there was no point in saying it. They wanted to hear what they wanted to hear, and I'm not really in the business of placating assholes."

"I get it," she said. "It's kind of sad, though."

"What?"

"You feeling like you can't trust anyone."

"I wouldn't call it sad," he said. "That's how life is."

"Sounds lonely."

Lonely, yeah... that he would admit. The life he chose was a lonely existence. People always surrounded him, but very few were ever actually *there*. Forced smiles, frozen faces, the warmest greetings known to man. All of it, every second, every moment, was calculated, fabricated, little more than premeditated motions. People rarely smiled at him to be friendly. No, they smiled to hide their fear. They smiled to get on his good side, to gain some leverage, to feel like they had the upper hand. Nobody wanted to be on his bad side, so they smiled, grinning from ear-to-fucking-ear, dreading what would happen if they didn't.

Dante hadn't intended to become this person. Hell, he still wasn't sure it was even him. He was little more than a caricature, a face attached to a name. That was what it meant to be a Galante. People came with a predetermined set of beliefs about what kind of man he would be, and he spent his life struggling to live up to that. The loyal soldier, following his father's orders, fighting a war that had almost cost him his life. He hadn't enlisted... he'd been drafted at birth.

He never complained before. Complaining was pointless. He did it because it was his duty. He did it because it was his birthright. And he'd always believed what he was doing was for the best, but now? Now he wasn't so sure.

Because being that soldier had cost him a lot, more than he'd been willing to pay.

He wanted a fucking refund.

"It's not so bad," he said. "As long as I can count on myself, I don't really need anyone else."

"Well, that's something, I guess," she said. "So... how are you feeling?"

He cut his eyes her direction at that question. *How are you feeling?* She stared at him eagerly as she awaited his answer, like she truly wanted to know.

"Dead," he admitted. "I feel dead."

"That's normal," she said, before amending, "well, maybe not *normal*, but it's understandable. You almost did die. You're lucky to be alive."

"So shouldn't I be rejoicing?" he asked. "Shouldn't I be celebrating getting another chance?"

"Probably," she said, "but I guess it depends."

"On what?"

"On whether or not you value your life."

He was quiet, stewing over those words, as he picked at his fingernails. "I'm not suicidal. You don't have to sit here and talk me off of a ledge."

"I don't think you're suicidal," she said, "but suicidal people aren't the only ones who jump."

He shook his head. "You don't know me."

"But I know people like you," she said. "People who value pride and loyalty. People who keep fighting because it's what they think they're supposed to do. People who refuse to let go out of stubbornness. People who jump, believing they'll land on their feet."

Dante clenched his hands into fists. "Like I said, Nurse Russo, you don't know me."

"It's Gabby," she said, her voice calm despite the hint of anger in his tone that should've warned her away. "And I don't have to know you, Dante. Not really. But I had a brother once. I had a brother who was strong, and stubborn, and the furthest thing from suicidal. But he was also someone who valued his pride more than his life. I had a brother who jumped off the Brooklyn Bridge. He didn't do it because he wanted to die. No, he did it thinking, somehow, he'd live. Someone told him he wouldn't, and so he did." She stood, placing a hand on Dante's shoulder, squeezing. "I hope everything works out for you. If you ever need someone to talk to, you know... if you ever decide you want to trust someone again... I'd be more than happy to listen. Just try not to jump, you know, unless you're certain the consequences are worth it."

Dante watched her as she walked away. His stomach twisted in knots. She'd gotten under his skin. He didn't like it. They'd only had a handful of conversations and yet she had him nailed down like he'd been an open book.

The worst part was that she wasn't wrong. His pride was all he had left at that point.

Standing up, he straightened the set of paper-thin borrowed scrubs he wore, ones the hospital had provided before showing him the door. His clothes had been cut off of him on arrival, had been taken as evidence by the police, along with any belongings that had been in his pockets... if the Barsantis had left him with anything. He didn't know. He hadn't asked. Until then, he hadn't even cared. But suddenly, he was itching to get his hands on his wallet.

Without it, he couldn't even afford subway fare.

No money. No phone. Not even a friend.

"Nurse Russo?" he called out, catching her before she entered the hospital.

She paused. "Please, call me Gabby."

He nodded, acknowledging that. His stomach churned. He could see her hope, that wide-eyed innocence, like she thought she'd gotten through to him.

He hated to have to squash it.

"I was just wondering if you had a few bucks you could lend me," he said, hating every syllable that came from his lips. He loathed himself for asking. He felt small. Emasculated. "I wouldn't ask... fuck, I know I shouldn't ask... but I've got nothing on me, and it's hard to get around this city when you've got nothing, you know?"

He wanted to dig a hole in the ground and crawl right in it, throw some dirt on him and call it a fucking night.

"Oh, uh, yeah..." She opened her purse and dug around inside of it, whipping out a yellow card. "Actually, I've got a MetroCard, if that'll help?"

He hesitated, not because it wouldn't help—it would—but because his pride was strong. So, so fucking strong. Asking for help was hard enough. Accepting it, taking it, almost proved to be too much. She seemed to get that, because she rolled her eyes, stepping toward him and forcing the card in his hand.

"Go home," she said, her small hand on top of his, squeezing, forcing him to grip the card. "Or go to a friend's. Go somewhere, anywhere, but don't just hang around here."

"Tired of looking at me?" he asked.

She shook her head, letting go. "I just think maybe other people might be missing you, instead."

She headed into the hospital then, disappearing through the front entrance. Glancing down at the MetroCard, he set off toward the subway. She was wrong. They didn't miss him. They missed who they thought he was.

They missed who they expected to come back.

An hour and a few connections later, Dante ended up standing on the lawn in front of the house he grew up in, north of the city, in Westchester County. Sweat pooled along his brow, beads of it running down the side of his face. He felt woozy, more exhausted than he'd ever been before. His legs weren't what they used to be. His knees shook, wanting to give out on him as he stood there, taking it all in.

The house looked like home. It looked like *his* home. But it didn't quite feel like home anymore.

Right out front, prominently parked, were two familiar cars: his black Mercedes, and behind it, Genna's BMW. That twinge of hope flared deep in his bones but he pushed it back, knowing if he gave in to the sensation, it would only hurt worse. If anything, her car was confirmation of the truth. Like his mother's belongings tucked away in the attic, their cars would've sat there forever, rusting away, collecting dust, tangible keepsakes their father clung to like maybe, if he kept it around, he could say he had a piece of them left.

Carefully, Dante approached the house, reaching for the doorknob, surprised to find it unlocked. It turned smoothly, his grip slipping a bit because of his sweaty palms. He pushed it open, stepping in the doorway, just as someone walked by. The familiar form skidded to a stop in the foyer, swinging around, on defense, a hand going straight for a waistband where Dante knew they kept their gun. It didn't faze him, though, not in the least—not even when they drew their weapon and aimed it at his head.

"You shoot me, Bert, and I won't be the only one who winds up dead," Dante said, stepping into the foyer and closing the front door.

Before him stood Umberto Ricci, arguably one of Dante's closest friends, although he doubted how far that sentiment went now. Weeks in the hospital and Umberto hadn't stopped by at all.

Not a peep from the guy.

Umberto lowered his gun, pointing it at the floor near his feet. "Dante?"

"Last I checked." Dante eyed him peculiarly. "You did know I was alive, right?"

"Yeah, uh... I mean... of course, yeah." Umberto nodded, seeming to shake off the surprise as he tucked his gun away. "I knew you were alive, that you'd survived, but knowing is one thing... seeing you is completely different. Just... wow. You're here. You're... alive."

"Again, last I checked. What are you doing here?"

"I've just been helping your father out, keeping him company and all that."

"Is he home?"

"Your father?"

Dante nodded.

Who the hell else would he be talking about?

"Oh, yeah... he's in his office." Umberto motioned toward the office, like Dante wouldn't remember where it was located. "He's asleep, though... was up all night. Hell, he's up most nights. Didn't expect you home for a few more days. I can wake him..."

"Don't bother," Dante said, shrugging it off as he set his sights on the stairs. "I could use some sleep myself."

"Of course," Umberto mumbled. "You, uh... sure."

Dante shot him a peculiar look. Nervous, he realized. Umberto was *nervous*. Genna used to call the guy a bumbling idiot, and he was certainly acting like one now.

Dante didn't have it in him to deal with that, though. Shaking his head, he walked up the stairs, leaving his old friend alone in the foyer. He went straight to his old bedroom, looking around when he opened the door. It was spotless, nothing out of place, all of his belongings right where he'd left them, like it had all just been sitting there, awaiting his inevitable return.

Curiosity nagged at Dante as his gaze drifted across the hall to his sister's bedroom door. Quietly, he stepped over, gripping the knob, hesitating before opening it.

A disaster greeted him.

Clothes were strewn everywhere. It was nothing new where Genna was concerned. The girl lived in chaos, while Dante always preferred order. Something in the room drew his attention, though, and he stepped further inside, careful not to trample on any of her things. Across the room, near her closet, on the floor, was a black duffle bag. A few pieces of clothing had been tossed in it, but otherwise, the thing was empty.

They were going to run, Gavin had said.

Guess they weren't fast enough.

After looking around, Dante headed back across the hall. He hadn't lied about needing some sleep. As exhausted as he felt, he could've slept for *days*, but he'd been out of commission already for too long. Anarchy had reigned in his absence. As much as he wished everything could go back to normal, it was impossible, because normal was gone.

So as he stood there, stripping out of the scrubs, he thought about where to go from there.

He considered his options. All of them sucked.

Stepping into his connecting bathroom, he turned on the shower, leaving the water scorching hot. What would Genna do? What had she done?

She'd rebelled.

It was in her nature. If you told her she had to go left, she'd deliberately veer right. Unlike Dante, the obedient soldier, Genna forged her own path. She was free-spirited like their mother. Dante always admired that about her. He'd been raised to be unyielding like his father. He saw only black and white. But Genna saw the gray area. She'd lived in it.

The gray area. That was what Nurse Russo had called him. She saw in shades of gray, too.

Maybe I ought to be more like that.

* * *

"Oh God, yes," Genna moaned, tossing her head back and closing her eyes. Sweat coated her flushed face. Goose bumps sprung up along her skin. "Holy fuck, that feels so good. Don't stop. Never stop. More. More. More."

Laughter rung out from across the room. "Should I be jealous?"

Genna peeked an eye open. Matty stood in the doorway to the kitchen, filthy from head-to-toe. Sweat soaked him, his dirty clothes clinging to his bronzed skin. He'd spent so much time working under the sun that parts of him, like his shoulders and his cheeks, were pink with sunburn. *Ugh, that's gotta suck.*

"Probably," Genna replied, closing her eyes again. "I'd definitely be jealous, you know, if it weren't happening to me."

Footsteps started in her direction, careful and measured. A soft smile touched Genna's lips as he approached. Cool air blew down on her from the vent in the kitchen ceiling. It wasn't cold, no, but compared to the desert heat, it felt glorious. She could stand there forever, in that exact spot, and die a happy woman. For over two weeks, Genna had felt like she'd been *baking* in that house.

"I can't remember the last time you looked so… satisfied," Matty said. "Starting to make me question my skills in bed."

Genna's smile grew. "You're alright."

"Just alright?"

"Well, I mean, I wouldn't say it's anything to write home about."

More laughter. Genna opened her eyes, gazing at Matty. He stood just a few feet in front of her, close enough to reach out and touch him if she wanted to.

"What a shame. I would've liked to see you write home to tell your father about all the spectacular sex we've been having."

"Right?" Genna sighed dramatically. "What a shame. Instead, I'll have to tell him about the ancient air conditioner and how it's blowing my goddamn mind by, you know, blowing."

Matty grasped her hips, stepping even closer. "I'm definitely getting jealous now."

"I told you—you should be." Genna wrapped her arms around his neck, gazing at him, as her fingers ran through the hair at the nape of his neck. His hair was getting longer. He needed to get it cut. Hell, he needed to shave. He could use some better deodorant, too, because whatever he'd been using hadn't been working. The man was a mess... a filthy, smelly, desperately-needed-a-shower kind of mess. But he was *her* mess. "You know, it's totally true what they say: you don't know what you've got until that shit is taken away."

He grinned. "Is that what they say?"

"Yep. You don't appreciate it until you don't have it anymore... like air conditioning. And Wi-Fi. Even a computer. Hell, any kind of technological device, for that matter. This place doesn't even have an electric can opener. They have one of those that you gotta crank with your own hand."

Matty gasped in mock horror. "What monsters."

She rolled her eyes. "I'm serious. It's so disconnected from reality... from *my* reality. I miss movies. And music. And Netflix."

"Porn," Matty chimed in.

"Even porn," Genna agreed. "Maybe that's what you need to spice up that mediocre sex you've been dishing out."

He nudged her. "I don't know. I don't think a lowly commoner like me is fit to please royalty. Might take more than porn to get me up to par."

"More like what?"

"Like practice," he said. "Practice makes perfect... that's another thing they say."

He leaned in for a kiss, but Genna's hand shot up, coming between them to cover her mouth. She stepped back, his hands falling from her hips. "No offense, but you kind of reek."

"I reek?"

"Yeah, you smell like... ugh, I don't know how to describe it. You smell like a man, but times ten. You need to take a shower. Like, STAT. Before the neighbors think something died out here."

"There are no neighbors."

"Then the buzzards. Or vultures. Or whatever those freaky ass birds are that look like Grim Reapers with faces like Red Skull."

His eyes widened. "Is that a comic book reference?"

"It's a movie reference. They make them into movies, you know. I watched it. The red dude was ugly. He was freaky looking, like the birds. But quit changing the subject."

"The subject being that I smell like a corpse."

"Pretty much."

After she dropped her hands, Matty carefully leaned in, leaving a small peck of a kiss on her lips, one she didn't attempt to ward off. "Enjoy your air conditioning, Princess. I'm going to go hose off."

He headed upstairs, leaving her in the kitchen alone. It lasted a minute or so before the silence grew too much, the novelty of the cool air wearing off. She trekked after him, hearing the shower running in the bathroom, and considered barging in but thought better of it. Shower sex, while hot in theory, was one thing that should *only* happen in porn. Something about being drenched and sliding around on slippery porcelain while trying to get some kind of rhythm going without drowning spelled disaster for Genna.

So instead, she wandered around, ending up in the boy's bedroom again. She plopped down on the old Batman comforter and grabbed a book from his bookshelf, mindlessly flipping through the pages. Matty finished in a matter of minutes, exiting the bathroom naked except for the towel around his waist. It was white and flimsy, stolen from one of the cheap motels they'd stayed in.

"You smell better," Genna called out as he started to pass by. "Or well, I *think* so. You don't stink from here."

Matty strolled into the bedroom, ignoring her comments. "Give up on your orgasmic air conditioning experience?"

Genna motioned toward the ceiling above the bed, to the perfectly placed vent. "I still feel it. Novelty kind of wore off, though."

"I suspect you'll be saying that about me someday."

Genna laughed as he sat down, nearly flashing her when the towel came loose. "What makes you think I don't already say it?"

He glanced around. "Because there's nobody around for you to say it to."

"Touché."

"Got you on a technicality." Matty cupped her cheeks with both hands, framing her face. "Guess that means I win for now."

"For now."

Matty kissed her, another peck like the one downstairs, before deepening it, his tongue gliding along her lips. Shifting positions, he pushed her back against the bed, leaning overtop of her. Genna kissed him back, losing herself in the moment, until his hand slid up her inner thigh, finding its way through the bottom of her shorts.

Breaking from the kiss, she pushed against him. "No, wait, we can't..."

Matty pulled away, sighing, and removed his hand. He grabbed the towel as he stood, attempting to wrap it around his waist, but Genna snatched ahold of it. "No, I mean, *wait*."

He shot her a confused look, loosening his grip on the towel, letting her yank it away. She tossed it on the floor behind her, discarding the thing, as her eyes drifted along his torso, following the happy trail right down to her happy place.

Wow.

He was hard, without a doubt, harder than Genna had probably ever seen him. Poor guy had blue balls. They'd been joking earlier, about the mediocre sex, but the truth was sex had been scarce.

"I wouldn't call myself modest or anything," Matty said, "but you're examining my dick pretty hardcore and I'm starting to get a little self-conscious about it."

Genna's eyes darted to his face, her cheeks growing warm.

"Hey, it's okay," he said, cupping her chin and tilting her face up. "We don't have to do anything. You owe me nothing. I can knock it out in the shower if I need to, if you know what I mean. Not a problem."

His voice was playful, and she knew he was genuine, but man, those words made her feel guilty. *You owe me nothing.* He truly believed that. She could tell. But it was a lie, because she owed him the universe. She was his world, maybe, but Matty was the sun. Without the world, the sun would keep on burning, but without the sun, eventually, the world would die. Not to be melodramatic, but that was how she felt. Matty burned so bright that he kept her breathing, he kept her living, he made it so that she could create life. Without him, she'd be lonely, dark, and cold, withering away until there was nothing.

And he didn't even know it.

"I want to," she said, placing her hand on his thigh. "But it's just, you know... we can't do it *here*."

Matty's brow furrowed. "Why?"

"Because it's a little kid's room."

"Not anymore," he said. "They're long gone, Genna. They left before getting an electric can opener, remember? The kid who slept in this room is probably a hell of a lot older than us now."

"I know, but still... there are baseball posters and Boxcar Children books and I'm sitting on a freaking Batman blanket."

He looked around. "We can get rid of it all."

"No," she said quickly. "Ugh, that feels even worse. I can't throw away the kid's things just to ease my guilt over defiling his room."

"So, what, the shower?"

She rolled her eyes, standing up, and pushed him toward the doorway. "No, we'll just go across the hall. There's a bed in there."

Matty let her drag him to the room across the hall. "Pretty sure a kid slept in here at some point, too."

"Probably, but it doesn't matter," she said, wrapping her arms around him as he backed her up to the bed. "There's no Batman blanket."

Matty laughed, laying her down on the bare mattress. It was old, and not so comfortable, and she cringed to think of how unhygienic it might be, but goddammit, it was a *bed*, and they were going to use it. "What's your problem with Batman?"

"It just feels so innocent," she whispered. "Everything in there seemed so pure."

"And this room is, what? Not so innocent?"

"You could say that," she said as he nuzzled into her neck. "It feels cold. Figuratively speaking, and not literally, because it's still hot as fuck in here."

He hummed in response, placing a kiss on her throat, his teeth grazing her skin and lightly biting. Genna gasped, tilting her head, as she ran her fingers through his damp hair. Matty made easy work of her clothes, slipping them off and tossing them on the floor. She lay beneath him, stark naked, goose bumps springing up along her skin. His hands were all over her, touching, caressing, and leaving a trail of fire from his fingertips.

Matty reached between them, his hand drifting between her

legs, stroking her inner thighs before he made his way to her middle. A chill radiated down Genna's spine, tingles encompassing her.

"So soft," he whispered, rubbing her clit with his fingers. "I've loved that about you since the very beginning. The Ice Princess had a soft spot."

"For you," she mumbled.

"For me," Matty said. "All mine, nobody else's... it'll never belong to anyone but me."

Genna smirked. "You're kind of hot when you get possessive."

He pulled back a bit to look at her. "You think so?"

She playfully scrunched up her nose. "Maybe."

Matty laughed under his breath, pulling his hand away from her to grasp himself. He stroked a few times, not that he needed to. He was still rock hard.

Shoving her knees further apart, Matty settled between her legs, not hesitating before lining up and slowly pushing in. His eyes fluttered closed, practically rolling in the back of his head, as he filled her, a soft growl escaping. "Fuck."

He rocked against her, pulling out before pushing back in. It was slow and sweet, and Genna waited for him to increase his pace, to give her more.

It didn't happen.

"More," Genna whispered, coaxing him. "Please."

Matty moved a tad bit faster, a barely noticeable increase. Genna dug her rigid nails into his back, repeating her words.

"Please, Matty. *More.*"

If he heard her, he certainly didn't listen, because he kept moving at the same pace. Genna gave him a moment, thinking maybe he was just trying to get his bearings, figuring he'd pick it up soon enough, but when it didn't happen, she lost a bit of her patience, realizing it was intentional.

He was being careful. *Too* careful.

"I'm not breakable," she said. "You're not going to break me. I'm pregnant, not helpless."

Matty pulled back a bit, propping himself up on his elbows, as he stared down at her. After a moment, he kissed her lips, softly and sensually, barely a peck before whispering, "I know."

Yet he went right back to what he'd been doing.

"I swear to God, Matteo Barsanti," Genna growled. "If you don't *fuck* me—"

In a blink, Matty shoved her knees up, opening her legs wider, as he slammed into her. Genna gasped, eyes widening with surprise, as he looked down at her, his expression serious. "Is that better?"

Genna nodded. "Uh-huh."

A smile cracked his face. Leaning down, he kissed her, a few quick pecks. "Whatever the lady wants."

That was it. Those were the last words spoken. Genna's knees were forced against her chest, her legs over Matty's shoulders, as he thrust hard... as he started fucking her. She whimpered, grasping at his skin. He gave her all of himself, not holding back, but he never went too far.

He was still, somehow, careful.

He knew her limits. He knew her needs. He knew what made her tick. He knew what she wanted from him. And he gave it to her—fucking her, yes, but with mercy. Fucking her so she knew who was in control, so she knew he wouldn't dare hurt her.

The pressure built inside of her, an orgasm coming on. She clung to Matty, gasping, as it rocked through her. Her body convulsed with pleasure, and Matty let out a throaty groan. It didn't take him long after that. Her orgasm was just waning when he let loose. Genna felt him spilling inside of her, the warmth spreading between them. He nuzzled into her neck, grunting, forcing her legs so far against her that her thighs ached.

After a few more thrusts, he stilled, just lying there.

"Matty?" Genna whispered.

"Yeah?"

"You're killing my legs."

He laughed, letting go of her, and pulled out as he moved. Flopping over on the bed beside her, he stretched out and closed his eyes. Genna rolled over onto her side, gazing at him. Sweat glistened from his skin. He hadn't stayed clean long after that shower. Her eyes scanned him, from his face and down his chest, drifting right toward his cock. She let out a laugh, shaking her head.

How was he still so hard?

"Never—and I mean *never*—look at a guy's dick and laugh. That's just all sorts of messed up."

Genna's gaze drifted back to Matty's face, seeing his eyes open again. "Did it bruise your ego?"

"I've got no more ego left to bruise," he said. "I left it back in New York, along with everything else... certainly my pride and most of my common sense... probably my dignity, too."

Genna smiled. "You've got me, though. And we've got this place. That counts for something, right?"

"Counts for everything." He squeezed her to him, kissing the top of her head. "Who needs self-respect when you've got decent sex and a half-ass working air conditioner?"

* * *

Business as usual.

As Dante stood in front of the open refrigerator in the kitchen, he realized life had continued as usual around there. Every day was like the one before it, like nothing had changed.

Like everything was normal.

Leftovers piled the shelves. The kitchen was stocked full of groceries. Wine had even been chilled. Primo Galante hadn't missed a beat. Life went on. The world kept turning. The calendar affixed to the wall had been changed, the month flipped.

Time hadn't stopped for them.

Dante shifted through the containers of food. Not that he was hungry, but he couldn't remember the last time he ate something that wasn't Jell-O.

The pizza from Nurse Russo.

Spaghetti. Lasagna. Some other kind of pasta. None of it caught his attention. Definitely not the chicken salad... he couldn't stand the sight of it. He grabbed a bottle of water and took a sip, hoping it would help settle his stomach.

The faint sound of footsteps registered through the downstairs, reaching Dante's ears as they moved through the foyer, coming his direction. Dante didn't look. He did nothing but stand there, sipping water in front of the open refrigerator, as whoever it was entered the kitchen.

Silence overwhelmed them.

It sucked all the air from the room.

95

"Dante?"

Primo's voice was quiet. Hesitant. Dante took another sip of water before screwing the lid back on. Shutting the refrigerator door, knowing he wouldn't find his appetite now, he turned to the doorway to greet his father. "Dad."

The second Dante spoke, Primo's expression shifted, relief relaxing his features, like he'd feared Dante was a figment of his imagination. *Maybe I'm not the only one waiting for ghosts to pop up.*

"It's good to see you, son," Primo said. "Good to have you home. I never thought—"

"Never thought you'd see me again?" Dante guessed.

Primo nodded. "Not alive. I thought—"

"They killed me?" Dante guessed again.

"Yes." Primo took a step closer. "They sent me a message—a son for a son. The blood in the car... there was no sign of you anywhere."

"So you looked?"

Primo stared at him.

He didn't respond.

The son of a bitch didn't look for me.

"You looked, right?" Dante asked again, not dropping that. He knew his father well enough to know his silence meant he had no answer, but Dante wanted an explanation. "You said there was no sign of me anywhere, so I'm guessing that means you looked everywhere?"

Primo stared at him some more before offering an answer. "They had you. There was no point."

No point.

Maybe Primo hadn't meant that the way it sounded, but those words were like a knife to Dante's gut. On one level, he got it. He'd even told his sister once: when the Barsantis got their hands on you, there would be nothing left. But that didn't mean they shouldn't still *look*.

That didn't mean there was *no point*.

"Well, what do you know," Dante said, motioning toward himself. "They left some part of me to be found. Not sure how much is salvageable, but here I am."

Something in the tone of Dante's voice, or maybe it was the

bluntness of his words, sent Primo's guard up. Dante saw it in the way the man's shoulders squared, the way his jaw clenched. The relief dissipated as fast as it came about. Primo's eyes studied Dante's face.

Dante knew the tactic. He'd seen it employed hundreds of times. His father stared people down, breaking them with silence, using intimidation as a form of punishment. He'd done it to countless men. Hell, he'd even used it on Genna. But he'd never tried with Dante before. He'd never had to.

And as they stood there, Primo staring him down, Dante realized it wasn't working. He was immune. He felt nothing but anger, the kind that burned cold and not hot. It wasn't volatile rage.

He was numb.

"We should talk," Primo said, breaking first, to Dante's surprise. He'd never seen his father let someone else win that game. "A lot has happened."

"Like the explosion in Little Italy?" Dante guessed. "I heard all about it."

Primo's eyes narrowed with a flash of rage, a flash of *suspicion*, before he straightened his expression out. His voice, though, betrayed his calm demeanor. "From *who*?"

Dante considered concocting some story to avoid what he knew would become an argument, but that was just a part of him that wanted to save face. *Fuck it.* "Amaro."

That answer shocked Primo. "Johnny Amaro?"

"No, his son."

"What the hell does that boy know about anything? When did you even talk to him?"

"He visited me," Dante said. "Came to the hospital."

"He did *what?*"

"He heard I was alive so he stopped by to see how I was doing." Dante paused, intending to drop it, but words kept flowing from his lips instead. "It's kind of fucked up, really... Amaro being the only person who bothered to check on me."

That struck Primo hard... just as hard as the mention of Genna had hit him at the hospital. The man flinched, his face paling, like he couldn't believe those words had come from Dante.

"I came to the hospital," Primo said, taking a step forward, pointing at Dante. "You *know* I did. You saw me there. That woman—that nurse—told me to leave. But I called every day to check on you. I called to make sure you were getting better. So don't give me that bullshit about Amaro being the only one who bothered, because no one named Amaro cares about you. No one named Amaro gives a fuck if you live or die."

"Maybe not," Dante said, "but someone named Amaro respected me enough to tell me the truth."

Primo scoffed. "Respect? You think he *respects* you? If you think he told you anything out of respect, you've lost your mind! And truth? What does he know of the truth? He was probably there to gloat!"

"He's got nothing to gloat about," Dante said. "He lost a cousin, you know."

To be technical, Dante thought, Gavin lost *two*. Enzo died at Dante's hands. He personally had taken away one of Gavin's cousins.

"I'm well aware of their relationship to the Barsantis," Primo spat. "It just furthers my point. Whatever truth you think he gave you is skewed. His loyalties lie with *them*. He's not your friend. No Amaro is, nor will one ever be, not as long as you're a *Galante*. You need to get that through your head and get over this 'he respects me' nonsense, and you need to do it quickly."

Primo turned, intending to walk away, like he considered the conversation over, but Dante wasn't done talking. "So tell me."

Primo stalled. "Tell you what?"

"The truth," Dante said. "Tell me the version that isn't skewed. Respect me, since Amaro doesn't, and tell me what happened."

A moment passed, and then another, before Primo looked at Dante again. His expression was calm. He'd pulled himself together with ease. "You want to know the truth, son?"

"You know I do."

Primo took a few steps forward, his demeanor casual, like the man was just strolling through the room. *Unruffled.* It was a facade, Dante knew. A mask to hide behind, to not let Dante see he'd gotten under his skin, but it was too late. Dante knew he'd struck a bad nerve, one he might never recover from. Primo had, even momentarily, questioned his son's loyalty. Was there any going back from that?

"The truth," Primo said, "is that I did what I swore I would do. I went after Matteo Barsanti. I blew up his car. And if you expect me to feel even an ounce of regret about that, you're going to be disappointed. I refuse to grieve for a Barsanti."

"But what about my sister?"

Dante kept his voice even as he asked that. Emotion was vacant in his voice. He felt it, though. He felt the anger. He felt the pain in his chest. Man, it burned.

Primo said nothing.

Dante wondered if he planned to answer at all.

What could he say? How could he twist it? How could he justify harming his own daughter?

But eventually, Primo let out a deep sigh that almost... almost... sounded coated in regret. When he spoke, though, Dante realized he'd been mistaken. Not regret. *Shame.* He was ashamed of her. "Genevieve knew. She knew, and she turned her back on us, on this family, and she chose him instead. She chose a Barsanti. So do I grieve her? Absolutely. I grieve the loss of her every day. But not for the reason you're thinking. It's not because of anything *I* did. Your sister committed suicide, as far as I'm concerned. She did it to herself. I'm not to blame."

Primo strolled out then, just as coolly as he'd approached. Dante listened to his footsteps as they headed to his office.

Dante followed but paused in the foyer, hearing voices. His father was talking to someone. It took just seconds for him to recognize the other voice. Umberto. Dante debated interrupting, torn between confronting his father and wanting to get the hell out of there. His dilemma ended when the office door opened, Umberto walking out and closing the door behind him.

He frowned at Dante as he started toward him, carrying some stuff. Dante realized, as he approached, that it all belonged to *him.* His wallet, his car keys, and even his cell phone.

"Your father figured you'd want this stuff back," Umberto said, holding it out. "He said you'd want to leave, to cool off, clear your head, you know... that you're upset about things."

"Upset about things," Dante repeated, grabbing his wallet to scour through it. Everything was still in there, as far as he could tell, even a couple twenties. They hadn't bothered to steal his money. *What kind of half-assed criminals...?*

"Yeah," Umberto muttered as Dante shoved the wallet in his back pocket. "Sorry about all that, by the way... sorry about what happened."

"What do you have to be sorry for?" Dante grabbed his keys and phone next. The battery was dead, but Dante guessed it still worked, considering his father returned it. "It's not like *you* killed my sister."

Umberto didn't respond to that.

He just stood there.

No. Dante groaned as he slipped the phone in his pocket, clutching his keys. "Come on, man, don't tell me *you...*"

Umberto half-shrugged. Dante didn't have to finish where he was going with that. Nobody knew the ins and outs of cars like Umberto Ricci, the guy who had done time for stealing them *twice*. He knew all about circuits and conduits and whatever the fuck else it took to get power flowing.

Of course he'd been involved.

He'd certainly know how to wire a bomb.

"You were gone," Umberto said, trying to explain. "Your father wanted it all to be over. He figured, you know, it should come full circle. He wanted the bomb to be exactly like the one that killed your brother. Key in the ignition... *boom.* And your sister, man, I didn't know. Nobody could've known she would go after him, that she would risk her life like that, knowing there was a bomb."

"I would've," Dante said. "I would've known she'd run straight for him, because that's who she was."

"An enemy sympathizer."

An enemy sympathizer. Dante laughed bitterly at that. She'd been put in a box with a label, like she'd never been anything more than someone in love with someone so wrong. Fucking *Romeo & Juliet* in the flesh, dying stupidly over forbidden love. Dante wasn't surprised. He'd feared that for her. But it made him sick to hear it. She'd always been so much more.

"I meant she was the kind of person who would risk her life to save someone," Dante said. "Say what you want about my sister, but nobody can deny she was one of the good ones. She was innocent... a hell of a lot more innocent than any of us."

Dante walked out before Umberto could respond. Dante was in no mood to hear whatever he'd say to that. He didn't want to start off his night by punching the guy who had at one time been his closest friend.

Besides, the world was out there, waiting.

And wherever his sister was, wherever she'd ended up, he was going to make her proud. He was going to show her he hadn't forgotten the promise he made.

The promise that he'd be there anytime she needed him. He might've been late this time, but it was never *too* late to make things right.

CHAPTER 7

Darkness cloaked Manhattan.

It had moved in hours earlier, coming on like a fog and swaddling everything around Dante. He found a strange sense of peace in it. He always had. As the sun went down, he felt himself growing calm.

More than anything, especially then, out there felt like home.

It hadn't been a particularly gloomy night. Nothing out of the ordinary. In a city like Manhattan, even in the darkness, everything still seemed to be lit up. Buildings, streets, and even the sky. Enough light radiated out that it made it damn near impossible to see any stars. But still, after nightfall, the world turned dark. It was like walking in the shadows.

Being invisible.

Invincible.

Dante sat on the metal bench outside of the hospital. He wasn't sure how long he'd been there but it had to have been a few hours. People came and went, moving in fast-forward, while he pressed pause, just existing in the moment. After darkness reigned, the sky again started to grow light. Dawn was coming. A new day happening. He'd survived another night.

Noises came from the entrance to the hospital near sunrise as a few people scattered. *Shift change.* Dante watched as a woman approached. Head down, eyes fixed on the ground, she walked at a brisk pace.

He almost let her keep going. Almost let her slip away. But his lips moved, his voice sounding out while she was still in earshot. "Nurse Russo."

She skidded to a stop. "Dante? What are you doing here? I thought you left."

"I did," he said, reaching into his pocket to pull out the yellow MetroCard. He held it up, clutching it between two of his fingers. "Figured I'd return this."

"You didn't have to do that," she said as she stepped to him, carefully taking the card and holding onto it. "You could've kept it."

He shook his head. "Returning it was the least I could do."

He didn't mention the fact that he'd loaded it with money, too.

"Well, thank you," she said, her voice hesitant, "but I'm serious... you didn't have to. You probably shouldn't have. Just because you got discharged doesn't mean you're healed. You should be in bed, recuperating, not hanging out here."

"I'm fine," Dante said. "Feeling good as new."

She rolled her eyes as she muttered under her breath. "You know, I didn't think it was possible, but you seem even more hardheaded now than you did in the hospital. And that was some next-level stubbornness. That was so stubborn they called in *psychiatry*."

Dante smiled at that. Her frustration amused him. "What can I say? I'm full of surprises."

"So I've heard," she said. "*More than what meets the eye*. That's what they say about you. A wolf in sheep's clothing."

"I guess my reputation precedes me."

"That it does."

Dante stood up from the bench then, lingering in front of her. He almost defended himself, but it seemed pointless.

"Look, Nurse Russo..."

"Gabby," she corrected him.

He hesitated before nodding once. "Do you want to, I don't know, grab a drink or something?"

She gaped at him. "A drink?"

"Yeah, I mean, I'm guessing you're old enough..."

"I'm twenty-six," she told him. "Which makes me older than *you*, but that's beside the point. You're asking me to get a drink with you, at seven o'clock in the morning, when you just got out of the hospital. Literally, just hours ago. You shouldn't even be on your feet right now. And you want me to go with you to get a drink? Are you *insane*?"

"I'm not sure. I didn't bother to read the psychiatrist's report."

"You should've. It said you suffer from a personality disorder, but you otherwise seem mentally fit."

"Huh, good to know. Did it give a name to the disorder?"

"The doctor was leaning toward Antisocial."

"Antisocial," Dante repeated. "So a sociopath, basically."

"Basically."

"Do I seem like a sociopath to you?"

She hesitated before mumbling, "I'm not a psychiatrist."

"I know you're not. I'm not looking for a medical opinion. I'm asking for your personal one."

"My personal opinion is that he knew your reputation and had you diagnosed before he even stepped in the room."

"So no, then."

"No," she agreed. "What's wrong with you isn't a disorder. I think something else."

"Like?"

"I'm torn between stupidity and grief."

Despite himself, Dante laughed at that.

"So," he said, drawing out the word as he cocked an eyebrow. "About that drink?"

"Aren't you on medication? Didn't they prescribe you stuff? Do you really think it's wise to drink under those circumstances?"

"Wise? No. But that's never stopped me before."

She shook her head, running her hands down her face in exasperation. "This goes against everything I stand for. I'm a nurse, for crying out loud. You were my *patient*."

"I'm not your patient anymore," he said. "Besides, I'm not asking Nurse Russo to have a drink with me. I'm asking Gabriella."

He expected to be shot down. The odds were stacked against him. She was her and he was him, and they existed in different worlds, and she didn't really know him. She'd been acquainted with the reputation. She'd been introduced to someone who didn't exist, as far as he was concerned. But yet, she'd somehow seen through that, she'd seen a part of the real him in that hospital, and that was what gave him the courage to ask.

Still, though, he expected a flat-out refusal.

So when she hesitated, something stirred inside of him. *Son of a bitch.* She was considering it.

"One drink," she said finally.

"One," he agreed.

"And then you go home," she said. "I'm dead serious, Dante. If I have a drink with you, you have to promise that afterward, you'll go home, and you'll rest. You'll let yourself heal. None of this hanging out around hospitals to pick up nurses nonsense, like this is Pearl Harbor and you're about to be shipped off to war. You're charming, but not *that* charming. I'll give you this, but it's not going to work any more."

A smile touched Dante's lips. "You think I'm charming?"

"Right now, I think you're an idiot," she said. "Even more of an idiot than I am for going along with it."

"Yeah, well, you only live once, right?"

"Or in your case, twice. You've been given a second chance."

"A third, technically," he corrected her. "This wasn't the first time. I escaped death once before."

"You must have a Guardian Angel."

"Maybe," he said. "Or maybe the Grim Reaper hasn't caught up with me yet. Someday he will, though. But until then..."

"Maybe the third time's the charm."

"I guess I'll find out."

She offered him a tentative smile then before glancing around the neighborhood. "So, where are we going to get that drink?"

"Where do you want to go?"

She shrugged. "Surprise me. You're full of surprises, right? Just... make it a good one."

"Right." He reached into his pocket and pulled out his keys. "I can do that. My car's parked just down the block."

"Oh, you're driving?" A conflicted look passed across her face. "So you'll be drinking and driving on top of taking medication. *Awesome.*"

"Relax," he said. "I'll get you home safe. I promise."

"It's not *me* I'm worried about."

He was getting to her. He could tell. Frustration was mounting into something more. She was worried. Hell, maybe she should've been. Maybe his head wasn't in the best place. Maybe there was something wrong with him. But it felt nice, he thought, to have someone worrying about him again, even if that someone was a stranger... a stranger that was too nice for her own good, frankly.

Dante motioned for her to come along as he headed away from the hospital. Gabriella scowled, keeping in step with him as they strolled down the sidewalk. When he reached his Mercedes, parked cockeyed beside the curb, he opened the passenger door for her.

She stalled on the sidewalk, eyeing him warily, like she was debating backing out.

Dante wouldn't have blamed her if she did.

"I'm so going to regret this," she muttered as she climbed in.

"Probably," Dante admitted before closing the door.

When Dante got in, he noticed Gabriella's eyes were glued to his seat, to the discolored patch on the tan leather. *Blood stain.* His body covered it when he sat down. He knew, because the blood had come from him. He'd been sitting right there, in that exact spot, when it had been spilled.

Genna got out of the car, waving goodbye to her brother, and stood along the curb as he drove away. Dante watched her from his rear view mirror... watched her watching him. A sick feeling settled in the pit of his stomach. It had been brewing for days. Nothing was going as it should've. Their world was imploding. The family was at odds.

His sister was in love with one of them.

Of course, he'd known for a while, since he'd found Matteo in her bedroom, but he'd suspected it before that. Suspected it, but ignored it, hoping he was wrong. If you didn't see it, it didn't happen. If it's not happening in front of you, maybe it's not happening at all. Ignorance and naivety. That was what he blamed. His own ignorance and naivety in expecting it all to just go away.

He didn't blame Genna. He could never blame her. She was just being who she was.

Dante circled the block, coming back around, planning to wait outside of the community center as she worked her last shift. He whipped into an open spot along the curb, barely having a chance to park before the passenger door opened.

In that split second, he thought it was his sister. The terror didn't come until later, until a gun pointed at his face.

Tweedle-fucking-dum climbed in, holding a 9MM, his finger on the trigger. The door behind Dante opened, someone sliding into the backseat, both doors closing at the same time.

A glance in the rearview mirror told Dante it was Tweedledee.

The Civello brothers, two of Barsantis men.

They'd been close to Enzo.

"Drive," one of the brothers said. "Take a left at the red light and head down to Little Italy. Cooperate, and we won't kill your sister. We'll make sure she makes it home tonight."

Dante stared straight ahead, his eyes drifting toward the community center. "She has nothing to do with this. She's never hurt anyone."

"I said we wouldn't kill her." Tweedledum pressed the gun against Dante's cheek. "What more do you want?"

What did he want? More than he'd ever be able to have. After a moment, he closed his eyes, taking a deep breath, before putting the car back in drive.

He followed their directions. He drove where they told him. He even pulled into the quiet, vacant alley, knowing it didn't lead anywhere.

Dante stopped the car, his heart racing. He had maybe thirty seconds... thirty seconds to try to save his own life. In broad daylight. The middle of Manhattan. At the hands of two idiots. This wasn't how he was supposed to die.

Where was the honor in that?

It was a snap decision. He didn't even think it through. The second he had the car in park, he swung, hitting the guy beside him, stunning him enough to make him lower the gun. Dante reached into his waistband, grabbing his own gun, whipping it out and aiming it. His thumb switched off the safety as his trigger finger shook. All he needed was ten more seconds. Ten more seconds and he'd kill them both.

The guy lunged from the backseat, grabbing Dante. Before he could pop off a shot, pain tore through him. A scream echoed from his chest as a knife ripped into him, piercing his side.

Again.

And again.

Those ten seconds passed.

It wasn't enough time.

A car showed up, pulling in behind them. It wasn't help, though. Reinforcements. Burning pain radiated. He was losing too much blood.

The driver's side door opened. Someone grabbed Dante, pulling him out of the car and throwing him on the ground. He was disarmed, his pockets rifled through. A kick to the side sent blood gushing out.

"That's enough," a voice said.

Roberto Barsanti.

Dante forced himself up, clutching his side. Roberto approached, stopping to intercept Dante's wallet from whoever had gone through his pockets. He stood in front of Dante, the two of them eye to eye.

"You killed my son," Roberto said. "You murdered Enzo."

"I didn't mean to," Dante said, spitting blood onto the ground. "I wanted to kill Matteo."

Rage took over Barsanti's face. "You think this is a joke?"

Dante shrugged.

Barsanti's cheek twitched as he took a step back, motioning to his men. "Take him to The Place, get him fixed up, then put him in the basement. Don't let him die. He hasn't suffered enough yet."

"Dante?" Fingers snapped in his face. "Are you okay?"

Blinking, Dante glanced at the passenger seat, meeting a pair of concerned eyes. "I'm fine."

"You don't look *fine.*" Gabriella grasped his face, feeling his forehead. "You're pale and sweating."

He grabbed her wrist, stopping her as she tried to examine him. "I'm fine."

"But—"

"You're not Nurse Russo right now, remember? I don't need a diagnosis."

"You need *something.*"

"I need a friend."

When Dante let go of her wrist, Gabriella shifted in her seat, resting her hands in her lap. "A friend."

"Yeah. And I know we don't know each other. I'm just that guy who was brought in, the one everyone talked about, the gangster." He grimaced when he said the word and noticed she did, too. "You're the nurse who drew the short straw. Tough break. So I get it, if being friends isn't in the cards. Hell, I wouldn't want to be my friend. Look at me. I'm all fucked up. But I don't know if I can count on myself right now, not like I should. So I need someone. Someone who can listen to me, someone who hears me, someone who can help me make sense of it all."

She was quiet before saying, "It sounds like you need that psychiatrist."

"I can't trust them, either," he said. "I can't trust a man who judges me by my name, who can diagnose me based on some bullshit reputation. I need a friend. And I'm not asking for some lifelong commitment, none of that BFF bullshit. Don't expect me to make you friendship bracelets, and I know sleepovers are out of the question. You can keep this as your dirty little secret. When you pass me on the street, act like I don't exist. It won't hurt my feelings, I promise. But I need someone..."

He trailed off. Maybe what he asked for was selfish. Maybe it made him an asshole.

She wasn't responding, which made him think that was exactly how it sounded.

"Nothing to say?" he asked, turning to her.

She stared at him.

"Seriously? Nothing?"

Gabriella pursed her lips. "But what if I *want* friendship bracelets?"

Dante put the key in the ignition and started the car. "Then you ought to make them, because that's a bit out of my range of skills."

"Really? You just braid some string together. You can braid, can't you?"

"Maybe," he said, pulling out into traffic. "Never really tried before."

"Unbelievable," she muttered. "Take a class or something."

Dante navigated the streets, making his way down to Little Italy, to the old sports bar he used to hustle at on the weekends. He neared Mulberry Street, swinging into a parking spot along the curb.

Gabriella climbed out of the car and paused on the sidewalk, waiting for him. They walked in silence down the block, Dante's mind wandering.

"Maybe we should cross the street," Gabriella suggested, her voice hesitant.

"Why?"

She didn't answer. She didn't have to. Dante's gaze shifted, his footsteps coming to an abrupt stop. Yellow caution tape quartered off most of the sidewalk, leaving just a small path to squeeze through. The surrounding buildings were blackened, scorched by fire, chunks of bricks missing and glass shattered. Plywood covered doors and windows, signs posted along some of them.

Danger. Do not enter. Condemned.

He saw, quite clearly, the center of the destruction. A small crater had been blown into the asphalt.

He had to look away.

He knew. He did. Gavin had told him it happened there. But knowing and seeing were different. It was physical confirmation.

It was a slap in the fucking face.

Something struck him as the two of them stood there, him trying to come to terms with what he was seeing, while Gabriella stood in silence, not questioning his reaction.

She knew about the explosion.

Of course she did.

Why wouldn't she know? Rumors ran rampant at the hospital. An explosion like that would've made the news.

"Are you okay?" she asked eventually, her hand on his arm.

"No," he admitted.

"Let's go get that drink," she said. "We can go around."

They crossed the street, and Dante kept his head down, his eyes trailing the sidewalk until they made it to the bar. Familiar faces greeted him, watching him with stunned looks.

He ignored them, motioning to a table. "Take a seat. I'll get our drinks."

"You don't know what I want."

"You look like a margarita kind of girl."

She scowled. "Really?"

"Fine," he said. "I take it back. What do you want?"

"A margarita."

Before he could respond, Gabriella skidded over to the booth to wait. Dante approached the bar, tucking in at the side where the bartender lurked.

"Galante," the man said, plastering on a smile. "Great to see you!"

"I'm sure," Dante muttered. "I'll take a margarita on the rocks and a Heineken."

"Coming right up."

The bartender made the drinks, refusing Dante's money when he tried to pay. He knew he should've been grateful for that, and back in the day he would've probably expected the special treatment, but it irked him now.

He threw the cash on top of the bar and walked away.

"Your margarita," he said, sliding it on the table in front of Gabriella before sitting across from her.

"Thank you," she said, offering a smile, one that felt a hell of a lot more genuine than the bartender's. "Guess your reputation precedes you everywhere."

He took a swig of his beer. "What makes you say that?"

"Everyone is staring at you with awe," she said, "but in that pretend-I'm-not-looking way that isn't really subtle at all."

"How do you know they're looking at me? Maybe they're looking at you."

She rolled her eyes as she sipped her margarita. "Why would they be looking at me?"

"Because you're beautiful," he said, that word making her blush. *Huh.* "Besides, I'm nobody special."

"That's not what I heard."

"Yeah, well, you shouldn't believe everything you hear. People like to talk, and none of it's true. It's nothing more than gossip."

"It's all false?"

"Yes."

"Huh. So, true or false—your father is mob boss Primo Galante."

"Alleged mob boss," Dante corrected her. "He's never been convicted of anything."

"You're involved in organized crime."

"True," Dante admitted, before saying, "allegedly."

"You were caught up in a violent turf war. You were kidnapped and assumed dead. Those people tortured you and almost killed you out of revenge."

"Oh, that's all true. Allegedly, anyway."

"Allegedly," she muttered. "So which part was false?"

"The part where they made me out to be a bad guy because of it."

"You think you're a good guy?"

"I know I am."

"Even though everything else is true?"

Dante regarded her. "I like to think what defines a man aren't

111

his circumstances or his mistakes. What defines him are his intentions, and mine have always been good."

"That's deep," she said, continuing to sip her drink.

"So, I get it, you think I'm a bad guy..."

"Whoa, *I* never said you were a bad guy. I'm just riddling out where your head is."

"Moonlighting as a shrink again."

"Being a friend," she said. "And just for the record, you know, I didn't draw the short straw."

"What?"

"In the car, you insinuated I got stuck with you, but that's not true. I volunteered."

"Why would you do that?"

She shrugged. "Because you needed somebody. Everyone else was being all weird about it. I don't think it was *you*, really... I think it was your father. He barked orders and demanded things, and it freaked them out. Nobody wanted to be *that* person..."

"The person who killed Primo's kid."

"Yep," she said. "Because I gotta tell you, you looked bad."

"But yet you volunteered. *Ballsy.*"

"I wasn't worried. I'm more worried *now*. You were fighting hard then, but now..."

"Are you saying I gave up?"

"More like you're currently in the process of shutting down."

"I've told you before—you don't know me."

"Oh, but I do now." Gabriella motioned between them. "Friends, remember?"

"Right, my mistake. How could I forget? Of course us being friends now means you know everything about me."

"I know you use sarcasm to hide how you're feeling."

"How do you know that?"

"Because you just did it."

"How observant."

She smiled, sipping her drink some more, sucking every last drop from her glass. "You know, you're kind of cute when you're annoyed."

"Cute, on top of charming? If I didn't know any better, I might think you have a thing for me."

A sharp bark of laughter burst out of her as she shoved her glass aside. "Puh-lease. You're hardly my type."

"What's your type?"

"The opposite of you."

Ouch.

"Loyal, upstanding citizen, you mean? The kind that doesn't get kidnapped and tortured?"

"More so the hair and the eyes." She scrunched up her nose as she waved her hand around in the direction of his face. "More Nate Archibald and less, you know, Chuck Bass."

He gaped at her. "Did you just...?"

"No offense, of course."

"Of course," he said. "I thought everyone liked Chuck Bass."

She laughed. "Do you even know who Chuck Bass is?"

"*Gossip Girl.*"

"How...?"

"I had a sister," he said with a shrug. "She was more of a Carter Baizen girl, though. She wouldn't shut up about it."

Had. Past tense. Dante threw back his drink, swallowing what was left of it. It wasn't very strong. *Not strong enough.*

"Had?" Gabriella asked. "Genna, you mean?"

"Yeah."

"What happened to her?"

Dante's eyes flickered to meet Gabriella's gaze, seeing an innocent curiosity that nagged at him. "Are you fucking with me? We *just* walked past the spot outside."

It seemed to take a moment for his words to register. "You mean where the car blew up?"

"Ding, ding, get the girl a cookie, she solved the riddle."

"I, uh... I don't know what to say."

"You don't have to say anything."

"But I just... I had no idea. I mean, yeah, the car blew up, but your *sister?*"

"What? It hasn't been on the news?"

"Well, I don't *watch* the news, but..."

She sat there, staring at him.

Dante let go of his empty bottle, pulling away to stand up. "Anyway, a deal is a deal. We said one drink."

Gabriella stood, smoothing her scrub top. "Yeah, I should be getting home."

Dante reached into his pocket for his keys. "I can drive you."

"No need," she said as they stepped out into the warm Manhattan morning. "I can walk."

"Don't be ridiculous," he said, stalling on the sidewalk in front of the bar.

"Ridiculous would be driving me, considering my apartment is closer than your car."

"No shit? Which one?"

She pointed at a tall brick building across the street, three lots down. "Top floor."

Interesting.

As much as he hung out in that area, it was a wonder they hadn't met before. How many times had he passed her on the street without noticing? How many times had they unknowingly crossed paths? He'd been inside that building a few times.

Small world.

"Thank you," Dante said, grasping her arm and rubbing it. "For humoring me."

"That's what friends are for," she said. "And I'm around, you know, if you need a friend again."

"That goes both ways," he said. "Anything you need."

Gabriella turned away, taking a few steps before stalling again. When she glanced back at him, a look of confusion crossed her face, like she had something she wanted to say but was afraid to spit it out.

Jesus Christ, was she going to ask him to come up?

He would, without hesitation. The condition he was in, he'd probably disappoint. He wasn't sure he could satisfy her through his exhaustion, or if he was even strong enough to be on top, but hell, she could always *ride* him, right? *If my dick cooperates...* Regardless, she wasn't the kind of girl a guy said no to, but then again, she wasn't really the kind of girl who asked a stranger to come to bed with her... was she?

"Dante?"

"Yeah?"

"I'm really sorry about your sister," she said, "and I just think you should know... well... nobody has mentioned her being involved. I honestly had no idea. I wondered why she never came to the hospital. I didn't know you believed... that she was ... there."

Dante's expression fell.

Gabriella left then. He watched her as she crossed the street, his eyes glued to her until she disappeared inside the building alone, leaving him with those parting words.

It made no sense.

Barsanti knew.

His father knew.

Hell, Gavin knew.

So why didn't the rest of the world know?

CHAPTER 8

"I got a job."

Four words. Hell, four syllables. They came together to make a sentence that just didn't compute in Genna's brain. She heard them, sure, but it didn't make sense. *I got a job.* What the hell?

What was that jibberish?

"A job," Genna said. "You got one."

"Yep."

Matty grinned, looking damn proud. It was cute, she thought. He was cute. Something about the moment felt just so wholesome. But she couldn't quite enjoy it, thanks to her confusion. How the hell did he get a job? She didn't even know he was looking.

"What kind of job? You're gonna need to elaborate, Matty."

"The kind that earns money. We're okay at the moment... we've got more than enough to get through. We don't have many bills, not while we stay here, but still, we're having a baby, so..."

"So..."

"So I got a job."

He said it just like that, like that was all there was to it. He got a job so that he can earn money, because obviously he hadn't been doing enough, seeing how he was only doing *everything.*

"A job doing what?" Genna asked. "Because you're being kind of vague and it's making me think the worst."

"It's legal, don't worry."

"Prostitution is legal in Vegas. I'm still worried."

"Well, technically, prostitution isn't legal in Vegas, it's only—"

"Matty," she growled.

"—legal at brothels around the state." He sighed, holding his hands up. "Fine, it's cooking."

She gaped at him. "Cooking."

"Yeah, I was in town, running errands, when I passed this small diner that had a 'help wanted' sign hanging on the door. I got curious, asked what kind of help they were looking for. The manager said they needed someone who could cook."

He shrugged then, like that was that, like there was no need to go any further with the story.

"So... you volunteered?"

"More like I applied," he said. "I filled out an application... or *Matthew* did. I figured it was a long shot, considering I'm twenty-five and have no work history, nor do I have any references, but they were desperate. I start tomorrow."

Genna wasn't sure what to say. Congratulations? Thank you? Are you fucking *crazy*? She didn't know which sentiment fit best. They were in uncharted waters. When leaving New York, they hadn't given much thought about the future. Sure, they talked about the possibilities, but they hadn't stopped to consider the specifics. They both had an ungodly amount of family money, but touching a single penny of it was out of the question.

That would be dangerous.

Way too dangerous.

So all they had was whatever cash Matty had pulled together from whoever had helped them. He'd said it was enough to get by, but how much *was* that, exactly?

"It's only making ten bucks an hour, but it's something," he said. "Thirty or so hours a week, after taxes, we're looking at an extra grand or so every month."

A thousand dollars. Genna used to blow that in ten minutes at the mall. She bought shoes that cost more than he'd make in a month. She couldn't wrap her brain around it.

Matty's smile fell. "Why are you looking like that, Princess?"

"Like what?"

"Like you're about to cry."

Tears burned Genna's eyes, a lump forming in her throat. "Probably because I am."

He full on frowned and opened his arms, pulling her into a hug. "I thought you'd be happy."

"I am," she whispered, tears streaming down her cheeks. "I'm just sorry you have to go through this because of me."

"Whoa." He pulled back to look at her. His hands framed her face, holding it in place. Fresh calluses had sprung up on his thumbs, the skin rough as he stroked her flushed cheek. "This isn't something I'm going through because of you. This is nothing you did. It's not some kind of punishment, Genna. This is living. This is how other people live. It's a lot of work for not a lot of pay, but it's money I'll earn, money I'll deserve, money I made for *my* family."

Matty's right hand drifted down, leaving her face, and settled on her stomach instead.

"And that's enough for you?" she asked.

"It is," he said. "We've got plenty of cash. And I still have people I can turn to. I don't have to work, but I need to. I need to do this for us. Can you get that?"

It took Genna a minute, but she got it. It wasn't about the money. He got a job to contribute. He needed to feel like he was working toward something. For weeks they'd been holed up in that house, doing little more than just existing, venturing out only to get what they needed.

"I get it," she said. "I do."

"Good. If you start to get lonely here and want me to quit, I will." He kissed her forehead. "Anyway, since it's my last night of freedom before I become your average everyday working man, I thought we could go out and celebrate."

"Celebrate how?"

"Vegas is just down the road," he said, his smile returning as he nodded toward the vacant highway. "I'm sure we can find some trouble to get into there."

Genna grinned. "Trouble sounds fun to me."

They didn't have many clothes, and most of Matty's were stained from working around the house. And Genna had little more than tank tops and shorts... shorts that kept getting shorter because she insisted on cutting them up and tops that got tighter because— *whoa, mama*—the breasts seemed to balloon overnight. But upstairs, in the bedroom with the scattered bottles, Genna had found a slew of clothes hanging in the closet. Most of it was gaudy, some even falling apart, but a few things Genna encountered had been salvageable, some dresses and even a pair of heels that miraculously fit just right.

"You don't think Mrs. Whatever-Her-Name-Is would mind me borrowing her clothes, do you?" Genna asked, pulling a hanger out of the closet and holding the black dress up to her as she turned to Matty, who lurked in the doorway.

"I don't think she'll ever know," he said, leaning against the doorframe. "Besides, finders-keepers. Not sure how much you want, though, since half of it looks like it came out of the 80s."

"More like the 90s," Genna said. "80s were all about big shoulders, but the 90s went sleeveless a lot."

"I stand corrected."

"And the shoes," she said, reaching down to snatch up a pair of pointy-toed heels, "are more like early 2000s, without a doubt. 2004 or so, I'd say. Shoes were so pointy you could stab a man with them. So someone was still here then, or else *these* wouldn't be around."

Matty raised his eyebrows. "You should've been a P.I."

"Hardly," she said with a laugh as she stripped out of her clothes to try on the dress. "I've got the pieces, yeah, but none of them fit. Downstairs there's a rotary phone and an old ass television without a remote, which is totally more the 60s, right?"

"Right."

"And the car out back is a 64, I think. But in the boy's room, there are books that weren't published until the early 80s. The poster on the wall, of the White Sox, was of the '78 team or something. I can't remember. Anyway, but in here, you know, shit is more modern. That wine bottle right there on the dresser even says 1998 on the label."

"Wow," Matty mumbled. "That's a lot of numbers you just tossed out."

"Yeah, well, who the hell knows what they all add up to." She slid the black dress over her head, letting it fall down around her body. "I'll figure it out, though."

"You seem invested."

"We kind of got dropped in the middle of someone's life, in their house, with their things, in the middle of fucking nowhere, where nobody with an ounce of sanity would want to live. It makes me feel like we might be in an Amityville Horror sequel."

"I don't think it's anything that bad."

"So you don't know?" she asked, eyeing him. "You have to know *something*."

"I told you what I know. It was a favor from a friend of a friend. They offered the keys, said they didn't need the place."

"It's weird."

"It is," he agreed, "but I'm not going to look a gift horse in the mouth, Genna. Besides, the last thing you do with people like them is get curious."

"Yeah, I know," she muttered, slipping her feet into the high heels before reaching into the back of the closet, pulling out an old dry cleaning bag. "Here, put this on."

Matty took it carefully. "What is it?"

"A suit. A crazy expensive one, too, from what I could tell."

"How do you know it'll fit me?"

"I don't," she said. "Won't know until you try."

Matty unzipped it to pull out the suit. It was gray with a subtle pinstripe pattern, paired with a black button down shirt. "You seriously want me to wear this?"

"Yes."

Letting out a resigned sigh, Matty walked away.

Genna tinkered around as he showered, fixing her hair and putting on a bit of makeup. It wasn't much, whatever she'd acquired at the drugstore in town. It made her feel better, though.

Amazing what a pair of heels and some lip-gloss can do...

Genna was lingering in the kitchen when Matty resurfaced, making his way downstairs. He'd ditched the coat but the pants fit him, maybe a bit tighter in the ass than he might've liked, but Genna certainly enjoyed that view. *Wow.* The shirt hugged him in all the right places, the buttons stopping around his chest, showing off a flash of skin. He paused in front of her, rolling his sleeves up to his elbows, exposing his tattoos.

"You look nice," he said, eyes scanning her.

"Right back at you." She grinned. "Vintage."

"I look like a walking cliché," he said, glancing down at himself. "Like I stepped right out of *Scarface*."

"That's the 80s," she said, "but it's totally making a comeback, you know. And hush, because seriously... those pants? *Wow.* That suit does a body good."

Matty tugged on the pants, trying to adjust them. "You're lucky I'm secure with my manhood. These pants are so tight I'm pretty sure they're cutting off the circulation to my balls."

She laughed. "They're not *that* tight. I can't even see your, you know…"

He cut his eyes at her as she pointed toward his crotch, wiggling her finger. "My balls?"

Another laugh. "Yes."

"You can't see them because they're gone. They shriveled up and died from the lack of oxygen."

"You know, you've been talking about them a lot lately…"

"That's because they're important," he said, stepping close enough to grasp her by the hips. "We can't have more kids if I've been de-nutted."

"Whoa, buddy," she whispered. "I haven't even popped out this one and you're already planning others?"

"I've been planning them since the second I laid eyes on you," he said, his voice low. "The moment you stepped onto that elevator, the first thing I thought was, '*damn, we'd make pretty babies*'."

"Is that right?"

"Yep."

"How many babies are we talking? Two? Three?"

"Seven."

She coughed, choking on thin air. "Seven?"

"It's a good number," he said. "A lucky number."

"Yeah, well, two feels pretty lucky. It's a good number. I like it. What's your problem with two?"

"No problem with it," he said, grinning. "It's not seven, but I won't object to two. All I know is that I'm more than happy spending the rest of my life knocking you up."

"Knocking me up," she mumbled, wrapping her arms around him as he kissed her. "So romantic."

"Romance. Is that what you want?"

"Maybe."

"You want me to wine you and dine you? Bring you back home and sixty-nine you? You want me to take you out for another ten-inch steak?"

"Kiss my ass."

"I can certainly do that," he said, not missing a beat. "I can do even more than just kiss it, if you're down. I can take you upstairs, strip you out of that dress, and turn you out until sunrise, Princess."

"*Mm... can you?*"

"Absolutely." He kissed along her jawline before whispering in her ear. "You wouldn't have to ask me twice. Anything you want, however you want it... I could make love to you all night, over and over, or you know, maybe just fuck you senseless for a few hours. Fuck you with my mouth, my tongue... caress every inch of your body, whatever you want. Just ask and it's yours, Genna."

She hummed. "Anything?"

"Anything," he promised.

"What I really want is pickles."

The second that she said that, the spell broke. Matty let out a laugh as he pulled away. "Pickles?"

"Yeah." She scrunched up her nose. "It's weird, but I would seriously kill for some."

"Well, then," Matty said, running a hand through his chaotic hair, still not cut, the ends curling. "How about we go find you some pickles? Maybe, I don't know, some ice cream to go with them."

She yanked him toward her, pressing a hard kiss against his mouth. "Now you're speaking my language. You better watch yourself, Matty. If you don't stop seducing me, I might just be inclined to keep you around."

* * *

Pickles. *Unbelievable.*

Matty sat across the small table from Genna, watching as she gnawed on a pickle spear. Her fourth, as it was. She hadn't eaten anything else. An entire plate of food was going untouched because of goddamn pickles. They'd stopped at a small restaurant just inside of the Vegas city limits, both of them ordering cheeseburger platters, with Genna requesting *'an ass-ton of extra pickles'*.

Much to her delight, they'd brought her a whole bowl of them.

"Do you like cucumbers?" he asked.

Her face scrunched up. "Gross."

"Pickles are just pickled cucumbers. You know that, right?"

"I'm aware," she said, pointing what was left of her pickle at him. "I don't even like *pickles*, but I started craving them."

"Pregnancy cravings."

"It's funny, because I was eating one the day I found out. It actually made me sick. Dante—" She cut off after saying her brother's name, silence taking over for a moment, before she continued. "He joked about me being pregnant. It never crossed my mind until then, but it probably should've. He realized his joke wasn't a *joke*, so he bought a test and made me take it. I was in shock, but he, well… he went to find you."

Matty knew the day she referred to. He'd riddled out the timeline, having not much else to do while on the road except dwell on what happened. It made sense, looking back. Something had set Dante off the night he showed up in Soho looking for a fight.

It was the night he'd taken Enzo's life.

It was meant to be me instead.

"I asked him why," Matty said. "Your brother, you know… he was who he was, but I never took him to be malicious. So I wanted to know why he'd come after us."

"What did he say?"

"He said I gave him no choice, that because of me you were as good as dead."

Genna took a bite and muttered, "He *so* overreacted."

"I don't know," Matty said. "I don't know if there's such a thing. He just… reacted."

She damn near dropped her pickle. "Did you just…? No, seriously, did you just *defend* him?"

Matty stared at her. *Huh, guess I did.* "I just think about your father and what *he* would've done. You being pregnant would've set him off, regardless. He coddled you; we all knew it. *Nobody* touched his little girl. Add in that it was *me* that did it, someone he already hated, and he would've lost his fucking mind."

"My father wouldn't have killed me."

"Maybe not, but he would've killed *me*, Genna, and there's no way he would've accepted this baby. It's impossible. The hate runs too deep. It's a part of you, yeah, but all he would see is the part that's me."

123

"He wouldn't hurt a baby," she said. "Children are *innocent*."

The moment she said that, her expression shifted, reality hitting her. Even she didn't believe her words. History had taught them that when it came to their fathers, innocence was irrelevant.

"I was innocent once," Matty said. "You were, too. So were Joey, and Dante, and even Enzo. None of us started out as monsters. I don't know that any of us even became them. But it didn't stop people from seeing us that way. So maybe your father would've kept you breathing, but breathing doesn't always mean living. Dante was right—you were as good as dead."

Genna tossed the rest of her pickle down on her plate before pushing it away. "Never in a million years did I think I would hear you defend a Galante."

"Don't get used to it," Matty said. "In fact, I'm wishing I could take it back."

"Whatever," she said, smiling. "It's burned in my brain. You'll never live it down. You're practically aligned with the enemy now."

"Practically? I was aligned with the enemy the moment I felt what it was like to be inside of you. There was no coming back from that."

"What did it feel like?"

"What?"

"Being inside of me."

Her voice was dead serious, but the twinkle in her eye told Matty she was teasing him.

"You really want me to describe it?"

"Yep."

He considered that. What did being inside of her feel like? *Everything.* It was Heaven. It was Hell. It was the most beautiful torture he'd ever felt. "Let me put it in words you'll understand."

"I'm listening."

"It's chocolate cake with strawberry icing, covered in chocolate sprinkles, eaten straight out of the pan."

Her eyes widened. "*Damn.*"

"Anyway..." Matty motioned for the waitress to bring the check, even though neither of them had eaten much. "The night is young. What do you want to get into?"

"What are my options?"

"We could see a show, maybe. There are musicals and concerts—"

"And strippers," Genna chimed in. "Aren't those Chippendales guys in Vegas? You know, the dudes with the little G-string banana hammock looking thingies with the black bowties?"

Matty ignored that. "And magicians and comedians and who knows what else. There's gambling—"

"And prostitution."

"And nightclubs where we could go dancing, I guess, if we want to be around a bunch of drunk people when we're sober."

"I think that describes the *entirety* of Vegas, but go on."

"There are shooting ranges and roller coasters and racecar tracks—"

"And wedding chapels."

"And..." That stalled him. "And wedding chapels."

"They've even got those drive-thru ones," Genna said. "You could make an honest woman out of me without even getting out of the car."

Matty laughed. "What comes after that? Road-head for the honeymoon?"

"You wish," she said, balling up a napkin and smacking him square in the chest with it. "It'll be a cold day in Hell before I suck a dick in a stolen Honda."

The waitress approached, damn near tripping over her own feet when she heard Genna. Her eyes widened, cheeks flushing, as she glanced between them. "I, uh... I'll just take this when you're ready," she muttered, dropping the check on the table before scurrying off.

Matty shook his head, picking up the check, when Genna muttered, "Oh fuck, I did that."

He pulled out his wallet, grabbing a few bills to pay. "Traumatized the waitress? Yeah, you did."

"No, I sucked a dick in a stolen Honda," she said just as the waitress again approached. The woman took the money, dashing away, as Genna rolled her eyes. "You remember when we met at the courthouse? I said I was there for stealing that car?"

"I remember," Matty said. "I'm guessing it was a Honda?"

"An Accord," she said. "*Wow*. I can't believe I actually sucked a

125

dick in a stolen Honda."

An exasperated sigh echoed around them as the waitress tossed Matty's change down on the table before stalking off. Genna glared at the woman's back.

"Well, then," Matty said, leaving his change on the table. It was more than he'd usually tip, but he figured the waitress deserved it this time. "Guess it's a cold day in Hell, Princess."

"Yeah, well, it's not happening ever again," she said, pointing at him. "Don't go thinking I'm some cheap floozy just because I let you fuck me on a pool table that first night."

"I wouldn't dream of thinking that about you. No *baby mama* of mine will ever be a cheap floozy."

"Ugh, don't call me that." She grimaced. "This isn't an episode of *Maury* we're living. If you cheat on me and deny my baby, I'm not going to give you some DNA test on national television. I'll cut your dick off and make *you* suck it in a stolen Honda. You got that?"

"Jesus Christ," someone muttered nearby.

Matty glanced to the next table over, watching the waitress shake her head as she delivered a few plates. Leave it to Genna to shock a woman who works in Vegas, a woman who has probably seen and heard *everything*. He almost felt bad for her. It was hard to tell sometimes with Genna whether or not she was being serious. There was still a bitter coldness to her exterior, the rigid façade that had earned her the *Ice Princess* nickname. It wasn't really her, of course. The Genna that Matty knew was warm and loving.

Loving enough to see past his name, to judge him for *him*, knowing it was a risk. The fact that he was a Barsanti should've scared her away, but she gave him a chance. She was one of a kind. There was nobody else like her—nobody as brave, and as beautiful, and as downright *crazy* as Genevieve Galante.

"Got it," he said, turning back to Genna. "How do you feel about being called a Barsanti?"

"I don't see how that's *better*."

"It's probably not," he admitted, "but you wouldn't be my baby mama anymore… you'd be my wife."

"What?"

"Like you said, there are a lot of wedding chapels in Vegas. I'm sure one can squeeze us in."

She stared at him, her expression blank.

Matty wasn't sure what that meant.

"Are you joking?" she asked finally.

"No," he said. "I mean it."

"You want to get *married*."

"Yes."

She stared at him a bit longer, long enough for him to question if maybe he'd screwed up by suggesting it. He got that it wasn't ideal, and she deserved more than a quickie wedding in Vegas that wouldn't even be legal, considering they couldn't use their real names, but it would still count where it mattered. They'd know, even if nobody else would.

"I'll marry you," she said quietly, "under one condition."

"Anything," he swore.

Genna leaned closer to the table, her voice dead serious as she said, "There can be no goddamn Elvis Presley in the building."

A smile slowly formed on Matty's lips as he mirrored her, leaning her direction. "Deal."

Two hours later, as the sun set over Vegas, Matty and Genna found themselves in a little chapel on Las Vegas Boulevard, one that didn't even have a name. A blue sign stood out front of the old stone building, 'wedding chapel' shining bright in lights. A few white pews lined the sides of the aisle, soft lighting bathing everything in gold. The room was vacant except for them and the minister, the lady who worked the front desk stepping in as a witness. It hadn't taken long to secure a marriage license, a hundred bucks and a form filled with lifetimes of lies that nobody questioned. Another two hundred dollars later, there they were, a wedding in progress. All that remained were the vows.

Matty took her right hand, holding it as he gazed at Genna beside him in a little black dress she'd taken from a stranger's closet. She was nervous. He could tell. Her left hand clutched a tiny rose bouquet so tightly her knuckles glowed. He hadn't spoken a single word yet but tears already brimmed her eyes.

"We've been through a lot," he said, not sure where to start, but it was enough to send the tears streaming down her cheeks. "More than most people go through in a lifetime. The world tried to tear us apart in the worst ways, but we didn't let it, and I know I'll never let it, because you *are* my world now. No matter what happens, I'll always be here for you. I'd follow you to the end of the Earth and back again, if I had to, if you needed me to. I wouldn't hesitate. I love you."

Genna tried to wipe away her tears with her arm, still clinging to the bouquet. Matty reached over, brushing them off her cheeks, as the minister motioned for her turn.

"I love you, too," she said, staring at him, her mouth opening and closing a few times, like the words were caught inside of her. Damn near a minute of silence passed before her face contorted and she let out a cry loud enough to startle their makeshift witness. "Ugh, that's all I've got!"

"Ah, come on, that was weak," Matty said playfully. "I know you've got something else in you."

"Matteo," she whispered. "Kind of rhymes with potato."

Matty laughed, wrapping his arms around her and pulling her to him. "Good enough for me."

"Fucking hormones," she whined into his chest. "Yours was perfect and mine's over here all jumbled in my brain and I don't know what to say except I love you, I really do... I love you more than chocolate cake with strawberry icing."

"With chocolate sprinkles?"

"Don't push it."

He kissed the top of her head before turning to the minister. "What's next?"

The old man smiled. "Rings."

Matty frowned. "Got none of those yet."

"Then I suppose that's it," the man said. "By the power vested in me by the State of Nevada, I now pronounce you husband and wife. You may kiss your bride."

Matty cupped Genna's chin with one of his hands, the other still around her. Slowly, he leaned down, kissing her, taking his time to savor the moment.

"Mrs. Barsanti," he whispered against her lips, loud enough only for her to hear.

"I'm *not* taking your last name," she whispered back.

"I don't blame you," he said. "So, how about that honeymoon now?"

"You can suck your own dick in the Honda."

"Tempting, but I was thinking about Paris, actually."

"Paris?"

"Paris Hotel and Casino," he whispered. "How about we go see that other Eiffel Tower?"

CHAPTER 9

Soho.

Dante could count the number of times he'd visited the neighborhood on one hand. He'd driven through it while on missions from his father. Once, he threw caution to the wind and went home with a girl who lived there. And then there was that time, not long ago, when he confronted the Barsanti brothers, when he'd lost control and somebody ended up dead.

It was a mistake, he knew. He'd had no business going to Soho.

It was just asking for trouble.

So why, yet again, did he find himself there?

There, on the wrong side of that invisible boundary. It was pointless now, he figured. *Nowhere* was safe. He'd been attacked in East Harlem, somewhere the Barsantis just didn't go. That had all changed, though, because of Matteo. He'd flown into town in that goddamn red sports car, violating every rule the families had established, blurring lines and inviting himself where he didn't belong.

Dante didn't blame Genna. She'd been innocent. She didn't know what their world was like. She didn't remember. But Matteo should've known better.

Because of him, everything was different.

Dante hesitated on the sidewalk in front of the brick building, gazing up at the faded sign near the entrance. *The Place.*

Here goes nothing.

Opening the door, Dante stepped inside the busy bar. Chatter echoed throughout the place, dozens of men hanging around, socializing. There was almost a happy undercurrent, an excited buzz in the air, but it didn't last long.

Someone noticed him, recognizing his face, and that was all it took. The whispers started, passed along from person to person like a game of *Telephone*. It was so blatant that Dante trailed the gossiping with his eyes.

It took less than a minute for the whispers to reach everyone. Men gawked, and sneered, a few even prematurely reaching for weapons. The only person who didn't seem to react was the man standing at the far end of the bar. His back was to Dante, his shoulders relaxed, like he had not a care in the world.

Roberto Barsanti.

Dante took a deep breath before approaching the bar near where Barsanti stood. *No sudden movements. Gotta stay calm.* Even a hint of agitation could get him shot.

"A Coke," he ordered, stopping in front of the bartender.

The guy glared at Dante, blinking a few times. He made no move to get the drink or even acknowledge Dante had spoken at all.

A throat cleared. "Get the boy his drink."

The bartender's posture slumped as he muttered, "Yes, sir."

"I'm not looking for trouble," Dante said right away as he glanced beside him at Barsanti.

"Oh, I don't buy that for a second," Barsanti said. "You wouldn't have come here unless trouble was what you were looking for."

The bartender set a small glass filled with ice against the bar, pouring some soda into it before shoving it toward him. Dante nodded his gratitude as he picked up the drink. "How do you know I wasn't just *so* appreciative of your hospitality that I decided to come by for another visit?"

A slight smirk touched the corners of Barsanti's lips. "In that case, how about a tour?"

"I think I've seen most of it," Dante said. "Saw the basement, now I'm seeing the bar... all that's left is whatever's up above."

"Nothing's upstairs," Barsanti said. "My boys used to live up there, but not anymore."

Dante's eyes flickered to the ceiling. *Huh.*

Barsanti rubbed his mouth, tapping his fingertips against his chapped lips. He was thinking, probably about what to do with Dante. Kill him or humor him? Dante figured he had fifty-fifty odds. After a moment, the man turned, motioning to the bartender. "Give me a bottle of our best Scotch."

The bartender snatched an unopened bottle off the wall behind the bar. Barsanti took it, swiping two clean glasses.

"Come." Barsanti motioned for Dante to follow him. "Join me."

A part of Dante wanted to plant firmly in spot, refusing to follow that order, because it went against everything he'd always stood for. Just being there made him sick to his stomach. It felt inherently wrong. But another part of him, the part that had led him to Soho in the first place, reminded him he had nothing to lose.

Kill him, Barsanti might, but he could've done that weeks ago if he'd wanted. Besides, killing him at that point would've been *merciful.*

So Dante trailed the man to the back of the bar, into an offshoot room filled with pool tables. Barsanti set the bottle of Scotch and the glasses down on a small table inside the door before sticking two fingers to his lips and letting out a loud whistle that stalled everyone.

"Out," he barked, not needing to say another word. The handful of men shuffled toward the door, shooting Dante some unpleasant looks.

"Do you play?" Barsanti asked once they were alone, picking up a pool stick that was leaning against a nearby wall.

"I'm sure you already know the answer to that," Dante said.

Barsanti returned the stick to the holder before grabbing another, cleaning up. Dante watched the man make a quick sweep of the room, straightening everything up, before returning to his bottle of Scotch.

"I've heard about your occasional hustle," Barsanti said. "I've heard a lot about you, in fact. I like to stay on top of things, and people, they always seem to have a lot to say about *you.*"

"I can't imagine why."

Barsanti opened the bottle, pouring a bit in each of the glasses. He nudged one toward Dante before picking up the other and swallowing the liquor. "Word on the street is that you don't remember anything, that you have no idea what happened to you, but the fact that you're here tells me differently. You wouldn't have come without a reason."

Dante hesitated, eyeing the liquor. He set his glass of soda down beside it, having no interest in drinking either one. "I want to know why you didn't kill me."

Barsanti considered that as he poured himself more Scotch. "Would you rather I did?"

Dante didn't answer.

"You know, I was about your age when I came into power," Barsanti continued. "It wasn't easy, but it worked, because your father and I had come to an understanding. We respected each other. We worked together. He even made me your godfather, you know."

Dante glared at him. "I know."

"But something changed. I don't know when, or why, but we lost it. Respect turned to suspicion, and eventually, we cared about territory more than anything. So your father attacked, and I retaliated. Figured that would be the end of that, but Primo, ah... he doesn't know when to let things go."

"You killed his son."

"And you killed *mine*," Barsanti said, a hard edge to his voice, as he pointed at Dante with his glass. "You can be angry, and you can hate me, but don't be a hypocrite."

"What happened to Enzo wasn't intentional."

"You aimed your gun at him and pulled the trigger. It doesn't get much more deliberate."

"Then why let me live?"

Barsanti swallowed his Scotch before setting the glass down. "Because I stood along that street in Little Italy as my son's car burned, and I realized that nothing I could do to your family would *ever* be as bad as what Primo did. We want revenge for losing our children. Believe me, I'd love nothing more than to see you dead for what you've done. But Primo's got no one to blame for his loss now except himself."

"He doesn't blame himself," Dante said. "It wasn't intentional."

Barsanti let out a sharp laugh, a bitter edge to it. "You Galantes and your *unintentional* excuses. Your father used a bomb. A *bomb*. He had every intention of letting that bomb go off, regardless of who got caught in the blast."

"He wouldn't have—"

"Your sister had enough time to get there," Barsanti said, cutting him off. "Your father knew where she was going, so why did it still happen? Why didn't he stop it?"

"Why didn't *you*?" Dante asked. "I remember the night my brother died. Your people were lurking. They knew kids were there. So why'd you still let that bomb go off? Didn't you care who got caught in the blast?"

Barsanti was quiet for a moment before saying, "No."

"No?"

"No, I didn't care."

"You're *sick*."

"Maybe I am," he said, "but at least I'm honest about it."

Rage simmered in Dante's bloodstream. He felt himself shaking. *Despicable son of a bitch.* Clenching his hands into fists, he turned away, knowing if he didn't get out of there, he'd likely do something that *would* get him killed.

"To answer your question," Barsanti called after him. "I let you live—not for him, not even for you—I did it for *myself*. I've lost my children, and I could blame your father, I could blame *you*, but the fact is, I brought this on them. *I* did. It was my job to protect them, and I failed. So I let you live, because I'd murdered a son once and look what that got me. I didn't want to murder another. It wasn't worth it."

Dante walked through the bar, heading for the exit. He'd damn near made it when someone stepped right into his path, blocking him. Dante's muscles coiled at the familiar faces.

The Civello brothers.

Spineless motherfuckers.

That rage he'd tried to quell boiled over, flowing out of him, prickling his skin. He stepped forward, not stopping, bumping right into one of them. Dante looked the guy dead in the eyes. If they expected him to cower, they'd be disappointed.

"Move," Dante said, "or I'll move you myself."

"I'd like to see you try."

Dante shoved against him, knocking him back a few steps, right into his brother. Before the guy could try to come at him, Dante took another step forward, toe-to-toe again. "If you think I'm afraid of you, you're wrong. You're nobody. You're *nothing*. You might've got one over on me before but never again. Next time you get in my way, you'll be cut down. *Permanently*."

"Ohh, strong words from such a weak little boy that couldn't even protect his baby sister."

Dante didn't think. He didn't care. Those words hit him and he *swung*. His fist collided with a jaw, knocking the guy back, making him lose his footing.

At once, people swarmed them.

Hands grabbed Dante, yanking him back as others threw punches. Pain tore through him, rippling down his spine when he was thrown into a nearby wall. He gasped as the air was forced from his lungs, a fist slamming into his gut, over and over. Dante fought back, blindly swinging, a blur of bodies surrounding him, attacking.

The Civello boy got up from the ground, reaching into his pocket. Dante spotted the knife in his hand as he flipped it open, coming at him. Before he could defend himself, the door to the bar swung open.

Fucking reinforcements.

Panic threatened to consume Dante, but when his eyes darted that way, he saw a familiar face. *Umberto.* Galante soldiers flanked him, rushing inside, ten seconds too late to stop what was happening. The blade sliced into Dante, searing pain tearing through his side. He growled, clenching his teeth, as chaos erupted. Weapons were pulled, guns aiming at heads.

"Enough!" a voice bellowed through the bar. *Barsanti.* He didn't approach, but the lone word was enough for them to press *pause.* Barsanti's men lowered their guns as Dante was released, the hostile mob around him retreating.

Dante clutched his bleeding side, staggering toward the door, shoving through the crowd. He stepped in front of Umberto, his old friend's gun inadvertently pointing at him.

Dante continued to the door, moving around his father's men, not addressing any of them. Stepping out into the warm night air, Dante inhaled sharply, pulling up his shirt to examine his side. Blood streamed from the wound. Not so much that he would bleed to death in the street but enough be concerning.

"What the fuck, Dante!" Umberto spat, storming out of the bar behind him. "What the hell is wrong with you?"

Dante groaned. "The son of a bitch got me."

Umberto looked at the wound as he shook his head, muttering under his breath, "I can't believe you fucking did that. What were you *thinking?*"

Dante dropped his shirt, covering the wound, as the rest of the Galante men resurfaced. What was he thinking? It was hard to say. "How'd you know I was here?"

"Lucky guess."

"Bullshit," Dante said. "Are you following me?"

Umberto hesitated, not wanting to answer that question, which was all Dante needed to figure it out.

"He *ordered* you to follow me. Unbelievable."

Truthfully, he wasn't surprised. How many times had his father told him to shadow Genna, to keep an eye on her? Every damn day since the moment she'd learned to walk.

"He was concerned," Umberto said. "You're not acting like yourself."

"Stop following me. I don't need a fucking *babysitter*. I'm fine. I can take care of myself."

Dante turned, taking a few steps, trying to apply pressure to his side to stop the bleeding.

Umberto quickly caught up, grabbing his arm. "Look, let's get you to the hospital, okay? Get you seen by a doctor."

Dante yanked his arm away. "I don't need a doctor."

"You're hurt."

"I'll live."

"Come on, don't be this way, man. We're friends."

"Are we? Because I thought we were, Bert, but seems to me I was out of sight, out of mind."

Umberto gaped at him, jaw slack. No defense to that.

It would've been nice, he thought, for just a moment, to have someone put him first. It would've been nice to have someone care about him... to have someone *miss* him.

It would be nice to have someone need him again.

It would've been nice, but that wasn't how it happened. It was never about him. He was just a pawn. Umberto hadn't hesitated to fill his shoes, hadn't hesitated to take his place in the game.

"I have to go," Dante said, walking away.

"Where are you going?" Umberto called out.

Dante didn't stop, mumbling to himself, "To see the only friend I've got."

The town was just a few miles down the highway, not even the size of a Manhattan neighborhood, so small that Genna wasn't sure of its name. *Did they bother to give it one?* A picture-perfect community, the kind she didn't think existed outside of television. No stoplights. No police. It was Mayberry without Andy Griffith.

Parking the Honda in the small dirt lot, Genna climbed out and glanced around. It was quiet. *Too* quiet. Birds chirped in the distance as bugs buzzed by her head, but where were the revving engines? The people shouting? The horns blowing?

She'd never get used to it.

Turning, she approached the square building, eyeing it with distaste. The red paint was chipped, exposing tattered old wood, surrounded by stained concrete and topped with a rusted metal roof, like some sort of makeshift barn. Old gas pumps lined the right side, a pair of garage doors raised to the left, with a span of dingy shop windows between them. It looked as if someone had plucked it right out of the 50s and plopped it down in front of her.

Jerry's Garage

It was still functional. Cars surrounded it, two pulled inside with the hoods raised. A guy in blue coveralls leaned over the front of a little Toyota, checking fluids as he whistled along to some song playing on a nearby radio. He caught Genna's eye. "Can I help you?"

He was young, mid-twenties, with sandy-blond hair that looked dirty as hell, somewhat slicked back on his head. Stains covered the front him, grease streaked down the thighs from wiping his hands. A smell clung to him, like some cologne of motor oil with a dash of body odor mixed in. *Gross.* The guy smiled, his eyes kind, so Genna forgave him for that.

"I was wondering if there were any stores around here where I could buy car parts," she said. "Like a NAPA or a, I don't know... Pep Boys, maybe?"

"I'm afraid not," he said with a laugh before slamming the hood of the car. A small white patch sewn to his chest displayed the name *Chris* in blue stitching. "Closest you'll find one is Vegas."

"Ugh, I was worried about that."

He pulled a rag out of his pocket to wipe his hands. "We might have what you're looking for here, though. Car giving you trouble?"

His eyes flickered to the Honda out in the lot. Genna shook her head. "Oh, that's working fine. There's actually a car back at the house that needs some work. It's kind of, you know, not working. *At all.*"

She was guessing, anyway. She wasn't sure what was wrong.

Her response surprised him. "Oh, you new in town? I haven't seen you around. Figured you were passing though like others."

"We're staying just outside of town, a couple miles down the highway. The place is kind of by itself in the middle of nowhere."

His brow furrowed. "The old Moretti house?"

"Maybe." *Moretti.* The name sounded familiar to Genna. "If you're thinking about a wooden house that looks like it might be haunted, then yep."

"That's the one," he said. "Never thought I'd see it inhabited. Always heard rumors about a lady living there, though, some crazy recluse. Guess that's not the case. You don't seem to fit the bill."

Live there long enough and I might. "What happened to the lady?"

"Don't know. Not sure she ever existed. Probably just some local urban legend, but anyway..." He leaned back against the Toyota, crossing his arms over his chest. "This car you've got... what do you need for it?"

"Everything, probably. It's been sitting there, rusting away."

"For how long?"

"Years."

"I'm guessing you're trying to get it running?"

"That's the plan."

He stared at her, almost as if he were looking through her, his mind drifting somewhere. Just when his silence was starting to grow uncomfortable, he opened his mouth and rattled off a laundry list of issues. Battery... fluids... tires... brakes... any gas left in it would need to be replaced... carburetor probably shot, would need rebuilt... an oil change was essential... hopefully the engine hadn't suffered damage... "Basically, if it's liquid or rubber, it's gonna need to be replaced."

She gaped at him. "I feel like I should be taking notes."

He smiled. "I can write it down for you, if that'll help."

"Immensely."

He motioned for her to follow him as he headed through the garage to a small office along the side. Two other guys hung out in there—one behind a desk on the phone, while the other lounged in a filthy plush chair.

Chris walked over to the desk, grabbing a pen and a piece of scrap paper, before meeting her again outside the doorway. He scribbled things down, muttering to himself about wires and rodents and *oh god—there might be rats living in the damn thing?* "This is all worst case scenario, of course. If you're lucky, a lot of this will have survived."

"I'm not lucky," she said. "If it's possible for it to be fucked up, chances are it will be."

"The worst thing you can do for a car is to just let it sit there," he said. "I've seen cars start again after thirty years, but I've seen others with a host of problems after just three. Sometimes you've got to consider that it might not be worth it. What kind of car is it?"

"A '64 Lincoln Continental."

He shot her a surprised look before muttering, "Definitely worth it." After writing down a few more things, he handed the list to her. Most of it seemed simple enough… she could change a tire and replace a battery, take old hoses off and put on new ones… but a few things seemed out of her skill range.

"So, how does one rebuild a carburetor?" she asked. "Is there a book I can buy? *Carburetors for Dummies?*"

"I'm sure there are books," he said. "That's best left to a professional, though."

"I'd rather just buy a book."

"Okay, then." He laughed. "Most of that stuff we can get for you. We have shipments that come in a few times a week, so tell us what you need and we'll order it."

"How about we start with whatever's easiest and go from there."

Twenty minutes later, Genna had the makings of a plan, a few parts ordered along with some tools the guy suggested. Chris filled out the rest of the order sheet, jotting down details. "Do you have a number I can reach you at when all this comes in?"

"Uh, yeah…" Reaching into her pocket, Genna pulled out the

burner phone Matty had gotten for her when they first got on the road. She'd never used it, having no reason to, but Matty insisted she carry it. As soon as she flipped it open, she saw the message: **Missed Call**. Matty. *Shit.*

Scanning through it to find the number, she read it out loud for Chris to write down.

"908," he said, repeating the area code. "Where about is that?"

"That would be New Jersey."

"Yeah? You a Jersey girl?"

"Something like that."

"What brought you to Vegas?"

"What brings *anyone* to Vegas?"

She'd gotten kind of good at deflecting, she thought. *Answer a question with a question and you never have to lie.* Her brother had taught her that. Of course, it never worked with him. Dante always knew that meant she was hiding something.

"Good point," Chris said with a laugh. "Anyway, I'll give you a call when it's in. Shouldn't be more than a week or so."

Genna left then and drove straight to the small diner across town. It was a little white building with big windows and blue awnings, *Morningside Diner* written in block letters along the glass. The clock in the Honda showed it as a few minutes past six, stuck on east coast time. Matty had been working at the diner for a week, from eight in the morning until three in the afternoon, Monday through Friday. She drove him there and picked him back up at his insistence, making her keep the car just in case she needed it.

In case my invisible friends and I want to go for a joyride.

She parked in front of the diner and walked inside, a bell above the door jingling to announce her arrival. Bright colored booths lined the walls, blue barstools dotted along the counter, as the black and white checkered floor glistened. There was even a jukebox in the corner.

A jukebox.

All that was missing were those little white hats that kind of looked like paper boats. The first time she'd walked in, seeing Matty at work, she'd said that to him. He hadn't found it funny.

"You're late."

Genna rolled her eyes, finding Matty perched on one of the

stools near the register. "I'm like, three minutes late."

His eyes flickered to a clock up on the wall. **3:16 pm**.

"I was worried," he said. "Thought something might be wrong."

"Sorry." She pulled the phone out to wave it at him. "I'm not used to this thing. It flips and has all these buttons. I don't even know if it works, honestly, because I didn't hear it *ring*."

He took it from her, flipping it open, and handed it right back. "You had it on silent."

"Oh." She glared at it, pressing random buttons. "How did I do that?"

Laughing, Matty blocked her hand before she could press anything else. "Probably by doing *that*."

Rolling her eyes, Genna slid the phone back into her pocket before plopping down on the stool beside him. She felt Matty's eyes studying her, like he had something else to say.

"Are you hungry?" he asked.

"Starving."

"Order something," he suggested, grabbing a menu off of the counter and holding it out to her.

Genna glanced at it, settling on the first thing she saw. The middle-aged woman behind the counter approached. *Doris.* "You ordering something, sweetheart?"

"Uh, yeah… can I get the grilled cheese platter?"

"Sure," Doris said, grabbing an ordering pad from her apron to jot it down.

"And can I add some bacon to that grilled cheese? Like, inside of it? Oh, and some pickles, too? *Oh my god.* Pickles. Inside the grilled cheese."

Doris looked at her with confusion before writing it down. "Grilled cheese, add bacon and pickles. Something to drink?"

"Strawberry milkshake."

Doris nodded. "Anything for you, Matt?"

"I'll take what she's having… minus the pickles and bacon."

"Matt," Genna grumbled when the woman walked away. "It just sounds so generic."

"Okay, *Jen*, you're not much better."

She rolled her eyes, childishly sticking out her tongue.

It took a few minutes for their food to arrive. Genna dug in

141

right away, devouring every bite, while Matty picked at his, his attention more on her.

"Not hungry?" she asked, snatching one of his fries and popping it in her mouth.

"Not really," he said, pushing his plate her direction. "Help yourself."

He didn't have to tell her twice.

* * *

"Yep. Okay. Uh-huh."

Gabriella nodded, even though nobody was around to see, as she glanced at the cell phone on the kitchen counter. The chipper voice babbled through the speaker about everything imaginable: a new chick-flick was coming out that weekend, a neighbor was pregnant, it was supposed to rain on Tuesday...

Or was it Wednesday?

Gabriella wasn't really listening.

She glanced in the small foggy window on the oven, glaring at the frozen pizza. Was the dang thing even *cooking*? Six o'clock in the evening on a Friday, Gabriella's first night off after a grueling rotation at the hospital. She had the weekend off and planned to do nothing except sleep and eat... after she got her mother off the phone.

"And your Aunt Lena, oh my goodness, you won't believe this... she called to tell me they were having a potluck this Sunday for Bobby's birthday. She wanted to have it here. *Here*, at the house! I told her, you know, that was fine, I'd be happy to host, but if he didn't show up because of the location, that wasn't *my* fault, you know?"

Gabriella sighed. "Please tell me I'm not expected to go to this thing."

"I told her I'd let you know."

"Mom..."

"Don't '*Mom*' me, Gabriella Michele. You can show your face for a few minutes."

"But it's my day off."

"Which means you've got plenty of time. Family is family, like it or not."

"Not," Gabriella muttered.

"You come, you eat some food, and you go back home. How hard is that?"

A heck of a lot harder than her mother would understand. "I'll consider it."

"There's nothing to *consider*. Bring some kind of appetizer. Stuffed mushrooms. Got it?"

"Got it." Gabriella barely got those words out before a loud buzz echoed through her apartment. Her eyes darted to the intercom on the wall by the front door. "Mom, hold on a second."

"Why? What's going on?"

Gabriella ignored those questions as she walked over to the door. The buzzer went off again, so startlingly loud that she flinched. She'd lived there for a year and could count the number of times someone had buzzed her apartment on one hand... and most of those had been accidents.

Needless to say, she didn't get many visitors.

Pressing the 'talk' button, Gabriella mumbled, "Who is it?"

Nothing met her ears for a moment... nothing except the sound of the noisy street below. She was about to chalk it up to a glitch when the voice spoke. "It's Dante."

Dante.

Something stirred inside of Gabriella at the sound of his name. She'd wondered if she'd ever hear from him again. "Dante."

"I know I shouldn't be here," he said, something off about his voice, something that Gabriella couldn't pinpoint. "I just, I need... *fuck*."

A groan filtered through the intercom, loud enough to be distinguishable. While he didn't elaborate about what he needed, Gabriella could guess what he thought he needed was *her*. And that went against her better judgment. Heck, part of her screamed in alarm. This wasn't normal. He *shouldn't* be there. But without giving herself a chance to second-guess it, she pressed the 'door' button, buzzing him in.

"Gabriella, I swear on your father's life, if you don't answer me right now—"

Rolling her eyes, Gabriella headed back into the kitchen. "Sorry, Mom. I'm still here."

"Where'd you go? Is somebody there?"

"Yeah, it's, uh..." Crap, how to explain that? *Not even trying.* "It was nobody, just someone pressing buttons."

Liar, liar, pants on fire.

God, had she *ever* lied to her mother before? Maybe as a kid, but she'd never felt the need to keep secrets from her parents. But this was secret-worthy. A lie would go down a lot easier than this truth.

"I need to go, Mom," she said, her heart pounding like crazy when a knock echoed through the apartment, loud enough that she knew her mother heard it. *Crap.* "I'll see you Sunday."

"Gabriella, don't hang up this—"

Gabriella tapped the button to end the call. Her nerves frayed as anxiety swelled in her gut when he knocked again. *Ugh, pull yourself together, nitwit.*

Walking over, she fiddled with the locks before pulling the door open a crack, coming face to face with Dante, the chain still latched. His warm brown eyes were dark, so damn dark they appeared black in the dim lighting, but the whites of them were strikingly bloodshot. He blinked, the movement exaggerated, as he stared at her from the hallway. She clearly wasn't the only one tired. Dark circles, puffy eyes, pale skin... had the guy slept at all since leaving the hospital over two weeks ago?

She opened the door further as a slight smile turned his lips, barely detectable, before his expression fell again. He cleared his throat, his voice gritty as he whispered, "Nurse Russo."

"I thought you were going to call me—"

Gabriella didn't finish her sentence, getting a good look at him, her gaze settling on his filthy white shirt. His *bloody* white shirt. A patch of red covered the side, where one of his blood-covered hands gripped, while streaks were smeared along his stomach like he'd finger-painted with it.

Gabriella undid the chain before yanking the door open the whole way.

"What happened?" she asked, reaching for him as her gaze darted along the hallway, hoping nobody was around to see him. She grabbed his arm, anxiously pulling him into her apartment before slamming the door. "You're bleeding!"

"I got stabbed." Dante glanced down at his side. "Again."

"You got stabbed?" she asked. "*Again?*"

Was that *seriously* what he said?

"I didn't know where else to go," he explained, looking back up at her.

"The hospital. You get stabbed, you go to the hospital. You go to the *emergency room*. That's why it exists! For emergencies!"

"I couldn't."

"Why not?"

"Because they ask questions."

She groaned. Mandatory reporting. Any gunshots or stab wounds have to be reported to the police by the hospital. "Yeah, well, you've proven before that just because they ask doesn't mean you have to *answer.*"

"I just... I can't do it." He shook his head. "If you want me to leave, I'll go, but I've had my fill of hospitals, and at this point, I'd rather bleed to death than walk into that fucking place, so I came here hoping..."

"Hoping I'd help you?"

"Yeah."

"This goes against everything I stand for," she said. "This is wrong on *so* many levels. It's unethical. It's dangerous. I can't just *help you* when you've been stabbed. That's crazy! *You're* crazy!"

As she ranted, Gabriella dragged him through the apartment and into the small bathroom, flicking on the bright light, both of them squinting from the harsh glow. Dante leaned back against the white counter as Gabriella dug her first aid kit out of a drawer and grabbed a clean towel.

"I need to..." She stood in front of him, flailing her hands toward his side. "You know."

Did he know? Did it make sense to him? Gabriella had to wonder, because nothing about any of it made any sense to *her*. What she needed to do was call the guy an ambulance. What she needed to do was the opposite of what she was about to.

I can't believe I'm doing this.

Dante nodded, like he understood, and yet he hesitated, like he wasn't sure what was going on. After a moment, though, he pulled his bloody shirt up, gritting his teeth as he tucked it beneath his chin. He stood still as Gabriella put on a pair of rubber gloves.

"You should really lay down." Gabriella glanced around her minuscule bathroom. There was barely enough room for the two of them to squeeze in there, much less space for him to lie down. "The bedroom is, uh, right through there…"

"I'm fine," he said. "I don't need to lay down."

"But—"

"Just do what you have to."

"You seriously need a doctor," she told him, kneeling in front of him. "There's no way for me to be sure that they didn't hit anything."

"I'll take my chances."

She rolled her eyes. "Maybe what you *really* need is another psych consult, because this isn't normal. This isn't what normal people do when somebody *stabs* them."

"I never claimed to be normal. Besides, I'm pretty sure normal people don't get stabbed at all."

"Oh, they do. Just not as often as it seems *you* do. Something about you I guess just makes people want to stab. Kind of like *stick a fork in it*, you know, but with a friggin knife."

Dante laughed at that, his hands gripping the counter on each side of him as Gabriella washed the wound. "If it makes it any better, it was the same person every time."

"That doesn't make it any better."

"You sure?"

"Positive." She glared up at him. "If anything, it makes you an *idiot* for going near them."

He stared down at her, his expression unruffled, like her calling him an idiot didn't bother him. His gaze was so intense that Gabriella still felt it when she looked away. She tried to ignore him and focus on his injury, flushing the wound and sterilizing it. His body tensed, hands gripping the counter so tightly she was surprised he didn't break off a piece of the cheap plaster.

He'd applied enough pressure to stop most of the bleeding, so at least he wouldn't bleed to death in her bathroom. *Thank goodness.* After Gabriella was sure she had it clean, she used tape to close the wound, gluing the edges, before covering it with a large bandage.

Standing up again, she met his gaze. He was still staring at her. After an awkward moment, where Gabriella swore the temperature rose a hundred degrees, he lowered his head and looked down at her handiwork.

"Give it to me straight," he said. "Am I going to live?"

"Most likely," she said. "You're not very good at this dying thing, you know."

"I'll have to try harder next time."

Gabriella tore her gloves off and tossed them in the trashcan as Dante let his bloody shirt drop, covering his chest.

"You should wash up," she suggested. "I'm sure I've got a shirt you can change into around here somewhere."

She didn't give him a chance to argue, jetting out of the bathroom and closing the door, shutting him in there alone. Nervously, she made her way into her bedroom, cringing at the mess. Clothes were flung all over the place, clutter piled up on the dresser and bedside stands. Gabriella waded through it, heading to her closet. She found a Mets shirt hanging in the back and yanked it off the hanger, a startled scream escaping when she swung around.

Dante stood in the doorway, watching.

He'd made a half-assed attempted at cleaning himself up, at least washing the blood from his hands.

"Uh, here, this should fit you," she mumbled, holding the shirt out to him, but he made no attempt to come any closer, not crossing the threshold into her bedroom.

Brow furrowing, she approached him. Once it was within his reach, he took the shirt she offered. He was even paler now than when he'd shown up. Sweat formed along his brow. Instinctively, Gabriella grabbed his wrist, checking for his pulse, counting the faint beats. He tolerated it, again staring at her, not attempting to pull away.

"You sure you don't want to lay down?" she asked, nodding her head over to the bed.

Dante waited until she let go of him to answer. "If I ever find myself in your bed, Gabriella, it'll be under entirely different circumstances."

There went the temperature rising again.

Her cheeks flushed as Dante observed the shirt, cringing like it hurt him to look at it. "Didn't take you for a Mets fan."

"What did you take me for?"

"Someone with class."

He draped the shirt over his shoulder before walking into the living room. Gabriella followed, watching as he staggered a few steps, swaying. Her heart nearly stalled when his knees buckled. Ten seconds and he was going to slam right into the floor.

Darting forward, she grabbed him before he fell. *Oh crap, he's heavy.* She managed to get him to her couch, dropping him on it. He leaned his head back, closing his eyes, as he ran his hands down his face, the softest whispered apology escaping his lips. "I'm sorry."

"Don't apologize," she said, sitting down on the coffee table in front of the couch, her knees pressing against his. "You lost blood, so it's not surprising if you're feeling weak. Besides, no offense, but you look like you could use some beauty sleep."

He peeked an eye open. "You calling me ugly?"

"Maybe."

Absolutely not. She could think of a few words to describe him— reckless, fearless, most definitely cocky—but ugly didn't come close to registering on that chart. Even looking like *Casper the Less-than-Friendly Ghost*, there was something captivating about him, something charming in his smile and kind in his eyes. She couldn't quite explain it, because he was *far* from being her type. She'd always dated architects and athletes, not the kind of guys who got stabbed on Friday nights.

She'd purposely avoided dating those guys.

She dwelled on that as he leaned forward, moving around enough to finally tear his bloody shirt off. He dropped it in his lap and exchanged it for the one she'd given him. Her gaze flickered to his bare chest when he pulled the clean one on. It was instinctual, a reaction to having a half-naked man in her living room.

She averted her gaze, not wanting to be caught ogling him. *Control the friggin hormones, girl.*

"I was five," he said, his voice quiet. "My shirt caught on fire."

Gabriella met his gaze. "What?"

"Car blew up. I was close to the blast. That's how my chest got all fucked up."

She frowned. He thought she was reacting to his *scars.* "I wasn't... you know... and I actually knew that. I know what happened."

"Of course," he said. "You live like a block from there."

"I didn't live here then," she said. "I grew up in Jersey, but something like that... word travels. They said you were lucky to survive."

"I'm not lucky." He leaned forward, propping his elbows on his knees, his face mere inches from hers. "I almost died. I *should've* died. But I didn't. I survived because I'd been busy that night looking out for my little sister. That's all I ever did... look after her. But here I am, years later, with nobody to look after. Doesn't get much more *unlucky*, does it?"

Gabriella didn't know what to say. She had so much she *wanted* to say, so much she wished she could tell him, but her voice didn't seem to work. Maybe it was fear that silenced her, or maybe it was self-preservation, but when her lips parted, all she could do was exhale.

Dante's eyes scanned her face, like he was seeking the answer to his question, before his gaze settled on her mouth, like maybe he thought he'd find what he really wanted *there*. Gabriella's breath hitched as he licked his dry lips, inching closer so slowly she wasn't sure he was actually moving.

Was she imagining it?

But then he tilted his head, and Gabriella's heart raced. Her hands trembled in her lap, her fingertips tingling with the urge to do *something*. Push him away. Pull him closer. She wasn't sure which, because both options were horrifying. This shouldn't be happening, but geez, how something inside of her wished it would. He shouldn't even be there. She shouldn't have let him in. But there he sat, just a breath away from her.

The bad, bad boy with the horrible reputation. When she looked at him, she saw a broken man who couldn't heal from all of his wounds. His pieces no longer fit together like they should. She could close the gashes in his body, but what about the gaping holes in his soul?

Dante inhaled deeply as Gabriella's eyes fluttered closed. Her hands clenched into fists to keep them from shaking, and she tiled her head to match his. He was so close she felt his warmth and tasted his breath on her tongue. She waited for him to kiss her, wondering if his lips would be soft, but seconds passed with nothing happening until she heard his voice. "Do you smell that?"

149

Her eyes opened right away. The tips of their noses nearly touched. "What?"

His eyes narrowed as he pulled back. "It smells like something's burning."

Something's burning. "Oh crap!"

Gabriella jumped up, nearly falling over his legs as she darted for the kitchen. The closer she got, the stronger the smell grew, assaulting her nostrils. Grabbing potholders, she yanked the oven door open, a blast of smoke slamming her right in the face.

She gagged, fanning it away, as she grabbed the pan, tossing it on top of the stove. The smoke detector across the room screeched, a little too late to be of any help. She turned the oven off, slamming the door closed.

"Un-friggin-believable," she muttered, tossing the potholders down on the counter near her phone. She'd been so distracted by Dante that she'd forgotten she had food cooking.

Annoyed, she spun around, about to dismember the offensive smoke detector, when she slammed right into something in her path. Gasping, she stepped back, stunned to be face-to-face with Dante, having not heard him follow. She stammered, unable to get a word out, when he cradled her face with his large hands, his thumbs stroking her flushed cheeks as he stared into her eyes. It was only a few seconds, but it felt like a lifetime—a lifetime of anticipation before he smashed his lips to hers.

The kiss was rough and needy, his mouth moving eagerly as he drank her in. His teeth nipped at her lips, his tongue mingling with hers, as he kissed her like she was the air in his lungs, the blood in his veins. He kissed her like he *meant* it. He kissed her like she'd never been kissed before. He kissed her until she was breathless, until her knees went weak, as he backed her up against the kitchen counter.

A minute felt like an hour, the world a fast-forward blur. The smoke detector was still screeching when he pulled away. Her chest ached and lips tingled, her eyes watering from the lingering smoke. She gaped at him, stunned, as he blinked rapidly. Time stopped as the world hit pause.

She saw it coming before it happened.

His hold on her face loosened, his hands slipping from her skin.

In a blink, his legs gave out and he hit the tile floor.

BAM

Out cold.

Gabriella snatched her phone off of the counter before dropping to her knees beside him, rolling him over onto his back. She grabbed his wrist, feeling his racing pulse. "Dante? Can you hear me?"

No answer.

"Idiot," she said, letting go of him to scan her phone, about to dial 911. "I swear there's something *seriously* wrong with you."

A hand reached up, covering her phone. "That's the second time you've called me that."

Her eyes darted to him, relief rushing through her. He was awake again, so at least he hadn't gone into shock. "If you don't want me to call you that, stop acting like one."

"Not my fault," he said, trying to sit up, but she forced him back down, sternly pointing him in the face, warning him to stay put. He obliged as he draped his arm across his sweaty forehead, drawing his knees up. "If anyone's to blame, it's you."

"Me? How do you figure?"

"You're the medical professional," he said. "You should know better than to seduce someone in my condition."

"Seduce? Ha! I did no such thing!"

"Then what do you call the way you were kissing me?"

"Kissing you? You kissed *me*!"

"You kissed me back."

"I, uh…" She scoffed. "Whatever."

"There's no excuse for that," he said, his lips curving into a smile as he raised his hand, tapping her on the nose with his pointer finger. "You siphoned the air from my lungs and the blood right out of my brain. You ought to be ashamed."

"I am," she said. "We're *both* idiots."

"Ah, don't be so hard on yourself." He caressed her cheek with the back of his hand. "I think it was worth the headache."

"You've got a headache?"

"I'm assuming I just hit my head pretty hard."

"You did, which is yet another reason I think you should go to the hospital."

"The hospital can't help me," he said, his hand shifting from her

151

cheek to run his fingertips across her lips. "I trust you to give me CPR if I stop breathing."

He sat up then, ignoring her this time when she tried to stop him, and managed to get to his feet. Gabriella watched as he staggered out of the kitchen, following to see him flop down on the couch again. He laid across it, running his hands down his face.

"Is there seriously no one I can call for you?" she asked. "Other than 911?"

"Please don't call 911."

"How about a cousin? *Someone?*"

"Are you forgetting nobody visited me in the hospital? Actually, that's a lie. Someone did come. Gavin Amaro. He was nice enough to stop by and tell me my sister was dead and that my father had been the one to kill her."

Those words shocked Gabriella. "He told you that?"

Dante closed his eyes. "So no, there's still no one you can call for me. I've got nobody left. Just give me a few minutes to pull myself together and I'll leave."

"You don't have to," she said, stepping over to him. "But there's something I should tell you."

Anxiety ravaged her as she awaited a response from him, but one never came. She placed her hand on his forehead, feeling his warm skin, before running her fingers through his hair. He stirred a bit but his eyes remained closed, a soft snore escaping his parted lips.

Asleep.

She didn't want to leave him alone in his condition, but she was too exhausted to be of much use. Fishing a blanket out of a hallway closet, she draped it over him and turned off the lights before heading for her bedroom, leaving the door open.

Sleep proved to be evasive, as she tossed and turned, straining her ears for noise from the living room. Eventually, she drifted off, waking around sunrise. She strolled out of her bedroom to check on Dante, her footsteps stalling a few feet from the couch.

The living room was empty, the blanket folded on the table.

No Dante.

CHAPTER 10

It was a warm afternoon in the New Jersey suburb outside of Elizabeth, a soft breeze blowing, rustling the scattering of trees along the property. Gabriella sat in a chaise lounge chair in the backyard of the house she'd grown up in, one of those cheap plastic get-ups, her legs spread out along it. Her black flip-flops lay discarded in the neatly trimmed grass to her right, her bright red toe polish gleaming in the sunlight. It was the only stitch of color on her that afternoon: black sundress, black sunglasses, and black wide-brim sun hat.

Black soul, too, according to her superstitious grandmother.

'*You look like you're in mourning!*' she'd declared when Gabriella showed up forty-five minutes late. '*You'll never find a husband looking like that!*'

Never mind the fact that Gabriella hadn't been *looking* for a husband. Her grandmother wouldn't understand that, though. Her family, for how unique they were, tended to be conservative when it came to relationships, but getting married wasn't exactly her priority.

Nor was it even something that *interested* her.

"So, are you gonna tell me why you were late?"

Gabriella glanced up, meeting her mother's stern gaze, grateful to be wearing sunglasses. They felt like a shield, a protective barrier to keep her mother from digging too deep. Victoria Russo was a no-nonsense woman, the kind that went toe-to-toe with men twice her size, a product of her upbringing. And while Gabriella had been raised to cower from *no one*, her mother was one of those rare folks who scared the day lights out of her sometimes.

She shrugged, figuring it was best to be honest. "I really didn't want to come, so I almost didn't."

"I'm glad you came to your senses. You would've been missed."

"That's under debate." Gabriella looked over her shoulder, back toward the house, where most of the guests gathered. "Half of these people don't even remember I exist. Unless you're packing a penis in your pants, your existence means nothing. Can't measure it to prove my worth, therefore I must not be worthy."

Victoria stepped over to her, reaching down and grasping Gabriella's chin, pulling her face up to look at her. "What's wrong with you today?"

"Nothing."

Her response was immediate. It was also a big, fat *lie*. She'd woken up the day before to find Dante gone from her apartment, and there had been no sign of him since. She wasn't sure when it happened, or even how, but somewhere along the way she started to really care about the guy. Worry consumed her. Was he well? *Alive?* Had he passed out in an alley somewhere and ended up in another hospital? *Or geez, maybe he made it to the morgue this time...*

A lot was wrong with her.

She was losing her friggin mind over a guy.

A guy who had no regard for his own safety.

A guy who once told her he felt dead inside.

"Your father's in the house," her mother said, not buying her *'nothing'* nonsense. "Why don't you go say hello?"

Gabriella knew better than to argue. "Yeah, maybe I will."

Standing, Gabriella snatched up her flip-flops before trudging through the back door. People packed the house, all of them *family* in some way, although Gabriella only recognized maybe half of their faces. They ran the gauntlet of Italian surnames, mixed through marriages, with a few notables missing.

One being the whole reason any of them were there to begin with. *A birthday party with the birthday boy skipping it.*

"There's my girl!"

Gabriella's attention turned to the source of that voice when she stepped inside, seeing her father sitting at a table in the kitchen, accompanied by a few other guys as they played a game of *Texas Hold 'Em*. Alfie Russo, card shark extraordinaire, was a car dealer by trade, specializing in high-end vehicles for a select clientele, playing a role in a scripted show most people thought was reality. He sold bright colored Ferraris to the filthy rich while driving a plain black

Ford Crown Vic. Whatever they asked for, he it got for them with a smile, no matter how insane or absurd he thought it was. He had one heck of a poker face.

God, she wished she'd inherited *that*.

"Hey, Daddy," she said, stopping beside him, eyeing the thick stack of crumpled cash on the table in front of him. "I see you're winning."

"Always," he said with a grin.

Laughter rang out from across the table. "That's because the bastard cheats."

Gabriella glanced over at her Uncle Johnny, the table in front of him pretty much cleared. Her father did cheat. That was common knowledge. He cheated at cards. He cheated on his taxes. He'd probably cheat on his wife, too, if she were the kind of woman to tolerate it.

Newsflash: she wasn't. She'd cut him up and serve him at the next potluck if he even *thought* about touching another woman.

"That's crazy," Alfie said, waving that assumption off. "I just play by my own rules."

"You *cheat*," Johnny said again. "You can't just make up rules as you go along."

"Says who?"

"Says everyone."

"Pfft, and who's going to stop me?"

Alfie laughed, tossing his cards down on the table, face up. Gabriella glanced at them, doing a double take. He had four of a kind, except two of them were exactly the same, both the Queen of Spades.

The men grumbled, tossing their own cards down, as Johnny flicked a card right at him, hitting him in the chest with it: the *real* fourth Queen.

"So, how you doing, baby girl?" her father asked, not at all ashamed as Johnny crumbled up and discarded the extra spade before sorting through the deck, making sure no other cards had slipped in. "How's that job of yours?"

"Good," she said, shrugging.

"What are you doing these days?" Johnny asked, cocking an eyebrow. "Last I heard you were still off at school in Caldwell."

"I graduated," she said. "Went into nursing."

"She's a city girl these days," her father told Johnny. "Working at a hospital out your way."

"Is that right?" Johnny's eyes flickered to her as he shuffled cards. "Which one?"

"Presbyterian."

"Presbyterian," someone else chimed in, one of the faces she didn't recognize—a cousin of a cousin of someone's brother-in-law or something. "Isn't that where they treated Galante's son?"

Way too many eyes darted straight to her with that question. She stood there, silent, and just shrugged a shoulder. No way was she approaching that topic with those people. HIPPA violation aside, she wasn't interested in breeching his privacy to appease their nosiness.

"Kid got put through the ringer," Johnny muttered as he dealt the cards out to the men. "The kind of hell he went through... I don't think it's the kind you ever come back from."

"Nonsense," a new voice cut through the room. "He seems to have bounced back just fine."

The men didn't give the newcomer a glance, while Gabriella looked at the doorway. *Guess the birthday boy decided to come, anyway.* He stood there, dressed in a black suit, his dark hair flecked with bits of gray. Gabriella wouldn't call him family. She'd never thought of him that way. He certainly never considered them to be anything more than strangers, like they were living a game of *Six Degrees of Kevin Bacon,* loosely connected through circumstances.

Gabriella's mother had five brothers and two sisters, one of which married the man in the doorway. The family tree she'd scribbled out in elementary school said that made him an uncle, but in her mind, he was just some guy they all called Bobby.

"Is that right?" Johnny asked. "You seen the kid lately?"

"Two nights ago," Bobby said, strolling into the room. "He showed up at my bar."

Someone let out a low whistle, but Gabriella didn't look to see who it was. Her gaze trailed Bobby as he grabbed a chair and joined them at the table.

"You didn't kill him for that, did you?" Johnny asked, snatching up all the cards to start over, to deal Bobby in.

"Of course not," Bobby said. "He had some questions, so I humored him. Besides, you know, he's angry about what happened with his sister."

"Rightfully so," Johnny said.

Bobby's eyes narrowed, but he continued on like Johnny hadn't interrupted. "He's angry, and anger makes people careless. Makes them reckless. Way I see it, I don't have to kill him, because he's already well on his way to being dead, thanks to his own father. Just gotta give him enough rope to hang himself."

Gabriella couldn't take much more of that conversation. It was making her stomach churn, her vision blurring around the edges. She gripped the back of her father's chair, shifting position in an attempt to shake off the dizziness, but all it seemed to do was garner attention.

Bobby gave her a quick once-over before turning to Alfie. "She yours?"

Alfie glanced up at her. "Yeah, you remember my little girl, Gabby."

"Of course," Bobby said. "She's just not so little now."

"They grow up quick," Alfie said.

Johnny cleared his throat. "The ones who get to grow up."

"Speaking of," Alfie said, "any word on Matteo?"

Bobby picked up his cards, sorting through them as he shook his head. "I keep calling, keep asking, and it's always the same answer. *Nothing.* No sign of him. They claim they'll keep looking, but I know better. They never bothered from the start."

"So what now?" Alfie asked.

"Now, I guess I put an empty coffin in the ground."

The air grew suffocating with those words.

Gabriella sensed it was time for her to go.

Leaning down, she kissed her father's cheek before slipping away from the table, nobody saying a word about it or trying to stop her. She headed right for the front door, having had her fill of family. She showed up, she brought stuffed mushrooms, so now it was time for her to get the heck out of there.

When she stepped outside, someone was coming up the small path that cut through the yard, leading to the front door. He strolled along, like he didn't want to come any more than she had, which explained why he was two hours late. She took in the sight of the black slacks and plain black button down, the short, dark hair and the steel blue eyes.

Gavin.

He looked at her with confusion, like he didn't recognize her, before smiling. "Gabby?"

"Gavin."

"Look at you," he said as he laughed. "Looking like you're heading to a funeral."

She rolled her eyes. "I'm not the only one."

Gavin motioned to the house behind her. "With these people? You never know."

"Tell me about it," she muttered.

"You leaving already?"

"Girls aren't really welcome in the big boys club, you know? The guest of honor showed up so I figured that was my cue to disappear."

"And sadly, my cue to get my ass inside," Gavin said, nodding as he passed her. "It was good to see you, Gabby."

He headed for the door, while Gabriella stayed rooted in place. Her feet were like lead, too heavy to move, no matter how hard she tried. Her lips parted, words on the tip of her tongue that she wanted to say but she just... *couldn't.*

Her family shared everything. They always had. When Gabriella was six years old, playing hide-and-seek with her father, she'd found a gun tucked beneath her parents' mattress. She'd never seen one before, except for in movies and on television, so she'd picked it up, to play with it, forgetting all about her father coming to find her. He startled her, shoving the bedroom door open, declaring, "Got you!"

So Gabriella did what any frightened kid would: she *shot.*

Swinging around, her finger squeezed the trigger, a loud bang echoing through the room. She'd dropped the gun with a shriek as a bullet ripped into the wall right beside her father, a mere few inches to the right of him. Alfie leaned against the doorframe, calm and collect, and glanced at the hole as he said, "Looks like we need to work on your aim, little girl."

It was her earliest memory. The world didn't really exist before then. Her father, while he *did* work with cars, lived another life within the Jersey crime family. It was her mother's family, a family that had happily welcomed Alfie Russo in. They were messy and blended, a dysfunctional tribe that branched out into other families through marriages, and not all of them got along. Occasionally, though, for just a few hours, they pretended they didn't want to shoot each other in the face, and they did it because of the women.

Their mothers. Their wives. Their sisters.

Sisters.

Taking a deep breath, Gabriella swung around to face Gavin, starting to ramble, but it was pointless. The front door closed as he disappeared inside the house.

Crap.

Crap. Crap. Crap.

She thought about following, sticking around, but she'd lose her nerve long before she got the opportunity to talk to him.

So she walked away, pulling out her phone to call a cab. She didn't own a car—although, once upon a time, her parents had given her a Ferrari. *Graduation present.* She left it behind when she moved to the city, much to her father's chagrin. She'd wanted a fresh start. She wanted to make her own way. She wanted to help people and make a difference.

The last thing she wanted was to get caught up in *that* world, but it seemed inevitable.

Fate was a *douchebag.*

* * *

"Fuck."

The curse slipped through Dante's clenched teeth in the form of a growl, loud in the otherwise silent room. *Fuck. Fuck. Fuck.*

Wearing nothing but a pair of white boxers, fresh out of the shower, Dante stared down at the wound on his side. He ran his fingers along the medical tape, wishing like hell he still had some painkillers left. It wasn't that it hurt so much as it bothered the fuck out of him. He wanted to forget it happened. He wanted to forget it *all* happened. In his short life, he'd been stabbed, punched, and kicked... his bones had been broken, his organs injured, his skin set on fire… he hadn't been shot, *yet*, but he figured it was only a matter of time before someone decided to put a bullet or two in him.

It was exhausting, being a goddamn magnet for trouble.

A knock sounded out from the bedroom door as he stood there, water still dripping from his damp hair. He ignored it, walking back into his connected bathroom. He grabbed a tube of antibiotic ointment, rubbing some of it along the wound, when the knock rang out again, this time louder.

"Whatever you're selling, I'm not buying," Dante called out, tossing the ointment back down before reaching for a bandage. Before he could put it on, his bedroom door opened, someone knocking again the same time they walked in.

Umberto peeked around the door. "Dante?"

"Do you make it a habit to go where you're not invited these days, Bert? Because I don't think I asked you to come in."

Dante's brash tone made the guy frown, but it didn't stop him from stepping even closer, further into the room, where he *really* wasn't welcome. "Says the guy I trailed to Soho."

Ignoring that, Dante stuck the bandage on and made sure it was secure before stepping back out of the bathroom to get dressed. He waltzed past Umberto to his closet.

"Look, Dante, I know you're upset, but don't be like this, man. Don't overreact."

Dante snatched a black shirt off a hanger and slipped it on. "You think I'm overreacting."

"Well… *yeah*. It's not that bad. Not as bad as you seem to think it is. I mean, you're alive. You're fucking *alive*! You bested those assholes. And they lost. We took his kids, his wife is gone, and maybe he's still got his territory, but for how long? We walked up in there, and what happened? Huh? Nothing."

"I got stabbed, Bert, in case you forgot."

"Of course I didn't forget, but Barsanti's weak, and you proved it. He's *beaten*. Everything is ripe for the picking now. I know you went through hell, but we won. *You* won."

"Nobody *won*," Dante said. "Not yet."

He grabbed a pair of jeans from his dresser and slipped them on before searching for his shoes.

Umberto sighed. "So, what are you going to do? Give up?"

Dante slid his feet into a pair of sneakers and sat down on his bed, cringing as pain tugged at his side. "Does it look like I'm giving up?"

"I don't know, man. *I don't know.*"

Dante glared down at his untied shoelaces. There was no way he could reach them without opening up his wound, tearing the tape apart that flimsily held him together. He was about to kick them back off when Umberto crouched down in front of Dante to tie his shoes for him.

"I swear to God, if you tell anyone I'm doing this..." Umberto muttered, double-knotting the laces so they stayed in place.

A joke was on the tip of Dante's tongue, slipping out before he could swallow it back. "You say that to every guy you get on your knees for?"

Umberto shot him an irritated look as he stood back up, but his expression cracked damn near instantly, a laugh replacing it. "Fuck you."

"Sorry, but you're not my type," Dante said. "I like them a little taller than four-foot-eight."

"Fuck. You."

"Again, I'm gonna have to pass, but I appreciate the offer." Dante stood up from the bed, running a hand through his hair. Just like that, in the second it took him to move, all humor was sucked from the room, the air around them growing stale once more.

"What are you going to do?" Umberto asked again.

Dante stared at him, dead serious as he said, "I'm going to make sure the man who tore apart my life pays for it. Then maybe I'll be able to piece something back together, some shred of an existence out of whatever's left."

A grin spread across Umberto's face. "See, I *knew* you had a plan. Tell me what I can do to help."

"What you can do is stay the hell out of my way."

Dante snatched his keys and cell phone off the top of his dresser before walking out, leaving Umberto standing there alone. He trudged downstairs, listening to the sea of voices coming from the first floor. Primo's office door stood wide open, half a dozen men sitting inside, drinking Scotch as they discussed business. *Typical Saturday.*

Strolling to the office, Dante paused in the doorway, scanning the men inside. The usual suspects: underboss, consigliere, along with a couple capos... the administration and a few of the supervisors, so to speak. They set the rules the rest of the family had to follow.

It only took them a few seconds to notice him, based on the shift in their demeanor, conversation dwindling, but it took a lot longer for any of them to acknowledge his presence. Primo regarded him with a cautious eye. "Son."

"Sir."

"You heading out tonight?"

"That's the plan."

"Where are you off to?"

"Depends."

"On?"

"On whether you've got any work you need me to do."

His father stared at him when he said that, stared at him as if he'd spoken in another language, like he just couldn't comprehend those words. Lifting a hand, he motioned toward the other men. "My son and I need a moment alone."

The others vacated, not a single one greeting Dante as they passed him. Suspicion clogged the air like smoke. Dante felt it in every breath, infecting his lungs and tightening his chest. They didn't know what to make of the kid who came back from the dead. They looked at him like they'd once looked at Matteo Barsanti— like he was a *ghost.*

"Shut the door," his father said after everyone cleared out. "Take a seat."

Dante shut the door behind him but made no move to sit down.

The man swirled his glass around, waiting, before he said it again. "Take a seat."

It was an order. He wouldn't tell him again. The man rarely repeated himself. Getting a *third* chance was unheard of, even for his own kid.

Dante's steps were slow as he approached, sitting in the first chair he came to, perching on the edge of it, not letting himself get comfortable.

"Heard about your incident the other night," Primo said.

"I'm sure you did."

"I want to know what you were thinking," he continued, "why you thought going there was a good idea. I want to know what you expected to happen when they saw you. You *just* got out of the hospital! You almost died. I thought I lost you! Do you know what that did to me? Losing you to them after I'd already lost Joey? And you just... go there again. Willingly. *For no reason.*"

Dante listened to his father's rant, the words going right through him, not stirring up the remorse Primo sought. If anything, it touched a nerve. A *bad* one.

"I need you to use your head. I need you to start *thinking* again. I can't lose you when I just got you back. Do you know what that would do to me? It would kill me!"

I... I... I...

Me... Me...

Why did he always make it about *him*?

Dante almost asked that, but instead he merely said, "Yes, sir."

Primo regarded him, that suspicion still weighing down the air. He knew something was off about Dante, that much was clear. Dante expected him to press for some sort of explanation, but he merely sighed, drinking his Scotch.

Nobody said anything else.

Eventually, Dante stood and headed for the door. His father wasn't treating him like he treated the Galante soldiers. They'd sit there all night in strained silence if he waited for a dismissal, because it wasn't business at that moment. It felt *personal*.

Was that how Genna had felt? Always on the outskirts, never allowed inside.

It was a helpless feeling.

Dante didn't *do* helpless.

He pulled the door open to leave when Primo's voice cut through the room. "I've got some guys down in Little Italy that owe money, if you're up for it."

Dante nodded. "I can take care of that."

"Good." Primo waved him away. "Take Umberto with you. He knows who they are."

Dante stepped out into the foyer, where Umberto lurked. He grinned at Dante, like a kid on restriction that finally had permission to play again. "So, where are we going?"

"To Hell," Dante muttered, pulling his keys from his pocket. "Otherwise known as *ground zero*."

"Little Italy," Umberto said. "Got it."

The drive took over an hour. Umberto yammered on and on, filling Dante in on every excruciating detail of what had gone down in his absence, noticeably skipping over anything having to do with Genna.

It was like she'd never existed.

Strange, Dante thought, since Umberto used to have a problem keeping Genna's name out of his mouth. All day, every day: *Genevieve this, Genevieve that.* His crush on her had been damn near intolerable.

"Is this weird for you?" Umberto asked when they pulled onto Mulberry.

"Which part?" Dante asked, whipping his car into a parking spot across the street from the blast. "The fact that you're acting like I never had a sister or the fact that she might've died *right there*? Because I wouldn't say it's weird for me. I'd say it's more fucked up than anything."

Umberto's expression fell as Dante cut the engine. "Look, about Genevieve…"

"You don't have to say anything," Dante said. "The silence told me enough."

"You know how I felt about her. She was amazing. Beautiful. Sassy. But she went another way. She went the *wrong* way. And when someone turns their back on the family, when they go against the family, what do we do? We make it so they don't exist. You know how it is."

"And that's why it's fucked up. Because she deserves more than that, *she* was more than that, but we're all too goddamn self-centered to admit it."

Dante got out of the car before Umberto could respond. His hands shook, and he shoved them in his pockets, hoping if they weren't accessible he wouldn't feel compelled to punch anyone. Umberto joined him on the sidewalk, uncharacteristically mum.

"The guys stay in some apartments around here," Umberto mumbled, glancing around the neighborhood. "It's Michael Parsons and his friend, uh, what's-his-face... the one with the glasses?"

Dante cut his eyes at him. *Well, that narrowed it down.* Didn't matter, though, because Dante knew where to find Parsons. "How much do they owe?"

"Parsons owes three grand, and his friend, about five hundred."

Dante walked down the street, heading for a deli on the corner at the end of the block, beneath a set of decrepit apartments. Umberto stayed in step with him, not asking any questions.

"Take the back," Dante told him, grabbing the door to step inside the deli. It was Sunday evening, nearing closing time, so customers were scarce, the last two leaving right as Dante appeared. Parsons stood behind the counter, cleaning the meat slicer, wearing a filthy white apron and smelling like cold cuts. Dante clicked the lock in place on the glass door before grabbing the *open* sign, flipping it over.

Parsons turned, smiling in greeting, the expression on his face freezing. Terror drained the color from his cheeks. "Dante, what can I do for you?"

"I think you probably know," Dante said.

A few seconds passed. Nobody moved. Nobody spoke. Parsons stood, frozen, until self-preservation kicked in.

Grabbing a stash of utensils, he hurled them across the counter before sprinting behind the refrigerated meat cases. Dante ducked from the flying knives, aggrivation stirring up inside of him. Of course the motherfucker would have to make this hard.

Jumping up on the counter, Dante dropped onto his feet on the other side, knocking displays over in his haste to follow. Parsons forced open the swinging door leading into the back storage room, grabbing metal racks and throwing them down, sending things spewing all over the place. Dante went after him, trying not to trip over shit as he ran, catching up to the guy just as he reached the back exit.

Dante grabbed his shirt, yanking on it, sending him stumbling. Parsons turned, panicked, and blindly swung, his fist connecting with the edge of Dante's jaw. The blow was strong enough to make him stagger, throwing him off enough for Parsons to slip from his grip. *Son of a bitch.*

Parsons yanked the door open, heading out into the alley, as Dante's aggravation turned to fury. He saw *red.* Springing out the door, Dante tripped the guy, knocking him to the ground, Parsons' face slamming against the grubby asphalt. He cried out, blood pouring from his nose.

Umberto appeared in the alley, pistol in his hand, finger hovering over the trigger. "Get the fuck up, Parsons. Don't do anything stupid."

Dante rubbed his jaw. *Too late.*

Parsons stood, blood streaming down his chin and dripping onto his apron. He held his hands up in surrender. "Please, don't hurt me. I don't want any trouble."

Again, too late.

"You owe Primo Galante money," Umberto said. "That's pretty much the *definition* of trouble."

"I'm under protection," Parsons blurted out. "They told me... I mean, they said..."

"They told you not to worry about us?" Dante guessed, stepping closer to him. "Told you if you give *them* money, they'll make sure no one comes after you?"

"Well..." He lowered his hands. "Yeah."

Dante snatched a hold of the guy's thick black hair, yanking his head down, making him hunch over as he dragged him back inside, to the front of the deli. He slammed Parsons against the counter, shoving his head toward the meat slicer. Pressing his face against the blade, tight grip still on his hair, Dante pinned him there.

"Three thousand dollars," he said, "or I turn the slicer on and make you pay another way."

"Please!" he begged. "Please, I didn't know!"

"You didn't know?" Dante asked. "Then let me tell you, so we're clear. I don't give a rat's ass *who* promised you protection, whether it be Roberto Barsanti or the fucking President of the United States. You owe."

"Okay! I'm sorry, okay! I'll pay!"

Dante snatched his head back up, shoving him away from the counter as he let go. Parsons turned to the cash register, his hands shaking as he pressed the button to open it. Yanking out fistfuls of cash, he attempted to count it, screwing up a few times. Umberto kept the gun trained on him from the other side, as Dante stood there, waiting. His side burned, his body aching. He wanted to sit the hell down but he knew that was out of the question.

"Three thousand," Parsons said, holding a wad of cash out. "It's all there."

Dante took it, passing it Umberto's way.

Umberto shoved it in his pocket and lowered his gun.

Parsons looked between them, starting to apologize again, when Dante drew his fist back and swung, clocking him right in the face. A loud crack echoed around them, stinging running up Dante's arm from the force. Parsons stumbled back into the cash register before his feet came out from under him and he slid to the floor.

"Don't *ever* swing on me again, asshole."

Dante walked away, unlocking the door to the deli and waltzing outside, stretching his fingers and shaking his hand. He glanced down at his side, pulling his shirt up, seeing the blood starting to soak the bandage. *Shit.*

Umberto lingered inside for a moment before joining him. Dante dropped his shirt, not mentioning it.

"His friend's at the bar," Umberto said. "Good timing, because I would kill for a drink after that."

The two of them started down the block, toward the bar. Dante's attention drifted, his gaze across the street as they walked, on the top right window of the brick walk-up. Light glowed from inside, the blinds raised, somebody moving around the apartment. He could see the shadows dancing.

"You think you got this?" Dante asked, stopping in front of the bar. "Can you handle this guy on your own?"

"Sure." Umberto's brow furrowed. "You not coming in?"

"I've got something else to take care of," Dante said. "Just do what you gotta do. I'll catch you later."

He didn't give Umberto a chance to respond before jogging across the street, dodging traffic. He reached the building just as someone else was entering and snatched a hold of the door before it closed, slipping in the building without needing buzzed in.

The building was a relic and hadn't been renovated in decades, everything in the place pre-dating him. A slight odor lingered in the hallways, like the wooden floor was starting to rot, the boards squeaking when he walked. The apartment was in better shape, albeit damn small, but instead of being suffocating, it felt cozy.

Maybe it's not the apartment, dumbass. Maybe it's the girl.

Dante stopped in front of her door, listening, before carefully knocking. At once, footsteps approached, locks jingling before the door opened a crack. The chain was still attached, catching the door after a few inches, giving Gabriella just enough room to look out.

Her eyes widened. "Dante?"

"Did you use the peephole?" he asked.

"I, uh... no."

"You should've," he said. "You should always check the peephole before you unlock the door."

Her brow furrowed as she glanced at the chain. "It's still locked."

"That one doesn't count," he said. "Chains are easy to break."

"Well, then, I guess it's kind of pointless, huh?"

"Pretty much."

"In that case, hold on a second."

She shut the door, and the chain jingled before the door opened the whole way. Gabriella stood in front of him, wearing a pair of black shorts and a matching tank top, showing a sliver of her tanned, toned stomach. He'd never seen her wearing so little before. He couldn't seem to stop his eyes as they roamed her body, meeting her gaze again when she cleared her throat.

"Are you going to come in?" she asked. "Or are you planning on just staying out in the hallway? Because I'd like to shut the door again, so I need to know which side of it you're hoping to be on when I do."

"Well, since you asked so nicely," he mumbled, stepping into the apartment.

She shut the door, securing the locks. "How'd you get in the building?"

"I slipped in behind someone. They didn't say anything about it, which you know, is another reason you should use the peephole. There's no telling who's roaming around this building."

"I'm starting to see that," she said. "Seems like the neighborhood has gone to Hell lately."

"It's always been Hell. It's overrun with Satan's minions."

"And who would *Satan* be?"

"Do you really want me to answer that?"

She paused, like she was considering his question, before shrugging. Wordlessly, she stalked off in the direction of the kitchen, and Dante followed, watching her. Something boiled in a pot on the stove, a torn-open blue box on the counter beside it.

Kraft Mac 'N Cheese.

"You like your macaroni doused in powdered cheese?"

"Don't judge me," she said, stirring the boiling water with a wooden spoon. "I don't judge you."

"Not judging," he said. "Just curious."

"Well, then, yes. I do." She grabbed the pot to drain the water out of it before tossing some milk and butter in. Ripping the packet of orange powder open, she sprinkled it in and stirred. "I eat hospital food most days, so I'm not exactly picky. Anyway, are you hungry? Do you want some of it?"

She glanced over her shoulder at him. He wanted to say no. He *was* picky. He hadn't eaten that shit since he was a kid. His mother hadn't been a good cook, and one could only eat food that came from a box so many times before they dreaded eating at all. Besides, Dante had experienced hospital food, too. It was half the reason he never wanted to go back. So he wanted to give her an emphatic *hell no*, but his stomach opted to growl, overruling him.

"I'm taking that as a yes," she said. "It's not five-star dining, but it's something to put in your stomach, and quite frankly, you look like you need it. If you're not going to sleep, you at least need to eat."

"Are you insinuating I look like shit?"

"I'm insinuating nothing. I'm telling you—you look like crap."

"Crap," he repeated. "Dang. Heck. Friggin. You got something against cursing?"

"I said 'Hell' a second ago."

"Hell's a location. Big difference."

"I have no reason to be vulgar. I think I get my point across just fine without it."

Gabriella dished out the macaroni equally into two bowls before holding one out to Dante.

He took it. "You didn't have to share with me. I didn't come here to steal your food."

"I know." She leaned back against the counter, pulling up a forkful of macaroni and blowing on it. "I'm curious why you *did* come, though."

"I was in the neighborhood and saw your light on."

"So you thought you'd come and talk to me about keeping my apartment secure?"

"It's a dangerous world."

"It seems you'd know." She took a bite of her food. "Speaking of, how's your side?"

He shrugged as he took a small bite. "Hasn't killed me yet."

"Well, that's something."

Silence surrounded them as they stood in the kitchen, eating. The air was awkward, a strange tension mounting that made Dante's skin prickle. He wasn't sure what to say or what to do. He set his empty bowl in the sink after he'd forced down the last bite and paused beside her. She smelled warm and sweet, like vanilla, with a hint of something uniquely her. He couldn't put his finger on it, as he breathed her in, but tingles crept down his spine at the sensation, like déjà vu was kicking in.

Her eyes narrowed as she set her bowl aside. "Why'd you *really* come here, Dante?"

"I don't know," he admitted. "Do you want me to leave?"

She hesitated. "I don't think so."

"Well, that clears it all up."

"Tell me about it."

He stared at her, contemplating, before slowly raising his hand, grazing the back of his fingers along her cheek. Her breath hitched—he could see it. Her body tensed, her skin flushing, an instinctual reaction to his touch.

"You know, since I woke up in that hospital, my life has been nothing but sorrow," he said quietly. "I'm fucking miserable. Everything I've done has been for nothing. Everything I touch, I hurt. Do you know what that feels like? I'm poison, Gabriella. And I want to touch you so bad I can taste it, but I don't want to hurt you, too. I don't want to poison you. It's tempting, though, so fucking tempting, because you'd be so goddamn sweet you might drown out just enough sorrow to keep me breathing. Because a bit ago, down on that street, I felt nothing, but then I saw your light on, and for a moment, I felt *something*."

"What did you feel?"

"Hope."

A smile touched her lips as she repeated the word. "Hope."

He dropped his hand from her cheek, putting a bit of space between them. "It's a pipe dream, thinking there's any hope left. Just look at me."

"I am looking at you. And I see a guy who is being *way* hard on himself." Her brow furrowed as she stepped closer, erasing the space he'd created, to run her hand along his jawline. "He's also a guy with a nasty bruise. What happened?"

"Some schmuck punched me."

"Same one who keeps stabbing you?"

"Different one this time." He grasped her wrist and pulled her hand away from his face. "I probably shouldn't have come here."

"You're probably right."

"And I probably shouldn't be doing this."

"You're probably right again."

"But I just..." He ran his hands down his face, cursing under his breath. "*Fuck.*"

"You like how it feels to have hope. It feels like maybe you won't die in the dark all alone."

Those words were like a lightning bolt striking his soul. "How do you know that?"

"You said that in the hospital," she said. "One of those moments you were in and out of it, you said you didn't want to die in the dark alone."

"That's... fucking embarrassing."

She laughed, the sound light and airy, and grabbed his arm when he tried to turn away. "Ah, don't be embarrassed."

"I ought to be," he said. "You sponge-bathed me, for fuck's sake. You touched my scars. You saw my *dick*. And there was a tube shoved up in it. You shoved a tube up my dick."

She was trying not to laugh at him. "Well, *I* didn't do it. You were already catheterized when you got to me."

"It doesn't matter. It still happened. You still saw it."

Shaking his head, he walked out of the kitchen, making his way to her couch. The room was spinning. He needed to sit down before he passed out.

Gabriella followed, lingering in front of the couch when he took a seat. Dropping his head down, he ran his hands through his hair, fisting handfuls.

"It grows, you know," he muttered under his breath. "It was cold in the hospital, so it was trying to shrink away. And I lost a lot of blood... probably didn't have enough blood left to make the damn thing hard if I'd even wanted to, but I wouldn't have, considering the fucking tube. It was traumatizing."

Loud laughter cut through the room, the kind that stole breaths and caused tears to stream down faces. Dante cut his eyes in Gabriella's direction. Unbelievable. She was seriously *laughing*.

"That's not helping, you know," he said.

"Sorry. Sorry!" She held her hands up, fighting to keep a straight face. "It's just... *that's* what you're worried about? I mean, okay, yeah, I did my job, but I don't even remember what it looks like. I wasn't looking at it like that. It wasn't a memorable moment or anything."

He groaned. "Still not helping."

She cracked again, laughing. "I didn't mean it *that* way. I'm not saying it isn't memorable."

"That's exactly what you said."

"I'm just saying I don't remember it. I wasn't checking it out, Dante. It was a penis. I see penis all the time. Every single day."

"Awesome."

"It's just a part of the body," she continued. "It's another limb, a smaller limb, no different than touching an arm or something. It's nothing special. It's just a penis."

"You know, sex with you must be *wild*."

"Oh, *hush*." She kicked his shin. "It's not like that. When I'm Nurse Russo, a penis is nothing. It's just skin and soft tissue and blood vessels and—"

"Careful," Dante said. "All this dirty talking might turn me on."

She rolled her eyes. "I'm just saying..."

"You're saying Nurse Russo didn't give a shit about my *penis*."

"Basically."

"That's good to know, because you should never judge a man by his dick when he's in the hospital."

"I don't think you should judge him by it *period*."

"By what?"

"His penis."

"Penis," he echoed, staring at her. "That's what Gabriella calls it, too? A *penis*?"

She blushed.

"Not cock? Not dick?" Reaching out, Dante grasped her by her hips, pulling her between his legs. "Tallywhacker?"

"You're terrible," she said, her hands resting on his shoulders. "*Horrible*."

"And you're too innocent for your own good."

"I'm not as innocent as you think."

Dante wondered what she meant by that, but he didn't have to question it. Gabriella's hands drifted, her fingers running through the hair at the nape of his neck, as she leaned down. A breath away, she hesitated, before kissing him.

Her lips were soft, the kiss gentle. It was sweet. *So fucking sweet.* He savored every second, making no move to deepen it. He'd let her have her way with him, let her do whatever she wanted, however she wanted it. All he knew was that being around her breathed life into him, and if he had his way, he'd kiss her *forever*.

But forever came way too soon for him, as ringing shattered the silence of the room. Dante's phone vibrated his pocket, shaking them out of the moment. Gabriella pulled away, and Dante groaned, his hands dropping from her hips.

Reaching into his pocket, he pulled out the phone, glancing at the screen. *Bert*.

"What?" he answered.

"Yo, this son of a bitch *hit* me!"

Dante pinched the bridge of his nose. "So hit him back."

"I did!"

Noise erupted in the background.

Cursing. Glass breaking. People shouting.

Umberto's phone dropped, hitting something, the bang echoing through the line. He yelled, his words jumbled, but Dante got the message.

The fucker started a bar fight.

Not the first time.

Hanging up, Dante slipped his phone back into his pocket. He got to his feet, his hands framing Gabriella's face. He kissed her then, hard and passionate, but he didn't linger. Pulling away, he pressed a soft kiss to her forehead before heading for the door.

"Where are you going?" she asked.

"Probably to get punched again."

"Are you coming back?"

"I probably shouldn't."

"So I can expect you, then?"

He paused at the door, looking back at her. Her expression was earnest, none of the amusement he thought he'd see. It was an honest question. She wanted to know if he'd come back.

God, how he wished he could answer that the way he wanted. How he wished he could say fuck it, that he wasn't going *anywhere*. Part of him wanted to, but there was still that side of him trained to follow orders and obey commands.

"Make sure you lock your door after I'm gone," he said. "Keep yourself safe, Gabriella."

He looked away when disappointment clouded her face. Unlocking the door, he walked out, closing it behind him. He stood there in the dingy hallway until the locks jingled, the deadbolt turning. Glancing back, his gaze caught the peephole.

He could practically *feel* her eyes on him through it.

CHAPTER 11

"You can do this. You can do this. *You can friggin do this.*"

Gabriella chanted the words under her breath as she hurried across the street in the crosswalk, the bright orange hand flashing at her, telling her to halt. She had no time for that, though. Not if she was going to do what she had planned.

Five-thirty in the evening. Rush hour traffic clogged the streets. She had an hour and a half before her shift was scheduled to start at the hospital. Three days in a row working twelve-hour stretches overnight with Cindy and the Grinch around. *Oh, joy!* Patients in the ICU required undivided attention, and Gabriella couldn't do that until she got something off of her chest. It was heavy, a weighted secret pressing down on her. She needed to let it out. She needed to tell somebody.

She wasn't religious, but desperation had her thinking about seeking out a priest.

One of those couldn't help her, though. A couple *Hail Mary's* wouldn't solve this problem.

Maybe what she needed was *sanctuary,* protection from whatever trouble this secret would invite into her world.

Gabriella approached the small cafe near the end of the block, her gaze scanning along the lettering on the fresh glass: *Casato.* The explosion had blown the windows out of the place, but it managed to escape most other damage, back up and running within a week.

The door was propped wide open, the cafe busy, as it always seemed to be at the time. Gabriella walked by it on her way to catch the subway, but it was the first time she'd gone inside, the first time she visited. The Amaros owned the café, so Gabriella knew the crowd that frequented it, but she tried to separate her private life from that part of the family.

Tables covered most of the space. Gabriella scanned them, looking for someone. Her stomach churned as her eyes fixed on a small two-seater table in the back corner, Gavin Amaro sitting alone, scribbling something in a notebook.

"You can do this," she whispered before stalking over to the table and sliding into the chair across from him.

Gavin looked up at her, his pen pressed to the paper.

"Hey, uh... sorry to interrupt whatever you're doing," she said, waving at his notebook. *Math equations.* "Your homework or whatever, but I need to talk to someone. I need to tell someone what I know. Or what I *think* I know. I've got to get it off my chest, and I'm not sure who to tell. And I mean, maybe I shouldn't tell anyone. Maybe I shouldn't tell *you*. But I can't keep it to myself anymore, and I figure out of everyone I know, you're the least likely to blow a friggin gasket over it."

Gavin cocked his head to the side. "Gabby?"

"Yeah."

He shook his head as he closed his notebook and waved the pen her direction. "You look different not dressed like Morticia Addams. What are you doing here?"

"Did you not hear what I said?"

"Not really," he admitted. "I was busy trying to figure out why some lady wearing scrubs was suddenly sitting across from me."

"Sorry," she mumbled. "I didn't want to interrupt, but I need to talk to someone."

"That someone being *me*?"

She shrugged. "I guess."

"Okay," he said, drawing out the word. "I have to warn you, though. I'm terrible at relationship advice, so if this is about a guy..."

"It's not." She paused. *Crap.* Was that a lie? "Well, it kind of is, but it's more than that. I don't need relationship advice. I need *help*."

"I'm better at helping." He leaned closer to the table. "What do you need?"

"I need to tell you something, but before I do, I need you to promise you won't go all crazy, or that you won't think *I'm* crazy."

"I'll do my best."

Gabriella glanced around the cafe, surveying the people near them, making sure nobody was around to overhear. She didn't recognize any faces, but it wasn't as if she would. She didn't know many people who belonged to *those* families.

"I, uh..." She turned back to Gavin. "I don't think they're dead."

She said nothing else. That, alone, had been hard enough.

He stared at her, expression blank. "Who?"

"Matty," she whispered, "and Genna."

She expected him to laugh or scoff or tell her to get the heck out of his face, like she was some conspiracy theorist without an ounce of common sense. But he continued to just sit there, nothing showing on his face. Not shock. Not awe. Not confusion. *Nothing.*

"You don't think they're dead," he said after a moment.

"No," she said. "I don't think they were in the car."

More silence.

"I live across the street," she continued, figuring she ought to explain. "I was home that night. My mom called to check on me, to tell me about Enzo's funeral. I felt bad, because I hadn't gone, and when I looked out my window, I noticed a car. *Matty's* car. I recognized it parked down the street. I thought about going outside to see him, to tell him I was sorry about his brother, but before I could..."

The car had exploded.

She could still see it when she closed her eyes.

It was as if it happened in slow motion.

The lights on it flashed, as if someone had unlocked it, seconds before it came to life, seconds before it *exploded*. The detonation had shaken her building, the fire escape rattling as the floor beneath her feet trembled.

It felt like an earthquake.

Windows shattered. Pictures fell from the walls. The fireball lit up the neighborhood.

Through it all, she stared at the car in horror.

Not a single soul had approached.

"I didn't see anyone," she said quietly. "I would've seen them."

Gavin shifted in his seat as his gaze turned to the table between them. He rubbed his mouth, as if deep in thought, like maybe he was considering what she had to say.

Her heart raced as she awaited his reaction.

After a moment, he sighed, leaning back in his chair. "Interesting. And you haven't told anybody else, right?"

"Right."

"Good," he said. "*Don't.*"

"Because I'm crazy?"

"Because you're right."

Whoa.

She blinked rapidly. "I'm *right?*"

Her words were louder than she meant, coming out as a screech, drawing attention from people around them. Gavin frowned, waiting until everyone looked away before nodding in confirmation.

"You *knew?* Why haven't you said anything?"

"Because I'm not going to," he said, "and you aren't, either."

"But—"

"Listen to me, Gabriella," he said, his voice dropping low, a hard edge to it. "You know what'll happen when people find out those two are alive? They'll *die.* That car blowing up wasn't an accident. It was a hit on Matty's life. They planned to leave before it happened and were committed to spending the rest of their lives on the run. This made it so they had a chance to get away without looking over their shoulders."

"You helped them," she whispered, stunned.

He didn't just *know*—he helped make it so.

"Of course I did," he said.

Gabriella couldn't believe it. Well, okay, she *could.* She suspected it, she thought it, but she figured she must be wrong. She wasn't, though.

"Dante," she whispered, her chest aching. She'd tried to tell him what she suspected a few times, but she'd been afraid to give him false hope.

"Galante?" Gavin asked. "What about him?"

"He'll want to know."

"Doesn't matter. He can't find out."

"But—" Gavin moved, like he was about to cover her mouth to silence her, but Gabriella held her hands up to block him. "It's not fair. It's not *right.* He's grieving. He deserves to know."

Gavin stared at her. *Hard.* "Were you and Enzo Barsanti close?"

She hesitated at the topic switch. "Not really. Only saw him a few times growing up. He started working for his father, and well…"

Unless you were a *Barsanti*, you meant nothing.

"But you and Matty were, right?"

"Close-*ish*. I saw him a lot more."

"So you care about what happens to him?"

"Of course."

"If Dante finds out they're alive, I'm telling you right now, Matty will end up just like Enzo."

She shook her head adamantly. "You're wrong."

"Look, I like the guy. He's not vindictive, he's not cold-blooded, but he's not innocent, either. When it comes to the people he loves, the guy has no limits. He did it before, and he'll probably do it again."

"Do what?"

"Kill."

Coldness ran through Gabriella. "Who did he *kill*?"

Gavin shifted in his seat, looking away from her. He wasn't going to answer that question. She'd asked too much. She knew how those things went. *Don't ask; don't tell.*

"Why does it matter to you, anyway? Have you ever met him?"

Gabriella didn't know what to say, so she just shrugged.

Gavin's eyes narrowed. "How do you know him?"

"Who says I know him?"

"Your face," he said. "Your face says you know him."

She scoffed.

Wrong response.

"Jesus Christ, Gabriella, don't…" Gavin ran his hands down his face, growling. "Don't tell me you know him *personally*."

"Is there another way to know a person?"

"Intimately," he elaborated. "Tell me you haven't seen the guy naked. Tell me you haven't touched his dick."

A smile cracked her face at that. She wiped it away as quickly as it happened, but Gavin caught it.

"You have got to be kidding me." Gavin threw his pen down on the table. "What is it with people in this family planting shit in gardens that don't belong to them?"

Her brow furrowed. *What?* "We're not *planting*—"

"Does he know who you are? Has he figured out you're connected?"

"No, but I don't think it matters."

"You don't think so, Gabby? You're just a step removed from being a Barsanti."

She scoffed. *Again.* "I am not."

"You went to the man's birthday party."

"I didn't *want* to."

"Proves my point. The only people they force to do that shit are family. Doesn't matter how you feel about him. Matty was never a fan, either, but that didn't stop Dante from going after him."

Gabriella didn't know what to say about that. The Dante he spoke of sounded a lot like the one from the scary stories, the tales of the big bad wolf out to devour his enemies. But that wasn't the Dante she'd come to know. He was like a puppy that had been kicked one too many times. He'd bare his teeth and he might even bite, but with enough patience, with enough understanding, he'd warm up to you in no time.

"He just could really use some good news," Gabriella said. "He's drowning in so much *bad*. He gets in fights and goes places he shouldn't go... I heard he went to some place that Bobby owns, some bar in Soho, knowing he didn't belong there."

"Jesus Christ," Gavin grumbled.

"And I just don't see what the point of keeping it from him is when he'll find out eventually," Gabriella said. "They *all* will. Sooner or later, they'll put the pieces together. I'm surprised they already haven't, if there's no trace of them in the car."

"That's not my problem. They can riddle it out, but I won't be responsible for the truth getting out. I don't want their blood on my hands, and you won't want it, either. *Trust me.*"

Gabriella's gaze headed to the window across the room, at the city outside. Instead of relieving the pressure on her chest, instead of purging her secret, she gained a bigger one.

How many lies would she have to tell to keep this one buried?

"Gabby!"

Gabriella glanced up at the sound of her name, seeing Johnny

Amaro approaching. "Uncle Johnny."

"What brings you to my little part of the world?" Johnny asked.

"Just thought I'd say hey to Gavin."

"It's nice seeing you cousins hanging out," Johnny said, squeezing her shoulder affectionately. "Family, you know, it ain't about a name. I always said it didn't matter what they called you... what mattered was what kind of person you chose to be."

Gavin laughed. "Too bad not everyone buys into your hippie-dippie shit, Pops."

"Yeah, too bad," he agreed. "They'd stop trying to blow up their kids if they did."

Johnny squeezed her shoulder again before walking away.

Gabriella glanced at her watch before clearing her throat. "I should go. I have to catch the subway."

"I'll walk you," Gavin said, grabbing his notebook.

Neither spoke as they walked down the block. Gabriella thanked him and headed down the steps, into the underground station, when Gavin called out to her. "Hey, about Dante..."

She turned, looking at him.

"Just be careful," he said. "He's been broken, and I'm not saying he can't be fixed, but just don't break off some of your pieces trying to put his back together, because then you'll both just be broke."

She shook her head. "You were right, Gavin."

"Yeah?"

"Yeah, you're *terrible* at giving advice."

* * *

"You got a death wish, don't you?"

The cracking of balls echoed through the room, nearly drowning out the sound of that question. Dante's gaze flickered from the green felt-covered table as he stood up straight, a familiar face greeting him, although he wouldn't exactly call it *friendly*, based on the judgmental eyes and serious scowl.

Rare expression to see on that face.

"Amaro," Dante said by way of greeting, looking back at the table to take another turn. He hit a solid red ball, sinking it in a corner pocket. "You come to throw away your money? Because I'll be more than happy to take it."

Gavin said nothing as Dante took another turn, slamming a blue solid in a side pocket but accidentally sending the cue ball down with it. *Fuck.* He motioned for the other guy to go, some cocky rich kid that went to NYU and had an ass-ton of his parents' money to blow.

"You know they *all* know your game by now," Gavin said. "They know how good you are, but they play you because they don't think they've got a choice. So it's not much of a hustle any-more... it's more like extortion at this point."

Dante shrugged. "It pays the same."

"I guess it does. Too bad you won't stay alive long enough to spend any of it."

The boy sunk one of his striped balls, completely missing the next—intentionally, by the look of it, the cue ball breezing right past the blue number ten. Usually that wouldn't annoy Dante, but something stirred inside of him, as the boy tried to step back, waving for Dante to go.

Dante grabbed him by the back of the neck, catching him off guard, and shoved him against the table, slamming his face against the worn, green felt so he'd look at the ball he missed. "I don't need your *help*, asshole. I can win on my own. So you hit this goddamn ball, and you sink it in that pocket, and *then* I'll take my turn."

"Okay, okay, I'm sorry!" the guy said when Dante let go of him. "My mistake!"

The guy hit the ball, sending it soaring, but it slammed the pocket at the wrong angle and bounced back out. Panicked eyes darted to Dante, but he shrugged it off. It wasn't worth the fight.

"Do you have some kind of brain damage?" Gavin asked. "Did they fuck you up so much that you forgot how things are?"

"There's nothing wrong with me," Dante said, taking his turn.

"I heard about your little field trip to Barsanti territory."

"You go there all the time."

"My last name doesn't typically get me shot *on sight*."

"On the contrary, it's never gotten me shot," Dante said. "Beat-en, stabbed, and blown up? Sure. But nobody's shot me."

"First time for everything," Gavin said. "In fact, I'm tempted to shoot you myself just to get it over with. It wouldn't be hard. I doubt you'd even put up a fight."

Dante sunk the rest of his balls, back-to-back, before pointing at a corner pocket. The eight ball flew right into when he hit it, ending the game. He wasn't done there, though, sinking the rest of the balls for the hell of it.

Grabbing the wad of cash from the edge of the table, Dante shoved it in his pocket. "Your concern is showing, Gavin."

"Somebody ought to be concerned."

Dante set his cue stick aside, leaning it against the wall, before grabbing his beer from a small table nearby. It was piss warm from being ignored, but Dante still drank it. "I appreciate it, you know, but it's starting to weird me out. Next thing you know you're going to be writing about me in your diary."

Gavin's expression softened. "Dear Diary, Dante Galante died today because he's a fucking idiot that forgot people wanted him dead."

Despite himself, Dante laughed at that, grasping his side as pain stabbed at him. *Still.* Most of him had healed, but that last stab wound was brutal. "For the record, I didn't *forget* anything."

"So you just elected to ignore reality?"

"More like I figured it was worth the risk." He guzzled the rest of the bitter beer. "Not sure why it matters to you, anyway."

"It matters to me because of my cousin."

"Your cousin, huh?"

"Yes, my *cousin.*"

"The one I killed or the one my father blew up?"

Gavin's expression hardened. "I'm talking about the one you're fucking."

It took a solid thirty seconds for that to register with Dante. "The one I'm *fucking?*"

"Gabby."

The sound of her name was a punch to his chest. "Gabriella?"

"That would be the one."

"Don't bullshit me, Gavin. I'm not in the mood."

"No bullshit."

Dante's guard crept up. He hadn't uttered a peep about her to anyone, choosing to keep her existence to himself, his small bright spot in a dark world. "How the hell do you even know about her?"

"I told you—she's my cousin."

"How?"

"She's a Brazzi."

"No, she's a *Russo*."

"Technically," Gavin said. "Her father's a Russo, but her mother's a Brazzi, so she's got Brazzi blood. And maybe that doesn't mean shit to you, since you've got nothing to do with the Brazzi family, but it matters to me. It makes her just as much my cousin as the one you killed *and* the one your father blew up."

Sickness churned in Dante's stomach. In a fucked up, twisted, roundabout way, it meant she was related to the Barsanti family, a fact that made Dante queasy.

He ran his hands down his face.

Fuck. Fuck. Fuck.

"Cousins," Dante muttered. "That means she always knew *exactly* who I was."

Did she ever deny knowing him? If she had, Dante couldn't recall it. From the moment he'd woken up, she acknowledged him by name, not at all intimidated by his reputation.

That's because she grew up around those assholes.

"This is..." Dante shook his head. "...*fucked up*."

"Look, I'm not in the business of telling anyone what to do. You're grown. I'm just saying, try to not get yourself killed as long as you're involved with Gabby."

"You don't have to worry about that."

"You're going to stop tempting death?"

"No, I'm going to stop seeing your cousin."

Dante walked away, heading to the bar at the front. Umberto sat on a stool in the far corner, angled to talk to a blonde girl seated on his left. Dante shoved in beside him, to the right, shaking his empty beer bottle at the bartender.

It was replaced instantly.

He took a long, deep pull right away, before turning, knowing Gavin had followed him. He wasn't going to let it go.

"That wasn't my intention," Gavin said.

"What *was* your intention?" Dante asked. "Thought you could use her to scare me straight? Thought I'd choose a piece of pussy over family loyalty?"

The moment he said that, Gavin snapped. Gone was the guy who had almost been his *friend*, replaced with an angry soldier from a rival family. In a blink, Gavin swung, punching him right in the mouth. Wrong choice, given he was the sole Amaro in a bar over-run with Galantes.

Dante stumbled, his vision blacking out, coming back hazy as pain vibrated his skull. *Shit, he hits hard.* Blood pooled in Dante's mouth as his teeth bit down on his lip. Before he could react, others around them jumped in. Umberto leapt right out of his stool, dropping his conversation mid-sentence. Gavin swung a few more times, defensively hitting a couple Galante soldiers before someone managed to subdue him. They grabbed him from behind, pinning his arms down at his sides, as Umberto swung, hitting him hard in the chest, forcing the air from his lungs.

Gavin *gasped*.

"Whoa, whoa, whoa!" Dante shoved Umberto away, nearly knocking him to the floor. "Fuck, guys, it's not that serious! I don't need your goddamn help. *Let him go.*"

They released Gavin, backing away as he inhaled sharply. They'd knocked the wind out of him.

"Come on," Dante said, grabbing his arm. "Let's take a walk."

Gavin yanked away from him, shoving around Dante to head for the exit. The second he was outside, he hunched over, hands gripping his thighs as he caught his breath. Dante stood in silence, waiting for Gavin to pull himself together, knowing he'd have something to say once he did.

As usual, he didn't disappoint.

"You," he said, standing up straight, pointing at Dante, "are an *asshole.*"

"Not the first one to tell me that."

"Seriously, what's going on with you? This isn't *you.* You were always a bit cocky, a whole lot hardheaded, but you weren't this reckless. You didn't pick fights for no reason."

"You hit me," Dante pointed out. "I didn't fight at all."

"But you knew exactly what you were doing."

"You fell for it."

"You called my cousin a *piece of pussy.*"

"Yeah, I shouldn't have said that." Dante wiped his mouth with the back of his hand, smearing blood from his busted lip. "I didn't mean it. I'm not even fucking her."

"Yeah, right…"

"I'm serious. She treated me in the hospital. I've seen her a couple times since then, but none of it involved fucking. So I'm not sure where you got that impression, but it hasn't happened."

"Yet?" Gavin guessed. "I sense a '*yet*' there."

Dante spit blood onto the sidewalk. *Disgusting.* "I'm not going to lie, I thought about it. She's, uh…"

"She's *what*?"

"She's beautiful."

"Yeah, well, Manhattan is full of beautiful women you can fuck with. Leave Gabby alone."

"Thought you weren't telling me what to do?"

"I changed my mind," Gavin said, waving at him. "You keep *this* up and I might really end up shooting you. Can't do that if you're seeing my cousin. Need to keep my options open."

"Noted."

Gavin took a step back, mumbling something about '*death wishes*' as he turned to leave.

"For the record," Dante called out, "when I called her beautiful, I didn't mean her looks. Because yeah, she's gorgeous, but she's a beautiful person, too. She kept me breathing long after I wanted to stop."

Gavin glanced over his shoulder at him. "Dear Diary, today Dante Galante became what he dreaded most: a sentimental fuck. Just a pity it took him too long."

* * *

"True or false."

Gabriella stalled, key in the front door of her apartment building, as the quiet voice registered behind her. *True or false.* She turned, seeing Dante standing along the curb. His hands were shoved in his pants pockets, his shoulders slouched, his head lowered. It was nearing eight o'clock in the morning, the sun still rising along the horizon, bathing the city in orange light that gave his tanned skin a healthy glow. It was an illusion, she knew. *Healthy* was the last word she'd use to describe him.

"Okay," she said, pulling her key back out to take a few steps in his direction. People strolled along, heading to work, their days just starting, while hers had been extraordinarily long.

And she knew, when Dante met her gaze, that her day was about to get even longer.

"You're a Brazzi."

No emotion registered in his voice. No anger. No sadness. No shock. *Nothing*. It reminded her a heck of a lot like Gavin's reaction when she'd approached him at the cafe before work.

His poker face was strong.

His *battered* poker face, as it was. His bottom lip was split and swollen. It hadn't been like that the last time she saw him, an added wound to the bruise along his jawline. It made him appear harsh, almost savage, like there was nothing soft about him.

Brazzi. She knew it was only a matter of time before he connected those dots, being who he was... only a matter of time before that name came up. It wasn't that she'd tried to keep it from him. As far as she was concerned, there was no reason to hide it. But at the same time, she didn't make a habit of shouting it from the rooftops.

"True or false, Gabriella," he said, voice still flat.

"True," she said, "although I'm pretty sure you didn't need me to answer that."

"I didn't," he admitted. "But I wanted to see if you could look me in the eyes when you said it."

"Why wouldn't I?"

"Maybe because I'm me and you're one of them."

"False," she countered. "I'm not one of *anything*."

His eyes narrowed. "You just said—"

"I know what I said." She glanced behind her at the building. "Look, do you want to come upstairs? I'd really like to change my clothes."

Dante didn't answer.

Gabriella looked back at him.

He stared at her. *Hard*.

He wasn't budging.

Okay.

"True or false," she said, staring right back. "The fact that I'm a

Brazzi is a problem for you."

She expected him to say the word. *True.* His lips twitched, like it wanted to come out, but he kept his mouth shut, breaking eye contact to look past her. She stood there for a minute or so as people streamed past them, going about their business, before she realized he was refusing to answer that question. The silent treatment. She'd seen him do *that* before.

"You don't play fair," she said, "so I'm done playing."

She walked back over to the building, leaving him along the curb. He must not have liked that, because before she could stick the key in the lock, she heard his voice, louder, coming closer. "*I* don't play fair? You're a part of that and you didn't even tell me!"

"First of all, I'm not a *part* of anything. You don't seem to be grasping that. And seriously, Dante, why would I have told you? What would the point be?"

"Maybe because it's relevant."

"Not to me."

"Oh, bullshit." He stopped beside her. "Don't act like my last name wasn't just as much of a problem for you."

"True, then. Me being a Brazzi *is* a problem."

"Well, it sure as shit doesn't make things *easy.*"

"Good to know." She shoved her key back in the lock. "Are you coming up or not? Because I just worked a twelve-hour shift and I'd like to get off my feet. Maybe this conversation will be more tolerable when I'm not wearing scrubs."

She was sweaty, and exhausted, and more than a little annoyed. She worked hard to make her own way, to make her own *name*, and the second *Brazzi* came into the picture she was boxed back into the label, like nothing else mattered.

Dante said nothing, sharply nodding toward the door. As soon as Gabriella had it unlocked, Dante yanked it open, nodding again for her to go ahead of him. He muttered something as he held the door, irritation grating every incoherent syllable, like a caveman torn between chivalry and savagery.

That about sums him up.

Gabriella made the trek up to her apartment, her footsteps heavy against the old stairs. Every groan and creek of wood was exaggerated to her ears as strained silence followed them, an unwelcome companion.

Once she got the apartment unlocked, Dante grabbed the door, again holding it for her. She should've thanked him, but the dead air wafting off the man was so maddening she forgot her manners. Inside, she dropped her things before going straight for her bedroom, kicking her shoes off along the way, leaving them lying on the living room floor.

Grasping the sliding bedroom door, she shoved it halfway closed and pulled her top over her head, tossing it on a pile of filthy clothes. A mountain of laundry begged for her attention but she ignored it, as she had for days, her mind preoccupied. She yanked the pants down, wiggling her hips and kicking them off, leaving them wherever they landed. She was about to pull off the white tank top she wore beneath her scrubs when something struck her.

Her feet changed direction, and she kicked her pants out of her path before pushing the sliding door open again and stomping out into the living room. Dante sat on the couch, still utterly *silent*, his gaze lifting to meet hers. His eyebrows rose as he regarded her, as if he might have something to finally say, but it was too late, because it was *her* turn to talk.

"You know, how dare you…"

He blinked at her. "How dare me?"

"Yes! How dare you come at me like this, confronting me, acting like I've wronged you, like I'm the a-hole here, when never once—*never once*—did you ask me about my family! If you're so concerned about avoiding those families, about making sure you don't get involved with *those people* in any way, if you want to be sure the woman who cleans your wounds and keeps you from dying isn't in any way connected to them—if that's such a big problem in your life, Dante—then maybe, *just maybe*, you should've friggin asked!"

His jaw hung slack, his eyes everywhere but on her face. If it weren't for his obvious shock, she would've wondered if he'd even listened to a word of her rant.

"So, yeah, *true*," she continued. "My mother's Victoria Russo, maiden name Brazzi, daughter of Victor Brazzi. I'm sure I don't have to tell you who that is. And true, my father Alfie Russo is part of that *family*. So true, I've got that blood in my body. True, I grew up knowing the Barsantis. And true, that also makes Johnny Amaro my uncle through marriage, but none of that makes me one of them. Because also true is the fact that I took care of you, the fact that I didn't judge you, the fact that I spoke up for you when nobody else would. I let you into my apartment and welcomed you into my life, even though I'm a Brazzi, which is apparently a problem for some reason, but whatever. Any more questions?"

Dante's gaze drifted to her face. "Where are your clothes?"

"My what?"

"Clothes," he said again, waving her direction. "It's kind of hard to pay attention to what you're saying when you're standing in front of me not wearing any clothes."

She glanced down at herself, rolling her eyes when she got a look at herself. Cheeky black panties. Threadbare tank top. Plain black bra. Hideous white tube socks that almost reached her knees. *Ugh.* Ridiculous, maybe, but she was far from *naked.* "You see people wearing a lot less than this at the beach."

"I don't go to the beach."

"Strip club, then. Is that more your speed?"

A small smirk cracked his expression. His whole face lit up when he smiled, no matter how slightly. He hadn't done it often since barreling into her life, usually surrounded by dark storms, but those rare moments he smiled, it felt like the sun coming out, peeking through the rain clouds. It *warmed* her.

"Been to a few of those," he said. "Never seen a woman this beautiful working the pole, though."

His gaze unabashedly scanned her, tingles trailing wherever his eyes went. Her face heated, her stupid heart doing some crazy pitter-patter in her chest.

"Stop flirting with me," she said. "I'm trying to be mad at you."

"Why?"

Why?

Why?

"Seriously? Did you just ask me *why?*"

His eyes met hers, his eyebrows raised. "What?"

What?

What?

"Are you seriously not listening to me? Like, no bullcrap... you legitimately haven't heard a word I've said."

"Oh, I heard you," he said. "Something about strip clubs and beaches and Brazzis. It just doesn't seem that important when you're not wearing any pants."

"Oh my God."

"Is that a birthmark on your inner thigh?" he asked, cocking his head, his gaze trailing her body again, going to her legs. "Looks like one, but I can't really see it unless you, well, spread your legs for me."

Oh. My. God.

"I swear, you…" She shook her head, flustered by his gaze as her words trailed off. She'd always considered herself confident, but he looked at her like he was memorizing every inch of exposed skin, and that made her nervous. Self-conscious. *More than a little turned on, too.* "You're the reason stupid dress codes exist these days, you know. Guys like you, blowing loads over seeing collar bones."

His gaze darted up to her shoulders and along her chest. "Those are nice, too."

"*Stop.* Seriously. Stop checking out my bones and stuff. I mean it, Dante."

Leaning back on the couch, he crossed his arms over his chest, his face alight with amusement. That smirk was still on his lips, not helping her predicament. The blush from her cheeks was spreading all through her body, and she knew there was no way he hadn't noticed.

"Fine," he said. "You were saying?"

"I was saying, you know…" *Ugh, what the heck was I saying?* "I'm a Brazzi."

"I know," he said. "We established that outside."

"And whatever, if that's a problem, I guess it's just a problem. There's nothing I can do about it. I can't change my DNA."

"Wouldn't dream of asking you to," he said. "Genetics gave you those collar bones and that birthmark. Would be a pity to never see them again."

"Well… good."

"Good," he repeated. "Are you done being mad now? Can I flirt some more?"

"Yes. Wait. *No.* I'm not, I mean… *ugh!*"

He laughed. Genuinely *laughed*. The sound was so light and

carefree that it drained away most of her irritation. Had she ever heard him laugh like that? She didn't think so. A soft chuckle here and there, always restrained, weighed down. But this laughter came from somewhere deep down, like some of those clouds parted, letting the real him shine through.

Standing, Dante strolled over to where she stood. The closer he got, the more her heart acted up, her body reacting to him. *Butterflies.* She had butterflies. They battered her stomach from the inside.

She felt like a lovesick teenage girl. *What the heck?*

Stopping in front of her, still keeping eye contact, Dante cupped her cheek, the skin of his palm rough. A hint of alcohol clung to him, noticeable only because he stood mere inches away, so close she could run her nose along his scruffy jawline and breathe him in if she wanted to.

God, how she wanted to.

"You smell like a bar," she told him.

"You smell like the hospital," he said in return.

She cringed. *Gross.* "Is that a problem for you, too? We can add it to the list."

"Oh, we're making a list now?"

"We might as well," she said. "Things that are a problem for Dante Galante."

"Ah, if I have to name everything that bothers me, we'll be here for days, so maybe we ought to focus on what doesn't bother me... like you not wearing any pants."

Rolling her eyes, Gabriella pushed him. "You're ridiculous."

"Am not," he said. "Baby, you've got the kind of legs that men would go to war for. That'll *never* be a problem for me."

Baby.

Her stupid heart almost leaped right out of her chest.

"Everyone tells me I got my mother's legs," she said. "They look great in a pair of heels."

"I bet they do."

"Yeah, it's those Brazzi genes... you know, because I'm a Brazzi, in case you've forgotten."

The humor in his eyes died at those words, the reminder sobering him up, his expression turning serious. He pressed his lips tightly together, regarding her in silence. She wondered if that was it, if he had nothing more to say, but he sighed after a moment.

"I have no problem with your family," he said. "We get along well enough. So it's nothing personal, you know... I'm not that kind of man. Or maybe I am, but I don't *want* to be that kind of man. I watched my sister get caught up in it all over a guy she was better off staying away from, and some things are just too close for comfort. I don't like it."

I don't like it.

Those words made her stomach sink, drowning those butterflies.

"But I like *you*, Gabriella. I do. I like you a lot, although I probably shouldn't."

"You totally shouldn't."

"I shouldn't have even come here."

"You're right."

"And you probably shouldn't be standing in front of me in just your underwear."

"Well, I mean, I've got my shirt on, but I get what you're saying."

"But still, I like you, and here I stand, and you're right there..."

"So now what?"

He reached for her, his hands grasping her hips, pulling her closer to him, his voice gravelly as he whispered, "Now I jump."

His lips smashed against hers, catching her off guard. She gasped, as Dante winced from his split lip, but it didn't deter him. He kissed her hard, backing her up toward the sliding door leading to her bedroom.

He stalled in the doorway, like he was waiting for an invitation, but Gabriella dragged him inside the room with her. It was too late to second-guess it now. They were already free falling.

Breaking the kiss, Dante grasped the bottom of her tank top, pulling it over her head. He dropped it to the floor right where they stood, discarding it, his eyes glossing over her chest and trailing along her stomach. His hands snaked around her, reaching for the clasp of her bra, unhooking it with just the flick of his fingertips.

He was better at that than even *she* was.

"Do you do that often?" she asked, curious.

"Do you really want me to answer that right now?"

She hesitated before shaking her head.

No, she didn't want to know.

The bra straps slid down Gabriella's arms, and she let it drop to the floor. Dante palmed her breasts, thumbs grazing over her nipples. They perked up at his touch, goose bumps trailing from them, radiating across her skin. It had been a long time since anyone had touched her like that... *way* too long. Warmth spread down her torso, settling in that spot between her thighs. She let out a soft moan as she wrapped her arms around his neck, drawing him even closer, absorbing his warmth.

Dante kissed her again as he pulled her onto the bed. She lay back, head resting on a pillow, as he hovered over her. His lips left hers, making their way along her face and down her jaw, a searing trail leading to her neck as she cocked her head, giving him better access. The skin prickled, tingling, as his tongue traced circles, drawing patterns on her flesh the whole way to her chest. His lips encircled a nipple, sucking. It was almost too much to take. The sensations flowing through her made her vision hazy, so she closed her eyes and tried to relax, running her hands through his thick hair.

Within seconds, his hand slid down her stomach, slipping inside her panties, his touch so gentle she writhed beneath him. Gabriella's breath hitched when his fingers grazed her clit, stroking it, rubbing, and driving her straight to the brink. Just a touch had her seeing stars. Parts of her ached for more. The guy *definitely* knew his way around a woman. Her body was a roadmap he skillfully navigated, exploring every twist and turn with his fingertips and mouth.

Gabriella lifted up when he tugged on her underwear, pulling them off and tossing them to the floor beside the bed. Her eyes darted open when he parted her legs and shifted further down the bed, settling between her thighs. The orange morning glow streamed through the nearby window. She was used to sleeping with so much light, but she wasn't used to *this* happening.

He could see *everything*.

She tried to sit up, but he grasped her hips, pinning them against the bed. Before she could object, his mouth was on her, his tongue flicking against her aching clit.

"Oh my God." She fisted his hair as she fell back flat against the bed. Every ounce of protest dissipated as her muscles turned to jelly, her body succumbing to him. He shouldn't be doing that. His face shouldn't be down there. His mouth shouldn't be on her, his tongue doing whatever it was doing, flicking and circling or some-thing. She didn't know. But frankly, she couldn't find it in her to *care*, either. Whatever he was doing was absolute perfection, and she never wanted it to end.

His mouth took her straight to Heaven.

The sensations built, layer after layer, as his mouth grew more frantic. Maybe it was a minute. Maybe it was an hour. It was an eternity wrapped up in a moment, one she wanted to exist in forev-er. The pressure built to the point of explosion. Her back arched, her jaw slack, noise catching in her throat.

Orgasm rocked her. Her legs shook, thigh clamping down around his head as she gasped, "*Don't stop*."

He didn't stop. He kept going until she couldn't take anymore. The sensations subsided, pleasure morphing, the ache growing painful. He seemed to know, because before she could tell him, his mouth moved, lips trailing along her inner thigh as she loosened her grip on him. Her breathing was labored, eyes closed. The jelly feeling returned to her muscles. She was floating.

"A dinosaur."

Her eyes opened at the sound of his voice. "What?"

A sharp sting shot through her inner thigh. Screeching, she shot straight up, realizing he'd *bit* her. Not hard enough to leave a last-ing mark, but hard enough for her to feel it. She shoved his shoul-der, and he laughed, sitting up.

"Your birthmark," he said. "It's shaped like a little dinosaur."

The fading imprint of teeth surrounded the discolored mark on her right inner thigh. She rubbed it, scowling, as he leaned toward her, kissing her lips. Soft, and chaste, and oh-so-sweet.

"Do you taste yourself on me?" he asked.

She kissed him back before pulling away. "You taste like *beer*."

"Well, you taste like sweat and sex and disinfectant."

"Ugh, gross." She grimaced. "I need to shower."

"Yeah, give me an hour and you'll *really* need a shower."

He kissed her again, rougher, pushing her back onto the bed. Hovering over her, he fumbled with his pants, unbuckling them. Gabriella's heart raced, so fast and so furious it thumped in her ears, electricity buzzing along her skin as anxiety kicked in.

Was this seriously happening?

He slowed his movements, breaking the kiss. "Shit."

"What's wrong?"

"I don't have a condom."

"There's a box in the bathroom."

Dante climbed out of the bed and disappeared from the room. It took him thirty seconds, a minute at most, but it was the longest moment of Gabriella's life. She lay there, practically naked, awaiting his return. A flood of emotions assaulted her, rattling her nerves.

When Dante walked back in, he started shedding his clothes. He pulled his shirt off but made no attempt to remove his undershirt, letting his jeans drop, leaving them in the middle of the floor.

Climbing back onto the bed, he tore open the condom and set the wrapper aside. He pulled himself from his boxers, stroking a few times, massaging the swollen head, before rolling the condom down over it. Gabriella watched his face, studying his look of sheer concentration, a smile touching her lips as her anxiety dissipated.

He was nervous, too. She could tell.

He met her gaze, returning her smile, as he climbed between her legs, hiking her knees up. Dante hesitated before lining up and slowly pushing in. Gabriella closed her eyes as he stretched her, hearing him let out a strained groan.

She certainly wasn't a virgin, but it had been a while.

"Fuck, you feel good." He pushed the whole way in before pulling back out, moving slowly, over and over. She chanced a peek at him, seeing his eyes fixed between them, watching where he disappeared inside of her. As if he sensed her gaze, he smirked. "It's a beautiful sight."

"Oh?" she whispered as he lay down on top of her, pulling her to him. She wrapped her arms around him as he increased the pace a bit, still taking it easy, his thrusts restrained.

It struck her, maybe too late, that he was still injured. He shouldn't have been exerting himself. She started to say something, worried, when he nuzzled into her neck, his husky voice wiping out all thoughts except for his words. "You've got such a beautiful pussy. *So beautiful.* I could lose myself inside of you for days, baby."

Her eyes fluttered closed. "I wish you would."

"I will, if you want. Stay right here and fuck you forever."

His teeth sunk into her neck, grazing her skin, as he sucked and licked at her flesh. She gasped, fisting the back of his shirt, wrapping her legs around his waist so he could fill her deeper.

Gabriella couldn't wrap her mind around it. It wasn't sinking in. Her world was becoming chaos because of this man. Feelings she'd never had before swirled inside of her, filling her up as he filled her to the hilt. Her chest ached as she shakily breathed, her lungs just not getting enough oxygen. Dante Galante was on top of her, *inside of her*, when just weeks earlier the world thought he was dead. But he wasn't—he was alive, and breathing, and so utterly intoxicating. She got drunk on the air around him, floating higher every time she breathed him in.

The stubborn, infuriating, reckless idiot had overtaken her carefully controlled life without even knowing it.

He rose up a bit, looking her in the eyes, shifting position to thrust harder. She moaned, leaning her head back, her voice catching every time his hips slammed into hers. Pain jabbed her insides, a beautiful ache brewing in her gut. "Oh God."

"You like that, baby?" He kissed along her collarbones. "Tell me how it feels."

"So good," she whispered. "I feel... uhh, there's so much inside of me, I'm going to explode."

As soon as she said it, she felt it—the undeniable swell of pleasure sweeping through her body. Tingles encased her as she trembled beneath him, her body convulsing around him.

"Fuck," he growled, his mouth on her throat. He bit down, yet again, as his thrusts grew erratic. He slammed into her hard a few times, groaning, before stilling on top of her, panting.

Gabriella loosened her hold on him, her hands slipping beneath his undershirt to rub his sweaty back, her fingertips grazing the bandage on his side. She tugged on the shirt, attempting to take it off, when he pulled away from her, pulling out to stand up.

He said not a word.

Dante headed straight for the bathroom and sat down on the edge of the bed beside her when he returned a minute later.

Gabriella sat up, covering herself with the sheet.

"Don't do that," Dante said, casting her a sidelong look. "You're beautiful. Don't be self-conscious."

"I'm not... usually." She frowned. "I'm kind of the only one naked here."

"Oh." He glanced down at himself. "I never bother undressing."

"*Ouch*."

"I didn't mean it that way, like you weren't worth the trouble," he said, reaching up to rub his chest. "Just not a fan of people pitying me, so I don't give them the chance."

"I don't pity you."

"I know."

"Are you okay, though? Your side, I mean…"

"It hurts like a son of a bitch."

Ugh. "Do you want me to—?"

She started to ask if he wanted her to look at it, but he cut her off, crawling into the bed and pulling her to him. "I'll be fine. Just out of practice. Need some time to recover, but Jesus *fuck*… that pussy was worth the pain, baby."

Tingles crept through her at those words. "If that's you out of practice, full-strength might be too much for me."

Dante laughed. Sweeping her hair aside, he kissed her neck, just a light peck against her skin. "When you want me to leave, just say so. I won't take it personal."

"Stay," she whispered, "for as long as you want."

She grasped his forearms, caressing them as she savored his warmth surrounding her. Almost right away, Dante's breathing settled, a soft snore escaping.

Out cold.

CHAPTER 12

The barrel of the gun viciously dug into Dante's side, twisting, tunneling into a stab wound through the gash in his filthy shirt. Dante ground his teeth together, his face twitching, a growl rumbling his chest. It felt like hot iron, like the muzzle was branding him. He wanted to scream, to curse, but he forced it down, refusing.

Refusing to react.

Refusing to give them the satisfaction.

"Tough guy, huh?" a voice said as the pain subsided, the gun pulled away, relief rushing through Dante. It didn't last long. In a matter of seconds, the gun was shoved beneath his chin, the blood-covered muzzle forcing his head up, forcing Dante to look at *him*.

Roberto Barsanti.

"This is a nice gun," Barsanti said, eyeing it as he gripped it, his finger on the trigger. The safety was off. It wouldn't take much for the guy to kill him—a simple twitch of a finger. "How many lives has it ended? Huh? Did you kill my son with it?"

Dante stared into his callous eyes. Desert Eagle Mk XIX, satin black, with a muzzle break installed. He'd had the gun for years, had pulled the trigger dozens of times, but he'd only ever taken one life. *Enzo.*

He didn't tell Barsanti that, though.

Didn't answer that question.

He could kill him if he wanted.

Wouldn't make a difference.

Barsanti snapped, shoving the gun so hard against him that it knocked the chair over, throwing it onto the ground, taking Dante with it. He cringed, smacking his head against the hard cement. He couldn't move, couldn't defend himself... couldn't *protect* himself.

Duct tape surrounded him, wound tightly around his chest, pinning his arms at the sides of the old wooden chair. His feet were wrapped at the ankles, secured to the legs so he couldn't escape.

Barsanti's foot planted dead center of Dante's chest, knocking the air from his lungs and crushing his ribs, the bones cracking. He gasped, inhaling sharply. He couldn't fucking *breathe*. Barsanti stepped on him, damn near suffocating him, aiming the gun at his head.

"Did you?" he yelled, rage turning his face bright red. "Did you stand over him like *this* when you did it? Did my son look *you* in the eyes when you murdered him?"

Dante struggled against the weight on his chest, trying to stay conscious. He'd been beaten beyond black and blue. His vision was going hazy. He couldn't even answer if he wanted to.

"But this is what you did to Matteo, right? You stomped on him, knowing he couldn't fight back. Knowing he *wouldn't*. He was on the ground, defenseless, and you kicked him! So how does it feel, huh? How does it feel beneath *my* boot? I'm guessing it doesn't feel good."

Barsanti moved, and Dante inhaled sharply, desperate to take a deep breath. It was only a few seconds of satisfaction as the air seeped into his lungs before the steel-toed black boot came back at him, aimed right for his face. He saw it before it happened. He felt it before it really registered. A kick to the face sent Dante's vision fading, his ears ringing as Barsanti said, "You're not the only one who can kick people when they're down."

BAM

Dante's eyes shot open, his gaze fixed on a dim white ceiling above him. He inhaled, a peculiar scent greeting his nostrils, musky with a hint of sweet vanilla. Not the dank basement he expected to smell. He blinked a few times, trying to pull himself together, before taking in his surroundings.

Gabriella's bedroom.

Reality came back to him in a flood of memories, like the pages of a flipbook rushing by, the picture steadily moving. He sat up, running his hands down his face. Sweat drenched him. His muscles were stiff. Outside, the sun was setting.

He was alone. *No Gabriella.*

How long had he been asleep?

Climbing out of the small bed, he snatched up his clothes, pulling them on before grabbing his phone from the back pocket of his jeans. The screen glowed brightly: 8:20pm.

Shit.

A dozen or so missed calls showed up in his notifications. He barely paid them any attention, wiping them off the screen, not in the mood to talk to anybody. He hadn't been home in two days, maybe three... he wasn't sure. He didn't consult a calendar. Every day was the same, blending together in a blur of *whatever*. He came and went, here and there, going all over but staying nowhere, like one of the city's vagrants. The only time the world slowed enough for him take a breath was when he was near her. It was the only time he felt like a person, like he'd lived through what happened. The rest of the time, he was still just waiting to flat-line.

He was about to leave, walking through the silent apartment, when he stalled at the front door. Covering the peephole, stuck there with a strip of medical tape, was a scribbled note in messy handwriting.

Working 'til 7 in the AM.
XO, Gabby
PS – You're welcome to stay.

He tugged it off the door, shoving it in his back pocket. He left, engaging the locks that he could, feeling guilty for leaving her apartment exposed. His head was a fog as he made the trek downstairs, groggy like he hadn't quite woken up yet.

"Are you deaf?" a voice asked when Dante stepped out onto the sidewalk. "Or do you just not listen?"

Dante turned, finding Gavin leaning against the building. "What?"

"*What?*" Gavin mimicked, shoving away from the wall near the intercom. "Twenty-four hours ago, I told you to leave Gabriella alone, but here you are, coming out of her building, still wearing the same damn clothes from yesterday. Oh, but you're not fucking her, right? That's what you said, isn't it?"

Dante slowly blinked at him, his eyes trying to adjust, but it was pointless. Shaking his head, he muttered, "I'm not awake enough for this bullshit."

He took a few steps before Gavin grabbed his shoulder. "Dante."

Dante pulled away from him but stalled. Annoyance swelled through him that he tried to keep at bay, but his patience was still asleep somewhere. "I swear to fuck, Amaro, I don't want to fight you, but if you put your hands on me *one more time*..."

Gavin raised his hands. "I'm not trying to fight you. I'm just trying to understand."

"Understand what?"

"What's wrong with you."

Dante blinked at him again. Gavin looked serious, like he was genuinely trying to understand, like he just didn't *get* it. "Do you have a girlfriend?"

Gavin's brow furrowed, his stance defensive. "No."

"Maybe you ought to get one," Dante suggested. "Someone else for you to worry about so you'll stop riding my ass. Because I'm flattered, you know, that you care, but you're starting to make me wonder if you're about to boil my bunny here, and I'm not down with that, G."

Gavin glared at him. "It's not like that and you know it. I just don't like what I'm seeing."

"Why?"

"My cousin—"

"Don't give me that *'my cousin'* bullshit. You started acting funny before you knew I was fucking her."

Surprise crossed Gavin's face. "So you *are*."

"Don't change the subject. Where I stick my dick is irrelevant to why you're acting like a sentimental bitch. Is it because of my sister? Is that it?"

Something flashed in Gavin's eyes, something Dante couldn't quite figure out. "What about your sister?"

"What about my sister? How about the fact that my father wrote her off and just went on living like she never existed? The fact that I wasn't here... the fact that I was gone... the fact that I didn't do anything to stop it. The fact that *nobody* did anything to stop it!"

Gavin frowned. "You're upset."

"*Of course* I'm fucking upset."

"It's not your fault, man. You didn't do this."

"Didn't stop it, either."

"You couldn't."

"I could," Dante countered. "I could've stopped it long ago. Could've done something the day she came home and said she'd met a guy named *Matty*. Could've done something when I ran into Matteo and realized he was the *Matty* she met. Could've done something when she started lying to my face. Because I knew. I'm not stupid. I knew, but I did nothing. I did nothing when I found him in our house—a *Barsanti*—because she begged for his life, and I couldn't bring myself to hurt her after she told me she *loved* him. I did nothing, when I could've. But instead, I waited until her fate was sealed, and even then I took out the wrong Barsanti! I fucked up *bad,* and because of that, I wasn't here to do anything when somebody needed to do *something*."

Gavin just stood there on the sidewalk, staring at Dante. People walked by, casting curious looks their direction, but Dante didn't care. It didn't matter who overheard. The facts were clear, as far as he was concerned.

After a moment, Gavin frowned. *Pity.* Dante could see it in his eyes. "When's the last time you ate, man? You're wasting away."

"Don't do that." Dante shook his head. "You pity me and I'll never fucking speak to you again."

"I don't pity you."

"Don't want your sympathy, either. I'm not a charity case. I'm not your responsibility. You don't have to look out for me, nor do you have to *worry* about me."

"You make it so easy, though," Gavin said. "Christ, just, why don't we go grab a bite to eat?"

"It sounds a lot like you're asking me on a date, G, and that's bunny boiling territory again."

"It's a friend buying a friend a slice. That's it."

"Friend? Is that what you are to me?"

"Always thought so," Gavin said, "but then again, I'm not one to judge people by their name. Barsanti, Galante, Brazzi... doesn't matter. I've met a couple of each I wouldn't mind seeing dead, but a few others I'd be happy to call my friend."

Dante considered that until his phone vibrated in his pocket. Pulling it out, he glanced at the screen. *Bert.*

He answered it, buying himself a moment. "Yeah?"

203

"Got something to do," Umberto said. "Where are you?"

"Little Italy. Across the street from the bar."

"Pulling onto Mulberry now," Umberto said. "Pick you up in thirty seconds."

The line went dead.

Dante waved the phone toward Gavin. "Seems duty calls, so maybe some other time."

A black BMW screeched to a stop in the middle of the street beside where they stood. Dante nodded to Gavin before heading to the waiting car.

"Don't get yourself killed," Gavin said.

Dante stepped out into the street, looking back as he grabbed the door handle on the passenger side. "Don't lose any sleep over me."

He climbed in the car, barely getting the door closed before Umberto hit the gas, the tires squealing. Dante shot him a look, not bothering to put on his seatbelt despite the constant dinging from the dashboard warning him.

"Was that *Amaro* you were with?" Umberto asked incredulously. "Did you forget that jackass punched you last night?"

"That was nothing." Dante rubbed his jaw. "You gotta admire the guy. Took balls to swing on me like that. Besides, it was my fault."

"How was it *your* fault?"

"Long story," Dante said. "So, where are we going?"

"Jersey."

Jersey.

That hadn't been the answer Dante expected. "What's going on in Jersey?"

"We figured out where Matteo had been living before he showed up," Umberto said. "Your father wants us to go check the place out."

"Why?"

"What do you mean, '*why*'?"

"What's the point? What's he hoping to find?"

"Anything," Umberto said. "We're talking about Barsanti's kid... who the hell knows what we might find."

Dante shook his head, looking out the window as Umberto sped through the city. If they thought they'd find anything about the Barsanti family, they'd be sorely mistaken. If Matteo had possessed anything important—and Dante doubted it—Barsanti would've retrieved it long before then.

He didn't say that, though.

Who was he to argue?

No matter how senseless...

"Where'd you go last night?" Umberto asked, giving him a brief once-over when traffic slowed them near the tunnel leading out of the city. "I know you never made it home."

"Hung around," he said. "Stayed in the city."

"With Amaro?"

Suspicion laced Umberto's voice. If Dante didn't know any better, he'd say his old friend was phishing for information. "Yeah, Amaro and I made pottery and watched the fucking sunrise."

Umberto looked at him like he actually *believed* that.

It was beneath him, but Dante rolled his eyes. "With a girl, Bert. I stayed with a girl."

"Making pottery?"

"You can call it that if you want."

Umberto whistled. "Look at you, back in the game! Was it that curvy broad, you know, the one with the big tits that you used to mess with around there? What was her name? Leslie?"

"Lisa, but no... I haven't seen her."

Not since what happened to him. He'd seen none of them, none of the women he used to occupy himself with on the weekends. Dante had never been a relationship kind of guy... it was never his style. Relationships took too much time, and he'd never met a woman he felt compelled to put in that kind of work for. Love was fleeting, a feeling akin to the sensation that rushed through his body whenever he was buried balls-deep inside a pussy. He loved women. He couldn't deny that fact. But he'd never been *in* love with a woman, not the kind of love others talked about. That kind of love was a myth, an urban legend. That kind of love didn't exist for him.

He'd always been glad for that.

Because that was the kind of love that had taken down Romeo and Juliet.

It was the kind of love that destroyed lives.

He'd watched his father grieve that kind of love, refusing to step foot in his bedroom or sleep in his bed again after losing his wife. He'd watched his sister lose herself in guys until one took her down. *'It's like my insides are too big for my body and I'm going to burst.'* Genna had told him that, how she'd described it to him sitting in the café in Little Italy. He thought she was fucking crazy.

Until last night.

Dante knew what his sister had meant, because maybe he wasn't in love, *yet*, but goddamn if it wasn't happening to him. If he wasn't careful, Gabriella would claw her way beneath his skin and she'd stay there.

"So who was it? Who'd you nail last night?"

"None of your business."

"Come on…"

"Ask me again and next time it'll be your sister."

"Ah, man, that's *foul*."

Umberto's sister was young, barely legal. He was protective over her, wouldn't even let Dante *talk* to her because of his hit-it-and-quit-it reputation. The threat worked, because Umberto dropped the subject, rambling about how he'd spent his night with the woman he met at the bar, filling the air with his incessant chatter.

They drove to a small suburb down near the city of Elizabeth, deep in the heart of Brazzi territory. They'd entered their terrain the second they crossed the state line, something they didn't do often, being as they never had reason. Brazzi stayed out of their affairs as much as possible, choosing to stay out of New York as long as *New York* respected their territory. You needed something there—you called, you asked, you negotiated, and they made it happen.

But as Umberto pulled the car into a small neighborhood after nightfall, blacking out the headlights, visibly nervous, Dante realized that hadn't gone down this time. "I'm guessing the Brazzis don't know we're here."

"Primo didn't want to risk letting them in on it," he replied, parking the car along the curb in the first spot he came to. "Since Matteo was living out here, you know, they must've been protecting the kid. Can't trust nobody these days."

Tell me about it.

The house was in a cul-de-sac just down the street, tucked in between similar cookie-cutter houses, a typical suburban neighbor-hood. The place was dark with blinds covering the windows. The grass hadn't been mowed in weeks. A sprinkler ran on the lawn across the street, a few lights peeking out from neighboring houses. Dante was on edge, his gaze darting around for signs of trouble, as Umberto fiddled with the front door, attempting to break into the house. He was dressed in all black, carrying a black bag, while Dan-te hadn't been prepared for this kind of work, wearing jeans and a white t-shirt that glowed under the moonlight.

Dante grew impatient, shoving him out of the way to take over before the guy resorted to violently kicking the door in. "How many times do I have to show you how to do this?"

Sighing, Umberto stood back, watching as Dante picked the lock on the front door. When Dante got it open, he held his breath, expecting an alarm to go off.

Nothing.

Umberto slipped around him, heading inside. Dante followed, closing the front door. A beam of light cut through the front room as Umberto retrieved a flash light from his bag, handing it to Dan-te, before pulling out one for himself.

"Are you sure this is the right place?" Dante asked, his flashlight glossing over the furniture. *Plain.* There was no other way to de-scribe it. No pictures hung on the walls, nothing personal around the room.

Dust tickled Dante's nose.

"Positive," Umberto said.

"How'd you find it?"

They'd sought Matteo for years. While they suspected he could've been in New Jersey, suspicion was far from having an ac-tual address.

"Tracked it down using GPS," he answered. "These new phones, you know, they have that feature enabled, in case you ever lose it or someone steals it, so you can track it down, see where it went. I told your father about it a while back, told him that's why I use burners. I don't want anything linked to me that can be monitored."

"So, what, he found a way to track Matteo's phone?"

"No, he tracked your sister's."

Dante pointed the flashlight at Umberto, illuminating him.

"She came here a couple times," Umberto continued. "She mostly frequented that place you went to in Soho, you know... *The Place*. Guess they hung out at the bar. But we saw some hits in Jersey and figured it had to be something for her to come into Brazzi territory, so we put the pieces together, and here we are."

Dante lowered the beam of his flashlight. "Matteo was staying in Soho, in the apartment above that bar."

"How do you know?"

"I just do."

Dante didn't elaborate. He didn't owe anybody an explanation.

Looking away, he strolled into the kitchen, glancing around the quiet house. Umberto set off in the opposite direction, disappearing down a hallway. The place was stocked with essentials, but nothing personal could be found. Nothing more than a safe house, Dante gathered, as he checked cabinets and drawers. It wasn't really anybody's *home*. He moved to the dining room, finding a table with a few chairs, and plopped down in one as he shined his flashlight around.

"There's nothing here," Dante called out. "This is a waste of time."

Not worth the trouble, either. They had enough problems. Why risk enraging the Brazzis for crossing borders and invading territory?

"You're right." Umberto appeared from the hallway, heading straight to the front door. "Let's get out of here."

Dante followed him, pausing in the living room when the slight scent of something infiltrated his nose. It smelled *rotten*. "Do you smell that?"

"I smell nothing," Umberto said, "but we've got to get out of here before somebody catches us."

A car pulled onto the cul-de-sac then, headlights flashing toward the window, making Umberto freeze. He cut his flashlight out at once, while Dante pointed his at the floor. Strolling to the window, he pushed two slats apart to peek through the blinds. A black car pulled into the driveway across the street, cutting the engine after parking in the garage. As the garage door came down, the man strolled toward the front porch of the house, swinging his keys around his fingers, in no rush to get inside. He was too far away for Dante to get a good look at him.

"You seriously don't smell anything?" Dante asked, shining the flashlight at Umberto. It wasn't a strong odor, but it was distinct.

Umberto shook his head, but under the glow of the light, Dante saw his nose twitch. Damn right he smelled it. Dante shined his flashlight down the hall, about to make his way there when another car sped into the cul-de-sac, whipping into the driveway of the house right next door. Dante turned off the flashlight, glancing out the window.

"Hey, yo!" a voice called out, way too close for comfort, as a shadowy figure cut across the front lawn, heading toward the street. "Russo!"

Russo.

Son of a bitch.

It couldn't be, could it?

Dante parted the blind again, watching as the man across the street paused at the sound of that name. He waited for the other guy to join him, the two of them chatting before going their separate ways.

They needed to get out of there.

As soon as both men went inside, Dante slipped out of the house, Umberto right on his heels. Panic wafted from him, his eyes darting around, his steps hurried, while Dante took the time to lock the house up again.

"Don't bother," Umberto hissed back at him. "We've gotta go. This neighborhood is full of Brazzis. I'm talking *top-level* Brazzis. We can't be caught here."

Dante said nothing, his gaze sweeping along the numbers affixed to the front of the house before trekking back to the car. He slid into the passenger seat, barely getting the door closed before they sped away from the neighborhood. Umberto was uncharacteristically quiet on the drive back into the city, drumming his fingers against the steering wheel as he kept glancing in the rearview mirror, like he expected something. Silence grew into something more, that suffocating cloud of distrust forming. Something was off about it. Something was *rotten*.

"What did you do?" Dante asked, his voice serious.

"Nothing."

His answer was immediate.

"What did you do, Bert?" Before he could once again spout out with *'nothing'*, Dante said, "You lie to me again and I swear to God, I'll run this car off the fucking bridge with both of us in it."

Umberto hesitated.

"Nothing," he said as he settled back into his seat. "Just a little gas leak."

Dante closed his eyes. A gas leak. The house was uninhabited. The gas would build and build, undisturbed. It was like setting a bomb dead center of Brazzi territory. All it needed was a spark and *boom*.

Dante said nothing more as they drove straight into the city, turning north after the bridge, heading up to Westchester County. Dante's car was still parked somewhere down in Little Italy, but he didn't say a word about it, staying silent as they made the trip to the Galante house. Umberto pulled his car beside Genna's BMW, still parked along the driveway like some sort of morbid lawn ornament.

Dante headed straight inside, leaving the door open for Umberto. Primo met them in the foyer. "Any problems?"

"None," Umberto said, shutting the front door behind him. "There was nothing there. No sign of anyone. And nobody noticed us that I could tell. We were in and out."

"Good." Primo's gaze turned to Dante. "Where have you been?"

"Around," Dante said.

"He was with a girl," Umberto said as he smacked Dante on the back. "You know how he is."

"Ah, yes." Primo's expression softened, something akin to pride shining from his eyes for the first time since Dante had returned, like finally something felt familiar to him. Finally something reminded him of *his* Dante. "It's good to see you."

Dante didn't respond, and his father didn't wait for him to, heading back into his office. Umberto lingered in the foyer, looking like he wanted to join Primo but was hesitant to leave Dante.

"I should head back to the city," Dante said. "Get back to what I was doing."

Umberto laughed. "Or *who* you were doing, right?"

"Right." Dante hesitated, staring at his father's open office door when Umberto strolled that way. "Can I ask you something, Bert?"

Umberto turned. "What's up?"

"You said you tracked Genna's phone. You ever track *mine*?"

"Of course not."

"Never?"

"Never."

"Not even when I was missing? You didn't think, you know, you might've been able to track it to find me?"

"Didn't really think about it."

Dante nodded as he left, not having much else to say. He took the subway back into the city, in a daze, lost in thought, stepping out of the station in Little Italy, down the street from Casato. He pulled out his phone as he strolled along, his eyes on the screen as he sought out a number, dialing it.

"New Jersey Natural Gas."

"I need to report a leak," Dante said, stalling on the street corner not far from Gabriella's apartment. "It's at a house in a suburb outside of Elizabeth."

Dante rattled off the address, hoping he remember the numbers right and was sending them to the correct place.

"We'll send a crew out right away," the woman said. "Can I get your name?"

Dante hung up when she asked that, staring at his phone for a second before dropping it to the sidewalk, stomping on it, crushing it.

Picking up the remnants, he tossed it in the closest trash bin before continuing on, heading to the bar.

He needed a damn drink.

* * *

The first cell phone Genna ever had was a hot pink Motorola Razr. A flip phone. She remembered talking on it all hours of the night, not having to worry about her father picking up the line from somewhere else in the house. Her ringtone had perpetually stayed *Hollaback Girl*, a fact that drove everyone around her insane.

After that came smartphones and new ringtones every week.

Always a song. Always music.

Never the obnoxious generic beeping.

So why the hell did she hear it?

"What the fuck is that noise?" she asked, scrunching up her nose as she glanced around the kitchen, sitting on the counter beside the stove. Matty was cooking burgers in a pan. Nothing special, just some frozen patties, but she was so hungry she wouldn't complain. Compared to what she'd scrounged up for lunch, it was practically a gourmet meal.

"Banjos," Matty said, pointing at the dingy little AM/FM radio on the other side of the counter, one he'd dug out of a closet in an attempt to fill the silence. "It was all I could get to come in."

"No, I'm not talking about the freaky *Deliverance* bullshit," she said. "That beep-bee-bee-boop noise."

He reached into his pocket and pulled his phone out far enough to see it. "Not coming from me."

Shit.

Genna dropped down from the counter and ran out of the kitchen, skidding to a stop in the foyer. Her cheap flip phone lay on the stand, glowing bright, steadily ringing. She snatched it up, flipping it open, pressing buttons in a panic, not sure which one would answer it. "Hello?"

"Hey, it's Chris down at *Jerry's*. Can I speak to—?"

"This is her," Genna said, walking back into the kitchen. "How are you?"

"Oh, I'm great! Just calling to let you know those parts you ordered are in, so you can pick them up any time."

"Awesome! Thank you! I'll see you soon!"

She hung up, tossing her phone down on the counter, before meeting Matty's curious gaze. "Who was that?"

"Chris from Jerry's."

"Chris from Jerry's," he repeated. "Who the hell is Jerry?"

"Oh, I don't know. I guess the dude who owns the place? I only met Chris. He called to tell me the parts I ordered are in."

"You ordered parts? For what?"

"For the car."

"The Honda?"

"The *Lincoln*. I went into the garage in town and ordered some parts so I can try to fix it."

He stared at her like she'd gone insane. "Do you even know what's wrong with it?"

"I'll figure it out."

"So you ordered parts for a car that you don't even know will work, and you gave your phone number to some stranger so he could arrange for you to come pick them up from him?"

"Yep."

"And you don't see anything wrong with that?"

"Nope."

"White girl in the horror movie," he muttered, reaching over to flick the burner off, cutting the heat from the burgers. "Can't even recognize danger."

Genna laughed. "Whatever, I *know* danger. I grew up around danger. That dude was harmless."

"We'll see," Matty said, setting the spatula down. "Come on, let's go."

"Whoa, whoa, whoa!" She stepped in front of him, blocking his path when he tried to walk away. "Nobody is going *anywhere* until I get my damn cheeseburger."

Matty turned on his heel, swinging back around to the stove. Grabbing a bun from the fresh pack on the counter, he slapped a burger and a slice of non-melted cheese between it and held it out to her. "Eat in the car."

She took a bite of the burger as she followed him, slipping her feet into a pair of flip-flops in the foyer. She ate as Matty drove them into town, still eating when they pulled up to the garage, finishing chewing as she followed him inside.

"Excuse me?" Matty said, approaching a grubby man with long hair, leaning over the hood of a car. "Are you Chris?"

Genna paused at the entrance. *Oh Lord.*

The guy motioned toward the other side of the garage. "Chris is over there."

Matty diverted that direction, approaching Chris as he sorted through boxes in the back. It didn't escape Genna's notice that Matty sized him up, his eyes picking the guy apart.

"Chris?" Matty held his hand out when the guy turned around. "I'm Matt. I believe you've already met my wife, Jen."

Wife. That word sent shivers down Genna's spine. She was somebody's wife now.

Chris shook Matty's hand, his gaze shifting her direction. "Yes, of course. Nice to meet you."

"Likewise," Matty said. "She mentioned something about needing to pick up car parts?"

"Yeah." Chris turned to some boxes before launching into a rundown of whatever he'd ordered for her. Some of it was gibberish to Genna, which made her wonder if she was in over her head, but she smiled like she actually knew what the hell an *actuator* did. Matty seemed to, though, nodding as the guy talked. Afterward, Matty pulled out his wallet, forking over damn near four hundred dollars for all the parts she got. *Whoa.*

He carried them to the car with Chris's help, loading the Honda down, the two of them still talking. Matty slid a box into the trunk, slamming it closed, as Chris lingered there.

"North Carolina, huh?" he asked, glancing at the plate, before looking Genna's way. "Thought you were a Jersey girl."

Matty's gaze flickered her way as panic flooded through Genna. *Oh shit.*

"Transplants," Matty chimed in, his voice casual, but she could tell he wasn't amused. "Stayed in North Carolina for a while, but you know... you never let go of your hometown."

Chris smiled. "Fresno, right here... born and bred."

"As in, California?" Genna asked.

"Is there another Fresno?"

She shrugged, pretty sure there probably shouldn't even be that one. "Let's hope not."

Chris laughed, strolling away. "Hold on a second, got one more thing for you."

When he disappeared back into the garage, Matty took a few steps toward Genna, speaking quietly. "A *Jersey* girl, are you?"

She made a face, pretending to gag. "Trust me, I got no enjoyment out of calling myself that."

"Then why did you?"

"Jersey phone number," she reminded him.

He looked surprised, like that hadn't registered with him. His gaze flickered to the license plate when Chris reappeared from the garage, carrying a book.

"There's a manual in one of those boxes," he said, "but I thought this might help, too."

Genna took the thick book from him, laughing. *Complete Idiot's*

Guide to Fixing Classic Cars. "It just might."

"You need anything else, you know where we are," Chris said, motioning to the garage.

They climbed into the car, and Matty set out onto the road, driving back to the house. He said nothing until they got there, until he unloaded the parts behind the house.

"You really think you got this?" Matty asked, dropping the last box by the back door.

Genna's gaze glossed over the car. "Pfft, piece of cake." *Oh...*"Do we have any cake? I could go for some."

"Of course," Matty said. "I brought some angel food cake home from work yesterday."

She scowled. "That's not cake. Cake has frosting. And sprinkles. And it's chocolate, hopefully. Angel food is a dessert bread."

"Well then, how about we have some dessert bread and I pick your brain about this project of yours."

"Deal," she said, "but only if I can pick your brain, too."

"About?"

"About what the hell an *actuator* is."

CHAPTER 13

"Order up!"

Matty slid the plate of French toast onto the pass beside the stack of pancakes for Doris to deliver to a table. He wiped his sweaty forehead with the back of his tattooed arm, grateful to have a second to collect himself.

It wasn't hard work, it wasn't manual labor, but he wouldn't call it easy, either. It was work, *real* work, for a genuine paycheck.

A degree in communications and a cushy job keeping up the family books hadn't prepared him for spending eight hours a day on his feet, sweating over a hot grill, smelling like food by the time the day was over.

"Order," Doris said, appearing on the other side of the pass, a baffled expression on her face. She looked almost shell-shocked for some reason. "Hashbrowns smothered in onions, peppers, mushrooms, and cheese... excuse me, *extra* cheese... and a three-egg omelet, also with onions, peppers, mushrooms, and extra cheese. The gentleman requested I tell you, and I quote... uh... *fuck 'em up good...* whatever that means. He seems a bit of a weird one. He also asked for a Roman Coke, but I told him the only Coke we served was made here in America. He seemed to think that was funny."

Matty stared at Doris, his blood running cold at those words, while she laughed it off, clipping the ticket to a hook and spinning it toward him. He stood there for a moment, after Doris walked away with the plates from the pass. Sickness churned through him, but he tried to push it down, holding himself together as he worked on the order, not wanting to cause a scene. His gaze flickered to the clock near the pass. His shift was over in twenty minutes.

He wouldn't last that long.

As soon as the food was done, he set it aside. "Order up!"

Doris grabbed the plate, and Matty's gaze trailed her to a booth in the back left corner. Carefully, he untied his apron and tossed it aside before strolling through the diner, leading there. He passed Doris along the way but didn't look at her, not wanting to explain. Every footstep sent his heart racing, and every pound of his heart made him even queasier.

His vision blurred from a rush of adrenaline by the time he reached the booth.

Sliding into it, he looked across the table at a face he hadn't expected to see again so soon. *Gavin Amaro.* He was the only one who knew where to find them, who knew where they had gone.

"*This,*" Gavin said, pointing to his plate with his fork, "wasn't worth the trip. Five and a half hours on a plane, another hour in a car, and you couldn't even fuck 'em up good for me. You ought to be ashamed."

"I am," Matty said. "Deeply mortified."

Gavin took a bite as he met Matty's eyes. His expression softened, a smile touching his lips. "It's good to see you, Matty-B."

"You, too, Gavin. A bit worrisome, though."

"I figured," Gavin said. "Don't panic. Nobody knows where I am. The Prodigal Son and the Ice Princess are still safe with their *happily ever after...* for now."

"That's a contradiction."

"Yeah, well, isn't life? It sure doesn't make any damn sense to me. But I'm not here about you. Just needed to talk to you."

"You couldn't call?"

"I thought about it, almost did it a few times, but it's not something you tell someone over the phone."

Matty's chest tightened. "Something happen to my father?"

"No, still the same coldhearted Uncle Bobby."

"Primo?"

"Still homicidal."

"Uncle Johnny? Aunt Lena?"

"They're fine."

Matty's frown deepened. "So, what happened? Who is it?"

Gavin hesitated. "It's Dante."

Dante.

"I'm assuming that means they finally found him?"

"You could say that."

"And I'm assuming my father did it… whatever *it* is."

"Well, that's definitely the assumption."

"I'm surprised he let anyone find him," Matty said. "When someone disappears, they usually stay gone."

"Tell me about it. Took us all by surprise. Happened weeks ago… about two months, actually, right after you left town. They dumped him out on Primo's front lawn."

Matty cringed. "I'm assuming they've had a funeral."

Gavin stabbed his plate of food with the fork. "Not yet."

"What are they waiting for?"

"Him to die, I guess."

It took Matty a minute. An entire fucking *minute*. Those words bounced around in his mind as he watched Gavin casually eating, something about them just not wanting to sink in. But then he got it, after those sixty seconds. "He's not dead."

Son of a bitch.

"Not yet," Gavin said again. "Although, if you ask me, it won't be long."

Matty ran his hands down his face. "How bad is it? Coma? Brain damage?"

"Worse."

"What's worse than that?"

"He's a fucking cocksure jackass," Gavin said. "Even more so than *before*."

Matty's eyes opened, his gaze going straight to Gavin. "What?"

"He's got no sense of self-preservation. He's out there playing fast and loose with his life."

"You're telling me he's *alive*?"

Gavin looked up, brow furrowing at Matty's incredulous tone. "We already said that."

"We said he wasn't dead yet, not that he was alive," Matty said, his voice grave. This was the last thing he expected to hear. "That's a big difference, as far as the damage my father inflicts in concerned."

"Yeah, well, don't get me wrong here—Uncle Bobby got him good. Him being alive is pretty much a miracle. And it's not going to last, at the rate he's going. He's mad at the world and it shows."

"Does he know about us?"

"He just knows what everyone else does—car went boom and you two got ghost. I think he's too wrapped up in the *'who did what'* to go any further with it, but he's smart. If he lives long enough to start using his brain, he'll ask questions. He knows better than anyone right now that just because someone vanished doesn't mean they're not still out there."

"Shit. Shit. Shit. *Shit.*"

"Tell me about it," Gavin said, continuing to eat.

"What are we going to do?"

"*I'm* not going to do a damn thing," Gavin said. "No more than I've been doing, anyway."

"Well, what am *I* supposed to do?"

"I don't know, man," Gavin muttered. "You can be like me and keep your mouth shut, act like you know nothing, and let it all play out. He'll probably get himself killed before anything comes of it. Or you can tell your girlfriend—"

"Wife," Matty chimed in.

Gavin faltered. "No shit? Mr. Ice Princess now? Congratulations."

Matty's lips twitched, itching to spew a comeback to that, but it wasn't worth it. There were more important issues. His eyes darted to the clock—ten minutes until his shift was over. "Or I can tell Genna her brother is back in New York, alive and well."

"I don't know that I'd say he's *well*," Gavin said. "But he's alive, and he's back, and she deserves to know. But it could change things. She might want to see him. Probably wouldn't want him to think she's dead, especially since thinking she's dead has him acting like a miserable jackass. So if you tell her, you'll probably end up back in New York, back where you started, with people trying to kill you both for stupid shit."

"So I either keep it from Genna and let Dante get himself killed, or I confess, maybe spare him, but in the process risk *her*? Those are my options?"

"Yep," Gavin said. "Sure glad I'm not you right now."

"You're an asshole." Matty ran his hands down his face as he leaned back in the booth. "I take back everything I've ever said about you being my favorite cousin."

"Oh, speaking of cousins, I almost forgot the best part."

Matty glared at him through his hands. "There's *more*?"

"Yeah, you remember Gabby? Alfie and Victoria's girl?"

"Of course I remember Gabby. What about her?"

"She figured out the truth," Gavin said. "Which wouldn't be such a problem if it weren't for the fact that she has, for some inexplicable reason, decided to take up with Dante."

"What do you mean *take up* with him?"

"They're, uh…" Gavin waved his fork around in circles before stabbing the air with it. "Well, they're *fucking*. I don't know how else to describe it. He's sticking it to her on the regular."

Matty just stared at him. He had no idea what to say. Every word from Gavin's lips just made it all worse.

"So regardless of what you decide," Gavin said, shoving the plate aside as he dropped the fork. "There's always a chance Gabby could crack. So… good luck with that."

Doris approached. "You finished with that, sweetheart?"

"Absolutely." Gavin picked up his soda and sucked the rest of it down. "I'd love one of these Americanized Cokes to go, if you don't mind."

"Not a problem," Doris said, smiling, looking between them. "You two know each other?"

"Nope," Gavin said. "Never seen this shaggy-haired bastard before in my life."

Doris's eyes widened as Matty sighed, running a hand through his hair. He hadn't touched it since leaving New York, the ends curling around his ears, the top covering his forehead, falling into his eyes. "He's an old friend of mine."

"I was just passing through town and thought I'd stop in and remind him to cut his hair." Gavin looked at Matty. "You're starting to look like a girl. An *ugly* girl. With a beard. And a mustache. The bearded lady. *Stop it*."

Matty laughed, grabbing the discarded straw wrapper from the table and balling it up, flicking it right at Gavin's forehead. Doris walked away, carrying the plate of food, to retrieve Gavin's Coke. Before Matty could say anything to his cousin, the bell above the door jingled. His gaze darted that way.

Three o'clock on the dot.

Shift over. *Shit*.

Genna walked in, distracted, her attention fixed outside at something.

"Afternoon, sweetheart," Doris said, greeting her.

Genna turned to Doris. "Whose car is that out there? Do you know? The BMW?"

Matty glanced out the window, spotting the BMW parked in front of the diner. Black paint. Tinted windows. He knew what she was thinking. The people they grew up around steered toward that kind of car—discreet luxury.

Her guard was up.

"Oh, that would be mine," Gavin said, standing up.

If Gavin thought that would alleviate her worry, he was mistaken. Genna's eyes darted right at him, every inch of her tensing as Gavin approached. She was a block of ice with no expression. He veered to the register, pulling out his wallet to pay.

The second his back was to Genna, she swung toward Matty, panic melting her face as she mouthed, '*what the fuck?*' and dramatically motioned his way. Matty walked over to her, grasping her elbow to pull her out of the diner.

"What the fuck?" she hissed. "What is *Pennywise the Clown* doing here?"

Before Matty could respond, the door to the diner opened and Gavin walked out, sipping a drink from a Styrofoam cup.

"Genna with a G!" Gavin grinned as his eyes scanned her. "You gained some weight."

"Amaro." She crossed her arms over her chest. "You can kiss my fat ass."

He tilted his head. "I wouldn't call it fat. Round, maybe. And those hips are getting wide... not to mention those thick thighs."

"I'm *pregnant*, asshole," she said. "And you're not supposed to say that shit to a woman. I thought your mother would've taught you better than that."

"My mother taught me that all women are beautiful and should be treated as so," he said. "But you're extra cute when you get angry, so I'm just doing my civic duty by pissing you off."

"Why are you even here?" she asked, not giving him time to respond before turning to Matty. "Why is he here?"

Matty paused, his gaze flickering to Gavin. "He was visiting Ve-

221

gas on business."

"Oh, so he was just *in the neighborhood*? Thought he'd drop in for a piece of cake or something? Pie, maybe? Some milk and cookies? Thought I'd bake him a damn casserole? Fix up a guest room? Maybe I can read him a bedtime story and tuck him in while I'm at it."

"How very domestic," Gavin chimed in. "I'm starting to like Genna with a G becoming a mommy."

"Fuck off," she growled.

"There's that Galante spirit," Gavin said. "Or maybe it's the Barsanti in her, since she's got some of that now, too."

Genna spun around, darting forward, like she was about to swing on Gavin, but Matty wrapped his arms around her from behind, yanking her back to him. "Gavin, you're not helping."

"Okay, okay..." Gavin held his hands up in surrender. "I'll stop."

"You're lucky," Genna said, "because I was about to knock some teeth out and I *know* your mother taught you better than to hit a pregnant woman."

"Actually, any woman, period," Gavin admitted, "but you're right. And I meant no offense."

Genna scowled. "Yeah, right."

"Seriously. You look good. And I'm not hitting on you with that. I just mean getting away from all that seems like it was good for you. You look *good*."

"Don't do that," Genna said.

"Don't do what?"

"Don't be nice to me," she said, pulling out of Matty's arms. "It weirds me out."

Gavin laughed. "What *can* I do?"

"You can tell me what you're doing here."

Gavin's eyes subtly shifted to Matty, just a fleeting, questioning glance.

Matty shook his head. He didn't think about it. He couldn't let himself. Instinct kicked in, the fierce protectiveness taking over.

He shook his fucking head.

"Truthfully?" Gavin sighed. "I missed you crazy kids."

"How did you find us?"

"Easy," he said. "I never lost you."

Genna seemed confused by that.

222

"Gavin's the friend who got the house for us," Matty explained. "Got everything for us. We wouldn't be here without his help."

"Seriously?" Genna glanced at Matty as she scrunched up her nose. "I've gotta be grateful to this fucknut?"

"I'm afraid so."

"Just when I think things are looking up, I find out I'm indebted to *him*." She turned back to Gavin, who grinned with amusement. "What do you get out of this arrangement? Because I'm not giving you my firstborn. That's off the table."

"What do I look like, Rumplestiltskin?" Gavin glanced at his watch. "Look, this has been a blast... no pun intended... but I've got a flight to catch. Just wanted to see your faces before leaving, to make sure you're settled and see if you need anything."

Genna plopped down on the hood of the Honda, parked behind the sleek BMW.

Gavin's gaze trailed her, his eyes surveying the car as he approached it. "This is what you're driving?"

"For now," Matty said.

Gavin did a circle around it. "Seriously, Matty-B? Out of state plates, screwdriver in the ignition... I bet your fingerprints are all through it, too."

Guilty.

Shaking his head, Gavin reached into his pocket, pulling out a set of keys. He dropped them onto Genna's lap.

"Take the BMW," Gavin said. "I'll extend the rental on it, make it a lease, and get rid of this *thing*."

Genna hopped back off the Honda, grinning as she clutched the keys. She didn't hesitate before practically skipping over to the BMW.

"Thank you," Matty said. "I wish there was a way I could pay you back for everything."

"Don't sweat it," Gavin said. "You owe me so much at this point that I *fully* expect you to name that baby after me."

* * *

The city of Elizabeth was one of the biggest in New Jersey, but compared to Manhattan, where Dante typically roamed, it almost had a small-town vibe. Even with his recognizable face, Dante felt like he could blend in if he needed to back in New York. But over there, he was an outsider and it showed.

The moment he stepped out of his car, he felt eyes all over him, studying his every move. Curiosity. Suspicion. Even a bit of hostility. He didn't blame them for it, but it made him hyperaware of his surroundings.

Fall had settled in, the summer heat long gone, giving way to cool days and cold nights. *October.* Despite a slight chill in the air, Dante's white button down felt stifling, even with the sleeves rolled up. He hadn't dressed up in a while. He hadn't had reason to. But considering he stood in someone else's territory, he figured it wise to put his best foot forward.

The car lot was small, only a few dozen high-end cars strategically parked in a pattern, arranged more for coveting than actually *shopping.* Dante looked around as those eyes watched him from inside the building.

It took damn near five minutes for someone to approach him.

"Mr. Galante," a voice said, coming up behind him. "What can we do for you this afternoon?"

Damn good question.

Dante turned, finding a tall guy with wavy brown hair parted to the side. Fifty or so, wearing an expensive gray suit tailored to his slim frame. His expression was relaxed, an air of friendliness around him, but his brown eyes were guarded.

"I'm looking for a car," Dante told him.

"Anything in particular?"

Dante glanced at his Mercedes parked by the entrance. "Just something different."

"And you couldn't find your *something different* in New York?"

"Didn't look there," Dante admitted.

The man seemed to consider that, pursing his lips, before holding out his hand. "Alfie Russo."

Russo.

He was the Russo Dante had encountered while scoping out the house with Umberto, which a bit of research told him was the same Russo that had blessed them all with Gabriella. *Her father.*

Dante took his hand, firmly shaking it. "Call me Dante."

"Dante." Alfie pulled his hand away. "Lucky for you, we tend to specialize in different. Whatever you want, we can get. If it isn't on the lot, we can have it within a week—*guaranteed*."

"Good to know." Dante scanned the cars. Lamborghini. Porsche. Audi. Maserati. "Got any suggestions?"

"I'm a Ferrari fan, myself, but I suppose it depends on what you're hoping to get out of it. Safety? Discretion? Attention? I'm a big believer that what you drive sends a message, so what kind of message are you looking to send?"

Dante considered that. "That nobody owns me."

"Then I'd probably recommend the McLaren 12C. Unique, maybe not as *popular*, but it holds its own. Not black, which is cautious, or red, which tends to be antagonistic... maybe blue. It shows up, it's strong, but it doesn't necessarily disrupt the order, yet there's character to it, not subdued."

Dante looked in the direction Alfie pointed, at a bright blue supercar off to the side. The second his eyes landed on it, he *wanted* it. "Sold."

Alfie looked at him with surprise. "Seriously?"

"Sure, why not?"

"Well, then, why don't we head to my office and talk specifics?"

Dante followed the man inside, those eyes still trailing him the entire way to a back office. He took a seat in a black leather chair as Alfie settled in behind his oversized desk.

"Cigar?" he offered.

"I don't smoke," Dante said.

"You mind if I do?"

"Not at all."

Alfie lit up, puffing away, before lounging back in his office chair. "You got any special requests? Any particular *needs*? Armor, maybe bulletproof glass? Shock sensors and remote starters tend to be popular these days. They come together in a, uh... bomb-proofing package, if you're interested."

"I think it'll be fine just how it is."

"A man with simple tastes. I can respect that."

Alfie sorted through paperwork, cigar wedged between his lips, while curiosity got the best of Dante. "What do *you* drive?"

"What do I drive?"

Answering a question by repeating the question was the first rule in the 'how-to' of stalling. "I'm just curious, given your profession."

Alfie turned back to the paperwork. Dante figured he wouldn't answer, but he eventually muttered, "Crown Vic."

Same kind of car the police often drove. "And what message does that send about you?"

"Step out of line, I'll take your ass down," he said, no hesitation. "It pays to look like the good guy, no matter how bad you really are."

It took about thirty minutes for Alfie to get all the paperwork together, asking questions but refraining from getting too personal. A simple sale, cash exchange. It would take Dante a night to get the money together.

"Go ahead, take the car home with you," Alfie suggested once they finished. "I trust you'll come up with the money."

Trust.

That word felt *heavy.*

"And if I don't?" Dante asked.

Alfie smiled, a *genuine* smile, as he handed him the keys. "I guess we'll see if it happens."

They walked outside to the McLaren. Dante ran his hand along the sparkling paint, unlocking the car and lifting the vertical butterfly door. It was definitely *something different.*

"I was sorry to hear about your sister," Alfie said, the sudden serious topic catching Dante by surprise. So few people had said those words to him that they felt raw against his skin. *Grating.* "Never met her, but I heard good things. What happened, you know, it shouldn't have."

"It shouldn't have," Dante agreed.

"I sold that car to him. Matty. Told him red was antagonistic but he disagreed. Said it had *heart.* Boy was naive." Alfie laughed, but there was no humor to it—bitterness, maybe even some sadness, oozed out with that laughter. "I asked him the same question I ask everybody: what message are you trying to send? He said, 'that I'm not like the rest of them'. So I recommended the Lotus, but black, because that little shit should've hid. Should've had bulletproof glass and armored panels, while he was at it, but all he wanted was a remote starter so he didn't have to turn the fucking key."

Dante stared at the man. *A remote starter.*

Alfie motioned to the black Mercedes. "Anyway, what do you want us to do with that one?"

"Burn it," Dante suggested. "Light it on fire, invite the family over, make a thing of it."

"That's a good idea," Alfie said. "Kids might enjoy making s'mores."

"While the adults get their rocks off pretending I'm still inside of it."

"Contrary to popular belief, there's no bad blood over here, not as long as you keep your war on *that* side of the bridge."

"It's not my war," Dante said. "I didn't start it."

"No, but you inherited it, so that makes it yours."

Dante wanted to refute that, but he figured it was in his best interest to keep his mouth shut regarding family *business*. He nodded, jingling the car key. "You'll get your money tomorrow."

"I trust I will."

Trust. There went that word again.

The guy dished it out way too easily.

Dante climbed behind the wheel and shut the door, adjusting himself in the seat before pressing the button to start the engine. The moment it came to life, a smile lit his face.

It felt good, he thought, to throw caution to the wind. To not be so damn careful all the time. To let his paranoia subside as adrenaline kicked in.

It felt good to *live*.

CHAPTER 14

It drizzled, a sprinkling of rain falling from the overcast Manhattan sky when Gabriella stepped out of the hospital a few minutes past seven in the morning. She had the next four days off and intended to spend them pants-less inside of her apartment, drowning in take-out and rotting her brain with television.

She couldn't wait.

Scouring through her bag, she shifted her hoard of crap around, searching for her MetroCard, as she took a few steps away from the entrance. Hairbrush. Bag of candy. Even an extra pair of socks. Everything except what she sought.

Where the heck is my card?

"Good morning."

She stalled at the sound of that voice. Dante stood along the sidewalk, dressed impeccably in the makings of a suit. The tie was missing, as was the coat, but the rest of it was accounted for, bright white and sleek black, slightly damp from the weather. "Where's your umbrella?"

He cocked an eyebrow. "Where's *yours?*"

"I didn't spend weeks in the hospital," she said, looking back into her bag. "Nor am I still recovering from a stab wound that got treated in a friggin bathroom. I didn't defy death in a basement somewhere, my organs used as punching bags, which means *my* immune system isn't the one that's still compromised."

"I'm perfectly fine," Dante said. "Good as new again."

She scoffed. "If *new* is like, secondhand garage sale-level shape, I might agree with that. You're a threadbare human being, barely held together with just a few strings."

Despite her seriousness, Dante laughed at that, the genuine kind of laugh that caught her attention, forcing her eyes right to him. He glowed, lighting up the gloomy morning so much that she was surprised he didn't cause a rainbow.

Ugh, I'm ridiculous. He's just a guy. A friggin gorgeous guy, but still... a guy. A dangerous guy, at that. A reckless idiot. If Evel Knievel and Michael Corleone made a baby, if that were in any way scientifically possible, they'd spit out Dante Galante. Guaran-friggin-teed.

Shaking her head, she went back to searching through her bag.

"What are you looking for?"

"MetroCard," she said.

"Forget about it," he said. "Let me drive you."

"You don't have to do that."

"I know," he said. "That's the beauty of it. I don't have to do anything. Nobody can make me do a damn thing anymore."

Gabriella knew of a few people who would've been *more* than happy to prove him wrong about that.

"But I'd like to take you home," he continued. "I promise to be a perfect gentleman. Hands to myself. Eyes on the road. *Safety first* and all that."

Giving up her search, Gabriella eyed him. "I guess there's nothing wrong with letting you drive me since we're friends."

He smirked. "The kind with benefits now?"

"Ugh, there are no *benefits* to being your friend, Dante."

"Ah, that's cruel," he said. "There are plenty of benefits."

"Like what?"

"Like rides home from work."

"Fine, okay, that's a nice perk."

He held his hand out to her. The skin was rough, his knuckles still bruised from whatever he'd last punched—likely a person. That hand seemed to frequently inflict damage, but it had also touched her, caressing her, bringing her breathtaking pleasure. *Such a contradiction.*

If she thought about it too much, she might panic, so Gabriella opted to not think about it for another second. She slipped her hand into his, and he squeezed, like a silent *thank you* for surrendering.

He pulled her closer, tugging on her hand, moving it around behind his back so she stood right up against him. His head tilted, his eyes darting to her lips, and the flood of panic kicked in... *oh, crap!*

"So, where's your car?" she asked, twisting her own arm trying to put some space between them, as she looked all around, everywhere but *at* him, evading his kiss. "I don't see it."

"What's wrong?"

Way too much, buddy.

"I work here." Gabriella nodded toward the hospital. "Somebody might *see.*"

As much as she'd insulted him over the weeks out of frustration, calling him names and questioning his common sense, he'd never actually seemed offended until that moment. Hurt flashed in his eyes. "Right. Somebody might."

"It's not..." She paused when he let go of her hand. "Look, morally gray area, remember? It's not that *I* care. Well, I mean, I *do* care, but what I'm trying to say is you kissing me on hospital property isn't cohesive with me being Nurse Russo."

He blinked a few times. "Not cohesive."

"Yes."

"Well, then." He ran the hand he'd pulled from hers through his damp hair. "To answer your question, my car's over by the parking deck."

He motioned down the sidewalk, and Gabriella started that direction, glancing back at the hospital to catch a pair of eyes watching. The Grinch stood beside the entrance. *Ugh.*

She hurried her footsteps, bumping into folks as they walked in her path. Her eyes scanned the neighborhood, searching for the black car, but Dante grabbed her arm to stop her before she spotted it.

"It's right here," Dante said.

Gabriella's eyes fell upon a bright blue car. Dante pulled a key from his pocket, motioning to it, like that thing belonged to *him.*

"Wait, what? Where's *your* car?"

"This is it," he said. "Bought it yesterday. Or well, I haven't *paid* for it yet, but the money will be wired soon, so I'm calling it mine. What do you think?"

He grinned, looking at her, like he wanted her opinion.

Oh, boy...

"I think it's like handing you a fully loaded gun with a very loose trigger."

"I've been handed a few of those," he said. "They were never this thrilling."

Gabriella shook her head, surveying the car. She knew enough to tell a make and model, thanks to her father, but anything beyond that resided in the *don't-give-a-crap* portion of her brain. McLaren 12C. Crazy expensive and insanely fast and a bit flashy for a guy who pretty much had a bounty on his head.

"It's definitely gorgeous," she admitted, not sure what to tell him. "Where'd you get it?"

"From your father."

Whoa. Those words nearly knocked her off her feet. She swayed, turning to him so fast she risked whiplash. "Tell me you *didn't*…"

He wouldn't have. He couldn't have. He shouldn't have. *He better friggin not have.*

"Relax, your name didn't come up at all."

"Why did you even go there? What were you thinking?"

"I was thinking it might be nice to drive a car that doesn't have my blood soaked into the seats."

"So you buy *this*? And you go the whole way to Jersey to do it?"

He shrugged. "Why not?"

Why not? Gabriella could spout off a whole host of reasons, but ultimately, it boiled down to the fact that it terrified her. He was still her secret and she'd told lies because of that, so those worlds converging meant having to face facts.

The biggest fact being that she was in a *whatever* with the Galante boy, and unless someone showed up with a DeLoreon or a Tardis, it was way too late to try to go back. And even if she could, Gabriella wasn't sure she *would*. Their lives were entwining, and that had been the last thing she'd set out to let happen, but now that it *was* happening, she couldn't imagine it not being so.

The rain started to come down a bit harder, warm drops splashing her face, running down her cheeks like salty tears. "So, that ride? Preferably before you catch pneumonia?"

Dante opened the passenger side door, lifting it up for her to climb in. It still had that distinct 'new car' smell, something that always reminded her of childhood. Every night, her father would come home smelling like leather and vinyl, the distinct odor clinging to him.

This is so wrong. So, so wrong.

Dante navigated the streets with ease. He didn't speed. He was in no hurry. When he reached Little Italy, he pulled into a spot down the street from her apartment, but he made no move to turn off the car.

"Do you not want to come up?" she asked.

"Wasn't sure I was invited."

"That's never stopped you before," she said. "Besides, I think it's pretty clear by now that you've got an open invitation."

"You think so? Because that wasn't clear on this end. I've been expecting to pop in one day and be greeted by a restraining order."

"Well, you still might," she joked, "but until then, you might as well come hang out. I've got exciting plans that involve walking around wearing no pants. I'm going to eat a ton of food, maybe binge-watch some *Grey's Anatomy* so I can roll my eyes and complain about everything they screw up, which is usually, well, everything."

Dante cut the engine. "You had me at 'no pants'."

"Figures."

When they made it up to her apartment, the first thing Gabriella did was kick off her shoes and start stripping, even before Dante got the door closed again. She left a trail on her way to her bedroom, which Dante stepped over as he headed for the couch.

"Make yourself at home," she told him, yanking her hair down out of a ponytail, letting the waves fall around her shoulders. "There are drinks in the fridge and the remote is on the coffee table. I'm going to take a shower and wash off the hospital stink."

Unlike the new car smell, hospital stink was *offensive.*

She waltzed out of her bedroom, carrying a pile of fresh clothes, wearing only her bra and underwear, and made her way into the tiny bathroom. It took her barely ten minutes to shower, but when she resurfaced, the apartment was empty.

Son of a…

She scowled, something stirring inside of her that she wasn't fond of—disappointment. Loneliness was a bitter sensation, one she didn't like to taste, but it coated her insides as she inhaled, breathing in the air she used to be grateful to not have to share. She loved living alone, being out on her own, being able to come-and-go as she pleased, but she hated not having anyone waiting for her, like whether or not she ever arrived was irrelevant.

Plopping down on the couch, she kicked her feet up on the coffee table and turned on the television. She wore a plain white t-shirt and her cutest underwear, a pair of lace boy shorts that made her sort of hate herself, because she'd worn them specifically for *him*.

I call him an idiot but look at me. Going bananas over a moron doesn't make you any smarter than him, dummy.

Her phone rang, and Gabriella pressed the button to answer it, putting it straight on speaker from the couch cushion beside her. "Hello?"

"Hey, sweetheart!" Her mother's voice was way too chipper for it being so early. "How are you doing?"

"Fine," Gabriella lied. Man, the more she did that, the easier it had become. "How are you and Daddy?"

"You won't *believe* how we are..."

Her mother launched into a rant, but Gabriella only caught bits and pieces of the story as she flipped through channels. Five... ten... fifteen minutes later, they were chatting about a cousin's wedding—one of those faces she never recognized was getting married. *Awesome.*

"Can I just send a gift?" Gabriella asked.

"Come on, you *know* better."

"How about some cash? Everybody loves cash. They won't even know I'm not there when there's money to be spent."

"Don't try it, Gabriella. We rarely get together anymore. Don't dare skip this thing. You come, you eat cake, you wish them well, and then you go back home. How hard is that?"

Way too hard. "When is it?"

"Christmas Eve. You should be getting your invitation in the mail soon, so make sure you clear your schedule."

"Awesome," she muttered, tossing the remote down just as the apartment door opened. She sat straight up, alarmed, her eyes meeting Dante's as he walked in. "Hey, Mom? I've gotta go."

"What? Why? Is somebody there? *Who is it?*"

"No one." The lie slid right off of her tongue as Dante carefully shut the door behind him. "I'm exhausted, you know, with work and everything. I can barely keep my eyes open."

"Fine, go get some sleep. Just be thinking about the wedding. Your grandmother's going to be expecting a '*plus one*'. Don't break her heart. She's getting old, you know. She might not recover."

Gabriella mumbled a goodbye before slapping at the buttons on her phone, desperate to silence that conversation. *Embarrassing.*

"Death by heartbreak," Dante mused, strolling over to the couch. "It's a terrible way to go."

"It's more like death due to unreasonable expectations," she said, "with a stubborn granddaughter aiding and abetting."

"Ah, let me see... settle down, marry a decent Italian boy, have some babies to carry on the bloodline. Do your duty as a Brazzi woman. Am I getting close?"

She feigned shock as she clutched her chest. "However did you know?"

"Lucky guess." He sat down beside her, his eyes grazing up her bare legs and trailing along her thighs. "My sister never went for that bullshit, either."

"She picked an Italian boy."

"I said a *decent* one. You and her both, terrible taste."

She shoved him playfully. "Do not."

"You do. *Terrible.* And Genna, she..." He trailed off, shaking his head, like he was trying to shake off the memories. "She dated this one guy, Jackson, who let her take the fall for a stolen car. My father paid him to go away, and he did. He left her high and dry, didn't think twice about it. That's how little he valued her. She couldn't compete with a paycheck. And then she traded him in for a *Barsanti*. Couldn't get any more terrible."

"You're not a terrible guy," Gabriella said, "and I hate to break this to you, but neither is Matty. He *was* decent. He was never the kind of guy to let a woman take the fall."

"Just the kind to get them killed, right?"

Ouch. Gabriella didn't know what to say. She knew what she *wanted* to say, but saying that was too dangerous. So she just sat there, mouth shut, torn between wanting to hug Dante and wanting to punch him in the junk.

"Look, I'm sorry," he said. "I shouldn't have said that. It wasn't fair. It just..."

He trailed off, not finishing his thought.

"It hurts?" she guessed.

He nodded.

Reaching over, Gabriella ran her hand along his spine, rubbing his back overtop his shirt. He'd woken up to find his world shattered, and she'd been there when it happened, remembering vividly the moment he cracked. She'd watched him come apart at the seams, but she'd done nothing to stop it from happening, nothing to slow his unraveling.

If anyone was terrible, it was *her*. She was letting him destroy himself over a lie when she knew the truth.

"Nobody talks about her," he said, his voice quiet. "It's like she didn't matter to anyone, but she did to me. She *does* to me. She's my fucking *sister*. You know? But that's not the worst part. The worst part is not knowing. It doesn't feel real because of that. None of it does. It doesn't make sense, and maybe it never will, but she doesn't *feel* gone. I keep looking for her. I keep *waiting* for her. Some part of me expects her to show up. Maybe that's stupid, but I can't shake the hope."

"It's not stupid," Gabriella whispered.

"Hell, maybe *I'm* just stupid," he continued. "Because she'd be here. If she were still out there somewhere, she'd be here. There's no doubt in my mind. Nothing would've stopped her from contacting me. So I know... I *know*... but I just don't feel it. I can't accept her being gone."

Gabriella briefly closed her eyes, having to turn away from him, steadily rubbing his back and hoping he didn't notice her reaction. "Saying goodbye's hard, especially when there's no one to say goodbye to."

He laughed under his breath, his eyes glossy, swimming with tears. "Where'd you get that nugget of wisdom? A fortune cookie?"

"No, that came from experience. My brother."

"Chazz."

"Yeah, did you know him?"

"Heard about him. They tell his story different over here, though, than what you said about him."

They'd declared it a suicide, considering he'd jumped off a bridge. Case closed, no investigation needed. But she'd known her brother. She'd known him better than anyone. The moment she found out he'd plunged into the water, she knew there was more to the story. Her brother had been *invincible*. It wasn't until his body surfaced that her hope faded, so she understood Dante.

"It doesn't matter what people say or what they think. Everyone has an opinion, but I refuse to let it affect my reality."

"Must be nice."

"What?"

"Trusting your own instincts. Believing something so deeply that nothing can change your feelings."

"You don't feel that way?"

"Used to," he said. "Now I don't know. My reality makes no sense. Spent my whole life fighting for something, fighting *against* someone, and I'm not sure why. What did I get? My house isn't a home, my family is fucked up, and there's nowhere I belong. I probably shouldn't even be *here*."

Gabriella rested her head against his shoulder. "Yeah, you probably shouldn't."

Dante wrapped his arm around her, pulling her to him, her head shifting against his chest. Tingles shot through her, her eyes closing when he pressed a kiss to the top of her head.

"Where did you go?" she asked. "While I was in the shower?"

"I had to pay for the car, remember? Figured I'd wire the money while you were occupied."

"Oh, I thought you decided you didn't want to hang out."

"Not a chance. Being with you is the only part of my reality that makes any sense."

She smiled. "That's funny, because you're the part of mine that makes everything a mess."

"I don't know about that," he said. "Have you *looked* at this apartment? It's a fucking disaster."

She nudged him in the side, careful not to hit his still tender wound. Grabbing her wrist to stop her, he poked her right back, eliciting a squeal from her as she jolted, sitting straight up.

He pulled her closer. "There's nobody else here, you know... nobody who can see us."

"I know," she whispered.

His gaze trailed along her mouth as his own lips twitched with a small smirk. His eyes flickered to meet hers, the glint in them enough to make Gabriella shiver. She wasn't sure how to describe it, the way he looked at her. It felt a lot like *hunger*, like he would eat her up if she weren't careful.

Leaning over, he kissed her then, softly at first before turning passionate. He nipped at her lips, letting go of her wrist, one hand grasping the back of her neck while the other rested on her hip. Gabriella wrapped her arms around him, running her fingers through his hair. Something came over her as he pulled her even closer, dragging her onto his lap.

"Fuck," he growled, breaking the kiss to look down. Both hands settled on her knees before running up her thighs, grasping ahold of the white t-shirt when he reached it. Gabriella lifted her arms, her breath hitching when he yanked the shirt over her head. He dropped it on the couch beside them, his gaze going right to her breasts.

He captured a nipple with his mouth, his tongue circling it as his hand drifted between them, sliding along the black lace separating them. She moaned, tossing her head back when he started rubbing. *Oh God.*

He knew exactly what to do, where to touch, which buttons to push. She was panting and squirming before his fingers even slid beneath the flimsy material. He stroked her clit, sending jolts of electricity through her.

It came on fast, a sudden rush of pleasure sweeping through her. "Oh God, I'm going to—*uh*!"

She couldn't even say the word.

Dante caressed her, not letting up until her muscles relaxed again. He kissed along her chest, cupping her center, as he whispered, "Another benefit to my friendship."

Gabriella laughed. "That might be my favorite."

"There's more where that one came from, if you're interested."

"Oh, I'm *definitely* interested," she whispered, pressing small pecks against his lips, kissing the corners of his mouth before working her way along his jawline, grazing against the scruff. Reaching between them, she fumbled with his belt, doing just enough to release him from his pants. Fisting him, she stroked a bit. He was already hard, pulsating in her palm as she ran her thumb along the head.

He groaned, wrapping his hand around hers, stroking himself

harder than she'd done. With his other hand, he reached into his pocket, retrieving a condom.

"You carrying your own now?" she asked when he tore the wrapper open with his teeth. "Expecting this to happen?"

"More like hoping for it," he said, moving her hand to roll on the condom. "I don't expect anything, but damn if I don't *want* it."

She couldn't fault him for that. He wasn't the only one who wanted it. She *shouldn't,* but she did. She wanted him, all of him, *everything* to do with him. She wanted him in her and on her and all around her, lighting up the gloom with his smile and breaking the monotony with his chaos, making her feel all those things she shouldn't be feeling.

God, she *craved* it.

Pushing her underwear aside, she sunk down on him, sighing as he filled her. Dante rested his head against the couch, his hands on the small of her back as she rode him. Slowly, at first, grinding against his lap, savoring the look on his face. Jaw slack, eyes closed, his tongue ran across his bottom lip, wetting it. It was a look of agonizing pleasure, a beautiful kind of torture, the kind he seemed to welcome.

Eventually, she increased her pace, coming down on him harder, faster, her breath hitching when he filled her deeply. His eyes opened, gaze on her as his hands ran up her back. Gripping her shoulder blades, he pulled her down on him harder as he bucked his hips, thrusting up to meet her.

"Fuck, you feel so good," he said, his voice bordering on a growl. "I'll never get over how good you feel. You're *perfect.*"

Gabriella smashed her lips to his, shutting him up with a kiss. Pressure built up inside of her. It didn't take much longer for it to rush out through her limbs, another orgasm rocking her, seizing her muscles, making her come to a brief stop. Dante kicked in, grasping her hips and pulling her off of his lap, knocking her onto the couch on her back. He was on top of her right away, back inside of her, her legs over his shoulders and knees pressed to her chest.

She cried out, unable to stop the sound, as he slammed into her. The orgasm that had almost subsided came back full-force. Gabriella ground her teeth together, trying to be quiet, but each thrust knocked the noise right out of her.

Uh... Uh... Uhh...

"Fuck," Dante groaned. "I'm gonna... *fuck*."

He didn't say the word, closing his eyes, his face contorting as he groaned, thrusting a few more times. Dropping her legs, he sat back on his knees, pulling out of her as banging echoed through the apartment from the floor beneath them.

Dante laughed, leaning over her, to kiss her. "Guess your neighbors didn't enjoy all of that squawking."

Her cheeks flushed. "I tried to be quiet."

"They'll get used to it," he said. "Because I'm hoping like hell they'll be hearing it more often, you know, if that's something you want."

"It might be," she whispered. "How often is *more often?*"

"As often as you want it."

"So all day, every day?"

He grinned. "I'll fuck you until my heart gives out, baby."

"Which will probably be like an hour from now," she said, "with the condition you're still in. We probably shouldn't be doing this kind of stuff, not while you're still healing."

Standing up, he laughed. "Ah, don't fret it. Death by pussy... it's the only way I'm ever going to go out."

* * *

"Does she know?"

The question was out of Gabriella's mouth before she was even planted in the chair across from Gavin at the small table in the corner of Casato. He scribbled in a notebook again, working out some sort of math problem, and didn't bother to look up at the intrusion. "Who?"

"Dante's sister," she clarified. "Does she know about him?"

Gavin kept his head down, facing the notebook, but his eyes lifted. Unlike the confusion that greeted her last time she showed up there, all she saw then was wariness. "Why are you asking?"

Why was she asking? Because she was detrimentally nosy. Because something had been bothering her. "Dante said something to me."

"Of course he did," Gavin grumbled. "And what, exactly, did

239

our mutual friend say?"

"He said that if his sister were still out there somewhere, she would've come to see him, so I was just wondering..."

"Why she hasn't come to see him?"

"Yeah."

Gavin didn't appear surprised by that question. He went back to his notebook, working in silence. Gabriella watched, trying to make sense of the messy math.

"What are you doing?" she asked. "Are you taking classes or something?"

Gavin closed his notebook the second she asked that and looked up. "Genna hasn't come, because she doesn't know there's a reason to come."

Gabriella gaped at him. "So she doesn't know he's alive?"

"No."

"Why?"

"Because like you said, she'd want to come see him, so it's for the best that neither of them find out until it's safe."

"Which will be when? Never?"

"I don't know, but it's not my business, nor is it *your* business, for that matter."

"But Dante—"

"Don't," Gavin said, cutting her off. "Whatever you're about to say, just don't say it, because I already know. He's grieving. He's crazy. He's lost. *Whatever.* Having his sister pop up isn't going to make that better. If you want him to be happy, Gabby, help him find a reason to be. *Make* him happy, if that's what gets your rocks off. Be with the guy if you want to be with him. He got over you being a Brazzi pretty damn quick."

"But we could never, you know... not really."

"Why?" Gavin asked. "Think the family won't approve? Brazzi women have picked Amaros, and Barsantis, and Russos. A Galante isn't much worse. Not any *better*, but still, not much worse."

"But he's *him.*"

"And I'm me and you're you. What does it matter? We're all just one big fucked up family. So maybe they won't be ecstatic about you getting mixed up in this, but as long as you're happy, well, that's what matters, isn't it? They'll get over it. But this whole wavering, hush-hush keep-it-on-the-low thing can't go on forever. Secrets always come to light, Gabby. *Always*."

Gabriella considered that as she leaned back in the chair. "You're contradicting yourself. You expect me to keep this massive secret about his sister, yet you tell me that keeping secrets never works. You can't have it both ways."

"Yeah, I can," he said. "I can have it any way I want to have it. There's no law against me being a hypocrite. We're *all* hypocrites. No one is consistent all the time. But it's okay, you know, because there are exceptions. There are *always* exceptions. That's the way life is. And this? This is an exception. This is where we get to be hypocrites, because this isn't our secret to tell. If it goes south, we won't be the ones to *die*, so it's not up to us to decide. But this thing you have with Dante? That's on you. That's your secret. The fallout is yours."

She sighed loudly. "It could get ugly, though."

"You play with a poisonous snake, you shouldn't be surprised when the son of a bitch bites you," Gavin said. "I don't make the rules. I just, for some reason, get to be the one that constantly has to suck out the damn venom."

He flipped open his notebook again, like that was the end of the conversation, like he had nothing else to say about anything.

"Russo?" a voice asked as a young woman approached the table, holding a small bag. "Your order is ready."

"Thanks," Gabriella said, taking it from her. Once the woman walked away again, she turned back to Gavin. "You seriously do suck at this."

"Yeah," he muttered. "I should stop doing it."

"You should," she agreed, pushing her chair back. She stood up to leave when she ran smack into somebody walking past tables through the café. She stumbled, cringing as she caught an elbow right to the chest, the blow nearly knocking her back into the seat.

"Whoa, shit, didn't mean to hit you," a guy said, grabbing her arms to steady her. "You okay?"

"I, uh… yeah." She blinked a few times as she rubbed her chest. *Ouch.* "It was my fault. I should've paid attention."

"Nah, that was all on me," he said. "A guy always yields to a pretty lady."

241

Gabriella glanced at the guy, something striking her as familiar, like she'd seen him around. He offered her a smile, nothing sinister about it, but it didn't seem sincere, either. It was plastered on his lips, deliberately carved there.

"Hands off my cousin," Gavin said, his voice flat.

The guy pulled his hands away from her at once, his smile growing a bit, some genuine amusement shining through. "My mistake."

He skirted around her and disappeared to the back of the café.

Gabriella glanced at Gavin, whose attention was still fixed on his notebook. "Friend of yours?"

"If by friend you mean I'd be happy for the chance to send flowers to his funeral, then yeah, we'll go with that."

Huh.

"Just be careful, Gabby," he continued. "You walk around with someone who has a target on their back and you're at risk of getting hit, because some guys, you know, they've got really shitty aim."

"I thought you were done giving advice."

"That was the last time," he promised. "You're a smart girl. I'm sure you can figure everything else out on your own."

Gabriella walked away, heading for the exit. Her attention bounced toward the back of the café, momentarily catching the guy's gaze as his eyes trailed her movements. The second he caught her looking, he smiled again, tossing off a small wave that sent her guard up, like a silent '*I'll catch you later*' when she'd rather he not *catch* her at all.

Gabriella spun back around, banging right into someone else. *What the heck is wrong with me?*

"Gabby, sweetheart, it's good to see you again!" Johnny Amaro grasped her arms to steady her. "You leaving?"

"Yeah, I was just grabbing some breakfast and visiting with Gavin." She motioned to his table as she clutched her bag of food. "I was helping him with his math homework or whatever."

"His math homework," Johnny said, eyes darting to where Gavin sat, working in his notebook. Johnny shifted out of the way, motioning for Gabriella to go around him, to step outside.

He followed when she did. *Uh-oh.*

"You doing okay, Gabby? No problems?"

"No. None. Everything's going great."

"That's good to hear," he said, the expression on his face betraying those words. He looked *concerned*. "You ever need anything, you know where we are."

"I'll keep that in mind."

She took a few steps when Johnny's voice rang out again. "That also extends to Dante."

Her footsteps faltered, but she didn't turn back around, forcing her feet to continue on, not wanting to go down that road with yet another Amaro.

When she reached the apartment, she stuck her key in the lock, but before she could turn it, the door flung open. Gabriella gasped, surprised, when Dante appeared, his hair a mess from sleep, wearing only boxers and his white undershirt.

"You're awake," she said, smiling at the sight of him. He looked almost *refreshed*, like he'd been plugged into a socket and given a fresh charge. His eyes shone bright, the dark bags diminished.

"And you were gone," he said. "That's the second time I've woken up in your apartment alone."

"I grabbed some breakfast," she said, shaking the bag at him as she walked into the apartment and shut the door.

"Casato, huh?" He eyed the bag as he took it from her. "*Nice.*"

"I didn't really know what you liked, so I just got sandwiches," she said. "Egg, ham, provolone, something. I don't know. I've never actually eaten anything there before."

"Me, either," he said, pulling out the sandwiches and handing one to her. "Used to go with Genna all the time, though. She liked the place."

Gabriella grabbed some drinks from the kitchen and sat down beside Dante, picking her sandwich apart while she watched him eat. She wasn't hungry, but she'd wanted an excuse to wander across the street.

"So, just out of curiosity, how do you feel about the Amaros?"

He cut his eyes at her. "The Amaros?"

"Yeah, like Gavin…"

"Did he ask you to ask me that? Because I swear to fuck, if he sent a '*Do you like me? Check yes or no*' note with you, I'm gonna lose my shit."

She laughed. "What? No. I was just wondering."

"In that case, he's okay."

"Just *okay*?"

"I mean, I've always liked the guy. He never gave me reason *not* to like him. But if I ever got arrested, I'm not sure he'd be my one phone call."

"Who would be your call?"

"I don't know. Guess we'll find out when it happens."

"*When* it happens?"

"It's kind of inevitable, isn't it?" He shook his head. "My sister called me, you know. I was her one."

"Did you bail her out?"

"Never got the chance. My father intervened. And I guess, you know, he probably would've been mine. He used to clean up all my messes, but now, hell, I think I'd rather rot in jail."

"You could call me," she suggested.

"Impossible," he said. "The one time I asked for your number, you wouldn't give it to me."

She gazed at him, surprised. That hadn't even crossed her mind. Waltzing into the kitchen, she ripped a piece of scrap paper off of a notepad stuck to the refrigerator and scribbled her number down on it before walking back over to him. "Here, now you have it, so no excuses."

"Ah, I *always* have excuses," he said, taking it from her. "Like the fact that I don't even have a phone right now."

"What happened to your phone?"

"Same shit that always happens," he said. "Couldn't trust it."

"You couldn't trust your phone?"

"No, but I'll pick up a new one sometime this week… or next week… or whenever I feel like it."

"Excuses and complaints," Gabriella grumbled. "I think that might be all you're good for."

"Orgasms, remember? Christ, Gabriella. Are you *already* forgetting those benefits?"

"My bad, how could I forget that?"

"And anything else you need, all you've gotta do is ask," he said. "That was the deal we made, in case you forgot. I know we joke around about this shit, but I'm not kidding about that. There are *perks* to being with me, Gabriella. I'm at your disposal."

CHAPTER 15

"Genna?"

Music rattled from the small radio beside the back door, plugged in with an orange extension cord that weaved into the house. Oldies. Fifties. Songs Matty heard at work from the ancient jukebox. It was strange, hearing Genna listening to it, jamming out to The Penguins and singing *Earth Angel* at the top of her lungs. A set of tanned legs jetted out from beneath the jacked-up broken-down car, filthy bare feet digging into the dry dirt.

"Genna!"

He yelled her name, louder, when the song changed. Genna stopped singing, shoving out from beneath the car.

For weeks, she'd been working on it, pouring herself into it every chance she got, buying extra parts and blowing money on better tools all in some quest to get the damn thing running. Matty didn't question it... *much*. It was a distraction. A project. Something to focus on. So, he got it, but it worried him.

What would happen if she never got it started?

Would she take it personal?

For now, though, she looked content.

He hadn't seen her so happy since that first day they met, back in New York, before she learned how wrong he was for her. She was adjusting and settling, some of that burden on her shoulders lifting, like she truly believed they could make it on their own.

Sweat coated her flushed face, smudges of grease smeared along her skin. Her dark hair was wrapped up in a knotted bun on top of her head—unwashed, he gathered, since there was a twig stuck in it. A pair of cut-off jean shorts barely covered her ass, while a dark tank top clung to her, especially around her stomach. Matty's eyes were drawn right to it. Twenty weeks along, already halfway through the pregnancy. Time seemed to be *flying*.

"What are you doing?" he asked, dragging his eyes away from her to instinctively look for a watch he *still* hadn't replaced.

"Uh, messing with this little bracket thingy near the thermostat. It's crooked, so I'm trying to do the *Lefty-Lucy* thing to straighten it up but I *Righty-Tighty*'ed so good that the bitch isn't moving now, so I might have to break it off." She sat up, eyeing him warily. "Something tells me that's not what you're asking. What's going on?"

"What's going on is we have a doctor's appointment in an hour," he said. "If we don't leave soon, we're going to be late."

"I thought that was on Thursday."

"It *is* Thursday."

"Oh." Her eyes widened. "*Shit.*"

Matty helped her to her feet. Dirt covered her from head-to-toe, the smell of sweat and grease clinging to her. Grime covered her hands, blood trickling down her right middle finger from a cut on her knuckle.

"You should be more careful," Matty said, looking at the small wound. "You should probably also get a tetanus shot."

She rolled her eyes, wrapping her arms around his neck as she kissed him. "What I *should* do is take a quick shower."

"No time." He stopped her before she went inside. "I'm not kidding, we have to go or we're going to miss the appointment."

"At least let me take a bitch bath. I'm *disgusting*."

"A bitch bath."

"Yeah, you know, wash the goods and all that."

She kissed him once more, her cheek brushing against his, transferring a black smudge along his jawline. Shaking his head, he wiped it off with his hand as she skipped inside, leaving the radio on, *Tutti Frutti* blaring from beside Matty's feet. He reached down and clicked it off before walking through the house, enjoying the stream of cool air coming from the vents. The air conditioner would never be strong enough to keep up with the outside temperatures, despite it being fall now. *October*.

He waited in the foyer, glancing at his watch. A minute passed, and another, and another… after five, he started pacing, and after ten, he grew anxious. "Genna, please, we've got to go!"

"Geez, calm your tits," she muttered, coming down the steps. "I'm ready."

Matty's eyes took her in. She'd pulled herself together, wearing a pair of black shorts and a crisp white tank top, all traces of dirt gone. Her hair had even been brushed. As she approached him, he could sense the perfume, the scent sweet and flowery, one he hadn't smelled before on her. "You smell nice."

"Yeah? It's kind of strong, and who knows how old it even is, but I figure anything's got to be better than how I did smell," she said. "I guess it belonged to the lady of the house."

"You are the lady of the house."

"The *other* one," she clarified. "Found it in a drawer in the master bedroom."

"I like it," he said, grasping her by the hips when she stepped into the foyer. He dipped his head, nuzzling into her neck, his nose running along her skin.

"Down boy," she said. "We've got to go, remember?"

He grudgingly pulled away. "I remember."

The small OB-GYN clinic was located in Las Vegas, a nondescript brown building near the University Medical Center. Guilt nagged at Matty every time he stepped foot into the place, every time he sat in one of those flimsy plastic chairs in the packed waiting room and looked around at those bland tan walls with nothing on them. The place was a non-profit, catering to the uninsured, the kind of place that didn't ask many questions and just did the work. Genna seemed to like the people, and she never complained about the care, but Matty couldn't help the feeling that she deserved so much more.

He should've been able to give it to her.

"Gallivant?" a nurse called, peeking her head out of the back. Genna just sat there, staring off into space, wringing her hands together. "Jen Gallivant?"

"Baby, that's you," Matty muttered, nudging her.

Genna's eyes widened as she stood, smiling at the nurse. "Sorry, I didn't hear you."

"No problem," the lady said. "Follow me."

Matty trailed behind as the nurse led them to a small room with no windows, barely the size of a walk-in closet. An exam table filled the center of it with a computer set up on the end. Genna climbed up on the table, her legs dangling, as Matty lingered beside her.

"They'll be with you in a moment," the nurse said, shutting the door to leave them alone.

"Are you nervous?" Matty asked as she wrung her hands together, picking at her fingernails.

"Why would I be nervous? I've had an ultrasound before."

True, but this time was different. The baby had been nothing more than a little blob on a monitor, a flickering dot of life, the last time they had one.

Matty reached over, grabbing her hand to stop the fidgeting. "It'll be fine."

She sighed. "But what if it *isn't*?"

"Why wouldn't it be?"

"Because that's our luck? Because that's *my* luck? Because the universe wants to punish me for all the wrong I've done?"

"You haven't done anything wrong."

She laughed. "Are you crazy? Have I ever done anything *right*? What makes me think I'm equipped to be a mother? Me. Seriously, Matty... *me*. A *mom*. This is wrong. What are we even doing here? We've got no business trying to be parents. We're going to fuck this up. We don't know how. Look at who raised us!"

Matty stepped in front of her, standing between her and the door when her eyes darted that way. He grasped her other hand with his free one, squeezing them both, as he looked her in the eyes. "I love you, Genevieve Galante."

"I don't know *why*," she said, tears in her eyes. "I'm a fucking mess, Matty."

"You are," he admitted, smiling. "You're messy and neurotic and the furthest thing from *domestic*, but you're not afraid to get your hands dirty. You're stubborn, and persistent, and brave—so damn brave. And that's how I know you'll be a damn good mother, Genna. Because you love deeply, you love selflessly, and nothing stops you. Any kid would be lucky to call you mom, because you'll love them, you'll protect them, and you'll let nothing stop them from getting everything they deserve. What more could a kid want?"

"Someone who can cook chicken without giving everyone salmonella poisoning."

"Ah, that's what they have *me* for." Matty wiped her tears before nudging her chin. "So relax, because there's no reason to be scared."

He leaned down, kissing her, as the door behind him opened and someone walked in.

"Everything okay in here?" a soft voice asked.

"Everything's fine," Matty said, moving out of the way. He glanced across the room at the older blonde woman wearing pink scrubs as she settled in front of the computer monitor.

"Great," she said, smiling. *Always smiling.* "How about we get this show on the road? If you'll lie back on the table and lift up your shirt, I'll get started."

Genna obliged, rearranging her clothes to expose her stomach. The woman squeezed some jelly onto Genna's skin before spreading it around with the small wand of the ultrasound machine. Matty watched, his eyes trailing the curves of her stomach.

The second the woman clicked the monitor on, his eyes darted straight to it. *Whoa.*

A baby appeared. A real, live baby. Arms and legs, hands and feet, fingers and toes, every inch discernible and utterly perfect. Matty blinked a few times, watching in awe as the tiny human squirmed on the screen.

His gaze shifted back to Genna's stomach before he glanced at her face. She lay there, still, her eyes glued to him. The monitor faced away from her, at an angle she couldn't see, as the woman took measurements.

He smiled, watching the panic drain from Genna's face as she took a deep breath.

"Here you go," the woman said, turning the monitor toward Genna. "Have a look."

Genna's eyes widened. "Holy fuck."

Matty laughed. "That about sums it up."

The woman moved the wand around to different parts, counting fingers and toes, showing off the little button nose.

"Are you interested in learning the sex of the baby?" she asked after a moment.

"Yes," Matty said, the same time Genna said, "No!"

"Wait, okay, yes," Genna said as Matty mumbled, "We can wait."

The woman laughed. "How about I write it down and stick it in an envelope? That way you can decide later if you want to know."

"Perfect," Matty said, glancing at the screen again one last time before the monitor shut off, the image disappearing.

"I'll print some pictures and you can be on your way," she said, standing up. "I'll be right back."

As soon as the woman left, Genna sat back up. "Holy fuck."

Her hands went right to her stomach, the panic returning.

Oh shit.

"You okay, Genna?"

"No."

"What's wrong?"

"There's a person in there."

"There is."

"It's got to come out somehow," she said. "A person is going to come out of me."

"It will."

"That's not normal."

He laughed. "It's probably the most *normal* thing there is."

"It's weird," she said. "We made a baby."

"We did."

"How the hell did we do that?"

"Well, when two people love each other…"

"*Shut up.*" She laughed. "I know *how* we did it, but wow. It's weird. I let you stick it in and part of you just stayed there, and it's growing. It's, like, *attached* to me. And then it's going to come out and be this person we're responsible for. We'll have to feed it, and water it, and keep it alive, when we can barely keep ourselves alive. Wow."

"*Wow* is right."

The door opened again, the woman returning, clutching a couple pictures and a small envelope. Genna took them from her, thanking her quietly, and the two of them left. Matty stopped by the front desk, paying some cash for the visit, as Genna flipped through the stack of photos, in a trance.

She said nothing as they left the clinic, nothing in the car on the way back home. She was still staring at the photos when they headed in the house.

"I'm going to shower for real this time," Genna said, handing the stack over to Matty. She held the envelope out also, hesitant to let go when he grabbed it. "I don't want to know yet. The fact that it's a baby is enough. Any more information might make my brain explode. But you can look, if you want. Really, you should. But don't tell me. Not yet. Okay?"

"Okay," he said.

She disappeared upstairs as Matty strolled to the living room, propping the ultrasound photos up against the broken picture frame beside the couch, the one of the peculiar family that Genna refused to let him throw out. He stared at the envelope before slipping his finger beneath the flap, tearing it open.

He pulled out the slip of paper, seeing the simple word scribbled on it in pen.

Boy.

* * *

"You sure you don't want me to drive you?"

Dante stepped out of the apartment building, holding the door open for Gabriella to follow. She offered him a small smile of gratitude at the gesture before shrugging off his question. "I'm sure. Besides, I kind of like taking the subway."

"Weirdo."

She laughed, stopping right in front of him. She had on her usual hospital get-up, her dark hair pulled back with some loose strands falling around her face. Wrapping her coat tighter around her, she shivered a bit, the air borderline frigid. The glow from the setting sun made her lip gloss shine, drawing Dante's eyes to her lips.

Damn, he wanted to kiss them.

"Are you going to be around when I get off?" she asked.

"I sure as hell hope so," he said, staring at her mouth, "because I plan to be the one getting you off."

She laughed again, shoving him. "I'm being serious."

"Fine, fine..." He held up his hands, forcing his eyes to meet hers. "I'll be around."

"Here?"

"Somewhere."

She groaned. "Ugh, you're impossible."

"Wait." He caught her arm before she could leave. *Of course* he'd be there. Wasn't he always? For weeks, he'd done nothing but linger around, spending every minute possible with her. She should've known he'd be around. "Why don't you let me pick you up from work? That way I'm around when you get off, then maybe we can, you know, talk about getting off."

She rolled her eyes, but the smile returned to her lips. "My shift ends at seven."

"I know. I'll be there."

He kissed her then, her lip-gloss sticky, smearing across his lips. Her cheeks flushed when she pulled away, and she dipped her head shyly, biting her bottom lip. "Have a good night, Dante."

"You, too, baby."

His tongue darted out, sweeping across his lips, tasting the strawberry stickiness. He watched her as she headed down the block, smiling to himself when he caught her peeking back at him.

"She's cute."

That voice, right behind Dante, made the hair on his arms bristle, his back straightening. He turned his head, finding Umberto lurking. "Bert."

Umberto raised his eyebrows. "Girlfriend?"

"Friend."

"Does she have a name?"

"Of course she does."

Umberto stared at him, like he expected more. In the past, Dante would've offered it. Girls used to come in and out of his life, weekend flings that he'd flippantly talk about, because they never meant much. They *knew* they didn't mean much, although he was sure a few hoped he'd have a change of heart, but he never did, because his heart had nothing to do with it. Too much scar tissue covered his chest for any of them to break through.

But her?

She was different.

She'd gotten in.

There was no getting her back out.

"Wow," Umberto breathed, realizing Dante had no intention of sharing with him. "Okay, well, your father wants to see you."

"I'm busy," Dante said.

"It's not a request," Umberto said, nodding toward a black se-dan parked along the curb a few spots down, all the windows tinted so he couldn't see inside. "So let's not make a thing out of this, okay?"

"And if I choose to make this a *thing*? If I don't get in that car?"

"You don't want to play it that way."

"What are you going to do, Bert? Drag me over to it? Throw me in the back? Hold me down? Put a fucking knife in my side?"

"Come on, man..."

"Because that's what Barsanti did," Dante continued, "so it wouldn't be the first time."

"Just get in the car, Dante." Umberto ran his hands down his face. "It'll be over before you know it and you'll be back to whatever-her-name-is, doing whatever the hell you've been up to all this time."

Dante considered it. He wanted to refuse. He wanted Umberto to *try* to force him. He knew the guy's weaknesses, where he was most vulnerable. There was no way in hell Umberto would get him in that car without adding some serious firepower to the equation. But Dan-te also knew his father. If the man was calling him in, he wouldn't take no for an answer. If Umberto failed, he'd just send others.

Frankly, Dante was surprised it had taken the man so long to come for him. Time passed. He'd missed Thanksgiving. December had snuck up on them, Christmas right around the corner. He hadn't been back to the house, hadn't had a damn thing to do with the Galante family since the trip they'd taken to Jersey.

He sure as hell didn't want to go *then*, but his options were lim-ited.

Sighing, Dante shoved past him, strolling over to the car. Umber-to followed, opening the back door and nodding for him to get in.

One of Primo's usual drivers sat behind the wheel, not acknowl-edging Dante. Umberto slid in beside him, the car pulling into traf-fic. The forty-five minute drive felt like hours, the sun setting along the way. Dante stared out the side window, anger stirring, mixing with a bit of trepidation. That obedient soldier inside of him was sweating.

The tension in Dante's muscles grew when they reached the house. Cars surrounded the property, a sea of black sedans. Dante's eyes scanned the place in the darkness, on edge.

"Inductions," Umberto said, answering his unasked question. "Party started twenty minutes ago."

Shit. Dante got out and hesitated. Twice a year, they opened up the books, inviting a few select guys to join the organization. The night always involved a lot of ass kissing, and Dante didn't have it in him. The last time they'd had one of these, he'd found a Barsanti hiding in his sister's closet, a Barsanti he almost killed that night. One he probably *should've* killed that night. Had he pulled the trigger, had he told his father, his sister would've never forgiven him, but at least she would've still been around.

Had it already been six months?

Umberto approached the house, and Dante followed, seeing his father standing on the front step, waiting.

The man wore a straight black three-piece suit, while Dante had on jeans and a sweatshirt.

"He give you any trouble?" Primo asked, his eyes on Dante, but that question was meant for Umberto.

"No," Umberto said. "He got right in the car."

"Good." Primo motioned for Umberto to go inside, waiting until they were alone before addressing Dante. "You haven't been answering my calls."

"I lost my phone."

Primo's eyes studied Dante's face, looking for signs of deception, but he stood still, stoic, his expression betraying nothing.

"Go upstairs and shower, change your clothes, pull yourself together," Primo ordered. "Come back down when you're ready to play your part."

Dante moved past him. "Yes, sir."

Eyes trailed him inside, following him as he made his way upstairs. He went straight to his room, seeing everything as he'd left it.

He took twenty minutes, showering and shaving, before dressing in the best suit in his closet. He stood in front of the mirror, staring at his reflection as he knotted the blue tie, straightening it. Noise filtered up the stairs from the floor below, rambunctious chatter and drunken laughter, music melding with it. *Classical.* It was a five-star black-tie event for the scum of the earth. *Myself, included.* He had more blood on his hands than some of those men.

Heading out, he paused in the dark hallway, curious when he noticed his sister's bedroom door cracked open. Stepping across the hall, he pushed on it, shock running through him.

Empty.

Everything was gone. *Everything.* No belongings. No furniture. Nothing. The room had been stripped, scrubbed and sanitized, like it wasn't enough that they'd erased her name from their vocabulary—they needed to wipe her DNA from inside the house, too.

Gone.

Dante made his way downstairs then, knowing the longer he lingered upstairs, the longer he *dwelled*, the worse the night would get. Eyes trailed him through the foyer as he headed to his father's office, where he knew the man would be.

Primo looked up, a smile lighting his face, like he appreciated the obedience, considering Dante had done what the man demanded. "Son, come in, have a seat! We were just talking about you."

Dante stepped into the room. "Oh?"

"I was telling them how you've been on a bit of a sabbatical," Primo said. "You've had a tough year."

"I have," Dante agreed.

"But it was a well-deserved break, I'd say. You earned it. You protected the family. You fought for us in the trenches. You even killed the Barsanti kid. That, alone, earned you one hell of a vacation."

Primo grinned, and others laughed, while Dante's stomach clenched. He felt sick. He looked away from his father, catching sight of Umberto standing off to the side. He wasn't laughing, his gaze on the floor. He'd been there that day, when Dante pulled the trigger. A knee-jerk reaction, a split second decision. Enzo had pointed a gun at him, and Dante panicked out of fear.

He'd fired once.

Just once.

He took a life with a single bullet.

"But it's good to have you back now," his father continued. "Good to have you all refreshed. You feeling better?"

"Of course." Dante turned back to him. "More than happy to be here."

The conversation shifted off of him then. Dante was grateful. He sat there as they chatted, gossiping, talking business and making plans. Card games. Strip clubs. Doubling up on bookies. They were pushing harder into Little Italy, most of the neighborhood under their thumb, the way they told it, although Dante doubted it. He'd seen Barsanti guys on those streets, watching them from the windows in Gabriella's apartment.

They stood on the corners.

They went inside the buildings.

They still considered it open territory.

Dante stood after a while to roam the room, pausing beside Umberto. He poured a bunch of whiskey in a glass before leaning back against the bar.

"You lie to him so easily," Umberto said.

"I'm not lying to him." Dante took a drink of the warm liquor and shuddered at the burn. "He knows the truth. I'm just saying what he wants me to say. He wants them all to believe everything is normal, so for tonight, I'm the perfect son."

"What happens after tonight? After the party's over?"

Dante gulped down the rest of the liquor before pouring more. "I guess he gets rid of all of my shit, too."

Dante walked away, leaving the office, strolling through the downstairs. Mingling. He fucking *mingled*. Smile plastered to his face, alcohol buzzing through his veins, he played the role he'd been dragged there to play, a role worthy of an Oscar. *Yep, I survived. Nope, I don't blame my father. You're absolutely right; we can't grieve for a traitor.* Hours passed in a haze, as he drank and mingled. He drank so much his vision grew blurry, and he mingled to the point that he was tired of hearing his own voice.

He returned to the office eventually, the room cleared out as people made their way through the house, a card game going on in the dining room, others in the den with cigars. It was late. *Too* late. The sun was starting to rise. Dante sensed it through the windows, despite the shades being drawn. He poured himself one last bit of whiskey, barely a swallow, standing there as he swirled it around in his glass.

"You did good."

His father's voice came from behind him. Dante threw the alcohol back, swallowing it, and set the empty glass down. "I did what I had to."

"You were always good at that," Primo said. "Never questioned orders. Never questioned *me*. I was proud. Proud to call you my son. Proud to call you my heir. And I'm still proud, Dante. Proud of the man you were. You could still be that man, you know."

Dante stared at him, those words running through him. "The day Genna—"

"I don't want to talk about it," Primo cut in. "I don't want to think about what she did."

"Just answer one question," Dante said, "and I'll never bring it up again."

Primo glared at him. "What's your question?"

"Why didn't you stop it?"

"Why didn't I *stop* it?"

"It takes forty-five minutes to drive from here to Little Italy. Forty-five. I've clocked that drive hundreds of times. If Genna ran out of here, heading for that car, for that bomb, why didn't you stop it? Why didn't you call it off? You had *forty-five minutes*."

Primo stood quietly as he thought that over. "I guess I didn't care enough to."

Those words were a punch to the gut.

"Collateral damage," he continued. "It happens."

Dante took a shaky breath. "She was your daughter."

"And Matteo was my godson," Primo said, "but it doesn't matter. Daughter. Godson. They're words. Genevieve, she was a lot like your mother. *Too much* like your mother. Bad judgment. They crossed lines that couldn't be uncrossed. Never wanted it to happen, but neither gave me a choice."

Neither gave me a choice.

Dread ran through Dante, turning his blood ice cold. "Mom died in a car accident."

"Funny how that happens, huh?" Primo turned away from him. "Since I answered your question, Dante, I expect you to live up to your end of the deal. Don't bring up your sister ever again. She's dead to us."

She's dead to us.

Dante just stood there after his father walked out, staring at the vacant doorway. His knees wobbled beneath him. His head was fuzzy. He damn near passed out. He'd always thought his father an imperfect man, but one who made mistakes out of love. He did what he did to protect the family, and Dante thought he'd inherited those flaws. But as much as Dante had woken up different, realizing the man he'd been had only been a facade, he knew wasn't the only one wearing a mask. He saw now that his father wasn't just flawed.

The man was cold and callous.

The man was selfish.

The man was dangerous.

The man needed to be *stopped*.

* * *

Gabriella stood in front of the hospital, sunshine streaming down on her through a part in the clouds. Despite that, the air was cold, winter coming on fast. It seeped through her scrubs, goose bumps springing up everywhere the air touched.

Most of the *city that never sleeps* still snoozed at that hour on a Saturday: a quarter after seven in the morning. Cars lined the curb, light frost covering windshields, but not a single one the car Gabriella expected to find.

She sighed.

Pulling her MetroCard out of her bag, she took the subway, almost falling asleep as she waited on the platform. By the time she made it to Little Italy, by the time her building came into view, she wanted to collapse right on the sidewalk face first, close her eyes and succumb to exhaustion, giving up.

Stupid. Stupid. Stupid.

She felt *stupid*.

She knew better than to get her hopes up, to expect something from somebody, somebody who owed her nothing. Not their time. Not their attention. Not even their word. Disappointment flowed through her, a bitter pill to swallow. And it didn't help her self-loathing when she spotted the blue car parked across the street, in the same spot it had been in when she left the night before.

It hadn't moved an inch.

"Idiot," she muttered to herself after trudging up the stairs and unlocking her apartment. "You know better than this crap."

After relocking the door, she stripped and headed to her bedroom, sliding the room door closed and falling into her bed wearing nothing but a pair of tube socks and her white cotton underwear. Cuddling up with her pillow, she closed her eyes. *Stupid.*

She'd almost dozed off when buzzing echoed through her apartment. Gabriella pulled her pillow overtop of her head, covering her ears with it, diluting the intrusive sound.

It buzzed half a dozen times before stopping. When silence took over, sleep stole Gabriella away.

It lasted only a few minutes, though, before another noise jarred her awake. She tore the pillow away with a groan and sat up, her gaze darting to the bedroom door. Through the hazy glass, she saw movement, her heart stalling for a beat before wildly kicking in.

Someone was there. In the apartment. *Oh crap.*

Jumping out of bed, Gabriella opened the drawer in the bedside stand, pulling out a small .22 caliber pistol stashed there. Creeping to the door, she took a deep breath, counting to three in her head before shoving it open. "Don't move!"

The person froze.

Gabriella's hands were steady, her finger on the trigger, her racing heart battering her insides. It took a few seconds for her adrenaline to wane enough for her to make sense of things.

Dante stood in front of her, dressed in a suit, gaping at her from the living room. "Jesus fuck, Gabriella, what are you doing?"

"Me? What are *you* doing?" Her eyes darted to the door, seeing the locks dangling. "Did you... did you just break into my apartment? *Seriously?*"

"You didn't answer when I buzzed you," he said. "Didn't answer when I knocked, either."

"So you just force your way in? You default to breaking and entering? I could shoot you for that!"

"You could," he agreed, taking a careful step toward her. Gabriella smelled it then. *Liquor.* The odor clung to him.

"I'd do it, too," she warned. "I swear I would shoot you right in the face."

"I believe it." Dante raised his hands. "Look, can you just... put down the gun?"

"Why should I?"

"Because it's really fucking with my head," he said. "Not to mention your tits are distracting. I don't know where to look. I don't know what to *think*. I don't know whether I'm supposed to be turned on or terrified, and Jesus, the fact that I'm terrified right now is kind of turning me on. So can you just... take your finger off the trigger? *Please*? Before I come in my pants here?"

Gabriella lowered the gun and crossed her arms over her chest. *Ugh*. Turning, she stalked back into her bedroom, grabbing a shirt from her closet to cover herself. She put the gun back into the drawer and went to close it when Dante called out from the doorway. "Can I see it?"

She hesitated before stepping to him, holding out the gun. "Just don't shoot me."

"You know I wouldn't," he said, taking the gun and checking it out. "Son of a bitch, it's actually *loaded.* "

"Of course it is," she said. "What's the point of having a gun if it doesn't have any bullets in it?"

"Damn good question," he said, handing it back. "Here, put it away, wherever you keep it."

She took it as she stared into his bloodshot eyes. "You're drunk."

"A little bit," he admitted.

She shook her head, looking away. "Well, then, it's a good thing you weren't planning to drive anywhere. If you drink and drive, you might kill somebody, and we wouldn't want that, would we?"

He sighed as she returned the gun to the drawer. "Gabriella..."

"What do you want from me, Dante?" she asked. "I'm not in the mood, so just tell me why you're here so we can get this over with and you can go on your way and do whatever it is you do."

"I thought I had an open invitation."

She walked back into the living room. "You do. You *did*."

"Did," he repeated, his expression hardening. "Meaning not anymore?"

"I don't know," she said honestly. "I don't know what you expect from me."

"I don't expect anything."

"Maybe that's the problem," she said, sitting down on the couch. "Because today, I actually expected something from you."

He frowned. "I'm sorry."

"Don't be." She dropped her head down and covered her face,

her eyes burning. "You owe me nothing."

"I owe you my life."

"No, you don't," she said. "I did my job, Dante. That's it. I went to work every day, and I took care of you. I was happy to do it. You lived, not because of me, but because you refused to die. And I'm glad for it. I'm glad you're alive. But you owe me nothing for that. So it was my fault, because I should've known better than to have expectations."

"Please don't do this, Gabriella."

"Don't do what?"

"Don't *regret* me," he said. "Don't say I'm just some mistake you made."

"You're not a mistake, Dante." Sighing, she peeked up at him as he stared at her, his eyes *pleading*. What did he want? "My mom told me never to fall for a man like my father, because when they don't come home, it's going to hurt. *It's going to break your heart*, she said. And they're bound to not come home sometimes. They're bound to not show up. Because they might've made a promise to you, but they made another promise, too, they swore an oath, and that other oath will always come first. *Always*. So other guys might break your heart once or twice, but mobsters? They'll break your heart every single night."

Dante stood in silence, like he had no defense to that.

After a moment, he walked over to sit down beside her. "I just had one of the worst nights of my life, but realizing I've hurt you? Well, that takes the cake."

"I'm fine."

"You're not."

"You shouldn't feel bad."

"But I do."

"Well, *phooey*."

He laughed, gazing her way, his eyes burrowing through her.

"True or false," he said. "You're in love with me."

Gabriella's insides coiled at that word. *Love*. "Maybe."

He nodded, like that was answer enough for him.

"I know I shouldn't," she explained. "I don't even really know if I do. But I feel *something*. When I think about you. When I'm around you. I can't shake you. And I know it's probably too soon to have those feelings, and maybe I shouldn't ever have them at all, but I feel it. Can you understand that?"

"Absolutely," he said. "I felt it the first time I heard your voice."

"You did?"

"And again the first time I saw your face," he said. "I felt it the first time I kissed you. The first time I was inside of you. Jesus, I felt it when you pointed a fucking gun at my face. So yeah, I can understand that. I know what you mean."

"You're in love with me?"

"I am."

Whoa.

Gabriella blinked rapidly, absorbing those words.

"I'm poison, though," Dante said. "I told you that, and I think I might've proved it to you today. I'm going to break your heart. I'll probably break it *a lot.* I won't want to, but I will, and you deserve better than that. You deserve better than *me.* But if you want me anyway, all you have to do is say so. We'll slap a title on this thing."

Slap a title on this thing.

While so much in her yearned to take him up on that, to throw caution to the wind, she knew they needed to talk about what *titling* it would mean. "That's kind of a big decision to make when you're drunk and I've had like three minutes of sleep."

"True," he said. "You should go back to bed."

She stood up. "I'm going to."

"I should leave."

"No, actually, the *last* thing drunk Dante should do is wander the streets of Manhattan without supervision," she said. "So I'd rather you just come to bed with me."

"Okay."

"No hanky-panky, though," she warned. "If we even tried, I'd just fall asleep on you, and I don't know if you'd recover from that."

"Doubtful," he said. "My ego has taken a real beating lately."

Dante kicked his shoes off and removed his coat before climbing into the bed with her. Gabriella snuggled into his arms. She wanted to tell him to get comfortable, but she suspected those words would fall on deaf ears.

"What made your day so bad?" she asked, stifling a yawn.

"Long story," Dante mumbled. "Maybe I'll tell you later."

SWEETEST SORROW

Before sleep took Gabriella, Dante's soft snores filled the room. He was out like a light, just like that, while Gabriella's exhausted mind ran circles, repeatedly drifting to a particular thought.

"I love you, Dante," she whispered. "There's no *maybe* about it."

CHAPTER 16

"Dinner."

The lone word sprung from Dante's lips the second Gavin Amaro stepped out from his father's café around nightfall. Saturday evening, and Gabriella had just left for another long shift at work. A headache plagued Dante, the makings of a hangover, but despite it, he *really* wanted a drink.

And he really didn't want to drink alone.

Gavin stalled there. "Dinner."

"But you're buying," Dante said, "because I'm broke as shit. I haven't been working much."

"Understandable."

"And no touchy-feely bullshit, either. If you get handsy or ask how everything makes me *feel*, I'm out."

"Anything else?"

"Yeah," Dante said. "I don't fuck on the first date."

"*Bullshit.*" Gavin laughed. "The Dante I knew would've stuck it in a girl he met five minutes ago."

"Yeah, well, *that* Dante didn't have a girlfriend."

Girlfriend. That word was like a foreign language to him. But Gabriella had looked at him an hour earlier, before heading off to work, and said the magical phrase: *I want to be your girlfriend.*

And, well, like he'd said before, turning down a woman like her was impossible.

"A girlfriend, huh? Color me surprised. Always figured that word was too big for you, too complicated for you to ever figure out."

"Your cousin taught it to me."

"Is that right? Gotta be honest... I'm not sure if I want to congratulate you or punch you for that."

"You can congratulate me over dinner," Dante said. "I'll give you plenty of reasons to punch me later."

"I don't doubt it."

They went to the bar a few buildings down. Nothing special. Nothing unusual. Some place they both often visited on Saturday nights. Dante sat at an empty booth in the corner with Gavin across from him.

"Hey, guys," a waitress said, eyeing them curiously as she approached, carrying menus. "What can I get for you?"

"Heineken," Dante said, handing the menu right back when she set it down, not needing to look. "And a cheeseburger, rare, with everything on it."

She smiled, nodding, as she turned to Gavin.

"Roman Coke," he said. "And I'll just take the grilled avocado and chicken sandwich."

"Awesome, I'll have that right out."

"Avocado," Dante said when the waitress left. "Seriously?"

"It's good."

"It's fruit. On a sandwich."

"So is tomato."

"But tomato makes sense."

"Only because you're used to it," Gavin said. "You always question what's new. It's human nature. While everything else, you know, no matter how strange, feels normal because you're trained to see it that way. You're *brainwashed*."

"That sounds a lot like something the jackass in the lab coat at the hospital would say," Dante said. "I'm not here to be psychoanalyzed."

"Why *are* you here?"

"It was your idea," Dante pointed out. "You wanted to hang out, so here we are, hanging out like friends."

The waitress approached again, slipping their drinks in front of them before scurrying away. Dante picked his up, taking a sip of the beer.

"Friends," Gavin mused.

"Sorry, G, but like I said, I've got a girlfriend now. *'Friends'* is all we can ever be."

"Funny," Gavin said. "Not long ago you were telling everyone you didn't have any friends."

"Yeah, well, don't take it personal. I spent a week being tortured in a basement and nobody even looked for me. That kind of shit makes you question things."

Gavin stared at him. "What makes you think nobody looked?"

Dante took another sip. "The fact that my father said they did-n't bother to look because there was *'no point'*."

Something flashed across Gavin's face then, something that looked way too much like pity. Dante swallowed more of his beer, trying to dull the swell of shame that caused.

"I hate to break it to you, because you seem to be happy settling into this *'woe is me'* persona, but we looked for you," Gavin said. "My family called for a meeting, trying to get information out of Barsanti about where he might've dumped you. We thought you were dead, yeah, but we *looked*. My father wasn't going to rest until you returned."

"Seriously?"

"Seriously," Gavin said. "Even Matty-B dug around. Barsanti was preoccupied with Enzo's funeral arrangements, but Matty wanted to make it so Genna could bury *her* brother, too. She took it all pretty damn hard."

Dante was quiet for a moment, his gaze on his beer bottle as he mulled over those words. "The whole time I was in that basement, I kept thinking about her. Seven o'clock. I was supposed to pick her up at *seven o'clock*. And I just kept hoping, you know, that she made it home all right. They tortured me, but I didn't care. I knew I was-n't making it out of there. I figured they'd get tired and end it, but still, I wondered, did *she* fucking make it?"

Weight pressed on Dante's chest. The air felt heavy as he breathed it in. He guzzled his beer, trying to wash down the lump in his throat.

"Come on, you knew she did," Gavin said. "The Ice Princess was resilient. She probably learned that shit from *you*."

"I tried to tell myself that," Dante said. "I know she made it home that night, and the next night, and a few nights after that, but a lot of good that was, because she's not home *now*. I was supposed to die. I should be dead. And I can't help feeling like something got fucked up and we somehow switched places. Why am I home and she isn't?"

Gavin frowned, sitting in silence. Dante didn't expect a response. He wasn't even sure why he'd said that. But it was in him, nagging, and he needed to let it *out*.

"Dante? I think this might constitute touchy-feely bullshit."

Dante laughed. "You might be right."

The waitress swung by then, dropping off their food, before grabbing Dante another beer and refreshing Gavin's drink.

They chatted about nothing of importance as they ate, everyone leaving them alone. Dante was finishing up his third beer when Umberto walked into the bar. Dante watched, on guard, as the guy looked around, not moving from the entrance.

His gaze settled on Dante. *Fuck.*

"Well, this was nice, but I think duty calls." Dante took the last little swallow of his beer before standing up, setting the bottle on the table. "Thank you, Amaro."

Gavin shrugged it off. "It was just a burger."

"For looking for me," Dante clarified. "Thank you for *trying*."

Dante strolled to the door where Umberto lingered, dressed in all black. He paused, nodding in greeting.

Umberto didn't nod back. "Your father's trying to reach you."

"I told him I lost my phone."

Dante refrained from mentioning that he'd gotten a new one, having no plans to share the number with them.

"Well, we've got another job to do, and your father wants you involved."

"Jersey?"

"No," Umberto said. "Soho."

Soho.

"He told me to stay out of Soho."

"He figured he'd make an exception for tonight," Umberto said, "since you've got a vested interest in the place."

"What place?" Dante knew the answer the second he asked. "*The Place.*"

"Bingo," Umberto said, pulling his keys from his pocket. "This one's personal."

Dante went along, not putting up a fight, riding in the passenger seat and watching out the window as the streets flew by. Darkness infiltrated the city and swarmed the car, the windows rolled down, an icy chill in the air that made Dante's blood run cold.

Something twisted inside of Dante as they approached The Place, parking in an underground garage, out of sight of the street. Umberto popped his trunk, again pulling out his backpack, perching a ski mask on top of his head.

"Here, put this on."

Umberto tossed a black duffle bag to Dante. Black hoodie. Black ski mask. Black leather gloves. Dante slipped it all on as Umberto tinkered around in the trunk, resurfacing with a gun.

A *big* gun.

Umberto held up the AR-15, sliding the fresh clip in. Dante's chest tightened at the sight of it. "What are we doing here, Bert?"

"Making waves," he said, glancing at him. "Do you have your gun on you?"

"No."

He didn't *have* a gun. Barsanti had taken it.

"Do you want one?"

"Do I *need* one?"

Umberto reached into his waistband, pulling out his Colt .45 to hand it to Dante. *Guess that's my answer.* He gripped it, getting a feel for it, although he hoped like hell he wouldn't use it for anything.

The darkness made it easy for them to move undetected, to slip into the stairwell beside The Place and head up to the apartment above it. Umberto tried the door. *Locked.* Before Dante could volunteer to do something, Umberto whipped out his tools and broke right in.

"You're getting better at that," Dante said as he stepped into the dark apartment behind Umberto.

"Guess I learned from watching the best."

Umberto pulled out a flashlight to hand to Dante before setting off through the apartment.

"What are we looking for?" Dante asked.

"Whatever we find."

Whatever we find.

A kitchen. A living room. Two bedrooms. Two bathrooms. Umberto headed straight to the left, walking with purpose, while Dante veered right, curious. He stalled in the doorway, the beam of his flashlight bouncing around a room he riddled out right away as having belonged to Enzo. It was a mess, things strewn everywhere, a *Scarface* poster on the wall. *Typical.*

Dante couldn't bring himself to step inside the room. Enzo was smart enough to know not to keep anything where someone could find it. There was no point rifling through his things.

Strolling away, he noticed a pool table off to the back, prominently displayed in the living room. Dante ran his hand along the blue felt, picking up the black eight ball, holding it in his palm. He wondered if his sister had ever played on it.

"Anything?" Umberto asked, reappearing, still carrying around the massive gun. The sight of it made Dante nervous.

"Nothing," Dante said. "You?"

Umberto shrugged, heading for the door to leave already. Dante dropped the eight ball back onto the table before following, locking the door as Umberto headed down the stairwell.

"Guess that was a bust," Dante said, joining him.

"Oh no." Umberto stalled at the bottom and peeked out. "We're just getting started."

Umberto yanked his ski mask down, covering his face. Dante's heart raced. *Shit.* Not having much of a choice, Dante covered his face and pulled the hood up over his head, cloaking him.

Chaos erupted. Cars pulled up outside, double parking, blocking the road around the entrance. Men stormed the bar.

"Let's go," Umberto said, stepping out of the stairwell and heading right for the bar. Dante followed Umberto, slipping in the door, but he paused there, not wanting to go any further.

It was a coordinated attack, every meticulous detail worked out. They'd planned it in advance, leaving nothing to chance.

Nothing except Dante.

Barsanti's men went for guns, panicked by the intrusion, but they could do nothing to stop the invasion.

"Drop your weapons! Get on the ground!" Umberto yelled, cutting through the crowd, his gun pointed at the ceiling as he fired off a few rounds in quick succession. "Cooperate and we *might* let you go home tonight."

Men dropped to the ground, surrendering their guns. Galante soldiers dressed in black swarmed them, securing their weapons, as others robbed the place. *Always take the weapons.* It was a Galante family rule. *You never know when someone else's gun might come in handy for a frame-up job.* They raided pockets and rifled through the cash register, stealing anything of value, smashing whatever they planned to leave behind. Glass shattered, liquor bottles exploding as bullets haphazardly ripped into the mirror behind the bar.

Dante watched it all unfold in slow motion.

Thirty seconds. A minute. Maybe two. It wasn't long at all, but it dragged on forever.

Umberto climbed up on top of the bar, walking along it, surveying the scene. Liquor soaked the floor, running along the tile in puddles, carrying shards of glass along with it.

Umberto aimed his gun at the bartender's head. "Where's your boss tonight?"

"I, uh... he, uh..."

Umberto fired some shots right past the guy, close enough he could've hit him. The guy collapsed behind the bar, crying.

"I'll ask you once more," Umberto said, aiming at him again. "Where is your boss?"

"He's, uh... he's somewhere with Johnny Amaro! A meeting or something. I don't know! Don't shoot!"

Dante wasn't sure what happened after that. It all moved too fast. Umberto jumped down from the bar, satisfied, as he announced, "Thank you, assholes, for your cooperation. Primo Galante sends his regards."

As soon as those words were out of his mouth, someone moved, lunging for Umberto. *For the AR-15.* Gunshots went off. People started shooting as others viciously fought, fighting for survival like caged animals. Blood spilled, splattering along the bar, running into the puddles of liquor.

"Light it up," Umberto hissed, his voice scathing as he slammed the AR-15 into somebody's face before running for the door. "Leave nothing."

Dante ran out behind Umberto, his vision blurry, ears ringing, his hands fucking *shaking.* They hurried around the corner, into the garage, heading for the car.

Three minutes. That was it.

It felt so much longer.

Sirens wailed in the distance as Umberto drove out of the garage. People ran, getting into the cars to flee. Umberto turned, speeding away, as Dante ripped his mask off and watched the side mirror.

Thick smoke rolled out of the side of the bar. They barely made it half a block when an explosion rocked the street, loud enough to make Dante flinch, strong enough to rock the car they rode in. Flames jutted from every crevice of the building. Dante tried to steady his breathing, but panic crept through his veins when police cars flew by them.

Neither of them said a word. They drove straight to Westchester County, to the Galante house, where Primo sat in the dining room, eating alone.

Umberto walked right in the room, pausing beside his boss as he shed his heavy black clothing. "Nothing."

"Nothing," Primo repeated. "There has to be something, somewhere. It's impossible for there to be *nothing*."

"I know," Umberto said. "We'll keep looking."

"I know you will," Primo said. "How'd it go otherwise?"

"Got a bit messy at the end, but we didn't lose anyone. Wrecked the place and left. Took the guns."

"Good," Primo said. "And Barsanti?"

"At a meeting with Amaro."

Primo shook his head. "Amaro, you say?"

"Seems that way."

"You did good, son." Primo waved his wand dismissively. "You can go."

Dante was about to chime in, to say he'd done not a goddamn thing, when Umberto nodded and responded. "Thank you, sir."

Umberto walked away, slipping past Dante. *Son.*

"Take a seat, Dante," Primo said. "Have dinner with me."

Dante didn't budge from the doorway. "I've already eaten."

"Take a seat, anyway."

That was twice.

The man wouldn't say it a third time.

Dante pulled out the chair, the same one he'd sat in every night for over two decades, and sat down, staring at the empty plates, ones his father set out every night.

Just in case.

The man said nothing for a few minutes, eating in silence, meticulously cutting his steak into bite-size pieces and drinking copious amounts of red wine before he acknowledged Dante's presence again. "Are you happy?"

Dante wasn't sure how to answer that so he didn't, instead tossing it back at him. "Are *you?*"

"I will be," Primo said, "once I get what I want."

"What do you want? What are you looking for?"

"What belongs to me."

"And what's *that?*"

Primo turned his head, regarding Dante, scrutinizing him. After a moment, he turned away again, picking up his glass of wine and taking a sip. "You always had too much heart, even as a little boy. *Softhearted.* I tried to pull that out of you. I tried to toughen you up. I thought I succeeded. Some days, I would look at you and see *me*, and I would be proud. But even now, looking at you, I still see those pieces of her that I failed to erase."

Dante's gaze shifted to the empty plate diagonal from him, where his mother used to sit. "Why?"

"She betrayed me," Primo said. "The GWB only leads one place."

New Jersey.

"She was acting strange, so I had her followed. I loved your mother, but I questioned if I could trust her. I found out she'd gone to Brazzi territory. I found out she was visiting Savina Barsanti behind my back. She thought crossing state lines would keep me from finding out. I confronted her, told her if she did it again, I wouldn't allow her to come back, and she had the audacity to tell me it didn't matter, that she was done being a Galante because she wasn't happy." He shook his head, looking at his son again. "So tell me, Dante, are you *happy?*"

He stared his father right in the eyes and said, "No."

Primo looked away, sipping his wine. "Guess it's true what they say... you can't fight your DNA."

* * *

Nine o'clock Sunday morning. A twelve-hour shift had turned into more like thirteen and a half.

To call Gabriella exhausted would've been offensively understating the fatigue she felt. Every inch of her, from the top of her frizzy head to the tip of her unpainted toes, was beat. Her eyes burned, her muscles ached, and her brain was seconds away from calling for a mental break. She wanted to soak in a hot bathtub, to soothe her body and unwind, but she was pretty sure if she tried she'd just fall asleep in the water and drown.

Sighing, she approached her apartment door, cursing the fact that she'd moved into a walk-up. *Elevators are the true unsung heroes.* Sticking her key in the lock, she twisted it, the knob turning smoothly. Unlocked.

Uh...

Pushing open the door, she stepped inside, so dead tired that self-preservation had vacated premises. If it was a home invader, she was screwed, because running down those stairs was out of the question.

The television in the living room played, some middle-aged blonde reporter on the screen.

"...that masked gunmen, one reportedly armed with a semi-automatic rifle, barged into the small neighborhood bar at around eight o'clock Saturday evening and opened fire on patrons inside..."

Gabriella's gaze shifted to her couch. Dante sat there, staring at the news, so still she'd think he were asleep if his eyes weren't open. *Uh, catatonic, much?*

"Did you break into the apartment? *Again?*"

Dante turned her way, looking about as fresh-faced as she felt. He obviously hadn't slept any of those hours she'd been gone. "I waited around, but you were late, and I kind of just wanted to sit down."

"It's okay," she said, shutting the door behind her. "Well, I mean, it's not really *okay*. It's kind of scary how easily you get in here. I'm seriously questioning the point of locks."

"They keep most people out," he said. "The ones who can get in, well, nothing short of pulling the trigger on your .22 will stop them."

"Good thing I know how to do that," she said, plopping down beside him on the couch. Kicking her shoes off, she lay back, throwing her legs across him, her feet in his lap.

He didn't flinch at all, yanking off her socks and tossing them aside, his nose twitching. "Your feet stink."

"Hold your breath."

He laughed as he rubbed her feet, kneading the soles. *Holy crap.* Sighing, she closed her eyes, her toes curling as tingles flowed up her legs.

"*...authorities say it's too early to speak of a motive, but the business in question, known to those in the neighborhood as* The Place, *is owned by alleged mob boss Roberto Barsanti...*"

Gabriella's eyes reopened when she heard that, her gaze going straight to Dante. She'd learned about the incident at work. They'd treated a couple of the patients at her hospital. Gunshot wounds, burns, and a bit of smoke inhalation, for the most part. Nothing yet fatal, but one or two were critical. It had made for a long night in the ICU.

Dante stared at the screen, listening intently, rubbing *expertly.* The man had a way with his hands.

"Are you, uh...?" She paused, not sure how to ask, her voice tentative when she continued. "You're okay, right? You don't have any injuries or anything?"

His brow furrowed as he turned to her, like he didn't quite understand the question, but it seemed to click. His expression went slack, trepidation in his eyes as they scanned her face. He licked his lips, opening and closing his mouth. He was trying to find a way to explain something, like she'd asked him questions he was afraid to answer.

Her heart sank. *Oh God.*

"I'm not asking," she said before he forced out any words he might regret. "I'm just making sure *you're* not hurt."

"I'm fine."

"No boo-boos that need bandages?"

"None."

"Good." Her eyes closed again as he continued to rub her feet. "If you keep this up, I'm going to fall asleep."

"Go ahead."

"Are you tired?"

"Very."

"Have you eaten?"

"I had dinner last night with Amaro."

Her eyes popped back open. *Whoa.* "Really?"

"Yes."

"Why?"

Dante reached over and picked up the remote, pressing the button to turn the television off. "You ask a lot of questions."

"Sue me," she said. "I'm curious."

"Something to do." He shrugged. "We ate, had a few drinks, and that was that."

"So... like a date? I'm kind of jealous."

"Don't worry, I didn't even kiss him." Dante made a face as he shuddered. "Oh, *ugh,* just the thought of that makes me want to drink cyanide."

"Kissing Gavin?"

He shuddered. *Again.*

Laughing, Gabriella sat up, pulling her feet away from him. "Anyway, I should probably do that."

She went to stand, but Dante grabbed her arm, pulling her back onto the couch with him. "Do *what*?"

"Eat something," she said.

"Jesus fuck, Gabriella, I thought you meant kissing Amaro."

"What? Oh God, no! He's my cousin!" Now *she* shuddered, shoving him. "That's gross!"

"Tell me about it." He ran his hand down his face as he stood. "Just relax and I'll find you something to eat. It's the least I can do after breaking in again."

"You're going to cook?"

"Maybe."

"Do you know *how* to cook?"

"Not really."

He headed into the kitchen, and Gabriella sat there, listening as he banged around. He talked to himself, words she couldn't decipher, as something slammed against the counter.

Just a few minutes later, he walked back in, and Gabriella laughed at the blue plastic container he carried. *Easy-Mac.* She took it from him, not even mad. Macaroni was *always* a good choice, as far as she was concerned.

"I'll take you out," he said, sitting down beside her as she ate. "On a date, I mean. Whenever you get some time off. I'll do it right. I won't even break in. I'll *knock*."

"Yeah, please stop breaking in," she said. "The neighbors might catch you and call the police."

"I promise to wait until you open the door for now on."

"Or," she said, blowing into the bowl, "I could give you a key."

"You don't have to do that."

"I know, but really, be honest, when you're not here, where do you go?"

He didn't answer. He couldn't. Where did he go? Everywhere. *Nowhere.* He was homeless.

"It's a benefit," she said. "A friendship benefit. A *boyfriend* benefit. I mean, you're here, and I'm here, and there's no reason you shouldn't have a key so when I'm *not* here you can still be here."

He stared at her. "Do you realize what you're suggesting sounds a hell of a lot like me moving in?"

"Does it?"

"Yep."

"Huh."

She continued to eat her macaroni in silence.

Dante leaned back on the couch, draping his arm around her, pulling her closer. She rested her head on his shoulder, finishing her last few bites.

"If you want to give me a key," he said, "I'll happily use it."

"Good." She smiled, trying to ignore those butterflies flapping away in her stomach. *Lovesick fool.* "So do I get any say on where we go on our date?"

"Of course," he said. "If you've got ideas, I'm listening."

"Well, how does a family wedding at my grandfather's estate sound?"

"Like trouble."

"So I can count on you to take me?"

"You know it."

CHAPTER 17

Dante fiddled with his blood red tie in the mirror of the small bathroom, his reflection hazy from the lingering steam of his hot shower. His hair was damp, a messy mop curling on top of his head, but otherwise, he was all put together. A fresh shave seemed to do wonders for his face. He looked younger, he thought—refreshed, almost—like his system had been rebooted.

It's about fucking time.

"You sure about this?" Dante called out to Gabriella, who was off in the bedroom, doing whatever it was she'd been in there doing for over an hour with the door closed. Putting on makeup. Getting dressed. Doing other feminine shit. Not playing with her pussy, though, like she was in Dante's imagination. *Pity.* It was the only reason someone should be locked in a room alone for so long. "It's not too late to change your mind, you know. I could just drop you off or something. Wait by the highway."

The door to the bedroom slid open, the clink of high heels echoing through the apartment as her voice chimed in. "Why? Getting cold feet?"

"Not a chance," he scoffed, glancing out of the bathroom and stalling when he caught sight of her. *Jesus.* Blood red dress, not too tight, but clingy enough to show off her curves, falling just above the knees, exposing more skin than was probably appropriate. The woman looked like pure *sin*. Dante's eyes scanned her, from top to bottom, greedily drinking her in. "Maybe we *both* should just stay home."

"Not a chance," she said, mimicking him.

He met her eyes, smiling at the twinkle that greeted him. Damn, she was beautiful. He would never get over it, nor would he ever understand what he'd done to deserve her in his life. *Goddamn Christmas miracle.* "You look like something I'd love to eat."

She laughed. "It's good seeing you with an appetite."

"You say that now." He stepped out of the bathroom and shut the light off behind him as he approached her. Grasping her hip, he pulled her to him, feeling her warmth. "We'll see how you feel after I'm done ravishing you."

He nuzzled into her neck, running his tongue along her skin, tracing her jawline. Gabriella wrapped her arms around his neck, cocking her head to give him more space, despite her words of protest. "We can't do this right now. There's not enough time."

"My car's fast," he said. "It buys us a few minutes."

"But—"

Dante pressed his pointer finger to her lips, silencing her, as he kissed back up her jawline before looking her dead in the eyes. "Shh, no talking. There's not enough time, remember? So unless what you're trying to say is *'fuck me, Dante'*, it needs to wait for later."

She clamped her lips closed, giving him a curious look, one that he didn't dwell on. She was right, after all. Time was scarce. Dropping to his knees, right then and there, he pushed her dress up to her waist, exposing her matching red lacy underwear. He kissed her through the fabric, a few small pecks, before he grasped the side of the lace and tugged them down her legs. She stepped out of them, kicking them aside, as Dante forced her legs apart just enough for him to come up between them. His tongue grazed across the slit, tasting her as she whimpered. Fuck, she was *sweet*, a bit tangy with a pinch of saltiness. He couldn't describe it, not really, but he'd bake a fucking pie of that pussy and eat it all day long.

"Dante," she moaned, the sound of his name in that low, gritty tone enough to make his dick stand up and notice what was happening. It grew hard, throbbing, but he tried to ignore the son of a bitch, focusing all of his attention on Gabriella. He licked, sucking her clit, as his fingers worked magic, sliding inside of her, pumping in and out. He curved his fingertips, seeking out that sweet spot. The second he found it, her knees nearly buckled, her breath hitching.

He took it easy on her, savoring the moment, before time started ticking away too fast. *Tick-tock, motherfucker.* If he didn't wrap it up, STAT, they'd never make it. And as much as Dante might not have minded, because he could've stayed like that forever, he was pretty damn sure her family would be furious.

Sorry, Mr. and Mrs. Russo, your daughter didn't come because I was busy making *her come... my bad.*

That would earn him castration, no doubt.

Pulling back, he pumped his fingers deeper, rubbing hard circles around her clit with his thumb, as he kissed along her thigh. She was getting close. He could tell. He was becoming in tune with her signals. She always tilted her head back, her jaw going slack, her throat flexing as she held in a cry.

It hit her at once, her body jolting, her knees locking to keep her upright as her legs tried to close. She held onto his shoulders, fisting his suit coat as whimpers escaped her throat. The second the pleasure ran through her, Dante sunk his teeth into her upper thigh. She screeched, her body quivering, and Dante smiled to himself, kissing the red mark he'd left on her skin, before his mouth moved back to her pussy. He kissed it, his tongue swiping along it a few times, before he stood up.

No hesitation at all, he pulled her to him, smashing his mouth to hers. He kissed her, nipping at her bottom lip, before whispering, "I could keep going, but we've really gotta leave."

He grabbed Gabriella's hand. She staggered, stammering, tugging her dress down as Dante pulled her to the door.

"Wait, hold on, let me lock up," she growled at him, her face flushed, when he tried to lead her down the stairs. He gave her a few seconds before tugging on her arm, dragging her away.

He glanced at his watch. *Noon.* "What time does this thing start again?"

"One o'clock," she said.

Shit. "We might make it if we take the Holland Tunnel."

"We *better* make it," she said. "This whole thing is going to be crazy enough. The last thing we need is to get off on the wrong foot."

He hated to break it to her, but getting off on the *right* foot was impossible. Because *any* foot he used to waltz into New Jersey under these circumstances ran the real risk of a gory amputation. Dante should've courted Gabriella, schmoozing with her father the same time he wooed her, but it was too late for that.

No, instead he was crashing a Brazzi wedding, in Brazzi territory, to let them know he was dating one of their Brazzi girls.

Maybe he *did* have a death wish.

The hour drive to Alpine, New Jersey, was cut down to damn near forty-five minutes, thanks to a heavy foot on the gas pedal and a healthy dose of luck for a change. The massive metal gate blocking off the sprawling estate hung wide open. Men dressed in all black stood guard beside the entrance, looking like the Secret Service, and waved them through, the McLaren sticking out in the sea of black sedans that swarmed the area.

"Last chance to change your mind," Dante warned her, pulling onto the property past the men, following the paved path toward one of the biggest mansions Dante had ever laid eyes on. He'd always heard Victor Brazzi lived in style, but he hadn't expected a fucking stone *castle*.

"Not changing my mind," she said. "Not a chance."

Brave, brave soul.

Maybe she has a death wish, also.

Dante followed a few other cars, driving right up to the front of the house. The moment he put it in park, both doors swung open. Dante climbed out, coming face-to-face with the Valet, a young guy in a red vest, wearing a bowtie. He couldn't have been more than twenty-one.

"Try not to fuck up the car," Dante told him, taking the yellow numbered ticket and slipping it in his pocket to pick his car up later. "It's still kind of new."

Dante waited for Gabriella to join him. She slid her arm into his, wrapping herself around him as they headed for the door. Staff covered the property, an older bald man with a clipboard standing on the front step, greeting guests, a smile on his face.

Until he caught sight of Dante.

"Name?" he asked as they approached, his eyes narrowed. *Uh-oh.* There might've been some recognition there, but his suspicion was blatant.

"Russo," Gabriella chimed in. "Gabriella Russo."

The guy's eyes flickered to the clipboard, scanning for her name, before he again looked right at Dante. "And *your* name?"

"He's my plus one," Gabriella said as an orchestra started playing off in the distance. "So he won't be on the list. But if you'll excuse us, we *really* need to go grab our seats before this thing starts without us."

She tugged Dante's arm, pulling him into the house. Dante glanced back, watching as the guy with the clipboard pulled out a walkie-talkie, radioing something to someone, his gaze trailing the two of them. "Pretty sure I've been made."

"Not surprised," Gabriella said. "I'm just hoping they won't make it some big *thing*."

More men, dressed in black, were positioned around the house, every set of eyes on Dante, watching like a hawk. *Too late*, he thought. *It's a big thing.*

Her high heels clicked along the shiny black and white marble, echoing in the vast foyer. A massive Christmas tree stood in front of them, decorated in gold and white, a crystal chandelier hanging above it, sparkling in the lights. It looked like the lobby of a five-star hotel.

The wedding took place in the back, the yard converted into a makeshift chapel with a massive heated tent creating an aisle. *Who the fuck threw an outdoor wedding on Christmas Eve?* Rows of stark white chairs filled it, most of them already claimed. Dante surveyed their surroundings, spotting men perched in the top windows of the house, giving them an open view of everyone in the backyard. He caught a gleam of something on one of the men, the sunlight hitting metal at just the right angle, giving away the assault rifle.

Snipers.

"Who did you say was getting married?" Dante asked as they headed through an open set of doors, going inside the tent, passing even more security. Gabriella darted for the back row, slipping into the first empty chair she came to.

"A cousin," she answered as Dante sat beside her. Gone was that cool confidence she'd exuded on the drive. Despite the frigid winter air, she was sweating. *Hard.*

"The bride or groom?"

"Groom, I think."

"You *think*?"

"Yeah, I don't know. I think the invitation said he was a Brazzi."

"Are we talking literally or figuratively here?" Dante asked. "Is he an actual Brazzi, or is he a member of the Brazzi *family*?"

Dante wasn't sure if she'd get the distinction, but she grasped the meaning quickly. "I'm pretty sure he's both. Last name Brazzi while also being one of those guys."

Those guys.

The wedding of a made man.

The firepower made sense, as did the excessive security. Weddings were notorious targets. Guards went down. Powerful men turned vulnerable. And there he was, in the thick of it, the exact thing all those men with guns were told to watch out for: the uninvited *rival*.

Dante slouched in his seat, draping his arm over the back of Gabriella's chair, pulling her to him as he rubbed her arm, warming her up. "Are you close to your grandparents?"

"Yeah."

"How close?"

"Well, my grandmother acts more like my fairy godmother, always trying to fix me so she can, uh, *fix me up*, but I can do no wrong in my grandfather's eyes. He always said I was his little princess and I'd never need a king in order to rule."

"So he likes you."

"Of course," she said. "Why are you asking?"

"I'm just gauging my chances here," he said, watching as the man from the front porch marched straight down the aisle, aiming for someone sitting in the front row. Dante didn't have to see him to know it would be Gabriella's grandfather.

"Chances of what?"

"Chances of living." Dante watched as the man leaned down, whispering something to Victor. "These guys tend to be the 'shoot first, ask questions never' kind, but seeing how Victor likes you, he might not shoot your plus one on sight."

Gabriella laughed, like he was joking, but Dante meant it. The man raised the clipboard, showing something to Victor as he continued speaking. Dante was nowhere near close enough to hear anything, but he pretty much guessed how that conversation went.

Got a wedding crasher. Think it's one of those Galante pricks. He came with Gabriella Russo, but he wouldn't tell us his name. You want us to put a bullet in him now or wait until they cut the cake?

Victor waved him off, and the man stalked back down the aisle, stopping beside Dante's chair. He leaned down, his voice low as he said, "Mr. Brazzi would like to speak with you after the ceremony," before continuing on.

Cake, it is.

"Maybe we should've stayed home," Gabriella whispered.

"Ah, don't get cold feet *now*," Dante said, his thumb stroking her shoulder. "Besides, you look beautiful. It would've been a pity not to get to show you off."

"I just... I *really* hope I don't have to do any running or jumping or army-crawling or scaling walls to help get you out of here," she said, tilting her head his way to whisper, "I forgot to put on my underwear."

Dante choked on thin air, coughing as her cheeks flushed, a mischievous glint in her eyes.

Weddings were one of Dante's *least* favorite things. He would've rather been water-boarded than have to sit through long, drawn-out vows ever again. He zoned out, damn near falling asleep, until a hand slipped into his lap. He dropped his head, watching Gabriella stroke his thigh, coming dangerously close to his dick.

Relief flowed through him when the guy kissed his bride, but that relief was short-lived. *Very* short-lived. Guests filtered into the house, the party shifting to a ballroom on the second floor. Gabriella slipped her hand in his, entwining their fingers.

Judgment time.

Eyes trailed Dante, security still monitoring his every move. It wouldn't have surprised him a bit if somewhere up above, a gun was trained on him.

The moment they stepped into the house, feet moving from stone courtyard to marble foyer, Victor Brazzi appeared in their path, flanked by two guards.

Victor looked the part of a typical Italian grandfather: mid-sixties, leathery skin, with thin graying hair combed back so it sort of just stood on end. He wore his age well, his smile wide and his eyes spry. The man was sharp; there was no denying it. He sat atop an empire that men both feared and envied.

"Gabriella! How's my sweet little princess?"

Dante let go of Gabriella's hand as Victor gripped her arms and kissed both of her cheeks.

"Hey, *Nonno*." She smiled. "I'm great! How are you?"

"Surprised," Victor said.

"*Pleasantly* surprised?" Gabriella asked.

"Let's just stick with surprised for the time being." Victor's gaze turned to Dante. "Mr. Galante, welcome. We haven't had the chance to formally meet yet. I'm Victor Brazzi."

Victor held out his hand. Dante shook it, fighting off a cringe when the man squeezed. *Hard*. "Please, call me Dante."

Victor turned back to Gabriella without acknowledging that. "Sweetheart, why don't you head up to the ballroom? I know your mother is anxious to see you."

Gabriella made a face. "I, uh…"

"Don't worry," Victor said. "Everything will be fine. I'd just like to have a word with him in private."

Her eyes darted to Dante, panicked.

"Go on." Dante nodded past the men. "I'll join you soon."

Gabriella hesitated before kissing Dante's cheek. She walked away then, falling into the crowd, disappearing. As soon as she was gone, Victor's expression hardened.

"Follow me, Mr. Galante," he said, stepping past. The guards waited until Dante followed before they trailed along, staying on his heels.

Victor headed to an office on the first floor, through a set of ornamental wooden doors. The second Dante stepped into the office, hands grabbed him from behind, stopping him, pinning him in place. His heart raced as his hands rose in surrender, the guards relentlessly patting him down, clearing out all of his pockets and yanking apart his suit, roughing him up as they searched for *whatever*.

"I'm not carrying," Dante said, cringing when those rough hands went places they didn't belong. "I've got nothing on me."

"Can't ever be too careful," Victor said, taking a seat behind an imposing mahogany desk. He motioned for the men to let go of Dante, those hands leaving him at once. "Have a seat. Let's chat."

The hair on the nape of Dante's neck bristled when the doors closed, a lock clicking in place, trapping him in there. The guards remained in the room, blocking the only exit. Dante sat down in a leather chair across from Victor. He remained silent, figuring it best to let the man lead the conversation.

"Tell me," Victor said. "How do you know my granddaughter?"

"I met her at the hospital."

"She was your nurse?"

"Yes."

"And, what, she's still nursing you back to health?"

"She, uh..."

"Look, let's skip the small talk." Victor glanced at his watch. "I have a speech to give in twenty minutes. How about you tell me how long you've been seeing my granddaughter and I'll tell you what we're going to do about that?"

Dante cleared his throat, shifting around in the chair. *Uncomfortable* put it mildly. He felt incredibly small sitting there. "Officially, a few weeks. Unofficially, a few months."

"*Unofficially,*" he said, "meaning not only have you been seeing her in secret, but before you were actually *seeing* her, you were, what? Just screwing around? Is that what you're telling me here?"

"No, I'm not—"

"Because it's bad enough you start seeing her without talking to us," Victor continued, raising his voice. "It's bad enough you don't go to her father and ask him how he feels about you seeing his little girl. But now you're telling me, up until a few weeks ago, she was nothing more than a body you *used* to keep warm?"

Victor slammed his hands down on the desk, the bang making Dante flinch.

This wasn't going good.

"It wasn't like that," Dante said. "She was a friend, and then something happened, things changed, and it turned into more."

"So it just happened, huh?"

"Yes."

"Nothing deliberate on your part? Not something you planned? You just happened to take up with one of ours?"

"Well, yeah." Dante laughed dryly, running his hands down his face. "I fucked up. I know I did. I did everything wrong. But I love her. I fell in love with her. And it had nothing to do with her being a Brazzi. If anything, it was *despite* her being one." His eyes shot straight to Victor. "No offense. I have utmost respect for you, and your family, but this was the *last* thing I needed in my life. I don't need more problems, but Gabriella? The way I feel about her? Let's just say she's worth the trouble to me."

Victor stared at him in silence.

Dante wasn't sure what that meant.

He didn't know Victor Brazzi well enough to judge if his silence meant he was considering being merciful or if the man was too busy envisioning his death to speak.

After a moment, the man glanced at his watch and leaned back in his chair, his posture relaxed, but it did nothing to ease Dante's tension.

"I heard something about you," Victor said, his voice quieter. "Something I didn't like to hear."

"What did you hear?"

"I heard you killed my grandson."

Every muscle inside of Dante seized up.

Victor stared at him again. He stared, and waited. Waited for Dante to find the words to respond. And Dante wished like hell he could deny it. He wished he could say it never happened. For years he hated that family, despising Enzo Barsanti with everything inside of him, but he'd give anything to be able to go back and keep that motherfucker breathing.

The moment Dante pulled the trigger, he regretted it. It was instant, guilt burning from within. Because it was the moment Dante became someone else.

When he became a murderer.

When the man became the monster.

He never expected to feel that way.

Never expected to *regret* killing a Barsanti.

He wished like hell the feeling would go away.

"You heard true."

Victor drummed his fingers against the arm of his chair, pursing his lips. "Why'd you do it?"

"He pulled a gun on me first."

"I didn't ask what *he* did. I know what he did. I asked why you killed him. And don't give me the cop-out answer. Don't say '*self-defense*'. You shot the kid in the face in his own territory."

Dante's eyes fixed on his hands in his lap. This was sounding a bit like that psychoanalytic bullshit he refused to entertain with everyone else. "Because he was a Barsanti."

"Because he was a Barsanti," Victor repeated.

"I've spent almost my entire life wishing them dead because of what they did to my family. It made it easy to give in to the anger, made it easy to go there, made it easy to pull the trigger. So yeah, you can say I killed him because he was a Barsanti."

"I bet your father hailed you a hero for that, huh? His brave boy. Bet he was proud."

Dante looked at the man, seeing he was smiling. *What the fuck?*

"Did you know your father started it? Did he tell you how he woke up one morning and decided to shoot up my grandson's birthday party?"

"Nobody died that day," Dante said. "He just wanted to send a message."

"And that message was received," Victor said. "Barsanti responded. Somebody died. There's no denying that. But just because he caused the first casualty doesn't mean he's responsible for the whole war."

Dante said nothing to that. What could he say?

"You want to hear my opinion?" Victor asked. "You want to know why *I* think you killed Enzo?"

Dante nodded, because that was the only thing he could do.

"You killed him because your father gave you no other choice."

Victor glanced at his watch yet again before standing. "Out of all my grandchildren, Gabriella was always my favorite. She's different. She has a big heart, my little princess. She's out to save the world. When she was knee-high, she found this squirrel once. Ugly thing. *Wounded.* Looked like a dog got a hold of it. She picked it up, brought it home with her. Thought she could help it. Most of my grandchildren were born with brutality in their blood, but Gabriella? She was just so *good*. Which is why I was so surprised to see her with you, but I guess I shouldn't have been. She picked up another wounded animal and brought it home."

Those words were like a punch to the gut. Dante clenched his hands into fists, stopping himself from reacting.

Victor walked around the desk, pausing beside Dante. "She can't save the world, but you know, maybe she can help bring an end to this senseless war. My kids—my daughters, especially— married into a few different families, so if my granddaughter wants to be with a Galante, I'll welcome one in. Call it a clean slate for the New Year. *Merry Christmas*, Dante."

"Thank you," Dante said.

"But you better treat her right," Victor said. "Because that squirrel she brought home? It bit her, you know. It got scared, and it bit her, so I snapped it's fucking neck, because *no one* and *nothing* hurts my family. Remember that."

* * *

Music played through the ballroom from the small orchestra. Tables took up a significant portion of the vast room, while the wedding party was propped up on a stage near the front, along a wall of spacious windows, soft sunlight streaming in on them, making the bride glow. The rest of the space was made up of a dance floor, empty at the moment, as everyone ate.

Gabriella pushed the food around on her plate, not taking any bites of the veal they'd forced upon her. The plate beside hers remained untouched, growing cold, the chair empty. Her *plus-one*.

Across from her sat her parents, also not eating. No, they were too busy staring. Staring at *her*, although neither had spoken a single word since she'd plopped down at the table. Their silence, though, said enough.

They were surprised, also not of the *pleasant* variety.

How long had it been? Ten minutes? A friggin *year*? She was growing antsy, tapping her foot, eyes scanning the room at the dozens—maybe hundreds—of faces, some of them familiar but none of them the one she hoped to see.

They wouldn't actually kill him, would they?

She grew impatient, about to go hunt Dante down, when she caught sight of her grandfather. Victor strolled into the room, smiling wide, his typical chipper self. He headed to the front of the ballroom and picked up a microphone.

Gabriella studied him, searching for some clue about what might've gone down, and startled when the chair beside her moved. She jumped, coming face-to-face with Dante.

He'd aged ten years in the blink of an eye. His suit was unkempt, the tie barely knotted. But the rest of him... well, he wasn't bleeding. There was no bruising that she could see, so he wasn't *physically* wounded. They'd just torn apart his soul, it seemed.

The moment his rear end hit the seat, Gabriella's father dropped his fork, the metal clanking against the plate as he gave up the pretense of attempting to eat.

Gabriella cringed.

"I'd like a word," Alfie said, finding his voice. "*Now.*"

Dante stood back up.

"Wait," Gabriella interjected.

Dante placed his hand on her shoulder, rubbing it. "It's fine."

Alfie stalked through the ballroom, heading for the door, as Dante followed. Gabriella watched them as they stopped outside, well out of earshot but still within view. Right away, Alfie laid into him, going on and on, while Dante just stood there, listening.

In the ballroom, Victor spoke, giving some speech about love and loyalty, but Gabriella wasn't paying attention. *Ugh, what the heck is my father saying?* She started to stand up, to go out there, her father's expression murderous as he got right in Dante's face, spewing words Gabriella suspected she didn't even have in her vocabulary, when a hand darted across the table, catching her wrist.

"Don't dare, Gabriella Michele!" Her mother glared at her from across the table. "What are you *thinking*?"

Gabriella turned as she was forced back into her chair, looking at her mother. Victoria looked quite a bit like her father, those Brazzi genes strong. *She also inherited the notorious temper.*

"I don't know," Gabriella said. "Maybe that you guys are overreacting like I knew you would."

"Overreacting?" Victoria raised her eyebrows, still gripping her wrist, manicured fingernails pressing into the skin. "*Overreacting,* Gabriella? Do you know who that boy is?"

"Of course I know who he is."

"He's a Galante."

"So?" Gabriella pulled on her arm, but her mother wasn't letting go, acting like a leash tethering her there. "I mean, okay, I get it, but I don't know why you're so upset about it."

"He's a *Galante*," she repeated.

"I know he is, Mom. But Aunt Savina married a Barsanti. Aunt Lena married an Amaro. Heck, *you* married a Russo."

"That's different."

"How?"

"We were *idiots*," Victoria said, that answer making Gabriella laugh, despite the circumstances. "I raised you to be so much smarter than this. We were lovesick young girls, marrying men we hardly knew. And you, Oh God, you... don't tell me you're thinking about *marrying* that boy!"

"What? No!" Gabriella scrunched up her nose, yanking her arm free. "We're not, I mean... ugh, it's *way* too soon to be breaking out that word."

"But some day? Is that what you're telling me? You might someday think about marrying him? A *Galante*?"

"Maybe. Ugh, I don't know! I don't even want to think about that right now. I'm a little busy trying to survive *this* wedding to be planning my own. We're just dating."

"Dating?"

"Yeah," Gabriella said, knowing she was underplaying it. The guy had already moved into her apartment. "I like him."

"You *like* him?"

She smiled. "I *more* than like him, Mom."

Victoria covered her face with her hands, shaking her head. "He's going to break your heart."

Gabriella's eyes shifted back out the ballroom, at Dante, as he still stood there, taking the verbal lashing in stride. "I know he is."

"That's it!" Victoria dramatically threw her hands up, disrupting people around them. "It's official. You inherited it."

"What?"

"The idiot gene."

Gabriella laughed again, a bit of relief washing through her as her grandfather's speech ended, the orchestra again playing as the bride and groom moved to the dance floor. Alfie walked back into the ballroom, his expression softening more with each step, his anger melted by the time he reached the table.

Dante followed, another ten years gone from his life.

"Dance with me, woman," Alfie said, holding his hand out to Victoria. "Make me the luckiest man in the room all over again."

Victoria rolled her eyes but took his hand, the two of them setting off for the dance floor, gone by the time Dante made it to the table.

He slid down into his seat, sighing.

"What did he say to you?" Gabriella asked.

"The same thing your grandfather said."

"Which was...?"

"When I break your heart, they're going to rip mine right out of my chest."

"Wow," she whispered.

"Wow," he agreed, grazing his fingertips along her cheek before running them down her neck, right to her chest. He pressed his palm flat against it over her heart. "Guess I need to be careful with this thing."

"Guess so, unless you don't need *your* heart anymore."

"What heart?"

"This one." Gabriella pressed her palm against his chest. "It's still in there."

"You sure about that?"

"Positive," she said. "In case you forgot, I spent weeks listening to it. I heard it every day. So yeah, it's still in there. I know it is."

Dante leaned over to kiss her. Gabriella's eyes fluttered closed, tingles engulfing her at the public display of affection, right there in front of all of those eyes, so many of them suspiciously watching him. She got lost in it, just enjoying it, when a chair pulled out at their table, scraping against the floor. "Fools."

Dante pulled away with a sigh. Gabriella scowled, not having to open her eyes to know who it was.

Gavin.

"And here I actually thought I might go a whole day without hearing that voice," Dante said.

"For the record," Gavin said, "you're not the only one who gets tired of hearing shit. You know what *I'm* tired of hearing? Your name. My father asked me to come here, you know, to represent the Amaros, since he works so early in the mornings and didn't want to make the trip out, so I said, sure, why not? I figured a wedding in Jersey would be a safe zone, a chance for me to get away from the stress hearing your name causes me, but nope. Dante Galante walks in, and it's all I hear. *Dante, Dante, Dante...*"

"I happen to like hearing that name," Gabriella chimed in.

"You would," Gavin said. "It's mostly your fault I hear it."

She smiled. "You're welcome."

"Seriously, though," Gavin said, looking between them. "Did it never cross either of your minds that this might not be the ideal time and place for your coming out party?"

"It crossed my mind," Dante said, "but I kind of figured there was no ideal time or place, so go big or go home, right?"

"*Wrong*," Gavin said, pointing at Dante. "When you go big, you don't *get* to go home. When you go big, you end up tortured in basements."

Dante's cheek twitched. "I went home."

"That time," he said, "but you're running out of lives, pussy-cat. You wasted the first eight. Playing fast and loose with number nine isn't smart."

Dante's eyes narrowed, and he started to counter that, when Gabriella laughed. "You two argue like an old married couple."

Gavin shot her a look, while Dante scoffed. "He wishes we were."

"Fuck you." Gavin flipped his middle finger at Dante before glancing at Gabriella, who again laughed. "You know what? Fuck you, too. Fuck *both* of you."

"Not interested," Dante said. "I told you I had a girlfriend."

"He does," Gabriella said, grinning.

"You," Gavin said, pointing at Gabriella. "You need your head checked. And you…" He pointed at Dante as he stood up. "I can't wait until somebody *finally* gets the balls to shoot you, because you know what I'm going to do when that happens?"

"Cry?"

"Laugh," he said. "I'm going to stand back and laugh, because your dumb ass will *deserve* it."

Gavin walked away, shaking his head.

"Is it sad that I think that jackass might be my best friend?" Dante asked, turning to Gabriella.

That declaration surprised her. "Really?"

He nodded. "These days, well, Gavin's pretty much the only one I trust… except for you."

Guilt. Gabriella never thought of it as a tangible sensation, but she felt it swelling like a wave, threatening to break and crash into her. "You trust him? You trust *me*?"

Dante's brow furrowed. "Why wouldn't I trust you?"

"You said you didn't trust anybody," she said. "You said you could only depend on yourself."

"Yeah, well, I said a lot of shit," Dante said. "I was angry. I'm *still* angry. But if I've learned anything, it's that maybe I just trusted the wrong ones."

Gabriella frowned. The two people he let himself trust were keeping a secret from him. A life-altering kind of secret. It was lying by omission, as far as she was concerned, and she was tired of lying. Would she ever be able to stop?

"Anyway." Dante motioned to the dance floor. "Did you want to dance?"

"Dance? To Beethoven? *How?*"

"Looks like you kind of just spin in circles."

She grimaced. "I'd rather just go home. I think we've been here long enough."

"Are we *allowed* to leave?"

"I'm grown. I don't need permission."

"Says the woman who didn't want to come in the first place but had to because her mother said so."

Gabriella scowled, close to taking a move out of Gavin's play-book by flipping him off for that. "Come on, let's make our escape while they're preoccupied."

Dante stood, and Gabriella took his hand, spinning around to head for the exit, when she almost smacked into somebody walking by. *Seriously?* Dante yanked on her hand, pulling her to him so hard she stumbled, her back flush against his chest. Everything inside of her froze when she came face-to-face with Bobby.

Whoa.

"Alfie's little girl, right?" he asked, eyes studying her. "Nice to see you again."

"Uh, hello," she said, smiling awkwardly through her panic. This was not how their great escape was supposed to go. "I was just, you know... *psheeeww.*"

It wasn't even a word.

What the heck was coming out of her mouth?

He nodded, like he understood, and stepped aside for her to pass. She kept a grip on Dante's hand, pleading with the universe under her breath. "*Please don't do it. Please don't do it. Please—*"

"Barsanti."

Gabriella closed her eyes at the sound of Dante's voice, sighing the rest of the words. "—*don't do it.*"

Why did he have to acknowledge him?

"Galante," Bobby responded. "I see you're well."

"Still breathing," Dante said. "My heart is still beating, too."

"Your heart? Wasn't aware you ever had one. Congratulations. Must be a big deal in your family, a Galante that isn't hollow."

Gabriella braced herself, expecting Dante to whip out a snide comment, but instead, he shrugged it off. "Who would've imagined?"

"Certainly not me."

"Yeah, well, if you'll excuse us, you've got to *vroom*, or whatever the hell she said."

"*Psheeeww,*" she mumbled.

Dante pushed against Gabriella, and she was more than happy to start walking again, leading him out of the ballroom, jogging in her high heels to get away. The man with the clipboard stood outside, radioing something into his walkie-talkie the second he spotted Dante.

Letting go of her hand, Dante felt around in his pockets. "Shit."

"What's wrong?"

"Your grandfather practically had me strip-searched. They took the fucking Valet ticket."

"Crap, I'm going to have to go back in."

"Fuck that," Dante said, heading straight to one of the lingering Valet boys. "Hey, do you remember me? You parked my car."

The guy shrugged. "I parked a lot of cars."

"It was the McLaren," Dante said. "12C. Bright blue. Hard to forget."

"Not ringing a bell."

"Can you go look for it?"

"Do you have your ticket?"

"If I had my ticket, do you think I would've bothered describing the fucking thing to you?"

"No ticket, no car."

Gabriella saw the frustration rising up in Dante, his expression hardening. She took a step down, to approach them, to try to calm the situation because it was obviously intentional, when someone stepped out of the house, placing a hand on her shoulder to stall her. "I've got this, sweetheart."

Her father walked past her. "Get Mr. Galante's car, Alonzo. It's parked in the main garage. I'm sure you remember it."

"Yes, sir," the guy said, saluting him before jogging away.

Dante's narrowed eyes trailed the guy.

"Thanks, Daddy," Gabriella mumbled, stepping beside him.

"Don't mention it." Alfie reached over, snatching her into a hug. He pressed a kiss to the top of her head, and she smiled. He smelled like the inside of a car. "I figure, you know, he had enough balls to come here and face us, so the least I can do is let him drive my little girl home when she's ready to go."

"He's good to me, you know."

"He better be."

"He is," she said. "He rubs my feet and makes me macaroni."

Dante shot her a look that made her laugh.

"Well, then," Alfie said. "What more do you need? Other than safety and security, that is."

"He gives me that, too," she said. "Although, I can take care of myself."

"I know you can."

The blue supercar came rolling up to the front of the house. Dante approached it, opening the passenger door and waiting. Alfie walked Gabriella over to the car, letting go of her once they reached it. She climbed in and Dante closed the door, pausing there, turning to her father as the man started to leave. "Mr. Russo."

Alfie stalled.

"A while back, my father figured out that your family harbored Matteo Barsanti, that you let him hide out in your territory."

Alfie stared at him, not apologetic at all. "He was just a child."

"Yeah, well, my father..." Dante looked away, like he was struggling to find words. "He figures if you're not his ally, you must be his enemy. This whole thing was always supposed to be about protecting the people we love, and my father... I don't think there's a person alive that he loves anymore. Nobody but *himself*. But the people *I* love, well..." He glanced back through the window of the car. "He doesn't call them allies anymore."

Alfie stood there, stewing over that, before he asked, "Are you living with him?"

"Not anymore."

"Where are you living?"

"An apartment in Little Italy."

Alfie's eyes narrowed. *Uh-oh.* "You living with my daughter?"

Lie, Gabriella thought, bracing herself as she stared out the car window at them. *Whatever you do, don't tell him the friggin truth.*

"Yes, sir."

Ugh.

Alfie let out a sound, like a strangled growl, as he ran his hands down his face. "You have gotta be fucking kidding me. My daughter let you *move in?*"

Gabriella pressed buttons in the car, tinkering with the knobs on the door, trying to figure out how to put down the window so she could join the conversation.

"Yes, sir," Dante said again.

"I'm telling you right now, if this comes down on her, I'm coming down on *you.*" Alfie pinched the bridge of his nose as he muttered to himself, "Already shacking up. She's trying to give me a fucking heart attack."

Giving up on the window, Gabriella grabbed the door handle, lifting it to push the door open. She protested, demanding she could take care of herself, when Dante reached back, slamming the door shut again and leaning back against it, so she couldn't open it anymore. *Rude.*

"She won't get hurt," Dante said. "I'll make sure of it."

"You better," Alfie said. "Because my Gabby, she's quick to pull the trigger, and I mean that in every way imaginable. She makes decisions in a snap. She jumps in headfirst but doesn't always look at what she's diving into, and that can get her in trouble. *Big* trouble."

"I can hear you guys, you know," she yelled, banging against the window with her fist, but the men ignored her, continuing with their conversation.

"She doesn't scare easily these days," Alfie said, "but she isn't bulletproof. I don't think she realizes that."

"Yes, I do," she grumbled, swinging her legs over the center console, careful not to jab any buttons or kick any knobs, and climbed over onto the driver's side, that door still open.

"So you need to keep that danger *far* away from my daughter. You keep it where it can't touch her. You got me?"

Gabriella jumped out of the car. "I can take care of myself."

"I got you," Dante said, walking around to the other side of the car, his gaze on Gabriella. "Get back in the car."

"Or *what*?"

"Or I guess we stay here."

Oh, ugh, no thanks.

Gabriella got back in the car and climbed over to the passenger side instead of going around. Her father tapped on the window, garnering her attention as she put on her seatbelt. Cautiously, she turned that way, looking him right in the eyes through the tinted glass.

"You and I are going to be having a conversation about this," he said. "Just as soon as I figure out what the hell I'm supposed to do about it."

Ugh. Ugh. Ugh.

Dante didn't waste any time driving away. He relaxed once he was away from Brazzi property, tearing off his tie and wrangling out of his suit coat as he sped through New Jersey, discarding the clothes in the small space behind his seat as he blasted the heat.

"Did you *have* to tell him we were living together?"

"Yes."

"Why?"

"Because he asked."

She scowled. "It's not like he's your boss."

"No, but he is your father," Dante said. "Look, I walked in there today with two strikes already against me. I can't afford a third strike, so if he asks me something, I'm answering. I don't care what it is. If the man wants to know how big my dick is, I'll offer to measure it for him."

"Well, *boo* on that."

Dante laughed but said nothing else, the drive back to Little Italy quiet. Finding no street parking, he pulled the car into a nearby garage, securing it, before the two of them strolled down the sidewalk to the apartment. Gabriella slipped her hand into his, holding it as they walked. His fingertips were ice cold.

"I always loved this neighborhood," Gabriella said, surveying the splattering of red, white, and green all around the buildings. Street vendors opened up shop on the corners where small one-way streets weaved together, merging with bigger traffic, creating a continual flow of people.

"That makes one of us," Dante muttered. "Too much has happened for me to see anything but the bad."

"I know, but you shouldn't blame the whole neighborhood for the acts of two men."

"It was more than two men. A lot of us contributed."

"What did I tell you in the hospital? About playing someone else's game?"

"You have to play by their rules."

"Exactly." Gabriella bumped against him as they stalled in front of the market below the apartment. "You know how my father always wins?"

"How?"

"Sleight of hand."

Dante turned to face her. "Are you suggesting I cheat? What happened to little miss *'gotta play by their rules'* from a second ago?"

"I'm not suggesting you *cheat*," she said. "I'm just suggesting you manipulate the outcome a bit."

"In other words, cheat."

She laughed. "It's another gray area. If you don't get caught, is it really cheating?"

"I don't know," he said. "If I fuck another woman and you don't catch me, did I cheat?"

She flinched at that, a surge of jealousy stirring inside of her. "You better not."

"Wouldn't dream of it."

"Good, because even *dreaming* of it is all kinds of wrong," she said. "Besides, all I'm saying is that when the odds are stacked against you, you should consider maybe changing the odds."

"Easier said than done."

"Nobody said it would be *easy*," she said. "But it just might keep you on top."

"Well, that's a certainly a good position to be in." Dante smiled a bit as he leaned over, kissing her. "Although, you know, I kind of enjoy *you* being on top."

"You're changing the subject."

"I am," he admitted as he kissed her again, whispering against her mouth, "because I'd much rather talk about that."

She kissed him back, wrapping her arms around his neck, barely having enough time to get into it when a loud commotion disrupted them from across the street. Angry shouts echoed through the neighborhood, brash enough to raise alarm over the usual city chaos. Scathing voices hurled insults as people ran, others swarming the area in front of the bar. Gabriella pulled away from Dante, glancing over just in time to see fists flying, a fight spilling out into the street, a guy in a red shirt pummeling somebody.

"Come on, it's cold. Let's go inside," Dante said at once, whipping out his freshly acquired keys and unlocking the door to the building, dragging her inside before she could get a good look at what was happening. He kept his head down, his footsteps hurried.

"I'm guessing you know those guys?"

"Unfortunately."

"Who are they?"

"Barsantis," he said. "Galantes."

"Ah." She eyed him warily as they walked up the stairs. "You sure you don't want to go see what's going on?"

"I know what's going on," he said. "They're beating the fuck out of each other. Nothing new. I can't tell you how many times I've gotten into it with someone in this neighborhood, how many bar fights I've been involved in across the street. Hell, I'm pretty sure I got my ass kicked in front of your building a few months ago."

Dante walked up to the apartment door, unlocking it before motioning for her to go inside. She paused in the doorway, raising her eyebrows, feigning shock. "You got your butt kicked? *You?*"

"Don't go getting excited—the ass-kicking was mutual. It usually is. That's just how it goes. They'll hit each other until they get tired of it, and then they'll go on their way, back to their separate corners, and start plotting the next time they're going to come out swinging. Same shit, different day. Now, will you go in the apartment, or do I have to keeping standing out here in the hall, explaining this to you?"

She didn't budge. "Testy, are we?"

"A bit," he admitted, grasping her hips and forcing her into the apartment since she wasn't moving on her own. He stepped in behind her, relocking the door.

"Understandable, I guess, since it's been a stressful day," she said, following him as he walked to the bedroom, watching as he kicked off his shoes and set them beside the dresser. Even with her stuff strewn about, he made sure his stuff had a proper place, always cleaning up after himself. Sometimes she wondered how *at home* he felt there. He seemed to always be preparing for the worst, still taking it day-by-day, like every morning he woke up expecting to be on his own again. It wasn't that she questioned his feelings for her, no... she questioned his *confidence*. For someone so formidable, Dante certainly thought little of himself, like he wasn't worthy.

It baffled Gabriella, because if time had shown her anything, it was that Dante Galante was a beautiful force of nature.

Dante plopped down on the edge of the bed, sighing. "I had my life threatened by two powerful men today—men who probably won't hesitate to kill me—while I breathed the same air as a man who previously *has* tried to kill me... more than once. And then we get home, and I see the asshole that stabbed me... *more than once...* beating the shit out of a guy I used to consider one of my closest friends. And while I probably should've stepped in, because God knows he's taken a lot of hits for me over the years, I walked away. So I wouldn't call that a *stressful day*. I'd call it a fucked up one."

She frowned. "I didn't know."

"I know you didn't. And I'm sorry for being so touchy. None of this is your fault. I shouldn't take it out on you."

"I can take it."

"You shouldn't have to."

"I don't mind," she said, strolling toward him. "Besides, I might like it, you being so... *rough*."

His eyes shifted to her. "Don't do that."

"Don't do what?" she asked, using her foot to force his legs apart further so she could stand between them. "Don't change the subject like that, you mean?"

"Yes," he said. "I'm trying to apologize and you're fucking with my head."

Gabriella ran her hands through his hair. "That sounds like a good idea."

Dante's brow furrowed, like he was trying to riddle out what she meant, but she didn't give him the chance. She dropped to her knees, unzipping his pants. Dante stared at her in stunned silence as she reached into his boxers and stroked him, getting him rock hard, before taking him into her mouth. The moment her tongue came into contact with his flesh, he let out a groan, his head lolling back as he closed his eyes.

Gabriella sucked as his hands settled on the back of her head. He didn't push her, didn't force her, merely holding onto her as she took him down her throat. It went on for a minute or so, not long at all, before Dante forced her mouth off of him. She looked up, confused, *dejected*, until she noticed his strained expression.

"Do you?" he asked.

"Do I what?"

"Do you like it rough?"

Oh. "Maybe."

"Don't *maybe* me. It's got to be one way or the other. True or false, Gabriella."

"Well, then... true."

"Seriously?"

"Yes."

"Why didn't you tell me?"

"I don't know."

"You should've told me."

She looked from him down to his lap. "Did you really stop me so we could talk? We're seriously going to talk while I'm, like... holding it?"

"You're not fucking with me, are you?" he asked, ignoring her question. "You're not just telling me what you think I want to hear?"

"Of course not."

Before Gabriella could say another word, Dante pulled her completely off of him, nearly knocking her down as he stalked out of the bedroom. *What the freak?*

"Where are you going?" she called after him.

"Hold on," he yelled. "Don't move."

She ignored that, standing up to follow him.

Dante stepped out of the bathroom, eyebrows raised. "Didn't I just tell you to not move?"

"My *boyfriend*," she said, pointing at him. "Not my boss."

He held up a condom. "Had to get one of these."

"Oh."

"Because, you see," he said, stepping to her, not stopping, backing her up into the bedroom again. "I've been dying to fuck you senseless—that back-breaking, heart-stopping, pussy-aching kind of fucking that makes you forget how to speak, how to think, how to *breathe*..."

"Oh," she said again, this time breathless, heat rushing through her, flushing her cheeks and pooling in her gut, an ache stirring up. "You want to...?"

"I've been taking it easy," he said, "and if you're telling me I don't have to, that I can fuck you the way I've been yearning to fuck you, then you're goddamn right I *want* to."

The back of her legs hit the edge of the bed. He stood right in front of her, eye-level while still in her heels.

"I can take it," she whispered. "If you can dish it."

The second those words were from her lips, Dante grabbed her, dragging her onto the bed. Gone was the soft grip, the slowly tracing fingertips, the gentle lips, replaced by strong hands and a rough kiss. She'd seen little glimpses of his passion all along, but he'd kept it locked up for the most part. Maybe he hadn't wanted to scare her. Maybe he'd been afraid to hurt her. But she wasn't afraid, and unless the ache between her thighs counted, she wasn't in agony, either.

This was the Dante that faced death and survived, the Dante that had been tortured and persevered. The Dante that fought, that endured. The Dante that never buckled, no matter what.

She longed for that Dante.

She longed for *all* of him.

Dante flipped her over onto her stomach, the condom wrapper crinkling as he ripped it open, rolling it on. An arm snaked beneath her, snatching her hips up off the bed as he shoved her dress up.

"Fuck." His voice was a strained whisper as his hand ran over her bare cheek, roughly squeezing it. "I forgot you weren't wearing underwear."

Tingles coursed through Gabriella, rippling down her spine as she arched her back, letting out a soft moan when he pushed inside of her. He gripped onto her, holding her in place as he slid in and out, moving excruciatingly slow, pausing with just the tip touching before pushing back in. Over and over, again and again, until she *was* in agony, until she squirmed, desperate for more, on the verge of begging. "What are you *doing?*"

"Watching."

"Watching what?"

"Myself disappearing inside of that gorgeous pussy."

"Can you watch yourself do it a little harder?"

"I could."

He kept his tormenting pace—if anything, moving slower, lingering longer before pushing back in. She tried to shove back against him but he kept his grip on her, controlling the pace. "Dante..."

"Tell me what you want, baby."

"You," she said. "*More* of you."

"You've already got all of me."

"Ugh, please," she whined. "Harder. Faster. You're supposed to be, *ugh...*"

"Fucking you? Is that what you mean?"

"Yes!"

"Tell me you want me to fuck you and I will."

"I want you to."

"Want me to *what?*"

She realized what he was doing, what he was trying to get her to say. He pulled out, pausing again, toying with her. She could even hear the amusement in his voice, the light laughter in his words, as he teased her.

Two can play that game.

"I swear, Dante Galante, if you don't give it to me like I want, I'll go find someone else who—*uh!*"

He drove into her so hard it knocked the words out of her, the air leaving her lungs in a gasp, his grip so hard she was sure he'd leave fingerprint bruises along her skin.

Before Gabriella could get her bearings, Dante started pounding into her, not letting up, each thrust harder... faster... deeper. He let go of her long enough to gather her hair, to sweep the waves back, wrapping them around one of his hands, fisting and tugging, pulling her head back, not enough to hurt but enough that she had no choice but to comply. Her back arched further, his free arm snaking beneath her, again pinning her hips in place against him as he slammed into her from behind. "This what you wanted?"

"Oh God," she gasped. "Yes."

"*Wrong*," he growled, a harsh edge to that word that made Gabriella shiver. "If you can still talk, I'm not fucking you hard enough."

She didn't think it possible, but he increased his pace, his touch rougher against her skin. His hand slipped down, fingers rubbing her clit, as his other hand pulled on her hair, tilting her head to the side as he leaned over her. Her eyes fluttered closed, cries escaping her throat, louder every time he filled her.

"Open your eyes," he said. "I want you to look at me, so you remember it's *me* fucking you, since you seem to think you need to go out and find someone else to give you what you want."

She blinked rapidly, trying to clear her vision. Her eyes watered, the sensations flowing through her intense. She held his gaze, his stare penetrating, burning through her, igniting a fire deep down.

"You okay?" he asked, his voice low.

She nodded, whispering, "Yes."

A smile tugged the corner of his mouth as he leaned further forward, kissing her hard, teeth nipping at her bottom lip before he said, "That sounded like another word to me."

Dante let go of her hair, the locks unraveling from his fist, falling around her shoulders, as his hand gripped the back of her neck, shoving her chest down against the bed, her face against the pillow. He hiked her bottom half up higher, shifting position, pinning her against the mattress. The first time he thrust, she let out a shriek so loud it stung her throat. Burying her face in the pillow, trying to muffle her own sounds, she fisted the sheets as he beautifully brutalized her body, destroying and rebuilding every inch of her with his touch, with his thrusts.

Orgasm erupted inside of her, her body convulsing, as the sound of skin slapping echoed around them. Dante cursed under his breath, his pace slipping momentarily. "Feel good?"

She could do nothing but squeal, letting out incoherent noises, as the ripples of pleasure wove through her. Dante laughed, thrusting a few more times before grunting, slamming into her as he let loose.

Gabriella slid down flat against the bed when he pulled out. The muscles in her thighs twitched, the spot between them throbbing, aching from the battering. The bed shifted, Dante disappearing.

She rolled over onto her back and stared up at the bland white ceiling, colored splotches marring her vision whenever she blinked. Dante returned, his pants unbuckled, barely hanging on. He smirked as he undid his white button down. "You look thoroughly fucked, baby."

She propped up on her elbows. Her dress was still hiked up, probably flashing him all the goods, but she couldn't find it in her to care. He'd seen every inch of it up close and personal on more than one occasion. "I feel that way."

Best Christmas present ever.

He pulled off the shirt, tossing it in the hamper, before letting his pants drop. He kicked them off, also putting them away. Gabriella's eyes scanned him, standing there in his black boxers and white undershirt, a heck of a lot more put together than she felt.

"What do you want to do?" he asked. "It's still early."

The sun was just setting outside, casting long shadows along the room, everything growing dim. They'd agreed not to make a big deal out of the holidays, so they had no plans. Gabriella knew he wasn't ready for all of that, not ready to *celebrate* without his family.

"Sleep," she said. "For like, a week."

"Sleep sounds nice," he said, taking off his watch as he stepped over to the bed, setting it on the stand. Gabriella's eyes trailed him, unabashedly staring at his backside as he faced away from her. She was so lost in a euphoric post-coital haze, thanks to the flood of endorphins, that it took her a moment to realize it when Dante tugged his white undershirt off. As soon as it clicked, Gabriella's eyes glided along the bare skin on his back.

Whoa.

They'd been together for months, technicality of titles aside, and they were living together now, but in all that time, he'd never taken that shirt off in front of her like that. He kept his chest covered, like it had become second nature to him, layering clothing like a second skin, shielding his scars from prying eyes. She never pressed the issue, knowing it made him uncomfortable. He slept with a shirt on.

He had sex with a shirt on. For all she knew, he might even shower with a shirt on. Of course, he changed clothes, sometimes with her in the room, but this was deliberate.

He was leaving himself exposed to her.

Dante sat down on the edge of the bed, glancing over his shoulder at her before scrubbing his hands over his face. *Nervous.*

Her chest ached.

She'd seen them, of course. Nurse Russo saw them every day in the hospital, but he hadn't had a choice then. She'd looked, because she had to, viewing a piece of him without his consent, and she could always tell he felt violated by it. He'd never look her in the eyes when she adjusted wires or listened to his heartbeat, like if he didn't look at her, maybe she wasn't looking at him, either.

"I got stabbed by a pencil when I was thirteen," Gabriella said, sitting up. "I fell asleep doing homework and got woken up by a sharp sting. Pencil was literally sticking out of my thigh. That's how I got this weird gray dot."

She pointed at the small mark on her outer left thigh.

"And I had my appendix removed the summer before I started high school, which is where *this* came from." She yanked off her dress and tossed it aside, sitting there in only her bra. She sucked in her stomach, trying to get a better view of the two-inch scar on her side. "The whole low-rise jeans and half-shirt combo was hot back then, so everyone saw it. I used to tell people I got stabbed in a fight, because it sounded much cooler than appendicitis, although in hindsight, wow... people actually believed that."

She laughed, chancing a peek at Dante, before continuing.

"Of course, there's also the stretch marks, like on my boobs, courtesy of puberty. I went from nothing to C-cups overnight." She palmed her breasts, catching sight of the small scar between her thumb and pointer finger. "Oh! And this one on my hand—a squirrel bit me. It's kind of a funny story..."

"You don't have to do this," Dante said. "Don't pick yourself apart. That's the *last* thing I want."

"I'm not picking myself apart," she said. "They're stories. That's what scars are. Some are full of self-depreciating humor. Some are medical dramas. Some are Young Adult novels. And then some... well, some are tragic. Like, Nicholas Sparks meets Shakespeare on the

Titanic-level tragic. But something I've come to realize, working where I do, is that having scars means you survived. Scars mean you're alive. Patients come into the hospital all the time with wounds that never get the chance to become scars, and that sucks. The people who do walk away with scars... well, they're the lucky ones."

Dante sat in silence as the room grew darker, the sun disappearing outside. Eventually, he shifted to face her. Gabriella held his gaze before slowly, her eyes drifted down to his chest. Scar tissue covered it in patches, some thicker than others. He'd had multiple extensive surgeries over the years, skin grafts to correct the damage and plastic surgery to hide the evidence, but nothing could erase all signs of his burns.

Reaching over, she ran her fingertips along the rough, rigid skin, not at all surprised when he stared at nothing to avoid seeing her face.

"I love you, Dante."

He looked back at her when she said that. It was the first time she'd said those words to his face, with him awake to hear them. Without responding, he pulled her to him as he climbed into the bed. Gabriella settled into his arms, her hand resting on his bare stomach, stroking the small trail of hair around his belly button. Nuzzling against him, she pressed a kiss to his warm chest.

"I love you, too, Gabriella. More than *anything*."

CHAPTER 18

"Dante..."

The room was pitch black, the kind of darkness you could feel, thick enough to overshadow the cloudy haze in the air. It swaddled Dante, infiltrating his lungs when he inhaled, breathing in the impurities. He stood in the middle of it, a safe house, empty except for a scarce scattering of furniture.

"Dante, please..."

Dante's back grew rigid at the sound of the feminine voice. He *knew* the voice. It surrounded him, soothing him, while somehow also setting off an alarm in his mind.

This isn't right.

"Dante, *look...*"

He turned, his blood freezing, sludge clogging his veins when those icy blue eyes met him through the darkness. He blinked. Still there. Blinked again. Still there. His forehead creased as those eyes held his gaze. "Genna?"

She stepped closer at the sound of her name, out of the shadows and into the haze, a sliver of moonlight coming from a nearby window catching her. The light glowed around her, and Dante's heart nearly stopped. Months had passed in the haze, a haze where he tried to not think about what might've happened to his sister.

She looked *exactly* the same.

"Genna," he whispered, tears stinging his eyes as he yanked her into his arms. "I've missed you."

"Dante," the panicked voice gasped in his ear, desperation clinging to every syllable. "It's on *fire*."

Fire. The word was like a command, a trigger in his brain. The second it registered, he felt the explosion of heat, flash fire blasting through the room and igniting everything. The ground quaked. He winced as pain rushed through his body, flames lapping at his skin. He guarded his sister, knocking her down, covering her with his body, a human shield from the fire, but he wasn't enough to keep her from harm. He was nothing but flesh and bone, muscle and scar tissue, thin skin and frail organs. He was no match for an angry blaze, one determined to consume everything around it.

A scream pierced his ears as his body shook. "Dante!"

His eyes shot open, the fire around him extinguishing at once, smothered by the thick darkness and leaving only the haze. He blinked, coated in sweat, panting as he tried to catch his breath. Another pair of eyes watched him—dark, concerned eyes.

Gabriella stood beside the bed, frightened.

"What's wrong?" he asked, forcing himself up, still groggy.

"It's on fire," she said, her voice trembling.

Dante's back straightened, his expression falling at those words, as he braced himself for a blast of pain that didn't come. *It's not a fucking dream*, he had to remind himself. *Not now. Not anymore.*

"What's on fire?" He looked around the room, not smelling any smoke. "What are you talking about? Come here."

He reached for her, having the desperate urge to hold her, to pull her into his arms and feel her breathing, but she resisted, waving toward the window. "I'm serious, Dante. Something is on fire!"

Dante stalked over, dragging Gabriella with him. Thick black smoke touched the night sky, orange glow lighting up part of the neighborhood.

"People were yelling," she said. "I don't know what happened, but it was loud enough to wake me. There were a bunch of bangs and I thought those guys were out there fighting again, but then it just *exploded*."

"It exploded?"

"The ground shook, and then something went *whoosh*. I don't know if it's a car or a building, but something's burning."

His stomach sank. She was right. Something *was* burning. And in this neighborhood? It likely wasn't accidental.

Hell doesn't burn unless the devil lets it.

Dante snatched up some clothes and pulled them on, not bothering with any socks before shoving his feet into a pair of shoes.

"Stay here, okay? Lock up the apartment behind me."

"Why?" she asked, following him out of the bedroom. "Where are you going?"

"I'm going to check things out."

"But—"

He kissed her before she could protest any more and ran out the door.

"Be careful!" she shouted.

Dante scaled the stairs, bursting out into the cold night. Four, maybe five in the morning, he gathered. Dante kept his head down as he hurried down the block, jogging across the street to the corner, his breath surrounding him in an icy cloud.

Flames spilled out the front of a building, shattered glass covering the sidewalk in front of it, mixed with glints of metal. As soon as Dante laid eyes on the place, he knew what was burning.

Casato.

People gathered around outside, shouting, pacing the street, nobody daring get too close to the fire. Dante sprinted to it, forcing his way through the crowd.

"Is everyone okay?" he called out. "Anyone hurt?"

"Don't know," a guy said, eyeing him warily. "If anyone's in there, well, hell, they're already dead. No point looking."

No point. Dante shoved the guy, not liking that answer, and went straight for Casato. The café door stood propped open, how Johnny Amaro kept it. Symbolic, he'd told Genna once. His doors were always open to everyone.

Fuck.

Dante's eyes darted around, hoping the man got out, but he knew better. The glints of metal mixed with the glass caught his eye. Shell casings. Someone had lit up the place with gunfire.

"Call 911!" he yelled.

"Already did," someone said.

"Well, fucking call them *again!*"

He edged closer the doorway, trying to get a good look inside, but the air was too hazy, already stinging his eyes.

"Jesus *fuck*," he whispered, grabbing his shirt and pulling the collar up, covering his nose and mouth. "Don't let *this* be the time I die."

He couldn't think about it, wouldn't chicken out, even though just the thought of fire made him want to pass the fuck out. Taking a deep breath, holding it, he burst through the doorway, dodging the flames edging the doorframe. He had maybe a minute, two at most, before he needed to get back out or he'd risk never making it out at all.

"Amaro!" he shouted, his eyes watering as he searched the smoky haze. "If you can hear me, make a noise or something!"

Dante rounded the counter, heading for the back, and slipped on something in his path. *Blood.* He grabbed ahold of the counter-top to catch himself, pain ripping through his forearm when it hit a patch of flames. Yanking his arm away, hissing, he caught sight of a pair of black dress shoes. Johnny Amaro lay on the floor, bleeding from the chest.

"Amaro!" Dante shouted, choking on the name. His chest burned, lungs begging for more oxygen. Kneeling down, he shook the man, trying to get his attention, trying to force him awake. "Wake up. We need to get out of here."

Johnny stirred, his eyes cracking open, his voice hoarse as he whispered something Dante couldn't understand.

Dante's head pounded in rhythm with his frantic heartbeat, and fuck, his arm *throbbed*. "We have to go. Can you—?" A coughing fit hit Dante, and he managed to get control of himself just as Johnny's eyes closed again. "Oh fuck no, none of that."

Dante grabbed Johnny, using every bit of adrenaline he had to pull him to his feet. Johnny was heavy, and Dante was growing weak, but he managed to drag him through the cafe, the man having just enough strength left in him to stagger. Dante lugged him outside, dropping him to the sidewalk in front of the burning building.

Dante tore off his shirt, yanking it over his head, and balled it up, pressing it hard against Johnny's chest. They needed to stop the bleeding if the man stood a chance. The crowd still swarmed, people shouting, red and blue lights flashing down the block, fast approaching.

For the first time in his life, Dante was *grateful* to hear sirens.

Johnny opened his eyes, wheezing. "Dante?"

"Yeah," Dante said. "Just relax, help is on the way."

Johnny's mouth moved, like he had something more to say, but a coughing fit hit him. He hacked, his eyes watering, blood streaming along his lips, managing to vocalize just a single word: "Sorry."

Dante scanned the area as the first responders arrived, having no desire to take some deathbed confession, not wanting to witness the man's last breath. As long as he fought, he'd survive. Police cars, ambulances, and fire trucks surrounded them. Others took over, and Dante felt like he could take a deep breath again when medics assessed Johnny, giving him the help he needed.

Dante moved out of their way, glancing down the street, catching sight of someone watching from the outskirts of the crowd, standing alone and dressed in all black. *Umberto.* The moment that Dante caught his eye, Umberto took a few leisurely steps back before turning away. *Son of a bitch.*

Dante started to go after him, feet moving on their own, but an officer intercepted him along the barrier they'd put up. "Whoa, whoa, where are *you* going?"

"There's somewhere I need to be."

"You're right," the officer said, "and that somewhere is over there with a medic. You're injured."

"I'm fine," Dante said. "I need—"

He couldn't finish before dissolving into another coughing fit, his face turning red as his lungs struggled, overwhelmed by smoke. Oxygen. He needed fucking *oxygen.* Doubling over, hands on his knees, he fought to catch his breath.

Medics were on him, leading him to an awaiting ambulance, the back of it wide open. He sat down on the bumper, not fighting them when they forced the oxygen mask over his face. He inhaled deeply, taking it in, as they checked his vitals, covering him with a thermal blanket when he shivered.

"Mr. Galante," a voice chimed in. "Fancy seeing you here."

Dante pulled the mask away, glaring at the redheaded monstrosity in front of him. "Detective Dick, didn't know fires were your jurisdiction."

"They're not, but certain names spark automatic calls to the division. You know how it is."

Yeah, Dante knew. Even a ticket for public intoxication would send the detective straight to him. A fire at a place owned by an

Amaro would be enough for the snakes to slither in.

"Look, I know nothing, so don't waste your breath asking questions. I saw the fire from the apartment window so I came down."

"Wrong place, wrong time?"

"Considering the circumstances, I'd say my timing was perfect."

"True." The detective watched as they loaded Johnny Amaro into the back of an ambulance, lights flashing and sirens wailing as it sped off. "And you saw the fire from an apartment window? Which apartment?"

"I don't think that's any of your goddamn business."

"It is," he said, "if that's part of your alibi."

"My alibi? You think *I* did this?" Dante coughed. "Are you fucking stupid?"

"There's no need to speak that way."

"I just pulled a bleeding man from a burning building, I've got soot in my goddamn lungs, and you're suggesting *I* might've been the one to cause it? That I might've shot him and set fire to the place? That's the *definition* of fucking stupid."

His eyebrows rose. "How do you know he was shot?"

"There are expended shells on the sidewalk. He had a hole in his chest. Seriously, Detective, do I have to do your fucking job for you? It doesn't take a genius to put those pieces together. Maybe if you were better at investigating, this shit wouldn't keep happening around here."

Dante slipped the oxygen mask back on, done with that conversation. He shouldn't have entertained it to begin with. He closed his eyes and lowering his head, trying to fucking *breathe*, until his name was shouted from down the street. "Dante!"

Gabriella ran right for him, wearing a t-shirt and tiny shorts with no shoes on, her bare feet slapping against the frozen pavement. She skirted around the barrier, slipping under the yellow caution tape. Officers tried to stop her, shouting for her to get back, but she ignored them.

Jesus, she's going to get tased.

Yanking the mask off, Dante tossed it aside and pushed away from the ambulance, heading for her. The officers backed off, letting her continue, and she slammed right into him, wrapping her arms around him, nearly knocking him on his ass. He winced, staggering, stroking her hair. She was *shaking*. "I told you to stay in the apartment."

"And I told you to be careful!" She pulled away, looking him over, a cloud of breath surrounding her as she damn near hyperventilated. "What happened? Where's your shirt? Why are you *burnt*?"

"Long story," he said. "I'm fine."

As if to accentuate that point, he hacked yet again, grasping his chest, coughing so violently his vision dimmed. It *hurt*.

"You're not fine." Gabriella forced his face up, studying it, before grabbing his arm and lifting. "You're suffering from smoke inhalation, and *this*? This is a second-degree burn. You need to raise it up to keep the swelling down. And you need oxygen."

"I was getting some," he said, motioning to the ambulance, "until you decided to defy law enforcement and burst onto a crime scene."

"A crime scene?" Her eyes darted to the burning building. The firefighters were busy putting the flames out, salvaging whatever might remain. "*Casato*? It wasn't open, right? So nobody was inside, right?" She turned to him, eyes wide. "*Right*?"

"Amaro was there."

"*Which* Amaro?"

"Johnny."

"Oh God." Gabriella grasped her messy hair as she paced in circles, teeth chattering. "Uncle Johnny? Did he…? Is he…?"

Dante lowered his arm. "I pulled him out."

"You *what*? Are you *crazy*?"

"I couldn't just stand around," Dante said, "not knowing he was in there."

"Was he okay?"

"He was alive."

"Did he get burned?"

"A bit, but more concerning is the bullet he took to the chest."

Gabriella stared at him, her mouth agape, tears in her eyes. Dante pulled her back to him, kissing her temple, before leading her past the barrier, away from the chaos, out of the damn cold. She was in too much shock to argue, saying not a word the whole way back to the apartment. Once inside, Dante headed for the bathroom and turned on the cool water, wincing when he put his arm under the spray. He leaned into the counter, his head resting against his shoulder, and closed his eyes as he waited for the searing pain to fade. Gabriella's voice rang through the apartment, on the phone, frantically calling her family.

Five. Ten. Fifteen minutes.

"They're trying to find Gavin," Gabriella said, stepping into the bathroom and turning off the running water. "Nobody has seen him since the wedding. He left around the same time we did, said he had somewhere to be, but he didn't tell anybody where."

Dante opened his eyes and stood up straight as Gabriella shifted seamlessly into Nurse Russo, tending to his burn. His jaw clenched as she rubbed ointment on it, her touch gentle but *son of a bitch* it stung.

"Gavin will resurface," Dante said as soon as the pain subsided enough for him to form words. "He always does."

Gabriella wrapped his arm in gauze. "You don't think he could've been there, too, do you? There's no chance he...?"

"No," Dante said. "He wasn't in there."

"You're sure?"

"If Amaro's son needed rescued, he would've made damn sure it happened."

"How do you know?"

"Because that's the type of father he is."

Gabriella seemed to accept that answer, reaching into her medicine cabinet and pulling out an orange prescription pill bottle, handing it to him. *Vicodin.* "Isn't sharing meds against the rules for you?"

"It's against the rules for everyone, but I've jeopardized my career a bunch already, so what's one more time? Besides, you deserve it, you know... deserve to feel better. You're a hero."

"I'm not a hero, Gabriella."

"You pulled a man out of a burning building," she said, smiling sadly. "Pretty sure that makes you *Superman.*"

* * *

Genna stood in the kitchen, scowling, as cold air trickled out at her from the noisy decrepit freezer. She shifted packages around, her stomach growling. She'd left Matty asleep in bed, since he had the day off of work, figuring she could fend for herself, but man, she'd never gotten better at being domestic.

What the hell to cook?

Pizza—pizza cheesesteak, pizza burger, flatbread pizza—pizza *something*, extra-cheesy with pepperoni, preferably fast. *Why can't I get delivery in the desert?*

Floorboards creaked as she stood there, footsteps on the stairs coming her way. They headed right to the kitchen, like a guardian angel sent to save her from impending starvation.

"Oh Romeo, Romeo, wherefore art the fucking Pizza Rolls, Romeo?" She closed the freezer door, her scowl deepening at the sight of the face in front of her. "Oh, *ugh*, not Romeo."

"And you're no Juliet, Genna with a G."

Gavin Amaro stood there, the epitome of the words *dressed to kill,* wearing a well-tailored black suit and a smirk. "When did *you* get here?"

"Last night, after you two were asleep."

"And what, you just let yourself in?"

"Pretty much," he said. "I'm surprised you didn't see my car or hear me come inside. You're getting complacent."

Genna rolled her eyes, peeking out the window, seeing the black rental car right beside the one he had given to them on his last visit. "What do you want, anyway?"

"Needed to get away for a bit."

"So you come to the desert? The middle of nowhere? *That's* your ideal holiday vacation?"

"Seems to be working for you. Besides, gotta occasionally bless you with my presence so you don't miss me too much."

She scrunched up her nose. "I don't think that'll be a problem, but I guess I can tolerate you for a while as long as you buy me breakfast."

"Buy you breakfast."

"Yep," she said. "But keep your hands to yourself, because I'm a married woman now."

He blinked a few times before pulling a set of keys from his pocket, muttering under his breath, "fucking Galantes."

Her brow furrowed at that, but she shrugged it off when he motioned for her to follow him. "Wait, seriously, you're going to?"

"Why not?" he asked. "Pretty sure there's a rule against denying a pregnant woman food."

Genna slipped on her shoes, trailing him to the door. "Should I wake Matty?"

"No, just let him sleep," Gavin said. "We'll bring him something back."

The two of them climbed in Gavin's rental car, and he drove down the bumpy dirt path leading to the highway.

"What do you want?" he asked. "Pancakes? Waffles?"

"Pizza."

"Where are we going to find pizza at seven o'clock in the morning on fucking *Christmas*?"

"I don't know," she said. "Figure it out, Amaro."

Gavin pulled out onto the highway, aiming the car in the direction of Las Vegas. He sped along, not saying anything, fiddling with the radio trying to get something decent to come in. The further away they got from the house, the more Genna questioned this decision. She'd climbed in the car with him after he showed up out of the blue, never even hesitating. *Ugh, maybe I am complacent.*

"You're not kidnapping me, right?" she asked. "Because Matty might be mad about that."

"Not a chance," Gavin said. "Even if I *wanted* to, I'm pretty sure you'd annoy me so much I'd just take you right back."

"Or kill me," she said, clarifying when he shot her a look. "Not that I'm suggesting it. I'm just saying… you're not gonna kill me, right?"

"I'm going to buy you pizza for breakfast," he said, "and then I'm going to drive you home, so that you can continue living and bring your whatever-it-is baby into this world. What is it, anyway? Boy? Girl?"

"One of those."

"Shouldn't you know by now? What are you, eight months?"

"Almost seven, and yeah, but I didn't want to know what it was yet. It's a surprise."

"What the hell? Wasn't getting *knocked up* surprise enough?"

She laughed. "Well, that was more shocking of the terrifying variety, but this is an exciting kind of surprise. Matty knows, though, so if you actually care and aren't just asking because you don't know what else to say to me, I'm sure he'd be happy to tell you."

"I do care."

"Do you?"

"Yeah, it would be nice to know if I'm having a niece or a nephew."

She eyed him. "You know this baby is more like your second cousin, right? I mean, I know you Amaro-Barsanti-Brazzi guys got your family trees all tangled up, but nowhere in that crazy ass mess does that make you my kid's uncle."

"Ah, I like to think I'm an honorary uncle."

"There's nothing *honorary* about you."

He laughed.

A few minutes before eight, they found a pizzeria in the heart of Las Vegas with a fluorescent '*open*' sign flashing in the window. Gavin parked in a small adjacent lot and the two of them went inside.

"What do you want on your pizza?" he asked. "Some weird pineapple artichoke broccoli combo? Is that what you pregnant chicks get down with?"

She grimaced. "Call me a *chick* one more time, and I'm revoking even the second cousin title. And gross. *No.* I want pepperoni."

"Pepperoni," he repeated as he stepped up to the counter to order.

"And pickles," she called out, finding a small table to sit down at.

He glowered, ordering a large pepperoni with pickles, before joining her. After the pizza came out, Genna tore into it, while Gavin plucked the pickles off a piece to take a bite.

"This is what I miss about New York," she said. "Good pizza."

"That's what you miss?"

"Yep."

"Nothing else?"

"Well, I mean, I miss other stuff, and what I *really* miss is nothing I can ever have back," she said. "I used to think living there was isolating, since my dad micromanaged my life, but I at least had my brother. I took that for granted, because now I know what isolation *really* is. It's weird without him, without having him to talk to."

Gavin stared at her, ignoring his pizza.

"I mean, don't get me wrong," she said. "I have Matty, and I love him. I *desperately* love him. And I'm happy building a life with him, having a family with him, but this baby will never know *my* life. It'll never have an uncle that's not *honorary*."

Gavin didn't respond. Genna didn't expect him to. For all she knew, he wasn't even listening. She finished scarfing down her pizza, boxing up the rest.

It was half-past nine when they made it back to the house to find Matty pacing, a nervous wreck. He burst out onto the porch wearing only a pair of boxers, hair sticking up all over the place, desperately needing a shave.

"Whoa, buddy." Gavin let out a low whistle. "You're about a banjo away from *Deliverance* here."

Genna laughed, glancing at Gavin. "I think I've told him that before."

"That makes two votes for Matty-B taking a damn razor to that mess he's calling his face these days."

"I woke up to an empty house," Matty said, ignoring them. "I woke up to my pregnant wife missing, the car still in the yard, and her phone still in the house. I woke up not knowing where the hell she could've gone. I damn near called the police until I remembered *that* was out of the question."

"We went for food," Genna said, carrying the pizza box as she stepped onto the porch. "Figured we'd be back before you woke up."

"You should've left me a note," Matty said, pulling her to him. "Just leave me a damn note next time so I don't think you've been kidnapped."

"See," Genna said. "Told you he'd be mad if you kidnapped me."

"Good thing that'll never happen," Gavin said. "Don't want to upset your baby daddy."

"Ugh, see, that's it," Genna said. "Just when I think maybe I can grow to tolerate you, you throw out a word like that."

She headed inside, leaving the men out on the porch. After putting the leftover pizza in the refrigerator, she settled into the living room, turning on the television to the one channel that got reception. *Cartoons.* Matty and Gavin joined her after a bit, Matty plopping down beside her on the couch, still wearing just his boxers.

"Are you not putting any clothes on today?" she asked, eyeing him.

"Wasn't planning on it," he admitted.

Her gaze shifted to Gavin, who lingered right inside the room, watching them with a goofy grin. "He told you what we're having, didn't he?"

Gavin nodded, straightening out his expression. "Do you have a phone I can use?"

"What's wrong with yours?" Matty asked.

"Nothing, but seeing as I'm here, in what's pretty much your *safe house*, I'm not going to risk turning it on and having it ping my location, but I ought to check my messages."

"Good point," Matty said. "Didn't think about that."

"Complacent," Gavin said.

"My phone's in the foyer, on the stand by the front door," Genna said. "It's kind of ancient, but you can use it."

Gavin nodded his thanks, disappearing from the room. Genna leaned over, curling up against Matty. After a few minutes, a noise rang out from the foyer, a rush of footsteps followed by an engine starting.

Genna and Matty shared a look before she got up, walking that direction, finding her phone on the stand beside a small gift bag with a red bow on the side of it. She glanced out in just enough time to see Gavin's taillights as he sped out onto the highway, dust flying. *Weird.*

She walked back to the living room, carrying the present. "Gavin left."

"Without saying goodbye? Did he even say what he came for?"

"He said he needed to get away for a bit," she said, shrugging as she sat back down, shaking the gift bag in Matty's face. "I think he left us a present, though."

Matty took it from her, looking inside, and froze. "Huh."

"What is it?" Genna asked, snatching it back, digging through the bag. She pulled something out, holding it up, her insides twisting, her heart aching in her chest. A tiny white baby onesie, *I love my uncle* written on it with a red heart.

CHAPTER 18

There was a certain unwritten rule in the business that was supposed to be non-negotiable, a rule that even the most rebellious mobster followed: *bosses were not to be harmed.*

A soldier never did anything without permission, and his boss would never sanction the death of another boss, not without a unanimous vote. The rule was designed to protect the delicate balance of power, but it didn't take into account there were more ways to harm a man than *murder.* Loved ones became surrogate targets. Innocent blood got spilled. Men were annihilated emotionally.

Murder might've been more merciful.

It was this rule that had kept Roberto Barsanti alive long after Primo Galante wanted him dead. For damn near twenty years, Primo had been seeking permission, calling meetings and asking for votes, but he came up short every time. There was always one holdout, one man who said there had been enough bloodshed.

Johnny Amaro.

The door to the house opened, animated voices streaming through the foyer. Primo stepped out of his office, greeting the half-dozen men coming into his home. His own little Helter Skelter crew, dressed in all black. The sun was rising outside, another day upon them, another night of anarchy over.

"There's food and drink in the kitchen," Primo told them. "Help yourselves."

The men scurried off, all except for Umberto Ricci, who lurked behind the pack although Primo considered him their leader. Something about his expression made Primo pause. He waited until the others were preoccupied to motion toward his office. "Join me, Umberto."

Umberto followed him without question.

"How did it go?" he asked, sitting down on the couch. "Did you handle it?"

Umberto nodded. "Amaro was at his cafe. We lit it up and then, well... *lit* it up."

"And you got him?"

"Had him," Umberto said. "He was hit and the building was on fire. There was no way he was getting himself out of there."

"But?" Primo raised an eyebrow. "I sense a *but*."

"But somebody pulled him out," Umberto said. "Somebody helped him."

"I told you to stop anyone who got in the way," Primo said. "I told you not to *let* anybody help him."

"I know, but—"

"Another *but*?" Primo sat up straight. "I told you this was too important for you to let anything get in the way. We had one shot at this. *One*. Failure isn't an option. So I want to know what you were thinking. I want to know who was so important that you ignored an order!"

Umberto hesitated, like he didn't want to answer, but he had no choice. "It was Dante."

Primo forced himself not to react to that information. *Dante*. His son had made himself scarce since his hospitalization, the Dante returned not the same one Primo had raised. An imposter walked around in his body, wearing his *face*, constantly getting in the way. He'd gone from being the apple of Primo's eye to the bane of his existence.

Primo hadn't been sure what to do about it. He'd held out hope that he'd come around, but months had passed and things progressed in the wrong direction, only getting worse.

"Did you confront him?"

"Dante?"

"Amaro."

"Oh, yeah. He took one look at me and knew what was happening, so my questions mostly fell on deaf ears. I did get one thing out of him, though."

"What?"

"That you were right."

While he should've felt *relief,* hearing confirmation, Primo was overcome with anger. "He told you that?"

"In not so many words," Umberto said. "I told him we were looking, that we wouldn't stop until we found what we sought. He told me we could tear the city apart all we wanted, but we weren't going to flush them out, because, and I quote, '*They left New York*'."

Primo stared at the wall as he tried to control the fury building up inside of him. Someone had to have helped them. Someone had to be *protecting* them. They'd conspired before to shield Matteo from his reach and someone was doing it again.

Only this time, they were hiding his *daughter* with him. His own flesh and blood, betraying him time and again, trying to get one over on him, but he wouldn't let it happen.

No bodies in the car. Primo wasn't stupid. Barsanti's defeated behavior told Primo that he had nothing to do with it, that he had no idea of the truth. His misery was genuine, his common sense clouded by grief. They hadn't been hiding anywhere they'd gone before, but they had to be somewhere.

And he'd find them.

"Bring Dante in," Primo said. "If someone tries to stop you, kill them... even if that someone is *him.*"

* * *

There's a particular smell in hospitals that most people associate with sickness, but Dante knew the odor came from a specific chemical. *Iodoform.* It treated skin infections as an antiseptic and cleaned corridors as a disinfectant, clinging to patients and everything around them, even following Gabriella home on her scrubs every morning.

Dante fucking hated it.

Because all the knowledge in the world couldn't keep him from associating the stench with dying. It was unconscious, a sensation that hit him the moment he stepped foot in Presbyterian hospital.

His chest tightened, his lungs on fire. Or fuck, maybe that was still the smoke inhalation...

Men packed the waiting rooms, filling the chairs and lingering in the corners, some wandering the hallways while others lurked outside the doors, waiting for news. Dozens of them, from bosses down to street soldiers, held vigil, a few different families present in a show of solidarity.

But Dante noticed, as he took in the crowd, that not a single Galante had come... no one except for *him*. It was no wonder, knowing what Dante knew, what Dante suspected every other man there believed to be true, based on the skeptical looks cast his way. The Galante family was the culprit. *The sins of the father fucking up his kids again.*

Dante didn't stop, didn't acknowledge anybody, heading for the elevator and heading up to the ICU. He stepped off onto the floor, pausing to collect himself. An alarm went off in the distance, a loud blare of beeping assaulting his ears.

"You're actually here."

Gabriella leaned against the wall beside the elevator, appearing exhausted, although her shift wasn't even halfway over.

"You look like you knew I was coming."

"I did," she said. "Someone called Gavin from downstairs, said you were spotted in the building. I was sitting there when they warned him."

Warned him, like Dante posed a threat. "What are the odds he welcomes my company?"

"I'd say you've got a 50/50 shot. He hasn't let anyone else come up since he got here, wanting to be left alone, but he didn't ask me to leave when *I* sat down."

"You're his cousin. I'm just the son of the guy who put his father here."

"You're his friend, and he's probably your *best* friend, remember? I'd say it's worth trying."

"Oh, I'm going to try," he said. "Just kind of hoping to not get punched today."

"He wouldn't do that."

"He's done it before," Dante said, giving her a soft smile as grazed her cheek with his knuckle. "He punched me because of a certain somebody he wanted me to stay away from, but I'm too hard-headed to listen."

Gabriella seemed surprised by that and started to respond when a stern voice cut through the hallway. "Nurse Russo!"

Her expression fell as she scampered away without another word. Dante watched her as she approached a familiar man in a lab coat. Dr. Crabtree.

Dante walked past the abandoned information desk to the waiting room. This one was mostly empty in the middle of the night, just Gavin sitting alone, hands clasped together, his head down, eyes fixed on the shiny floor as his knee jumped.

The guy was a live wire, ready to fucking spark.

Dante slid into the chair beside him, letting out a deep sigh. He wasn't sure what to say. He knew what common courtesy told him to ask: *How are you feeling? Do you need anything?* It was bullshit, though, and he refused to spew it.

How was he feeling?

Like shit, obviously.

Did he need anything?

He needed his father to *live*.

So Dante sat in silence, inhaling the putrid disinfectant, listening to the machines screeching, wishing like hell he could do something to fix everything. Gavin hadn't said a word, hadn't reacted to his presence, so Dante took that as an invitation to continue existing, planted in that chair so long his ass fell asleep.

Eventually, Gabriella resurfaced, approaching them.

"You guys okay?" she asked, the question making Dante cringe. He let it slide, giving her a small nod. "Just let me know if you need anything."

"A do-over would be nice," Gavin chimed in, his voice raspy, "but I'd settle for a Coke."

"I can get that for you," she said. "The soda, that is."

Gabriella retreated, leaving them alone again, as Gavin shifted in his chair, stretching his legs out.

"She means well," Dante said.

"I know she does," Gavin said. "I don't need you to tell me that."

"Yeah, well, what *do* you need me to tell you? That you look like shit? That you need to eat something?"

"I need you to tell me what the fuck happened."

Gabriella returned, carrying two bottles of Coke, handing one to Gavin before holding the other out to him. Dante took it, catching her wrist when she went to walk away, tugging her closer. "Have I ever told you how gorgeous you look in scrubs? What do they call it on that show you like? *McSexy?*"

She blushed as she tugged her wrist away. "You're a friggin idiot. Gray area, remember?"

He smirked, watching as she ran off. The moment she left, his expression fell, his amusement gone.

"Fools." Gavin shook his head. "Just as lovesick as Matty and Genna."

Those words were like a kick to the fucking face.

Dante set his soda aside. "Look, I wish I could tell you what you want, but I don't know what happened. All I have is speculation. Theories. *Feelings.*"

"Then tell me how you're feeling."

Dante laughed dryly. "My feeling, Gavin, is that some men just want to watch the world burn."

Gavin hunched over, propping his elbows on his thighs, cradling his head in his hands as he closed his eyes. *Burn.* Dante instantly regretted using that word.

"I just meant—"

"I know what you meant," Gavin muttered. "Don't walk on eggshells around me. Don't treat me like I'm some..."

"Sentimental bitch?" Dante guessed.

Gavin didn't deny it, sitting in silence, rocking in his seat. Eventually, he sat up straight, pulling himself together. "They have him sedated. He's in bad shape, but it could be worse. Could be *a lot* worse. They say he's got a good chance of pulling through this, that he got lucky, you know, because somebody got to him in time. Because *you* got to him. Any longer and we'd be planning his funeral."

"I'm glad he's alive."

"Me, too, but I've gotta tell you, if the roles were reversed, if it had been *your* father, I don't know if I would've done it. I don't know if I would've risked my life for him."

The elevators dinged on the floor, a group of people stepping off. The first face Dante saw belonged to Victor Brazzi, flanked by two men dressed in black—his bodyguards. Gabriella's parents were with him, along with a few others, Dante's eyes drifting to the woman in the center.

Lena Amaro.

Johnny's wife. Gavin's mother.

"Yeah, well, if it was *my* father, I wouldn't save him, either."
Dante stood as they approached, reaching over to squeeze Gavin's
shoulder. "I'll leave you to your family, G."

Dante tried to walk away, not wanting to impose, but Lena
stepped into his path, stalling in front of him. Her voice trembled
as she growled his name. "Galante."

Dante's eyes connected with hers. Rage. Devastation. Fear. Hatred. A flurry of emotion lit her face, her cheek twitching and bottom lip quivering, as tears coated those expressive, bloodshot eyes.
He tensed as she flexed her hand at her side. She wanted to hit him.
Shit. She was going to.

Lena came at him and he braced himself, standing completely
still as she swung, her open palm slapping his face so hard his head
jolted to the side. A sharp sting tore through his cheek, and he
winced but said nothing, taking the blow in silence. Mere seconds
passed, tears spilling down her cheeks, before she came at him
again, this time flinging her arms around him.

"Thank you," she whispered.

The hug didn't last long, barely a few seconds, before she pulled
away and went for her son instead. Loud sobs echoed through the
room, spilling out of her, and Dante used the distraction as a
chance to slip away. He stalked right for the elevator, grateful when
it opened.

Stepping inside, he pressed the button for the lobby, the doors
almost closing before a hand shot between them, forcing them back
open. Alfie stepped inside, pressing the '*door close*' button. Dante
leaned against the back wall of the elevator, rubbing his cheek.

When they reached the lobby, Dante made his way to the exit
while Alfie veered into the waiting room. Four in the morning, almost twenty-four hours passing since the café fire, and the city was
quiet. *Eerily* quiet. Dante headed for the hospital's parking garage
around the corner, going for his car on the second tier. Pulling his
key out, he approached it, his footsteps faltering when it came into
view.

Someone was sitting on the hood.

They wore all back, oversized hoodie. *Umberto.*

Carefully, Dante scanned the garage, looking for others, but black sedans packed the place and he couldn't differentiate between them.

His steps were measured as he approached the McLaren.

"Nice car." Umberto glided a gloved hand along the glossy blue paint. "Not really *you*, though."

"You don't even know me."

"I do. Or I *did*. Dante I knew was smarter than this."

"Smarter than what?"

"Smarter than driving a car that stands out so much."

"What are you going to do? Blow it up?"

Umberto slid off the hood to take a few steps his direction. "Do you really think I'd do that to you?"

"Yes."

His answer was instant.

Umberto would do *anything* that Primo ordered.

A car pulled into the garage, speeding around the corner, coming their direction. Dante's heart raced at the flash of headlights. The car skidded to a stop behind him, blocking him in.

"Your father wants another word with you," Umberto said. "Shouldn't take long."

"Just long enough to shoot me, huh?"

"Don't be stupid." Umberto opened the back door. "Get in."

"Can't do that."

"Why not?"

"Because I don't want to."

"Figured you would've learned by now that these things aren't negotiable."

"I'm not looking to negotiate," Dante said. "I'm just flat out fucking denying."

"It's an order."

"I don't give a shit."

Umberto reached beneath his hoodie for a pistol. He aimed it, hand steady, not wavering. "Don't make me do this, Dante."

"That's the thing," Dante said, glaring at him. "I'm not making you do this. This? It's not *me*. So shoot me if you want, Bert, but you'll have to shoot me in the back, like a coward."

Dante turned, taking a single step before the gun cocked.

"Last chance," Umberto said. "Get in the car."

Dante closed his eyes, swaying, as grabbed the door handle of his car, preparing to get in. Seconds passed. He waited for the gunshot. He waited, expecting it, until another voice cut through the garage. "I believe he was quite clear when he said he wasn't going anywhere with you."

Alfie stood nearby, flanked by a few others, guns drawn and aimed at the sedan with the back door standing wide open.

"This has nothing to do with you," Umberto said. "Mind your own business."

"You're wrong," Alfie said. "I've made it my business."

Umberto's expression hardened. "His father wants a word."

Alfie turned to Dante. "You got anything to say to your father?"

"Nothing."

"Then I guess his father is just shit out of luck," Alfie said. "So why don't you run along and go pass that on to your boss? Tell him his son has nothing left to say to him. If he has a problem with that, he can take it up with the Brazzi family."

Umberto hesitated before lowering his gun, his eyes on Dante. "You're making a mistake."

Dante didn't respond, watching as Umberto slipped into the back of the car. It sped from the garage, leaving Dante intact. He glanced at Alfie as the others disappeared into the darkness. "You just saved my ass."

"You dying would hurt my Gabby, which means we have to try to keep you breathing... you know, just until my little girl gets sick of your existence."

CHAPTER 20

"Where the ever-loving fuck could it be?" Genna muttered, looking through a dresser drawer in the master bedroom. She shifted things around, yanking out old clothes and tossing them behind her, onto the destroyed bed. Despite going through the rest of the place and fixing things up, making it more of a home, they never bothered with *this* room.

Admittedly, it freaked her out. She still wasn't sure what kind of people had lived there, but she'd never forgotten Chris's words from the garage, about the creepy reclusive lady living out there. Many days since then, while Matty worked and Genna stayed home, she imagined what that would be like—living there for decades, isolated, becoming an urban legend more than a genuine person.

The thought *terrified* her.

Once that drawer had been rifled through, Genna shut it, moving on to the next one to do the same thing. She raided the entire dresser before moving on to the bedside stands, giving up eventually and turning to the closet. Besides the clothes hanging up and the pile of shoes strewn beneath, a few small boxes were stacked together on a shelf, the last of the untouched leftover belongings.

Genna scowled at them.

Fuck it.

She stood on her tiptoes to pull the first two down, finding nothing of importance. She reached for the third box, yanking on it, her grip slipping as the cardboard tore.

"Shit!" she yelped, jumping back as the box came crashing down, everything spilling out. A loud clatter, followed by the sound of something rolling, like marbles scattering along the wood. Glancing down, Genna's heart nearly stopped, her jaw going slack.

A few inches from her bare foot lay a silver gun, the metal dull. Genna had no idea what kind it was. Despite growing up in the family she had, she knew little about guns. In a pinch she could pick one up and squeeze the trigger, maybe even hit something if she got lucky, but she wouldn't bet her life on it.

She didn't much *like* guns.

Genna stared at it for a minute, her eyes glossing around the rest of the box's contents, surveying the stray bullets that had scattered when it fell. Not finding what she wanted, she backed out of the bedroom and left the mess.

Not even going there.

She scanned the other bedrooms, knowing she'd find nothing. She'd already been through all of it, cleaning and organizing— nesting, as Matty called it. If she had come across it, she would've remembered.

She headed downstairs next.

No luck in the living room.

No luck in the dining room.

No luck in the kitchen.

What the fuck?

Sighing, Genna paused in the foyer, frustrated and out of places to search. She spotted the small stand near the door that held the telephone, eyeing the small drawer on it. *Huh.*

"Please, please, please," she whispered, tugging the drawer open, a frustrated groan escaping her. *Empty.* "Oh, fuck you!"

Slamming the drawer shut, she stomped through the house, giving up as she headed for the back door to storm out. It was around sixty degrees outside. Cool for the desert, maybe, but being as it was the middle of winter, snow likely covering every inch of her former home, it still felt almost like summertime to her. It was hard to gauge the passing of time when the weather seemed to only have two settings: hot and hotter.

The hard ground scraped against her filthy bare soles as she approached the Lincoln. For months, she'd slaved over the thing, rebuilding carburetors and rewiring systems and replacing parts and then redoing most of it when she fucked things up the first go around, pouring sweat and dousing herself in SPF as bugs ate her up under the scorching desert sun, throwing money into it that she was sure they couldn't afford as she followed directions in books and looked at diagrams and taught herself the in's and out's of renovating cars. She'd smashed fingers and dropped things on her toes, sliced her hands open and bruised already sunburned skin, carrying battle wounds from crawling under the damn thing, replacing everything that needed replaced to make it realistically work. Cosmetically, however, the car was still a wreck, parts of the frame rusted out, but Genna still found it beautiful.

Would be even more beautiful if I had the key to the damn thing.

Genna glowered as she stood there, resting her hands on her stomach. In all the time she'd been working on it, in all the time she'd spent *thinking* about it, she never considered the fact that she hadn't encountered the key anywhere. Chris had warned her not to start it without first fixing certain things, so she decided to kind of just… fix it *all* before trying. And there she was, the car as good as she'd get it, and no key anywhere.

Sighing, Genna snatched up a screwdriver from her pile of tools and opened the creaky driver's side door to climb in behind the wheel. Prying open the dash to reach the steering column, she fiddled with the wires, not needing a diagram for this part.

She'd hotwired her first car at fourteen after watching *Gone in 60 Seconds* and knew the older the car, the easier the stealing.

Piece of chocolate cake.

She stripped and twisted wires together, the dashboard coming to life. Grabbing the starter wire, she closed her eyes, whispering a prayer to the car gods, before sparking it against the others. The car hesitated before starting, and Genna pressed the gas, squealing with excitement as the engine revved.

The rumbling sound surrounded her, rough and gritty, the entire car trembling, but son of a bitch, it *started*. She sat there in awe, making sure it wasn't going to stall, before she climbed out and walked around to the front, popping the hood.

"Oh yeah, I'm the fucking *man*," she sang, dancing around, twirling as she grasped onto her stomach, damn near falling thanks to a screwy equilibrium.

She left the car running as she ran back inside, going for her phone in the foyer.

She needed to call someone. She needed to *tell* someone. So she dialed Matty's number, despite the fact that he was working.

"Genna?" He answered right away. "What's wrong, baby?"

"Nothing's wrong," she said. "I got the car started!"

He hesitated. "The car?"

"Yeah, the Lincoln! I got it started. Like, it actually *started*! I mean, I kind of had to hotwire it because I couldn't find a key, but it's running!"

Noise surrounded Matty from the diner, so loud she wasn't sure he could even hear her, but he repeated some of her words back. "You hotwired the Lincoln."

"Yep." She walked into the kitchen to grab a bottle of water. "I know I'm only supposed to call when it's an emergency, but I just *really* wanted to tell someone."

"It's okay," he said. "We're kind of busy right now, though, so we'll talk about it when I get home. I'm getting off early. Gavin's in town."

Genna made a face as she took a sip of her water, glancing out the window, catching sight of a black car out on the highway, pulling onto the property. *Speak of the devil.* "Ugh, okay, he's already here. I'll see you in a bit. Love you."

"Wait, what? He's—"

Genna flipped the phone closed and deposited it in the foyer on her way back outside. The car was still running, and she squatted down, trying to peek under it to make sure fluids weren't leaking, but her stomach got in the way.

Out of the corner of her eye, she caught sight of a pair of slick black dress shoes approaching, the steps measured. *Gavin.* "Look, I got the car running!"

"Should you be doing that?"

The voice was deep, kind of monotone, very matter-of-fact, not at all the smug lightness she expected. *Not Gavin.*

Genna hauled herself back to her feet, on edge. In front of her stood an unfamiliar man, six-foot-something and sturdy, wearing a well-fitted black suit. He was older, maybe forties, with dark hair that kind of curled. Italian, without a doubt, and Genna might even have called him handsome if it weren't for the fact that his expression was crazy intimidating. He carried himself with the same kind of swagger Genna used to see in her father, that untouchable 'I do what I want, just *try* to stop me' attitude. With just a look she pegged him as part of the mob. The question was *which* part... what family did he come from?

Not that one was better than another. The fact that *any* of them might've found them wasn't good at all.

"Why?" she asked defensively, taking a step away, creating some distance between them as she regarded the man. "Because I'm a woman? Because I'm *pregnant*?"

"Because it's not yours," he answered, approaching the car and peering inside of it.

"How do you know it's not mine?"

"For one, you hotwired it," he said, surveying the interior. "It would've been easier to just shove something in the ignition."

"I didn't want to damage anything." Was he seriously giving her grand theft auto *pointers*? "Figured I'd stumble upon the key eventually."

The man didn't respond to that, circling the car. Genna's eyes darted around, her gaze flickering back into the house, planning an escape route.

"Did you learn that from your father?"

That question damn near stalled Genna's heart. "What?"

"Hotwiring cars. Is that something your father taught you?"

Genna swallowed thickly. "I taught myself."

"Interesting."

"Why? Because I'm a woman?"

"It has nothing to do with you being a woman," he said, pausing beside the car, "and everything to do with your father being Primo Galante."

The sound of that name on the stranger's lips made Genna lightheaded. *Primo Galante.* "I don't know what you're talking about."

"You don't have to lie to me. In fact, I'd prefer you didn't. I'm not in the business of hurting pregnant women."

"What about the non-pregnant ones?"

"Only when necessary."

"Well, at least you're honest," she said, clutching her stomach.

"You can relax," he said. "I'm not here for you."

"Why *are* you here?"

"I was nearby on business and figured I'd check on the property."

Her brow furrowed. *The property?*

"I inherited it years ago," he explained, "but I have no use for it, so when Amaro asked about a safe house, I offered it up."

"Oh, it's *yours*."

"Technically."

The man reached inside the car, flicking the wires apart, cutting it off. It struck her then, as she watched him. He knew the car didn't belong to her because it belonged to *him*.

"I didn't know," she said, motioning to the car. "I knew it belonged to somebody, but it was just sitting there, and that was kind of sad, you know? Because it's a great car, and really, it's a shame to let it rot."

"It is a shame," he agreed.

"You said you inherited this house, right?"

"Yes."

"Can I ask you something about it?"

"You already did."

Genna couldn't tell if the guy had deadpanning down to a science or if he just legitimately left his sense of humor back wherever he came from. "Can I ask you some more stuff?"

"If you insist."

Something told her he wasn't the kind of guy who took kindly to insisting, so she treaded lightly. "The people that used to live here, the *family*... what happened to them?"

He didn't answer right away, his attention on the car still.

"I mean, I know it's none of my business," she continued. "But I've been living here in their house, surrounded by their stuff, and really, let's be real... there isn't shit to do out here except *think*. So I was just thinking, you know..."

"About what kind of people would live in his hellhole?"

She hesitated as his eyes shifted to her. "Basically."

"Long story short, they're dead, for the most part."

He didn't elaborate.

"Is this like an Amityville Horror type deal? You know, one goes nutso and kills the rest?"

"Not quite."

"Well, can you maybe make that short story version a bit longer?"

He walked around the car, coming closer, and leaned against the side of it. "The woman was psychotic. The man thought isolating her here would help, but isolation doesn't solve problems. It just narrowed the pool on which she could prey. She drank herself to death, alone and miserable, long after driving everyone else away. The man didn't live long enough to see that happen."

"What happened to him?"

"He got himself killed."

Whoa. "And the kids?"

"Girl grew up to be just like her mother. Got herself killed, too. Man didn't live long enough to see that, either."

"And the little boy?"

"He suffered the worst fate of them all."

"What happened?"

"He gets to stand here and entertain your questions."

She gaped at him. "You?"

He extended his hand. "Corrado Moretti."

"Genevieve Galante," she said, shaking his hand. "Call me Genna... or well, I guess it's actually Jen? I don't know what I'm going by these days, so call me whatever."

Corrado let go to turn back to the car. "The Lincoln was my father's pride and joy. He never let anyone else touch it."

Shit. "I didn't know."

Reaching into his pocket, Corrado pulled out a set of keys, unwinding one off the ring. He held it out to her, the sunlight gleaming off of the old metal. "I know he'd prefer you use the key if you're going to be driving it."

She took the key from him, eyes wide. "Are you sure?"

"I have no use for it, and like you said, it's a shame to let it rot."

Genna started to thank him when Matty's voice shouted her name from inside the house, his panic palpable.

"I should, uh, you know..." Genna motioned toward the back door. "You're welcome to come in or whatever, considering it's yours and all."

She didn't wait for his response before ducking into the house, running right into Matty in the living room. He grabbed her, pulling her to him. Her gaze flickered past him, catching sight of Gavin, gun drawn and firmly in his grip, wearing the most serious expression she'd ever seen him wear.

"Are you okay?" he asked, voice low. "Who's here?"

"Relax, it's okay," she said. "It's just—"

Before she could finish, Corrado stepped through the back door. Gavin *froze*.

"Amaro," Corrado said. "Didn't your father teach you not to point a gun at someone unless you plan to pull the trigger?"

Gavin lowered the gun. "My father taught me a lot, like how you can never be *too* careful."

"I imagine he did," Corrado said. "He's a good man, Johnny Amaro. Too bad I can't say the same thing about the rest of your fathers."

Matty tugged Genna with him as he took a protective step back.

"It's okay," Genna told him. "He owns the house. He's not here to hurt us or anything."

"Matteo Barsanti, Corrado Moretti," Gavin said, introducing them. "I guess you've already met Genevieve."

"Moretti," Matty said. "The DeMarco family."

"Correct," Corrado said. "As I told Genevieve, I just stopped by to check on things. I'll be on my way now."

"You don't have to rush off," Genna said. Man, the atmosphere was *tense*. "Stick around, maybe have dinner or something. I mean, I can't cook and we don't have delivery, but Matty knows how to use a stove and we can just, like, send Gavin away, since he's really annoying."

Gavin rolled his eyes while Corrado, who hadn't cracked a single smile since showing up, actually *laughed*. "I appreciate the offer, and no offense, but I'm not fond of being in this house. But if you need anything, Amaro knows how to get ahold of me."

Corrado slipped by them, walking through the downstairs of the house. Genna pulled away from Matty's grasp to follow the man onto the front porch. Matty lurked behind her, in the foyer, watching and listening, always skeptical of everybody. Would it be that way for the rest of their lives? *Isolation doesn't solve problems.*

"Thank you," Genna said. "For everything. For the house. The *key*. Not a lot of people would be so hospitable, given the circumstances."

"I know what it's like to suffer at the hands of your parents."

Corrado stepped off the porch. "It's unfortunate, children paying the price. That's why I was happy to hear about your brother."

Genna blinked rapidly, those words a kick to the gut.

The door to the house flung open, Matty stepping out, grabbing her arm. "Let's go inside, Genna."

Genna shrugged him off, taking a step forward. "You were *happy* about my brother?"

"Of course," Corrado said, pausing to look at her. "We say a lot of goodbyes in this life with not too many chances to ever say hello again. Dante's one of the lucky few. You get another chance."

Corrado got in his car to leave, while Genna rooted in spot like a tree. Those words kept flowing through her mind, a continual loop. *Dante's one of the lucky few...*

She shook her head. *No.* There was no way. It wasn't possible. Whatever he'd heard had been a mistake. It had been a *lie.* Her brother was gone and wouldn't be coming back. Dante had told her that himself. When a Barsanti got ahold of you, there would be nothing left to find.

Genna watched the car disappear down the highway. Sickness stirred inside of her, a sinking feeling in the pit of her stomach, like Corrado Moretti drove away and took all semblance of peace with him.

* * *

Certain moments of Matty's life were forever burned in his memory, moments that cut him to the core, altering him as a person. Finding out his best friend was gone. Seeing his mother take her last breath. Watching his brother bleed out in the street. They were moments that stole a piece of his soul, pieces he could never get back.

And standing on the battered porch, as Genna turned to face him, seeing the turmoil in her blue eyes, he felt it. Her expression branded itself into his subconscious. There would be no coming back from it. She was stealing his soul, like they always warned him she would.

"Genna," he whispered, reaching for her, his fingertips grazing her arm when she pulled back just enough for his hand to fall from her skin.

"Did something happen with my brother?" she asked. "Did they find something? Did they find *him*?"

The door to the house opened, Gavin stepping out onto the porch. Matty's eyes flickered to him, hoping his cousin had some way to smother the igniting fire, but it was too late to stop the flames.

"No, don't do that," Genna said, panic in her voice as she grabbed his chin, forcing him to face her. "Don't look at him. Look at me. *Me*, Matty. Not Gavin!"

His eyes shifted to meet her gaze. "Genna..."

"I asked you a question!" Tears welled in her eyes. "Why aren't you answering it? Why won't you answer *me*?"

"Look, just calm down, okay? You're getting yourself worked up. It's not good for the baby."

"*Don't!* Don't dare try to guilt me. Don't *belittle* me."

"I'm not."

"You are!" she yelled, the sound of her raised voice pebbling Matty's skin. "You're treating me like I'm just some irrational, emotional woman. You're not answering my question. I deserve the truth! And I'm asking you... I'm begging you... tell me!"

Reaching up, Matty pressed his palms to her flushed cheeks, cradling her face in his hands, his thumbs stroking her skin. He knew he had to tell her.

God, he didn't want to...

Not now. Not *yet*.

She was nearing the end of her pregnancy, already in the third trimester, and things back in New York were dangerous. She didn't need that kind of stress. The timing couldn't be worse.

"I love you, Genevieve. You *know* I love you. I'd do anything for you. I'd do anything you ask of me."

"I'm asking you to *tell me*."

Matty sighed. "They found Dante right after we left New York."

"*Alive?*"

Matty hesitated before nodding.

She cracked, those tears breaking through, streaming down her cheeks. Her knees damn near buckled, but he grabbed ahold of her before she collapsed, helping her sit down on the porch as he knelt in front of her.

"He's alive," she whispered, her face contorting as she tried to hold back a sob. "You knew the whole time?"

"I found out a few months ago," he said. "The first time Gavin visited."

"Why didn't you tell me? Why did you keep this from me? Why did you let me keep thinking my brother was dead? We had a *funeral*!"

She shoved against him, almost pushing him over, but he grabbed her arms to steady himself and to keep her from lashing out. "Because it wasn't safe in the city. It *isn't* safe. And I knew when I told you that you'd want to go back, that you'd want to see him."

"Wouldn't you?" she cried. "If it was your brother, wouldn't you want to see him?"

"Not if it were dangerous."

"Bullshit! You risked your life to visit your mother!"

"That's different."

"How?"

"Because it was just *my* life I risked. Jesus Christ, Genna... you're pregnant! We're about to be parents! It's not just about us anymore. We have to think about the baby."

"I am thinking about the baby. I'm *always* thinking about the baby. Maybe it's dangerous in the city, but at least they're living. We're just hiding!"

Matty scrubbed his hands down his face. "I can't let you go back there, Genna."

"But you can't stop me, either."

"Please," he begged. "Just please listen to me."

"I am listening, Matty. I hear what you're saying. And maybe if you said it months ago, it would've been different. But I just... I don't even know what to say to you right now. I don't know what to *think*. You let me mourn for months when you knew he was alive, and why? For what? Because you didn't *trust* me?"

"I do trust you."

"You don't," she said. "You didn't trust me enough to let me decide for myself. You made this decision on your own. You chose for me. You thought me grieving was better than me knowing my brother was alive. And maybe you meant well. Maybe you had good intentions. But you've hurt me, Matty, because you did the *one* thing you promised you'd never do—you treated me like that fragile ice princess."

She shoved up from the step and headed for the house, stalling on the porch, face-to-face with Gavin. "Have you seen him? Dante?"

Gavin nodded.

"Is he okay?"

Gavin hesitated.

"Don't lie to me," she said. "Please don't."

"He has his moments."

"Does he know about me?" Her hands ghosted across her stomach. "About us?"

"He knows what everybody else does."

"Which is *what?*"

"That you vanished."

She stomped past him, bursting into the house and slamming the door behind her.

"That girl," Gavin said, pointing to the door, "is *just* like her brother."

Matty ran his hands down his face. "This isn't how any of this was supposed to happen."

"I don't know," Gavin said. "Isn't this kind of what it's like to be a Barsanti?"

"What? All fucked up?"

"Pretty much."

"Story of my life," Matty said, "but this was supposed to be different. This was supposed to be a fresh start, a chance to do things right. This wasn't supposed to be like everything else."

"Yeah, well, you took the girl away from the Galantes but you'll never take the Galante out of that girl. And you know, I don't think you really want to."

Gavin strolled off the porch, stepping past Matty.

"I'm going to leave you to your wife," he said, heading for his rental car. "Not sucking the poison out of *this* bite."

Matty glared at him, watching as the car drove off, before heading inside. The downstairs was empty, silent, so he headed up to the second floor, finding Genna sitting on the top step, lingering in the dim hallway. Her phone was in her hand, and she absently flipped it open and closed, staring into nothingness, her mind off somewhere else.

After a few flips, her gaze went to her phone. She pressed buttons, fingers working fast, as she dialed a phone number.

"What are you...?" He trailed off, not bothering to finish his question as she brought the phone to her ear, listening. From where he stood, he heard the voicemail pick up without ringing, a male voice telling her to leave a message. *Dante.*

"I've called that number a few times, just to hear his voice," she whispered, flipping the phone closed again. "Not once has he answered. It stopped ringing long ago."

"I don't know what to tell you."

She nodded, standing up, like she wasn't surprised by his lack of explanation. "I need some time alone to think. So can you give me that?"

"Whatever you need."

A sinking feeling settled in the pit of Matty's stomach as he watched her walk down the hall, disappearing into the little boy's bedroom and closing the door, shutting him out.

So many times he imagined their own little boy moving into that room. Maybe it was naïve, but Matty thought it could work. He believed they would've been happy. It wasn't perfect, but hell, it was something. It was *their* something. But he knew, watching that door close behind Genna, that any hope of that happening had disappeared.

Matty wandered the house in silence before heading to bed alone after dark. It took awhile for him to doze off, in and out of a restless sleep, jolting awake sometime after midnight, that feeling inside of him growing stronger, rooting deeper. Throwing the covers off, he climbed out of bed, pausing when he noticed the door across the hall wide open.

No Genna.

He searched the house, seeking her out, sighing when he spotted her. Genna sat behind the wheel of the Lincoln out back, illuminated only by a sliver of moonlight. Matty walked outside, joining her, slipping into the passenger seat. A key stuck out of the ignition, the car turned off but her seatbelt clipped on, like she wanted to run but that first step was too terrifying. He wondered how long she'd be sitting there, how long she'd been contemplating leaving him. Tears coated her cheeks, her eyes bloodshot as she stared straight ahead. Besides her phone on the seat next to her, she had nothing with her... nothing except that old, worn out map she'd stolen from the truck when they first set out on their journey, those veins and arteries pumping life through a country that she'd scoured relentlessly, searching for the *heart*.

"I'm guessing you've finally decided where you want to go," he said. "Finally decided where you want to call *home*."

"I'm sorry," she whispered.

"Don't be," he said. "If anyone should be apologizing, it's me. I was afraid of losing you, afraid of losing *us*. Because I know he's your brother, Genna. I know he's your best friend. But he's also the guy who killed *my* brother. He's the guy who pointed a gun at my head. So I know there's a chance that when it comes down to it, it's going to be either me or him."

"How am I supposed to *choose?*"

"I don't know," he said, "and I'd never ask you to, but others might, and that terrifies me. You're right, though. I should've trusted you. And I made a promise. I said wherever you wanted to go, we'd go, so..."

"So..."

"So let's go."

* * *

Snow covered the icy Manhattan sidewalks, flakes drifting from the overcast late February sky as coldness clung to the city. A cloud of breath surrounded Gabriella when she stepped out of her building, a shiver tearing through her. She pulled her coat tighter around her body, scowling up at the sky, at a traitorous sun that hadn't shown its face in days.

She hated winter.

Everything died in the winter, the beauty of the world somehow getting lost, withering away and leaving only remnants behind. But life didn't stop, no... it trudged along, clinging to frigid breaths, holding on for another tomorrow where maybe the sun would shine again.

No friggin luck today.

"Excuse me," she mumbled, moving around someone lingering outside the building, attempting to walk away when they stepped in her path.

"Amaro's cousin, right?" the man asked, smiling at her. It took a moment for recognition to strike, for familiarity to sink in. She'd run into the guy before—*literally*—at Casato.

"Uh, yeah, and you are...?"

"A friend," he said. "Your name's Gabriella, right? Russo? You happen to have a boyfriend, Gabriella Russo?"

Her back stiffened at the way he used her full name. He was choosing his words carefully, every syllable deliberate, like he was trying to intimidate her. "I might, but even if I don't, I'm not interested. Sorry."

She attempted to go around him but yet again he stepped in her path, blocking her from leaving. "Ah, don't be like that. I'm just asking a question."

"One I'm choosing not to answer," she said. "If you don't like it, take it up with the Constitution. It guaranteed me life, liberty, and the pursuit of happiness without having to worry about persecution."

"I'm not the government, sweetheart."

"Could've fooled me," she said. "You seem to have the whole smug incompetence thing down."

She tried for the third time to move past him, managing to make it a few steps before his hand gripped her bicep hard enough to stop her. "Feisty one, aren't you?"

She yanked from his grasp, a surge of anger rushing through her. "Look, I don't know whose goon you are, nor do I *care*, frankly. Barsanti, Galante, doesn't matter. I'm not afraid of you."

"Maybe you ought to be."

"Well, tough cookie, because if you're hoping to scare me, you're failing miserably. You should work on that, you know, for the next time you try to intimidate one of Victor Brazzi's grandchildren."

She took a few steps, flexing her hands at her sides as her heart raced, prepared to swing if he touched her again, but only his voice followed her this time.

"Brazzi. You think I'm scared of that name?"

"Maybe you ought to be."

He laughed when she threw his words back at him. "That's funny. Damn near as funny as the look on your boyfriend's face when he's got a knife in his gut. Now *that* is a fucking riot."

Gabriella's footsteps stalled. She wanted to keep going. She *should've* kept going. Instead, she faced him again. "That was you?"

He held up his hands, as if in surrender. "Guilty."

She pointed at him, waving her finger all around at his cocky grin. "Smug incompetence. *Knew it.* You stabbed him and never hit anything important. Do you know how crappy you have to be to miss even a kidney?"

"That's not incompetence," he countered. "If I wanted to hit something, I would've, but I wasn't trying to kill the guy. Just wanted to poke the bear a bit. All in good fun."

She shook her head. "You keep telling yourself that."

"I will," he said, "and why don't you tell your boyfriend something for me, while we're at it? Tell him to watch his back."

He strolled away, not at all frazzled by their conversation.

"Why can't you just leave him alone? Huh? What did he do that was *so* wrong?"

"Oh, nothing much," the guy said. "He only killed my best friend."

Gabriella stared at him as he walked away. A sinking feeling settled into the pit of her stomach at his words, bile rising in her throat that she desperately swallowed back. He wasn't the first one to tell her something like that, but Gabriella struggled to fathom it. Dante was passionate, and maybe he could be dangerous, but she'd never seen a malicious side to him.

Her gaze flickered to the apartment above, part of her wanting to go back inside, to go up there and see him, but she was due at work in minutes.

She'd never been late for work before.

Despite rushing, Gabriella walked into the hospital a quarter after seven, a solid fifteen minutes after she was scheduled. As soon as she stepped out onto the ICU, apologies spilled out of her, but they fell upon deaf ears. Dr. Crabtree met her at the elevator, along with the charge nurse, Monica Burns.

"We'd like to have a word with you, Nurse Russo," Monica said, "if you don't mind."

Her brow furrowed. "If this is about me being late, I really am sorry. *Really*. I had this situation and I missed my connection and had to wait."

"This isn't about that," she said, "although, as you know, there are no excuses for tardiness."

"I know," she muttered. "Can I ask what this *is* about? Is there a problem or something?"

"Follow me, please."

Her refusal to answer that question sent red flags flying, but Gabriella had no choice but to follow the woman. They went to a small conference room on the floor, usually utilized for brief meetings about a patient's care. Monica and Crabtree sat down on one side of the long wooden table. Gabriella's anxiety flared as she slipped into the chair across from them. "Am I in trouble?"

Instead of answering, Monica reached pulled out a crisp white envelope, sliding it across the table. Gabriella picked it up. The return address in the corner said it came from the hospital, straight from the Chief Nursing Officer, the sight making her stomach churn. She wanted to ask what it was, why they were giving it to *her*, but questions were pointless. If they wanted to answer any of that, they already would've.

So carefully, she slid her finger beneath the loose flap and reached inside, pulling out the piece of paper. Unfolding it, her eyes glossed across the text of the letter, slamming right into a stream of words that made her stop short.

Improper relationship with a patient.

"I can't believe this," she whispered, her voice struck with a small tremor. Anonymous complaints that she'd used her position to prey upon an emotionally vulnerable patient.

"I'm sure I don't have to tell you how serious these allegations are," Monica said. "You'll, of course, be able to defend yourself when you meet with the CNO and clear up what I'm certain is just a misunderstanding, but you've been taken off the schedule until then as a precaution."

"But my patients…"

"We were able to pull others in to cover your shifts," she explained. "Your patients have been reassigned."

Dumbfounded couldn't begin to describe Gabriella. She scanned the letter again, like maybe the words would change, but no, there it was in ink, her fate sealed, officially calling that gray area a big black strike. "So that's it?"

"For now," Monica said, standing up. "You'll be back to work just as soon as it gets cleared up."

The woman walked out, and Crabtree lingered for a moment before standing up. "You should've known better, Nurse Russo. Maybe you *do* need that Ph.D. to spot an ethical issue."

He walked out, leaving her with those words.

She was *screwed*.

After shoving the letter back into the envelope, she made the trek back to her apartment. Snow came down harder, the hidden sun moving on as night set in. By the time she stepped into the building, her toes were frozen and her nose ran, chills covering every inch of her as she shivered.

She unlocked the door and stepped into the apartment, silence greeting her. "Dante?"

No answer.

He wouldn't expect her back for twelve hours, so there was no telling where he might've gone or what he might've been off doing. After locking the door again, attaching the chain lock, she dropped the letter on the living room coffee table before stripping out of her cold, damp scrubs, discarding them wherever as she headed into the bathroom. While drawing herself a warm bubble bath, she fired off a quick text message to Dante's new number. **Back home. Not working, after all. Be careful, wherever you are.**

She slid down into the suds, earbuds in her ears, her phone perched on the ledge of the tub, blasting music. It took a minute or so for him to respond, her phone lighting up. **Not working, either, so don't worry.**

Where are you?

At Michaels.

Who's Michael?

Fuck if I know.

Her brow furrowed. Why would he be at someone's house he doesn't know? **Why are you there?**

Because they got what I need.

What do you need?

A fucking psych consult for doing this shit, probably.

What are you doing?

Being a damn Girl Scout for you.

She stared at that, even more confused, when another text popped up from Dante. **Be home in a bit. You're distracting me.**

She scowled at that, typing **K,** figuring that to be the end of that, but her phone lit right back up seconds later.

Don't K me. I deserve that shit spelled out for all the trouble I'm going through.

She rolled her eyes, typing **OK.**

Setting the phone down, she closed her eyes, sinking further into the tub, hoping to clear her mind and forget about everything that had happened that evening. She mumbled along to the words, letting the warm water soothe her muscles, relaxing so much she dozed off.

Something startled her, drawing her out of her light slumber. Blinking, Gabriella sat straight up, a chill ripping through her as she turned her music off. Goose bumps coated her, the now cool water nipping at her skin. Her teeth chattered, the bubbles dissolved. Crossing her arms over her chest, she climbed out of the tub, snatching up a towel when she heard the faint sound of footsteps.

"Dante? Is that you?"

No answer.

Silence permeated the apartment. A door shut in the distance. Her heart stalled a beat before kicking in. It was hard living in the city, differentiating noises, the walls thin and floorboards creaky. Innocence felt alarming, while the dangers of the world registered as whispers on a breeze instead of fiery explosions. Up was down, and it all went round and round. Sometimes gunshots were just fireworks but occasionally the sparkling bangs masked the suppressed sound of a bullet from a silencer.

Gabriella shook it off, wrapping the towel around her before letting the water out of the tub.

Stepping out of the bathroom, she walked down the short hall toward the bedroom, stalling in the living room when someone moved. "Dante?"

Dante turned to her, holding up a piece of paper. "This is about me, I'm guessing?"

The letter from the hospital board.

"So it seems."

He glanced back at the paper before shoving it in the envelope. "*Emotionally vulnerable*, my ass."

"It's true," she said, taking the letter from him. "Technically. You were hurt and you were grieving. You had nobody. But I was there, advocating for you."

"Don't do that," he said. "Don't act like I was just some fucking wounded animal."

"I'm not. I'm just saying—"

"I know what you're saying. I was beat down, at my lowest, and you swooped on in and made me feel something, like I caught Stockholm Syndrome, but that's bullshit. Because I've *never* been that weak, Gabriella. I'm not going to roll over and beg for the first pretty face that comes along."

"I didn't mean—"

Dante cupped her cheek, his thumb roughly grazing over her bottom lip. "Look, I love you, and I could stand here and list dozens of reasons why I do—you're funny; you've got guts; you understand my life—but not a single one of those goddamn reasons will be because you saw that tube in my dick."

She cracked a smile as he wrapped his arms around her. "Too bad the hospital board won't see it that way."

"I'm sure you can convince them." He nudged her chin, making her look at him. "When in doubt, just tell them you'd rather have your pussy shrivel up and die than let Dante Galante inside of it."

"That's a horrible lie," she whispered. "The biggest lie ever told."

Leaning down, he kissed her. "That's good to hear, because I'm pretty sure *I'd* die if I never got to fuck you again."

He gazed at her in silence, and she stared right back, those goose bumps still coating her.

She shivered in his arms. "I should put some clothes on."

"Or," he said, "I might have a better way to keep you warm."

Dante backed her up to the bedroom as he yanked away the towel, dropping it. Her eyes flickered around the apartment in the darkness, ghosting across the unlocked front door, eyeing the dangling chain. "You broke in again?"

"No," he said, "I've got a key, remember?"

"Yeah, but the chain..."

He nuzzled into her neck, his tongue gliding across her cool skin as he palmed a breast. "What about it?"

"It's not latched."

"I know."

"But it was. I locked the door when I got in the bathtub."

"You sure about that?" His thumb grazed across her perky nipple, sending tingles through her. "Because it wasn't locked when I got home."

"I, uh..." She moaned when he kissed the spot right below her ear. "Maybe I forgot the chain."

He pulled away. "But you're sure you locked the door?"

"Pretty sure."

"*Pretty sure* isn't sure," he said. "Because I'm not fucking with you when I say the door was already unlocked when I got home. And by that I mean anyone could've turned the knob and walked right in. So if someone unlocked it, it wasn't *me*."

Her expression fell. "What?"

He glanced at the door before scanning the dark apartment.

"But I was here," she said, sickness churning her stomach. "I mean, I heard a noise, but then you were here, so I figured..."

"You figured it was me," he said, finishing her thought. "What kind of noise?"

"I don't know." She reached down to snatch the towel back up, wrapping it around herself again. "Like a door, maybe? The floor creaking or something closing? I fell asleep but then—" She stalled abruptly. "Oh God, do you think someone was in here? *Seriously?* Someone broke in while I was taking a friggin bath?"

"It's possible."

"Who would do that?"

Dante moved away from her to search the apartment, checking rooms and opening up drawers. "I have some ideas."

"Like?" She followed him around. "What are you looking for?"

"I'm trying to see if anything is missing," he said, pausing, "and making sure nothing was left behind."

"What would they leave behind?"

"Bombs? Bugs? I don't know. Jesus, baby, you're a fucking *Brazzi*. I need you to act like one. Can you think of anything else? Anything that'll tell me who might've broken in?"

"I, uh, *ugh*." She followed him into the bedroom, watching as he checked under the bed and rifled through the dresser. "Oh crap, there was a guy earlier today."

"What guy?"

"He wouldn't tell me his name, but I've seen him before. He asked me about you... he asked me about my *boyfriend*."

"What did he say about me?"

"He said you killed his best friend."

Dante opened the bedside stand and stood there, completely still, staring down into it. "He wasn't lying."

Gabriella closed her eyes to keep the room from spinning.

"Gabriella?"

She opened her eyes again. "Yeah?"

"Where's your gun, baby?"

"It's in the drawer, where it always is."

Dante stared into the drawer for a moment before closing it.

"Do you think it was him?" Gabriella asked, watching as Dante walked over to the door, checking out the locks. "The guy I saw?"

"I don't think so."

"Why?"

"Because your gun is missing."

* * *

Genna's car was gone from out front of the Galante house.

It was the first thing Dante noticed when he approached the property at one o'clock in the morning, lingering in the frigid darkness, careful not to slip on any ice or leave any distinguishable footprints in the snow. His car was parked down the block, out of sight, too noticeable to bring it any closer.

The irony of the situation wasn't lost on Dante. Months ago, Matteo Barsanti had done damn near the same thing, lurking outside the Galante house with a gun and a grudge, both aimed at Dante. And Dante had realized in that moment, when Matteo's finger hovered over the trigger, itching to squeeze it, that someday he would pay for what he'd done, but it wouldn't be with his life. No, his life wasn't worth enough. The world would want to destroy everything he loved instead.

He couldn't let that happen.

Umberto's car was right out front. After pulling his hood up over his head, Dante carefully approached it, ghosting his hand along the hood. *Still warm.*

He banged his fist against it, setting off the shock sensors, the car alarm blaring through the quiet neighborhood. Dante plopped down on the hood as it screamed, just sitting there and waiting, knowing it wouldn't be long before he surfaced.

Thirty seconds passed, maybe a minute at most, before the front door of the Galante house opened, the car alarm deactivated. Silence reigned for a few seconds before the alarm again went off when Dante shifted position.

Umberto strolled toward him, once more disabling the alarm. Again, it only lasted a few seconds before the screeching alarm echoed through the neighborhood.

"You mind getting off my car?" Umberto asked, stalling near him. "You know, before it disturbs everyone around here?"

"When did you get so neighborly?"

"About the same time you did."

Dante stood up, moving away from the car so Umberto could cut the alarm off for the third time. The neighbors would've heard it by then. Eyes would be looking, concerned about the Galante hoodlums, stalking their every move to ensure no trouble brewed. Dante purposely took a few steps to the left, away from the curb, standing beneath a glowing streetlight, visible to anyone who might've been watching. Umberto surveyed him as he came closer, knowing exactly what Dante was doing.

They'd been friends for years, after all. They knew each other's strengths and weaknesses. They knew the tactics they employed to stay safe, just as they knew what made the other one tick. The two of them had done countless jobs together, and while Umberto's crimes had seemed to escalate, a few stark details hadn't changed.

"Johnny Amaro, you know, they say he's going to be just fine," Dante said. "Probably get to come home soon. Figured you'd like to know."

Umberto nodded. "Guess we have you to thank for that, huh?"

"Guess so."

Umberto's gaze left his, scanning the darkness. "You come alone, Dante?"

"Does it make a difference?"

"Not really," Umberto said. "Just trying to figure out your end game."

"I've already told you my end game."

Umberto looked at him again. "Refresh my memory."

"To make sure the man who ruined my life pays for it."

"Ah." Umberto looked down at the asphalt, toeing a few small rocks, kicking them toward the curb. "And to think I used to believe you meant *Barsanti* when you said that."

"Who says I don't mean him?"

"The fact that you chose to draw me outside instead of coming *in* says so. Not to mention the fact that you made a scene and are steering clear of the shadows because you think I won't shoot you if people can see—that's kind of a dead giveaway, too. Toss in that you've thwarted our plans and that you outright refused to come when your father sent for you, and I'd say it's pretty clear who you see as the enemy."

"My father's not my enemy," Dante said. "He's a bully."

Umberto laughed. "Bully, huh? You gonna go tattle to the grown-ups about the mean ol' bully shoving kids around out on the playground, stealing lunch money and picking on your friends?"

"No, I'm going to protect what's mine."

"Like a certain female down in Little Italy?"

"Exactly."

"You know, I'm not sure *any* pussy is worth turning your back on your family," Umberto said. "But hey, what do I know? Your little Brazzi girlfriend is cute, so maybe she's worth it. Bangin' ass body on that one, that's for sure. I was certainly admiring every inch of it earlier."

Coldness swept through Dante before intense rage exploded in his gut. Before the last syllable even spilled from Umberto's lips, Dante swung, punching him right in the mouth. The blow was so hard he stumbled, knocking into his car, triggering those shock sensors and setting the alarm off. Umberto regained his footing, ignoring the obnoxious blaring as he reached up, wiping away the blood that streamed from the corner of his mouth.

Umberto looked at his hand, at the blood coating his fingertips. "Okay, I'll give you that one."

"Stay away from her," Dante warned him, flexing his hands as they itched to pummel him for those words, for having the fucking nerve to look at her, to invade her privacy and violate her body like some goddamn *pervert*. "I swear to fuck, Bert, if I ever catch you near her..."

Umberto spit blood on the asphalt and shut off the car alarm. He looked around the darkness, scanning the neighborhood, before his gaze settled back on Dante. "So you *are* alone."

"Does that surprise you?"

Umberto shrugged, like that was the only answer he had, before he took a few steps back, out of the light, into the shadows. He was considering doing something. Dante could tell. His tongue ran back and forth along his busted bottom lip, his eyes everywhere as he shoved his hands in his pockets. "It's not too late, you know. All you have to do is walk in that house right now and your father will welcome you back with open arms. I haven't told him about the incident at the hospital. Haven't told him you refused his order."

"You should tell him," Dante said. "He won't like you keeping that from him."

"Yeah, well, he's not going to give you another chance after this. *This* will be it. If I tell him..."

"I really am the enemy."

Umberto nodded.

"You should tell him," Dante said again. "Go ahead and pass along the message."

Umberto frowned, closing his eyes as he lowered his head. It was only a brief second, but Dante sensed the sadness. He felt it, too, stirring deep inside of him. It was the sensation of the last bit of lingering hope dying a miserable death.

"Get out of here, Dante," Umberto said, stepping up onto the curb, "while you still can."

"I'll go once you give me what you took."

"I don't know what you're talking about."

"You took the gun when you broke into the apartment. I know

you; that's what you do. *Never leave a gun behind.* I want it back."

Umberto considered that, staring at him again, before stepping over to the car and unlocking it. He reached inside, beneath the passenger seat, and pulled out the small .22 caliber pistol before slowly approaching. "This one?"

"That's the one."

"I'm guessing it's registered to her, huh?"

Dante didn't answer that.

Umberto stalled in front of him, standing toe-to-toe, holding the gun. He raised it, pressing it to Dante's chest, pointing it where his ribcage protected his rapidly beating heart. Even through layers of clothing, Dante could feel the muzzle digging into his scarred skin. "And what's to stop me from pulling the trigger?"

"I don't know," Dante answered, reaching up and snatching ahold of the gun, gripping it tightly. "But if you *wanted* to shoot me, you already would've."

Umberto let go, letting him have the gun, and started back away. Once he stepped up on the curb, he turned around. "I'm sure I'll be seeing you real soon, Dante."

"I'm sure." Dante watched him stroll back to the house, his steps leisure, and called out, "So what's to stop *me* from shooting you right now?"

"Integrity," Umberto said. "You'd never shoot a man in the back."

"You sure about that?"

"Absolutely," Umberto said, turning around to face him. "Besides, there are no bullets left in that gun. I've already used them."

Dante waited until Umberto was inside before checking the gun. *No bullets.* He slipped back into the shadows, concealing the gun in his hoodie pocket as he made his way to his car down the block. Taking a deep breath, he sped from the neighborhood, driving straight back to the apartment.

Gabriella was sprawled out on the couch, watching an episode of some medical drama. She sat up when he opened the door, her eyes wide, on alert. He locked up before strolling over to her, pulling the gun from his pocket and dropping it on the coffee table.

"Where did you...?" she asked as she picked up the gun. "I mean, how did you...?"

She didn't finish those questions. Good thing, too, because Dante didn't want to answer them. He yanked off his hoodie, tossing it on the arm of the couch. "Doesn't matter, but we're not keeping it. There's no telling what it's been used for."

As soon as he said that, she dropped the gun, letting it clatter back to the coffee table. She wiped her hands on her pajama pants, as if whatever figurative blood was now on the gun had somehow transferred to her skin.

Dante headed to the bathroom to shower, standing under the scorching hot spray until he no longer felt the sting, letting it warm his body and wash away the memories of that evening. After he was finished, he wrapped a towel around his waist and stepped back out, heading for the bedroom. He made it a few steps before he heard the male voice in the living room. He came to an abrupt stop, his blood running cold at the sound of it, but he was too late to turn back or do anything. The apartment was so damn small he knew he was spotted, especially when the clipped voice asked loudly, "Do you make a habit of walking around my daughter's apartment naked?"

"Daddy!" Gabriella groaned from the kitchen. "He lives here, too, remember?"

"I remember," Alfie said, glaring at Dante as he just stood there, trapped in that void of space between the bathroom and the bedroom, hoping like hell the towel stayed in place as he uncomfortably crossed his arms over his chest. "We're still going to be having a talk about that, young lady."

"I'm twenty-six, you know."

"Talk to me when you're forty-six," he said. "Until then, I don't think it's too much to ask for him to respect you enough to show some restraint. Hell, he at least ought to have enough self-respect to keep his clothes on when you have *company*."

"He didn't know we had company," Gabriella said as she appeared in front of Dante, grabbing him and forcing him past Alfie, shoving him into the bedroom. She slammed the sliding room door closed once they were inside and looked at him, smiling sheepishly. "Sorry, he kind of just... showed up."

"He's your father," Dante said, dropping the towel. "He can visit you whenever he wants."

"Yeah, well, he's not here for *me*."

Dante cut his eyes at her, brow furrowing, as Alfie shouted from the living room, "Put on your best suit, kid. We've got somewhere we need to be."

CHAPTER 20

Decades earlier, eight hundred miles away, a man named Al Capone believed the key to coexisting was *distribution*. The pie was big enough for everybody to have a slice of it. The bosses in New York at the time bought into that theory, divvying up their territory.

Five boroughs. Five families.

They believed it was fate.

And just as it all came to a screeching halt for Capone, the harmony in the boroughs didn't last long, either. Greed set in. Sharing was no longer caring. Everyone, it seemed, wanted Manhattan, staking a claim and nitpicking neighborhoods. The Amaro family had it all first, it had been rightfully given to them, but then the Barsantis and the Galantes swooped in.

As they say, the rest was history.

Some booms, a couple bangs, and a bunch of spilled blood later, Dante found himself again crossing the state line into New Jersey, sitting in the passenger seat of a black Crown Vic, with Alfie Russo steering them toward Victor Brazzi's property. A family meeting, he'd said, one that had been in the works for weeks. He'd called it a last-ditch effort to establish peace within the network, but Dante knew what they truly were heading into: an *intervention*.

They were going to try to stop Primo's reign of terror.

"When you say all of the families," Dante asked, his voice hesitant, "do you mean *all* of them?"

"All of them," Alfie confirmed. "Chicago, New York, and New Jersey."

"I don't think I belong at this thing."

"Why?"

"Because I don't represent the Galante family."

"I know," Alfie said. "You're coming as a Brazzi."

"A Brazzi?"

"Yeah, you got a *problem* with being a Brazzi?"

"No problem."

Dante wasn't sure how the hell that was going to work, but he figured he ought not ask, opting to remain silent. Tension bunched his muscles when they approached the gate in front of the house, two men dressed all in black standing guard yet again, barely detectable, blending into the darkness. It was late, or maybe really early, well past three o'clock in the morning.

The gate shifted open and Alfie drove through, subtly nodding to the guys as they saluted him. Cars lined the driveway, a chain of black sedans. Alfie pulled up near the door, parking.

As soon as they stepped in the foyer, Alfie raised his hands, letting himself be patted down by another guard, hands barely touching him before the guy moved on to Dante. His touch was rougher, the search more thorough. Dante gritted his teeth, standing still, enduring the prodding until Alfie laughed. "At ease. He's okay. He's with us."

Right away, the man backed off, and Dante fixed his disheveled shirt, tucking it back in.

He followed Alfie up the staircase to the same ballroom they had been in months ago. It had been altered, the small tables replaced by larger interconnected ones. Men filled chairs surrounding the tables, sitting around, food spread out in front of them. They chatted and ate, drinking Bloody Mary's as they laughed at each other's jokes. The atmosphere was easygoing, like they were nothing more than old friends catching up, enjoying pleasant company over buttermilk waffles and chopped up fucking fruit, instead of guys who would gut each other in their sleep without an ounce of remorse.

Dante's eyes scanned the array of faces, recognizing most of them, but not finding the one he sought. Primo was noticeably absent, as was everyone else from the Galante family. Barsanti, too, was nowhere to be found.

"Would've been here sooner," Alfie said, waltzing into the dimly-lit room, a smile on his face, "but someone took *forever* to get ready, like he's some broad that needed to put on his fucking face or something."

Alfie motioned to Dante, who lingered near the entrance, all eyes in the room shifting to him.

"Ah, young Mr. Galante," Victor greeted him, waving to an empty chair to his left. "Join us. Have some breakfast."

Breakfast... at three o'clock in the morning.

Dante wasn't going to question it.

He strolled over and sat down, while Alfie helped himself to the food before sitting to Victor's right. Not wanting to be rude, Dante grabbed a pastry, setting it on a plate.

"Something to drink?" a woman in a black uniform asked, approaching them. *Hired help.*

"Bring me a Mimosa," Alfie said.

"A *Mimosa*?" someone called out. Vince Genova, head of another of the five families, the one that stuck to Staten Island, away from the madness. "You got a cunt between your legs, Russo?"

"Oh, fuck off," Alfie said, shoveling eggs into his mouth. "I got a cock you can suck, Genova."

"You'd probably like it too much, you little Mimosa drinking bitch."

The men around them laughed. Even Alfie snickered, not offended by the insult.

"And you, sir?" the woman asked, looking at Dante. "Something to drink?"

"Uh, orange juice," he mumbled. "Vodka."

The woman offered a smile before scurrying from the room.

"What, nobody's going to say shit?" Alfie asked. "He practically ordered a Mimosa, too!"

"Don't even try it," someone else said. "The kid asked for a fucking *Screwdriver*, not that bubbly ass pussy shit you suck on."

"Says the schmuck over there drinking homemade Sangria."

"Your *wife's* homemade Sangria," someone chimed in.

A resounding chorus of "*ohhhh*" echoed around the room, guys drumming their hands against the table, creating a ruckus and laughing.

"Alright, alright," Victor said, fighting off a grin. "You guys rib Russo all you want, but leave my daughter out of it."

A few more joking jabs were traded as their drinks were delivered. Dante downed his, swallowing every drop, grimacing as the burn lit up his chest. It was damn near instantaneous, his nerves easing and muscles relaxing. He ordered another drink and took a few bites of the pastry, listening to their conversations.

Dante's eyes eventually fell upon Gavin, sitting at the end of the table, standing in for his father. *The head of the Amaro family.* He sat beside another man, one Dante recognized: Corrado Moretti out of Chicago. They were deep in quiet conversation, there at the table but not entirely present. After a moment, Gavin's gaze flickered Dante's direction. *Nervous.*

"You look confused," Victor said from beside him. "I know this isn't your first family meeting."

"No," Dante said, "but the others weren't this, uh…"

"Casual?" he guessed.

"Yeah." Dante watched in disbelief as Alfie used his fork to fling a strawberry down the table, hitting the boss out of Buffalo with it, interrupting the man's conversation. These guys… they weren't the type to tolerate insolence from others. They demanded respect; they prided themselves on strength. Dante had no idea half of them even had personalities. "They're acting like they're *friends.*"

"That's because they are," Victor said. "We've all known each other a long time. Hell, I remember when some of these guys were born. We've worked together, and sometimes, we fight… we don't always agree, or get along, but that doesn't mean we're not friends. You don't have to like people to love them."

"*Love* them."

"Look, when I die, these are the guys who will show up at my funeral, the ones who will make sure I'm sent off with the respect I deserve… the respect I've *earned.* One of them will probably put me there, you know, but the rest will carry my casket, and I trust them to do their part, whatever it might be."

"*Trust* them."

"Yeah, trust them. That's how family is. No one will ever understand you better. Appreciate that. This life is in our blood. We all have that in common. We all want the same thing here. So you know, maybe we'll wake up enemies tomorrow because of it, but today, it's what makes us friends."

Dante shook his head. "I don't know what to say."

"Not surprised, considering your father." Victor motioned

around the table. "He has a way of pissing on everyone's parade, if you know what I'm saying. Guy has no idea how to make friends, and on the off chance he does make one, he doesn't know how to *keep* them."

A voice cut through the room then, edgy but somehow still cordial. "Am I late to the party or something? You started without me."

Roberto Barsanti strolled into the room.

"You're always late, Bobby," Alfie said, still eating, "but is it ever a *party* without you?"

"I like to think not," Barsanti said, plopping down into the first seat he came to. The woman approached him, not needing to ask for him to answer her question. "Scotch, straight up. You know what? Just bring me the damn bottle."

"A bit late for a whole bottle, isn't it?" Victor looked at his watch. "Or rather, a bit *early*..."

"Yeah, well, I didn't choose the time. What happened to sundown? We used to do this then. That too late for you now, old man? Need to be in bed by seven so you're up at the ass-crack of dawn for the Early Bird Special?" Barsanti waved all around the table. "God forbid we eat breakfast at normal hours like civilized human beings instead of geriatric *animals*."

"You're sounding awfully bitter, Barsanti," Victor said. "Finally realize you'll never live long enough to enjoy a senior citizen discount?"

Barsanti cracked a smile at that, one that didn't last, as his gaze shifted to Dante. He stared at him in silence as the conversation moved on, downing some scotch as soon as it was brought to him. The atmosphere had again turned casual, laughter surrounding them. Gavin even relaxed, cracking a few smiles, although the man beside him appeared strictly *business*.

Dante had heard that about Moretti, though. He didn't associate with the Galantes, but Primo held a certain respect for him, anyway, appreciating a man who didn't bullshit.

An hour passed. Maybe it was only thirty minutes. As soon as it happened, Dante knew it hadn't been *enough* time. The change was palpable, a charge in the air sweeping into the room. Laughter died on a breath, smiles dwindling, eyes growing guarded as heavy footsteps approached the ballroom.

Dante didn't have to look to know his father was there. A sensation entered with him, foreboding and serious. This... *this* was how the meetings went. No love. No trust. No humor. Dante used to admire that about his father, the way people sat up and paid attention when he appeared. He took it for respect, for admiration, for apprehension, but he realized in that moment that it was none of those. It was revulsion. It was anger.

It was *hatred*.

Foregoing a greeting, Primo slid into the last empty chair, sitting to the left of Moretti and directly across from Barsanti. His eyes scanned the men, stopping when they reached Dante. His stare was a void. There was nothing there. The man was hollow.

"Galante," Victor said. "I'm happy you could join us."

"That makes one of us," Primo said, tearing his eyes away from his son to turn to Victor. "Can we get this over with? I'd rather not be here."

Victor motioned toward him. "The floor is yours, if you want to start. I'm just a neutral party."

"There's nothing neutral about you, Brazzi."

"Ah, I beg to differ."

"You can *beg* any which way you want... it doesn't make a difference. You chose sides long ago. You've insulted my family. You've insulted *me*. Then you have the audacity to call this meeting, to order me here, as if I owe you anything. As if I owe *anybody* anything."

"You want to talk about insults, Galante? Let's talk about them."

Primo flippantly waved his direction as he sat back in his chair. "By all means, get it off your chest. Tell me where the bad man touched you."

"Matteo Barsanti. Enzo Barsanti. My *grandsons*. You insulted me when you targeted them, when you used my daughter's funeral as an opportunity to strike against the ones she loved."

"Careful, Brazzi... you're not sounding very neutral right now."

"It's simple human decency," Victor continued. "There's a mourning period that should be observed. It's a matter of respect. It's how real men act. They don't kick each other when they're down. They wait until their opponent stands up again so they can look them in the eyes, face-to-face, man-to-man, making the fight fair."

"*All* is fair in times of war," Primo said. "I've tried for years to end this, to confront this head on, and I've been shut down every time. *Every* single time! So don't talk to me about fighting fair. Don't talk to me about following unspoken rules. Don't talk to me about respect. Where's the respect for *me*? You lecture me for targeting a man's family, yet where's the rage over what has come of *mine*?"

"We grieve for your losses, Galante," Alfie chimed in, "but more bloodshed isn't the answer."

"Then tell me... what *is* the answer?"

"Forgiveness."

A manic laugh escaped Primo as he threw his hands up. "You expect me to forgive him after what he's done? Forgiveness has to be *earned*."

"He returned your son to you, did he not?" Victor asked, motioning toward Dante. "That's more than we can say about you."

Dante's stomach churned, not wanting to be dragged into the argument, but it was futile. Eyes shifted his direction. Primo regarded his son, staring him dead in the eyes as he said, "Returning something broken doesn't make me whole again. I was better off believing he died with honor than seeing him here today, sitting on the wrong side of this table."

Ouch.

"There's no *wrong* side of the table," Alfie said. "We're adults. Let's fucking act like it. We talk about leaving the kids out of it, yet we drag them in every chance we get. I hate to break it to you fellas, but there's no honor in killing someone's unarmed son. No honor in blowing them up with a fucking car bomb." Alfie's angry eyes darted between Barsanti and Galante, those words meant for both of them. "Enough is enough. I'm sick and tired of waking up every morning, wondering if today will be the day someone decides to go after my daughter instead of being man enough to come after *me*."

A throat cleared, Barsanti's calm voice cutting in. "If it's any consolation, Alfie, I'd never go after your little girl."

"I appreciate that, Bobby, because I'd have your balls if you did."

Dante's eyes narrowed as Barsanti laughed. He should've stayed out of it. He knew he needed to keep his mouth shut. But damn if his voice didn't chime in on its own. "You didn't have a problem killing someone's child before."

His voice somehow amped up the tension in the room. Expressions turned severe as Barsanti looked at him. "You want to have this conversation again? I'm more than happy to sit here and discuss it if you want, because I guarantee I'm not the only guilty party at this table. I'm not the only one responsible for something reprehensible. I'm not the only one who killed someone's *son*. So I advise you look deep within yourself, Galante, instead of pointing fingers, before I snap that fucking finger off."

Dante stood, pointing right at Barsanti's face. "I'd like to see you—"

"Gentlemen!" Victor shouted, shoving Dante into his chair. "We're losing sight of the point."

"What *is* the point?" Primo asked. "Because as entertaining as this is, I've had enough socializing to last me a lifetime."

"The point, Primo, is that you've crossed lines, lines that we can't tolerate being crossed. Certain things you just *can't* do. There are rules for a reason, rules that keep us all safe, and when you break those rules you endanger all of us. If you want to make a move, you *have* to consult the others."

"Fine," Primo said, his attention going to the heads of the five families, lingering on Gavin before turning to Barsanti. He stared the man dead in the face, mere feet from him, as he announced, "I call for a vote."

The men grumbled... all except Barsanti, who stared back, straight-faced. "What do you want?"

"Permission."

"Permission to do what?"

"Permission to kill you."

"Have you asked for permission before?"

"At least once a year."

"And what, they all deny you every time you call for a vote?"

"Oh no, they don't *all* deny me. There's only ever been one hold out."

"Huh..." Barsanti glanced around at the others, considering that, his gaze settling on Gavin. "And am I right to assume that man isn't with us today?"

"Seems he's had an unfortunate accident."

"Ah, yes, unfortunate how he *accidentally* caught a bullet from one of your men."

"This is bullshit," Alfie said. "We're not here to—"

"No," Barsanti said, stopping Alfie. "Rules are rules. He calls for a vote, and New York gives it to him. So let's do this." Turning in his chair, Barsanti's gaze skimmed along the head of the three families, not giving them a chance to chime in before answering for them. "We've got a yes, a yes, and another yes..."

Genova cleared his throat. "Barsanti, I'm not going to—"

"Oh, don't change your mind on account of *me*," Barsanti said. "A yes is a yes. No hard feelings."

Genova fell silent, the other two refusing to speak.

Barsanti turned to Gavin. "You can speak for your father today, if you'd like to take on that burden, or I can just answer for him..."

Gavin opened his mouth before closing it again, waving toward Barsanti as he shook his head, clearly not wanting to get involved. Barsanti turned back around to Primo, a grin on his lips as he said, "I guess it's your lucky day, Primo, because today you get a big resounding *yes* from Johnny Amaro."

Primo's eyes widened. "A yes?"

"Absolutely," Barsanti said. "So, there you go... permission granted, Primo."

Primo slouched in his chair. "I appreciate it."

Barsanti nodded. "I'm sure you do."

Silence overtook the room, nobody sure what to say. Barsanti grabbed the bottle of liquor, pouring himself a bit in a glass before offering it across the table, to Primo. "Scotch?"

Primo shrugged. "Why not?"

Dante ran his hands down his face. "What the fuck is happening?"

"I don't know," Victor said quietly, "but I don't like it."

"Well, then..." Alfie shoved his chair back to stand. "I need another Mimosa."

"Of course you do, you big pussy," the head of the Buffalo family called out.

Laughter rang out, wiping away some of the tension. The others seemed to relax, but nothing eased Dante's anxiety. He tried to make sense of it, his thoughts jumbled as he watched his father, the man way too complacent, sitting there like he no longer had a care in the world. Every so often, Primo's eyes would shift Dante's way, a flickering glance. It wasn't until the third time it happened that Dante realized the man wasn't looking *at* him but *past* him. Turning his head, Dante glanced out the window, down onto the estate. Darkness cloaked everything but through it, he caught sight of a man dressed in all black strutting through the yard.

Victor turned, to look, and groaned. "The incompetence of some is astounding."

"Why do you say that?"

"Because my men *know* to hold their positions until they're dismissed."

Dante's stomach dropped. He turned back around once the figure was out of sight, again scanning the room, finding his father looking at him... for real that time. Primo picked up his scotch, taking a sip of it, the glass not enough to conceal the smile on his lips. *Fuck.*

"Something's wrong," Dante said.

A harrowing bang echoed from the floor below, violent enough to vibrate the floor beneath Dante's feet, the chandelier above them wildly shaking, the crystals clattering together. Dante's breath caught as he looked up at it, staring into the orange glow just as another rippling bang echoed through the house, carrying panicked voices along with it, followed by a hail of gunfire strong enough to make Dante's ears ring even from a distance.

There wasn't enough time to stop it.

Dante had seen it before.

He'd watched it happen.

He'd stood there, at The Place, witnessing one of Primo's sneak attacks. *You throw the whole gauntlet at them and they don't know how to react.*

The doors to the ballroom thrust open, men bursting in, cloaked in all black. They scattered, moving in disarray around the perimeter, as the figure front-and-center headed straight for them. Short, wearing a ski mask, carrying that AR-15. *Of course.* He jumped up on top of the table, kicking plates out of the way, knocking drinks over as he walked along it, finger squeezing the trigger and letting out a hail of gunfire into the ceiling above them, sending shards flying from the chandelier as bullets struck it. Men ducked from the spray, shielding themselves against the shrapnel, but nobody ran. Nobody cowered away. Nobody *begged*. They weren't like the men from The Place.

These men faced death every day.

"Gentlemen, it's in your best interest to cooperate," Umberto announced, removing his finger from the trigger when he stopped in front of Dante, staring down at him. "Play nice and maybe you'll get to go home tonight."

Dante caught his eye. "Bert."

"Dante." He nodded in greeting. "I passed along your message."

"I see that."

"Message?" Victor looked between them suspiciously. "*What* message?"

Alfie cleared his throat. "I told them to tell Galante that his son had nothing to say to him, and if they didn't like it, they could take it up with the Brazzi family."

"So here we are," Umberto said, waving around them as he continued stalking down the table, "taking it up with the Brazzi family."

Victor's angry eyes darted right to Primo as the man downed the rest of his scotch before setting the empty glass on the table. "Galante, you've got some *nerve...*"

"I do," Primo said. "A lot more nerve than the rest of you."

Primo stood, his hand held out. One of the men in black slipped a gun to him. Primo checked, making sure it was loaded as he strolled around the table, over to where Barsanti sat, pressing it to the back of the man's head. Umberto paced back and forth, watching them, making sure no one tried to intervene. Dante watched as Barsanti's eyes closed, his mouth furiously moving but his words too quiet to hear.

"Are you *praying*?" Primo asked. "You think that's going to stop me from blowing your brains all over this table? That I'm going to show you mercy?"

Barsanti's eyes opened again, his voice flat. "I don't want your mercy."

"Then what do you want?"

"Eye for an eye," Barsanti said. "Tooth for a tooth."

The second he said that, a gunshot went off, the loud bang echoing through the room as Primo angrily pulled the trigger, a bullet tearing right through the back of Barsanti's skull. He dropped, slamming into the table, but Primo didn't stop there. Umberto skidded to a stop in front of Gavin, damn near tripping as his boss unloaded bullet after bullet into Barsanti's body, unleashing his fury.

Before Umberto could get his footing, before he could pull himself together, someone reacted. It happened fast, the blink of an eye, the movement so instant Dante damn near missed it. Moretti swung, hitting the back of Umberto's knees, making his legs come out from under him. His ass hit the table with a bang, sending plates scattering. Moretti snatched up a steak knife before it clattered to the floor, gripping it firmly, and swung, jamming it right into the back of Umberto's hand when he tried to push himself up on the table. It sliced through his hand, the thrust so hard it pierced the table beneath, pinning him there as blood poured from the wound. A shriek tore from him as Moretti stood and snatched AR-15, slamming the butt of it right into Umberto's face. The crippling blow forced him to let go, to relinquish the gun to Moretti, who swung around, firing off a stream of bullets toward the door, sending the others scattering, fleeing from the room.

Moretti aimed the AR-15 at Primo's face. "You just *had* to do this when I was here."

Primo stared at him, motionless. "This isn't your fight."

"You're wrong," Moretti said, "because I have a wife to go home to, and anything that tries to stop me from doing that *becomes* my fight."

Dante's heart raced. Nobody else said a word, nobody *moving*. Nobody looked surprised, not even Gavin, who sat in the thick of it, watching with a blank expression, like none of it shocked him.

"You've got two choices," Moretti said, "the first being you drop the gun and walk out of here."

"The second?"

"You don't drop the gun and see how far you get," Moretti said. "Choose wisely."

Primo lowered his hand, and Dante relaxed a bit, but just like everything with his father, it changed like the flip of a switch. Primo moved, trying to get the upper hand, raising the gun fast, aiming right at Moretti's face and squeezing the trigger.

CLICK

Moretti just stood there, his expression blank. He looked *bored*.

Panic flashed in Primo's eyes as he frantically squeezed the trigger.

CLICK CLICK CLICK CLICK

His gaze darted around, looking for something. A weapon? An escape? A friend? Desperation poured from him in shaky breaths, but Moretti didn't appear sympathetic. Primo lowered the gun, tossing it on the table in a small pool of blood, resignation calming his expression. "Guess I was out of bullets."

"You wasted them," Moretti said, still aiming the AR-15 at him. "I counted."

"Check the house," Victor ordered then. "Find out where they went, how they got in here and why none of my men *stopped* them."

"I'm on it," Alfie said, jumping up, grabbing Dante's arm and yanking him out of his chair. "Come on, you shouldn't be here for this."

Dante didn't argue, watching over his shoulder as he followed Alfie to the door.

"Anything to say for yourself?" Victor asked, standing up, staring right at Primo.

Primo said nothing.

Sickness swirled inside of Dante, making every inch of him tremble. By the time they reached the stairs, Umberto's voice cried out, begging, a stream of "no, no, no," before rapid gunfire tore through the ballroom. The sound stalled Dante as he doubled over, dry heaving, but Alfie grabbed his arm again and made him keep moving.

The house was still, not a sign of anyone anywhere. Alfie armed himself, getting guns from Victor's office, before motioning out the front door. "Go get some air while we clean this up."

The world was a haze, and Dante was in a fucking daze, sitting on the front step of the house in the darkness, trying to breathe but bile burned his throat, making it suffocating. He put his head down, forcing back the sickness and pulling himself together.

A hand clutched his shoulder, Gavin sitting down beside him on the step. He said nothing, just staring off into space.

"No sentimental bullshit?" Dante asked.

"Not today," Gavin said. "Honestly, I'm not sure what to say."

"You don't have to say anything."

"But I do."

Men exited the house, starting to leave, to handle business or clean up or do whatever the hell they needed to do to fix what had happened in that ballroom. A lot of bitter, grief-stricken soldiers would be running the streets of Manhattan now without anyone to control them.

Dante tensed when Moretti stalled in front of him. "My condolences."

Unwelcome tears stung Dante's eyes. "Excuse me?"

"Your father," Moretti said. "I gave him a choice, but he didn't take it. He forced my hand."

"You're offering condolences over a man you killed?"

"Regardless of the circumstances, it's always regretful when a son loses his father."

Dante was stunned. "Thank you."

Moretti nodded as he turned to Gavin. "Tell him."

Gavin said nothing in response.

"I'm serious, Amaro," Moretti said. "You tell him or *I'll* tell him myself, and none of us want that to happen."

Gavin covered his face with his hands, muttering, "I'm going to tell him."

Dante watched Moretti leave, silence surrounding them again.

"Look, Dante..."

Dante got to his feet, wanting to get out of there. "Whatever it is, you don't have to say anything."

"But I do." Gavin stood up. "For one, because if he has to come back and tell you himself, he'll probably shoot me, but more so because I just... I have to. I have to tell you. You deserve to know. Hell, I should've told you a long time ago. I should've let Gabby tell you when she wanted to. But I, uh... I don't know how you're going to take it. I don't know, maybe you'll be happy. You don't have a gun on you, right?"

Dante turned to Gavin. "Just tell me."

"Your sister," Gavin said.

Silence.

"My sister," Dante repeated. "That's it? That's what you have to tell me?"

"Yes," Gavin said. "Well, no. Your sister... she, well..."

"Christ, Gavin, *spit it out.*"

"She wasn't in the car that night. When it exploded. Your sister wasn't inside of it."

Dante stared at him. "You think I don't know that?"

"What?"

"I'm not an idiot, Gavin. I graduated high school. I took a fucking science class. There would've been *something* left if they would've been inside. There were no bodies in that car. I know."

"What?"

"Besides, the car had a remote starter. Bert said he wired it to go off exactly like the one that killed Joey. My father insisted. So it would've been triggered as soon as he hit the button."

"I, uh... what?"

Dante sighed exasperatedly, running his hands down his face. "Say *what* one more time, Gavin. *One more fucking time.*"

"I'm sorry, I'm just... why didn't you say anything?"

"What's there to say? She wasn't in the car, but she isn't *here*, either. Something has kept her away, and that something probably means I'll never see her again... not in this life, anyway. And no offense, because you're not a bad guy, as far as guys go, but I'm not really down with the bearing my soul to another fucking man thing."

Dante walked back into the house, done with that conversation, but Gavin's voice caught him, trailing him, not letting go. "I know."

"Know what, Amaro?"

"Where she is."

Dante skidded to a stop and swung around. "You know where she is?"

Hesitantly, Gavin nodded. "Or, well, I *knew* where she was. They're not there anymore."

"They?"

"Her... Matty... the baby..."

Dante's blood ran cold. "The baby?"

"Yeah, I mean, she hasn't *had* the baby yet. She's still pregnant. Or she *was*, last time I saw her."

"Whoa... you saw her? You've *seen* her?"

Gavin nodded again.

"Alive?"

Another nod.

"You're telling me my sister is alive, and not only did you know, but you knew *exactly* where to find her?"

One more nod.

Dante's calm slipped, something inside of him breaking. The emotion he'd been holding back, forcing down, came flooding through the cracks. His vision blurred. His hands shook. The second a tear slipped down his cheek, he swung.

CRACK

CHAPTER 22

The first time Gabriella laid eyes on Dante, lying comatose in the hospital bed, she had a thought: *for someone with such a big reputation, he seemed so small.* People spoke of him like he was larger than life, but there he was, this fragile human, with a broken body and a shattered soul, desperately needing to be healed.

It took days before he smiled, weeks before he laughed, months before he loved, but once he did, she believed there was no stopping him again. He'd grown ten feet and his skin became steel, and the fragmented boy seemed almost whole, turning superhuman. He risked his life, moving fast as a speeding bullet, running into burning buildings and standing up for people. Small, he wasn't... larger than life had been right.

But still, the underlying sadness remained, never going away, buried down inside of him. *Sorrow.*

And the moment the apartment door opened and Dante walked in, Gabriella saw it again. He looked exhausted, and frazzled, and absolutely done with the world, but beyond that she sensed the sorrow. She saw it in his watery eyes. She saw it in his barely-there smile. She saw it, and she felt it.

God, it hurt.

It hurt to see him *hurting.*

"Dante," she whispered, wrapping her arms around him.

"I'm okay," he said, rubbing her back with one hand as he shut the door with the other.

She clung to him as he walked her over to the couch, plopping down on it and pulling her along. Her hands explored him, caressing his face as she kissed the corners of his mouth.

Reaching up, Dante grabbed her hands, pulling them away from him. "I told you... I'm okay."

He kissed her once, softly on the lips, before pulling away. Gabriella's eyes darted to his hands as he pinned hers in his lap, keeping her from touching him. Even in the dim lighting, she saw his knuckles swelling. "What happened to your hand?"

As soon as she asked that, he let go of her. "Gavin."

"Gavin?"

"Yeah, his face hurts about as much as you'd expect it to."

"His *what?*"

"I punched him," Dante said, grimacing as he flexed his hand. "Should know better than to hit that hard-headed bastard."

"You punched Gavin? Why?"

"Long story," Dante muttered. "Look, can we talk about this later? I need to take a shower and wash off this... *whatever.* It's been a long day."

"Sure," she whispered, although he didn't wait for her answer, disappearing to the bathroom. She stared down the darkened hallway as the water started running, the door open a crack. He hadn't even bothered to turn on the light. Gabriella took a few steps that direction, curious, when her phone rang in the kitchen.

Diverting that way, she pressed the button to answer. *Gavin.* "Hello?"

"Dante knows."

Two words. That was it. Two words that had the power to make her knees weak. "Knows what?"

"About his sister. I told him, and he clocked me right in the jaw for it."

"Oh God."

"It's been one hell of a night, and I can't get into it right now... it's not my place... but I just needed to let you know."

"Does he know that *I* knew?"

"I'm pretty sure he riddled it out. I mentioned that I should've let you tell him... I wasn't thinking, and well, point is, cat's out of the bag, and he's in a bad place right now—a *weird* place—so be careful, okay?"

"Okay," she whispered. "Thank you."

Gabriella hung up and stepped into the hallway, looking toward the bathroom. It was still dark, the water continuing to run. Gabriella edged that way, pausing at the door to push it open further. A faint noise, a sharp inhale and shuttering exhale, struck her like a punch to the chest. *Crying.*

Frowning, Gabriella undressed before pushing the flimsy curtain aside just enough to slip into the shower behind him. Dante stood in the darkness, under the hot spray, his forehead pressed against the white tile wall, his eyes closed and the water masking his tears.

Gabriella ran her hand up his back, her fingertips tracing his spine.

"I'm sorry," she whispered, "for whatever's making you feel this way."

Dante drew her to him as he reached over to shut off the water. He said not a word, pulling her out of the shower, dripping water all over everywhere as he led her to the bedroom. Right away, his mouth was on hers, his hands roaming as he dragged her onto the bed. Hitching her knees up to push inside, he nuzzled into her neck, nibbling on the skin near her shoulder, as he thrust hard, over and over.

"Dante," she moaned, wrapping her legs around him, lifting up to meet each stroke. Her hands ran through his hair, gripping the locks, holding onto him as he found comfort in her body. "Oh God, you feel so good…"

He groaned, increasing his pace, each thrust desperate, hands everywhere and mouth moving, tasting every inch of skin his tongue could reach. Pain nipped at her gut as he hit deep, so deep, every bit of him in every bit of her. She could barely handle it.

Tugging his head up, making him look at her, she whispered, "I'm so sorry… *so, so sorry.*"

He thrust hard in response, making her breath hitch as he stared her right in the eyes. As soon as she inhaled, he pressed his mouth to hers, kissing her roughly, stealing the air back out of her lungs. His hand drifted down between them, stroking her, bringing her to the edge. She gasped, arching her back, orgasm rippling through her.

Dante wasn't far behind, grunting, slamming his hips against her a few times before stilling, breathing heavily. Gabriella hugged him, holding him, not wanting to let go.

He pulled out, not letting go of her, tugging her into his arms, onto his chest, as he rolled over onto his back. Still, nothing was said as they lay in silence.

Gabriella could feel the sorrow closing in around them.

She wished, more than anything, she could chase it away, but she felt powerless to stop whatever was happening.

Sleep caught up to Gabriella eventually, the sun shining through the bedroom window when she awoke. Groggy, she rolled over, shielding her eyes from the light, tangled naked in the sheets. *Alone.* As soon as that struck her, she sat up and paused. Dante sat on the edge of the bed, fully clothed, his head down as he stared vacantly at the messy bedroom floor. "Dante?"

"I trusted you," he whispered. "I thought you trusted me, too."

"I do."

"Didn't trust me enough to tell me the truth. Didn't trust me enough to tell me what you knew."

"Gavin said—"

"*Fuck* Gavin. You're my *girlfriend*. You're not supposed to keep secrets from me."

"I didn't want to, but it wasn't safe. Your father—"

"Is dead. He's dead now, so it doesn't matter. It wouldn't have mattered *then*, either. I wouldn't have put them in danger. I told her… the last time I saw her, the last time I *spoke* to her… I told her she was on her own. I told her I couldn't help her anymore. And it would've been nice… it would've been really fucking nice… if one of those times I was grieving my sister you would've had the heart to tell me she was okay, that she'd made it on her own, that I hadn't doomed her."

Gabriella stared at him, stunned, her hand grazing along his back before he stood up, moving out of her reach. "Dante, please."

"I need some time to think."

"Time," she said, "to think."

"I need to clear my head, to figure out what all of this means for me, because right now, I can't make sense of it, so I need some time."

"How much time?"

"I don't know," he said. "I'll let you know when I figure it out."

"Where will you go?"

"Home."

He walked out, leaving her sitting there, tears stinging her eyes as she whispered, "But *this* is your home."

* * *

"Toto, I've got a feeling our asses aren't in Kansas anymore."

Genna stared out the side window of the Lincoln as those words tumbled from her lips, accentuated by an icy cloud of breath. The heat in the car was hardly working, likely something she screwed up. It hadn't been a problem in the southwest, where it didn't seem to get cold enough to run it, but New York's frigid temperatures were proving to be her nemesis.

"Tell me about it," Matty muttered, drumming his fingers against the steering wheel. He'd taken over driving not long after they'd set out on the road. It had been a long trip... more small towns, more rundown motels, and more evading local police. *Same ol' shit.* While the car wasn't exactly stolen, it wasn't legal, either. It hadn't been registered in years, the Illinois license plate affixed to the back damn near older than *her.* "It looks like a war-zone."

"It *is*," she said. "That's why Dante calls it ground zero."

Dante...

The mere thought of him made Genna's chest tighten.

The closer they got to New York, the more her anxiety acted up, nausea brutally rocking her during the trip. She blamed it on 'morning sickness', although that had long ago gone away, seeing as how she was nearing the end of the pregnancy. She was a wreck, unsure how to act, unsure what to think when it came to her brother. They'd barely been on speaking terms when he disappeared, finding themselves on different sides of a battlefield in a war she wanted nothing to do with, a war he'd spent his life fighting, a war—judging by the look of the streets as they drove along—that hadn't relented at all.

Little Italy.

Gone was the sunshiny neighborhood full of friendly faces and familiar shops. Buildings were burned down, windows boarded up, streets blocked off. Matty had filled her in on a bit during the trip, like how her father had tried to *kill* Jonny Amaro, but they'd just felt like stories. Tales of another life, of another place. It wasn't until they drove by the quarantined shell that had once been Casato, pulling onto the block that had been rocked just months ago by a violent car bomb, that it sunk in.

"It's funny, though, isn't it?" Matty asked as he stopped at a red light. "They want to control these streets so bad that they go to war over them and end up destroying it all."

"I wouldn't call that *funny*, Matty. Joe Pesci is funny. Our fathers are just assholes."

"Funny, how?" Matty grinned, leaning toward her. "Funny like a clown?"

"Don't even." She shoved his face away. "Don't be quoting *Goodfellas* to me right now. I mean, holy shit... that's like saying Bloody Mary in the mirror in the dark. What are you trying to do, conjure the fuckers? It's goddamn *Candyman* all over again!"

Matty laughed, pulling away from her when the light turned green again. He continued driving, veering west. Genna left him to his curiosity as he drove into Soho, navigating the familiar streets to The Place. He slowed as he passed the remnants of the building. It, too, had burned.

"My father's seriously gotta be pissed about that," he mumbled, continuing on, not wanting to linger too long in one spot. "And those guys who hung out there, you know, they weren't bad. They just got mixed up with the wrong crowd."

"Don't we all?" Genna watched in the side mirror as she frowned. She hadn't expected to feel so... *heartbroken*. "I'm sad I'll never see that pool table again. I lost my virginity on top of it."

Laughter burst from Matty. "You were *not* a virgin."

"How do you know?"

"Because I know. I didn't take it easy on you that night. Had you been a virgin, you would've been in tears, not mewling."

She scowled. "Mewling?"

"Like a cat in heat."

She shoved him, damn near making him swerve the car into another lane. "You just did *not* compare me to a cat in heat!"

"You practically backed that ass up into me, begging me to stick it in, baby."

"See, that's it... I'm done with you." She shifted around in the seat, slouching, trying to get comfortable but the damn seatbelt was tight on her stomach no matter how she turned. "Just take me to my father's house and drop me off. It's about time we go our separate ways."

"Over my dead body. That's the *last* place I'll be taking you."

"What if I demand it? What if I refuse to go with you?"

"Then I'll tie you up and throw you in the trunk."

"See, I knew it!" She lugged her body his direction again, groaning from discomfort, and waved her finger all around his face. "When I saw you on the elevator that day, I totally called that shit. *Creep.*"

Matty pulled her hand away from his face. "I'm not taking you to that house. *Ever.* But I know where we can go."

"Where?"

"Neutral ground."

Neutral ground. New Jersey.

"You sure the house is still there?" she asked. "Everything else seems to have been wiped off the map."

"Positive," he said. "Just like I'm positive you weren't a virgin."

"Whatever. I didn't mewl, though. I would *never.*"

"That sounds like a challenge."

"One we'll save for another day," she said, shifting around yet again. "Ugh, can you make it speedy? I've gotta pee here."

"You just did that."

"Yeah, well, tell that to the baby bouncing on my bladder."

Reaching over, Matty ran his hand along her stomach, rubbing. "Take it easy on your Mom, kiddo. We need her in one piece."

Genna rested her hand on top of Matty's, slipping her fingers between his as she smiled. She could feel the bumps, the baby shifting around in her stomach, kicking against Matty's hand, his thumb steadily stroking the spot that kept moving.

He was right, as it turned out, the house in New Jersey still there. Matty parked the car in the driveway, not having a way to open the garage, and hesitated as he approached the front door. "Shit."

Genna danced around behind him, her bladder about to burst. "What?"

"No key." He felt his pockets. "I didn't even think about it."

"Oh, pfftt, no problem." She headed back to the car, yanking the door open, and snatched a screwdriver off the floorboard. She wiggled it in his face as she returned. "Easy-peasy."

"Stealing cars... hustling pool... breaking and entering... just a few of your many talents."

"I also do that thing with my tongue," she said, slipping the screwdriver around the doorjamb, near the lock, surprised to find it already loose. "Uh, Matty?"

"Yeah?"

She popped the door open. "Someone has pried this thing open before."

He caught her arm to stop her. "Wait, it might not be safe."

She pulled away and walked right in. "Sorry, man, but I've gotta *go*. If someone wants to, like, stab me, they can do it after I'm done."

"Genna..."

Genna sprinted to the bathroom, relieving the pressure on her bladder. Closing her eyes, she clutched her stomach, a wave of pain sweeping through her—nothing alarming, but enough to be a nuisance. "Come on, kid, we can't do this right now. I need you to give me some time here before you try to make your grand entrance."

Matty passed her in the hallway when she stepped out, carrying a few bags of stuff they'd accumulated on the road.

"I'll get the rest," she said, heading for the car. She grabbed the last two bags, slamming the trunk closed. The moment she did, a swell of nausea ran through her. Blinking, she came face-to-face with a gun, a man clutching it that she didn't recognize.

He stared at her in stone cold silence. He was maybe twice her age, looking like Andy Garcia circa *Oceans 11*, sort of attractive but mostly like he might shoot her if she moved too fast. *Mobster.*

"Who are you?" he asked, his voice low.

"Depends," she said. "What answer won't get me shot?"

"Genna, did you get—?" Matty's question stalled when he stepped out of the house. The man glanced that direction, and Genna's mind moved fast. While most people had enough compassion to not harm a pregnant woman, especially one so far along, Matty was fair game when it came to target practice. Gaze darting around, she weighed her options, considering kneeing the guy in the junk, when Matty's voice rang out again. "Alfie?"

The man stared at him, his gun still pointed at Genna. "Matty?"

"Uh... yeah."

The man regarded Genna again. "I'm guessing that makes you the Bonnie to my nephew's Clyde?"

"Nephew?"

Matty took a few steps their direction, holding his hands up in front of him, like he wasn't sure whether it was safe. "He's my mother's sister's husband, Alfie Russo."

"So… your uncle."

"Yeah."

"That's nice." Genna stared at the man. "Do you think your uncle can, like, not point his gun at me anymore?"

Alfie lowered the gun. "Sorry about that. Can never be too sure these days."

As soon as the gun was tucked away, Matty approached.

Alfie turned his way, a full-blown grinning taking over his face. "Jesus, Matty, talk about a sight for sore eyes."

He yanked Matty into a hug, beating him on the back before grasping his face, patting his cheek so hard he practically slapped him. Genna leaned against the bumper of the car, watching.

"You don't look surprised to see me alive," Matty said.

"Come on, you think we'd write you off? Knew it was only a matter of time before you popped up again. But this?" Alfie motioned toward Genna. "*This* is a surprise. What the hell, kid? Don't you know to wrap it before you tap it?"

Matty's cheeks turned pink. "Had a little slip up."

"I see that." Alfie squeezed his shoulder. "Your mother, God rest her soul, would be thrilled. A *grandbaby*."

"That makes one parent," Genna said. "The others, not so much."

Alfie cut his eyes at her, his expression falling. "Come on, let's go inside. Got a lot of catching up to do."

"We're actually hoping to find Genna's brother," Matty said. "We know he's alive."

"Yeah, we'll get to him," Alfie said. "There's something else we should talk about, though. Something important. You'll want to sit down."

Genna didn't like the sound of that.

What was more important than her brother?

She followed them inside, plopping down on the dusty brown couch. Matty perched on the arm of it beside her, while Alfie sat in a chair, stretching his legs out, clasping his hands together in his lap. "You know the expression 'don't shoot the messenger'?"

"Of course," Matty said.

"Well, I'm only the messenger here, so don't shoot."

Words came flowing out of the man, a wild story that started with a meeting and ended with three people dead: Roberto Barsanti, Primo Galante, and one of Primo's men. Genna stared at him in shock, trying to keep up with it all, her stomach churning. She swallowed thickly, tears burning her eyes. *Don't cry. Don't cry. Holy fuck, don't cry. He tried to blow up the man you love. He wrote you off. He would've hated your baby. He would've probably killed you all. He might be your father, but he wasn't a good man. He wasn't a nice man. He was just a man... a man who used to tuck you in at night... a man who used to hug you tight. Oh God, don't fucking cry...*

Matty rubbed her back, his touch breaking her reserve. Silent tears streamed down her cheeks.

"Wish I was surprised," Matty said. "We knew a long time ago it would come to this."

"Yeah," Alfie said. "Despite everything, you know, they were powerful men, *important* men, so we figured they deserved a proper send-off. I'll spare you the details, but we made sure they'd be found."

"Thank you," Matty said. "We had our problems, but my mother always wanted to be buried with him."

"I figured," Alfie said. "And you know, Primo has his kids... Dante told us to shove the old man in a car and light it up, for all he cared, but you know, burying him is the right thing to do."

"My brother said that?" Genna asked, surprised.

"Your brother says a lot," Alfie said. "Don't know about that kid some days."

"So you know him?"

"You could say that."

"Where is he?"

"Hard to say," Alfie said. "My daughter should able to tell you."

Matty cleared his throat. "I heard about that."

"Yeah, can't say I was *thrilled*," Alfie said, "but he's not so bad, I guess. Could be worse."

"What are you talking about?" Genna asked, looking between them.

383

"Your brother's dating my cousin," Matty said.

"Dating?" Genna asked. "Are we talking every other weekend and the occasional Wednesday kind of dating?"

Matty cracked a smile. "She's his girlfriend."

"Girlfriend?" she asked. "Like a real live girlfriend?"

"They're living together," Alfie said. "They say they're in love."

"Whoa, whoa, whoa…" Genna sat up, holding her hands up to stop them from saying anything else. "Out of everything you've said, *that* is the craziest. Are you sure we're talking about my brother here?"

"Unfortunately," Alfie said. "They're living in an apartment in Little Italy. Neighborhood's wrecked, but it's safe, for the most part. Everyone's been quiet. You should be fine over there."

* * *

The loud buzz echoed through the apartment from the box affixed to the wall by the front door. Gabriella's back stiffened when she heard it, standing in the kitchen, stirring macaroni on the stove. It went off a few times, back-to-back, but she ignored it. The only person she cared to see was Dante, and he still had his key to get in, despite walking out and offering no sort of answer for when he might return.

If he even returns…

She had nobody to blame but herself. Okay, and Gavin… she blamed Gavin. And Primo Galante, and Bobby Barsanti… she blamed them, too—blamed them for starting the whole war that created the entire mess.

Ugh, she blamed the world.

She blamed all of her neighbors.

She blamed the friggin *mayor*.

She could throw blame around all day long, but it wouldn't change anything.

The buzzing stopped. Gabriella drained her macaroni and mixed it all together, scooping it in a bowl as she headed for the living room. Meredith Grey stood on her television screen, blabbing about being dark and twisty, her mess of a life seeming to pale in comparison to Gabriella's currently, but it still managed to make her feel better.

At least she wasn't the *only* screw up.

Gabriella had barely made it a few steps when knocking echoed from the door. She stalled and turned toward it, considering ignoring it, too, hoping they'd leave her alone to wallow, but curiosity was a strong contender. She crept over, not wanting to be heard, and glanced out the peephole.

The moment she did, her muscles declared mutiny.

Her knees almost buckled, the bowl of macaroni slipping right from her hand, hitting the floor with a clatter. *Oh my God.* Fumbling with the locks, her hands shaking, she yanked the door open, giving no regard to the fact that she wasn't wearing *pants*. Luckily, her shirt was long enough to cover everything, because nothing mattered beyond what was in front of her. "Matty?"

Matteo Barsanti stood there, in the hallway in front of her apartment.

"Gabby." He smiled. "Long time, no see."

"I, uh... *wow*. What are you...? Why are you *here*?"

"She's not really surprised, either," a female voice called out from behind him. "Man, we did a shitty job at this whole faking-death thing. I think the only one that got fooled was *me*."

Gabriella pulled the door open further, her eyes widening. "Genna? You're, uh... *oh my god*. You're..."

"Alive?" Genna bumped Matty with her hip, nudging him out of the way. "Here?"

"I was going to say pregnant," Gabriella said. "You're *pregnant*."

"Oh, yeah." Genna grasped her stomach. "I'm that, too."

Gabriella had no idea what to say. In all of their conversations, Gavin had never once mentioned that fact, despite acknowledging seeing her. "I had no idea. Gavin didn't say anything."

"My brother didn't, either?"

"Your brother?"

Genna eyed her warily. "Yeah, Dante?"

"How would he...?"

"He was the first one to know," Genna said. "He figured it out before I did."

Gabriella was stunned. "He never mentioned it."

"Oh... well, then. That sucks. Did he mention me *at all*?"

Gabriella sensed the apprehension in that question. "All the time."

Genna smiled, her relief palpable.

"I'm guessing he's not here," Matty said. "If he was, he probably would've taken a swing at me by now."

"Oh, no, Dante's not here."

"Do you know where he is?" Genna asked.

Gabriella hesitated, not sure how much Genna knew, not wanting to have to be the one to tell her. "He mentioned something about going home."

Genna pursed her lips as she looked at Matty. "And you said you weren't taking me to my father's house."

"I'm not." Matty pulled out a set of keys. "You can take yourself, though."

Genna took the keys, scowling. "I was kidding about the going our separate ways thing."

"I know." He nudged her chin before kissing her, pressing his palm flat against her stomach. "I just figure, knowing your brother, it might go over better if *I'm* not around when you see him."

"What are you going to do?" Genna asked.

"He can hang out here," Gabriella suggested. "I have macaroni... or well, I *had* some." She grimaced at the mess on the floor, shoved behind the door. "We can order a pizza."

"There you go," Matty said, slipping around Genna as he backed up into the apartment. "You go do what you gotta do, while I eat pizza... real pizza... *without* pickles."

Genevieve scrunched up her nose, lingering in the hallway. "That sounds terrible."

"I bet." Matty grasped her face, cradling it between his hands. "*Go.* See your brother."

Genna bit her bottom lip. "But what if—?"

"Don't do that," he said. "We just drove the entire way across this country for you to see him. The time for second-guessing was two thousand miles ago."

"Fine," she grumbled, shoving away from him. "I'll go, but you better save me some damn pizza, Matteo. *With* pickles."

"Whatever you want."

Genna pressed a quick peck to his lips and stalked away, grumbling. Gabriella couldn't make out most of the words, something about bossy Barsantis. Her footsteps echoed through the building as she stomped down the stairs.

"Does she not *want* to see Dante?"

"Oh, no, she does." Matty stepped into the apartment. "She just gets mean when she's scared. Galante family trait."

"Ah, right." Gabriella shut the door, bending down to pick up her bowl and clean up the macaroni. "I've seen her brother do that."

"So have I," Matty said. "It's what killed Enzo."

CHAPTER 23

Soft, fluffy flakes fell from the night sky, a splattering of white in the stark darkness. Dante sat on the damp railing of the second-story balcony, his legs dangling over the side. His laces hung loose, swaying, his shoes on the verge of falling off.

Coldness seeped through his dark sweats and the NY Mets shirt he wore, but the liquor running through his veins, radiating out through his pores, proved enough to keep him warm. He was probably dying from fucking hypothermia, but he sure didn't feel it.

His nerves were *numb*.

The doors to the balcony stood wide open, letting cold air burst through, into the quiet house. Behind him, Genna's bedroom. She'd always loved the balcony. How many times had he found her sitting out there? *It's too suffocating inside,* she'd say. *I can't breathe.*

Although true, Dante always told her she was being dramatic. Their father had her on lockdown, yes, but Dante never minded keeping her company. But man, what a pain in the ass, not being able to take a breath without somebody monitoring each inhale.

So he got it, why she found it suffocating.

He understood the feeling.

He wished he could tell her that.

"Christ, please tell me you're not planning to *jump*."

The incredulous voice echoed through the vacant room, striking him. *Genna.* Dante tensed, his muscles rigid as he clutched tight to the oversized bottle of whiskey, already half drank despite cracking it open just an hour earlier.

Did hypothermia cause hallucinations?

Drunken delusions?

Was he already fucking *dead*?

"Seriously," she continued, "because at most you'll probably just break your leg, and I am in *no* condition to try to carry your dumb ass anywhere."

Dante's eyes closed, his head lowering. "Am I dreaming again?"

"Again? Have you been dreaming about me? That's kind of weird."

He lazily shrugged a shoulder, hearing her approach, every footstep making his chest ache more. "I watch you die sometimes in my sleep."

"Okay, that's not weird. That's *morbid.*"

"Better than it happening while awake."

Dante took another swig of the liquor as he reopened his eyes. Shifting on the railing, he swung around, dropping his feet flat on the balcony to stand up. He swayed from the sudden head rush, his vision briefly blacking out.

As soon as it came back to him, he saw her. Dark hair, longer than he remembered. Bright, pale blue eyes. Fair skin, like porcelain. Pregnant.

Jesus *fuck*, she was pregnant...

Her black shirt stretched tight over her round stomach, like she'd shoved a basketball underneath. Dante blinked a few times, his gaze fixed on it, dumbfounded. A shuddering breath escaped him as he let go of the whiskey bottle, letting it drop.

CLUNK

"Genna," he whispered, his voice strained.

Going right for her, he yanked her into a hug, holding her tightly to his chest. One hand fisted the back of her shirt, the other grasping her hair, as he rested his cheek against the top of her head.

"Dante," she grumbled. "You're smothering me."

"Suck it up," he said. "I'm not letting go yet."

She didn't argue, hugging him back. Dante waited. For what, he didn't know. Waited for the moment to come to an end. Waited for the world to stop turning. Waited for life to be over.

Waited to wake the fuck up.

But nothing happened.

He stood there, unsteady, holding on to her, until she pulled from his grasp. The blurry image of her remained in front of him, her nose red and cheeks flushed pink, teeth chattering.

She was freezing.

But she was breathing.

She was standing right in front of him.

Tears filled her eyes, her voice cracking as she whispered, "I thought you were dead."

"I could say the same to you."

She hugged him again, smiling as she cried, those tears breaking loose. She burrowed into his shirt, wiping her face, wiping her *nose*. Her body shook, so Dante pulled her into the house and out of the cold.

"What happened to my stuff?" she asked right away, looking around the empty room as Dante shut the balcony doors.

"It's all gone."

"Why?"

"Someone crosses you, you erase them from your life."

"I, uh… *wow*." She spun in a circle. "Guess I pissed him off."

"He was already mad. He was mad for a long time. You just gave him a reason to show you his anger," Dante said. "But if it's any consolation, I discovered my shit's gone, too."

"Really? *Yours*? What did you do that was so wrong?"

"I wouldn't even know where to start."

"I've got all the time in the world to listen." Genna rubbed her hands over her swollen stomach. "Well, okay, I've got more like three weeks, tops, until this one barges in, but you know what I'm saying."

Less than a month. Where the hell had time gone? It had all passed in a blur, a succession of blinks, flashing images that propelled him through time. It still felt like just yesterday that he'd stood in that same room, damn near in that very spot, and stared at his sister as she clutched that plastic stick with two pink lines, the world as he knew it crashing down. Until that moment, nothing had been irreparable. Nothing had been permanent. Nothing had happened that they couldn't have come back from. He'd ignorantly believed that it would all work itself out, that she would've come to her senses, like the smart girl she was, and their father would've forgiven her, like the rational man he was, and they would've been a family again, like Galantes were supposed to be. But then she popped up pregnant and Dante made himself a murderer, swearing he'd clean up her mess when in reality all he did was make everything worse.

"I'm guessing, since you're *here*, you know about Dad."

"Yeah," she whispered. "I know he's dead."

Dead. The word felt strange. They'd all been dead a time or two, it seemed, but there was no coming back from death for Primo. Death, in Dante's life, never felt so permanent.

"Barsanti, too," Dante said.

"I heard," she said, toeing the carpet. "Feels weird."

"Them being dead?"

"Yeah." She made a face, cutting her eyes at him. "This is going to sound stupid…"

"What?"

"And it's probably insensitive, too," she continued. "Like, *really* insensitive. I'm talking worst person in the world kind of insensitive. *Dad*-level insensitive…"

"I'm listening."

"This war between them was basically our whole lives. I don't remember a single day where it wasn't a factor. It dictated what we did, where we went, what we could say… it dictated *everything*. And now it's just over and I can't help but feel…"

"Free?" Dante guessed.

"Robbed."

"Robbed?"

"They're both dead, and it's over, but like… who won?"

"Who *won*?"

"We just played a game of *Monopoly* that was almost twenty years long and nobody got the damn monopoly. Nobody put a hotel on Boardwalk. They just threw in all their cards."

Dante ran his hands down his face. "I'm pretty sure *we* won, Genna."

"Us?"

"Yeah, we're alive, aren't we? I'm calling that a win."

"I guess so," she muttered. "And it's freeing, too, but damn… worst game of all time."

"You're funny."

"And you're drunk. When's the last time you ate? You're looking kind of… like shit."

"I'm fine."

"Uh, no, you're not. You're rocking the 'I'll suck a dick for a cheeseburger' look." She waved her finger around at him. "And a Mets shirt? *Really?* Worst Yankees fan of all time."

He looked down at his shirt. "Yeah, it's... somebody's."

"A female somebody?" Genna asked. "Maybe one that hails from Jersey?"

He cut his eyes at her. "How'd you guess?"

"I didn't *guess*, dumb ass. She's how I knew where to find you."

"Oh."

That was all he could think to say. *Oh.*

"Oh?" Genna repeated. "That's all you've got to say?"

He shrugged. "What else is there to say?"

She stared at him with disbelief before shaking her head and grabbing his arm. "Come on, I'm sure there's *something* in the fridge we can eat to sober you up a bit so you can tell me about this girlfriend you supposedly have, because drunk Dante is acting like it's all completely normal and I don't know what to make of that."

Dante didn't resist, staggering along with her down the stairs. "I don't know if we can call her my *girlfriend* now."

"Why not?"

"Because," he said, "I don't know."

"Well, that clears it up," Genna said, dragging him into the kitchen. She flicked on the light, waltzing right over to the fridge, while Dante leaned against the wall. She shifted things around, pulling out leftover containers, yanking off lids and sniffing the contents. She walked back and forth across the room, tossing stuff into the trashcan.

Dante watched her, laughing as she stood in front of the microwave, absently rocking back and forth, heating something up. "You waddle."

She turned his way. "Excuse me?"

"You waddle when you walk," he said. "Like a penguin."

She pointed a fork at him as the microwave beeped. "Say that again and I will *stab* you."

"Won't be the first one to do it." Dante pulled up his shirt, looking at the scars on his side. One was smoother than the other, professionally sewn up, while the second was more of a jagged gash, like a chunk had been taken out.

"Who the hell stabbed you?"

"Tweedle-whatever." Dante dropped his shirt again. "One of those assholes. Got me right after I dropped you off for community service that day. Then he got me again, a few months ago, at a bar over in Soho."

"Why were you at a bar in *Soho*?"

"I went to see Barsanti."

"Seriously? Are you *crazy*?"

"That's the same thing Gabriella asked."

"Well, then, that means the motion has been seconded, which makes that shit law. You've officially lost your mind."

Genna filled two plates with food before heading to the dining room. Dante followed, watching as she set them on the table, sitting in the same chair she'd sat in for family dinner, not hesitating before sliding the second plate across from her. Dante glared at it as he walked over, plopping down in the chair at the head of the table, a chair no one had ever sat in except for Primo. Dante grabbed the plate and stared down at the food. It was a horrendous buffet of whatever she'd found, from leftover pasta to scraps of shredded lettuce and a crouton or two. "What is this shit?"

"Something to put in your stomach," she answered, taking a bite out of a pickle.

"I'm not hungry."

"Doesn't matter," she said. "You need to eat."

He stabbed at some lump of something with a fork. "You sound like Gavin."

"Oh, *ugh*... don't even mention that guy to me right now."

"He's my best friend these days. Or he *was*. Don't know if we can call him that now."

"I thought *I* was your best friend."

"You died," Dante said, taking a bite. "He knew the truth and didn't tell me."

"Same," Genna said. "Matty hid it from me, too."

"So did Gabriella, hence the might-not-be-my-girlfriend thing."

"Because she didn't tell you?"

"Yeah."

Genna munched for a moment before pointing her pickle at

him. "Do you love her?"

"Yes."

His answer was instant.

Genna seemed taken aback, needing a moment to find words again. "Well, then, can I give you some advice? From someone who has experience with the whole 'being in a relationship' thing?"

"I'm not sure I want relationship advice from someone with your track record."

She rolled her eyes. "I'm giving it to you, anyway."

Dante waved his fork, telling her to continue.

"When the right person comes along, they're worth fighting for. They're worth the risk. You shouldn't let anything get in the way. Because shit happens, and people make mistakes, and things get messy and ugly and sometimes it all really hurts, but at the end of the day, they're worth it, because they make you feel something nobody else can. And it's better, I think, to ride a roller coaster with them than to stand on the ground alone, watching everyone else."

Dante forced a bite down. "You don't know her. How do you know she's the right person?"

"Seriously? She got you—*Mr. Monogamy-is-for-Pussies*—to commit. The girl's gotta be a miracle worker. She's a saint. Like, the Pope should literally give her Sainthood."

"He should," Dante agreed.

"So that's how I know," Genna said. "And besides, I've met her father. I'm intimately aware of the fact that he carries a gun, so I'm about seventy-six percent sure if you dump her, he's going to shoot you."

"Oh, yeah, he'll do more than shoot me."

"And I kind of like having you around," Genna said. "I *just* got you back in my life about twenty minutes ago. Don't fuck this up for me, Dante."

He stabbed at the food on the plate in silence, shoving it all around, as Genna ate another pickle. "Aren't pregnant woman supposed to eat those with ice cream?"

Her gaze darted right to him. "Oh God, *ice cream*."

She dashed from the room. Sighting, Dante dropped the fork and followed, leaving the plate there, wanting nothing to do with it. He stepped into the kitchen, seeing the freezer door wide open as

Genna pulled things out, tossing them on the counter. "I doubt you're going to find any—"

Genna held up a black carton. "Ice cream?"

"That's gotta be *at least* a year old."

She shrugged. "It's been frozen."

Dante watched as she dished it out, handing a bowl to him. He grabbed a spoon out of the drawer before leaning back against the counter, glaring at the ice crystals coating the top of the chocolate ice cream. "It's freezer burned."

"Oh, quit your bitching." Genna struggled to haul herself up onto the counter, bowl in hand. "Seriously, I don't remember you complaining this much before. You used to be so agreeable. What happened?"

"I died."

"No, you didn't," she said. "And neither did I, for the record, which means our best-friendship pact is still intact, so I'm gonna need Gavin to take a seat on that one."

Dante smiled to himself as he swirled the ice cream around in his bowl, mixing it all together. "So, where are you staying?"

"I don't know," she said. "I was so focused on getting back to New York that I didn't really think about what happened afterward."

"Stay here," he said, shrugging.

"What about Matty?"

"What about him?"

"He needs somewhere to stay."

Dante swirled his ice cream around a little more ferociously at that. "I'm sure I can find a ditch somewhere for him."

"Dante..."

"I don't like it." Dante tossed the bowl down on the counter without eating any of it. "I don't like *him*. Not a fucking bit. There are few people I like *less*, frankly."

She narrowed her eyes, biting her ice cream, teeth clanking against the metal spoon. "Game's over, remember? World War Whatever has come to an end. He's the lone surviving Barsanti. Time for a peace treaty."

"I don't give a shit about him being a Barsanti. That's not why I hate him."

"Then why?"

"Because he fucked my little sister. He got her pregnant."

Genna rolled her eyes. "If it makes it any better, he married me."

"You *married* that asshole?"

"I mean, we had to use fake names so it's not really legal, but…"

"Good. That means don't have to go through the trouble of divorcing him, since it didn't count."

"It *did* count. It counted to me."

"And you call me crazy."

"At least I risk my life for love. You risk yours for nothing, going to Soho to see Barsanti, like you're welcome there or something."

"I went to ask him why he let me live."

"Did he answer you?"

"Yes."

"Why?"

"Because Matteo was dead."

"Seriously?"

"He said enough people died. He didn't want my blood on his hands. He thought Matteo was dead, so I guess that means I got to live."

"Huh, you know, in a way—"

"Don't say it."

"—that means—"

"Stop."

"—Matty *totally* saved your life."

"No, he didn't."

"Yep, he did," she said, "which means you owe him."

"I owe him *nothing*."

"You do, so you have to cut him some slack. Give him a break. He's a good guy, whole Barsanti thing aside. When we were away, he got a job. He worked in a diner for minimum wage just so he could try to give me a life, a real life… a safe one, like normal people have. He baked me cakes any time I wanted them. He didn't complain when I blew every penny he made on some project to keep myself busy. He ate pickles on pizza, for Christ's sake. Gabriella isn't the only Saint. The guy puts up with *me*. So you don't have to like him, but just… respect him."

"Does he respect me?"

"Doubtful."

That didn't surprise Dante.

He laughed under his breath, watching as his sister swirled her ice cream around, melting it, before drinking it right out of the side of the bowl. Silence surrounded them, and maybe it was the whiskey still sloshing through his veins, but Dante no longer felt the tightness in his chest, no longer felt that gaping hole that had been there when he woke up in the hospital.

"I need a drink," he said, pushing away from the counter to stagger through the kitchen.

"Wait, we're supposed to be sobering you up here, not letting you get drunker."

"I'll sober up tomorrow," he said, spinning her direction. "In the past forty-eight hours, I was dragged to a meeting with the heads of the families, I witnessed Dad kill Barsanti before somebody killed Dad, I punched my now ex-best friend Gavin after my former friend Bert was murdered, I walked out on my girlfriend, and my pregnant sister came back from the dead to tell me she married Matteo Barsanti. So I need a drink, Genna... especially if you expect me to give you my blessing. I *definitely* need a drink for that."

* * *

"Dante? *Psstt...* Dante!"

Genna grabbed her brother's shoulder and shook him hard. He barely moved, laying flat on his back across the black couch in their father's office, clothes disheveled and only one shoe on. His eyes were closed, his chest rattling from snores.

"Damnit, Dante," she grumbled, shaking him. "Wake up!"

He stirred a bit, rolling over, shrugging her off and grumbling, facing the back of the couch. Genna scowled, looking around the bright room. It was well after sunrise, and Matty had to have been worried, since she'd never returned. She'd spent all night at the house, going to sleep in her parents bed, while Dante passed out on the stiff couch... same one her father used to always sleep on.

It looked uncomfortable. How the hell had the man slept there every night for *years*?

"Wake up, Dante," she said once more, giving him a moment. No response. *Fuck this.* Sticking her pointer finger in her mouth, she sucked on it, getting it good and wet before plunging it right in his ear, *twisting*.

Dante jolted, rolling over so fast he damn near fell off the couch. Grabbing his ear, his eyes opened to greet her standing above him.

It took a few seconds. Confusion. Annoyance. Total fucking *shock*. Eyes wide, he sat straight up, staring like he was seeing a ghost and seeing that ghost for the very first time. "Genna?"

His voice was as gritty as sandpaper, obviously uncomfortable, based on the way he grimaced, gripping the side of his head. He blinked, the whites of his eyes painfully pink.

Genna sighed. "Don't tell me you were so drunk last night that you forgot I was even here."

"No, I remember." He scrunched up his nose, making a disgusted face. "Did you just *wet willy* me?"

"You wouldn't respond."

"I was sleeping."

"But I needed you to wake up."

"Why?"

"Because I need to leave."

And just like that, panic flooded his expression. "Leave? You *just* fucking got here!"

"I don't mean *leave*-leave. I mean I have to leave the house. Matty's probably worried."

"So?"

"So I need to go see him and let him know I'm alright."

"Ugh." Dante scrubbed his hands over his face. "What time is it?"

"Ten in the morning."

"What *day* is it?"

"Monday, I think..."

"Month?"

"March." She tried to stick her finger in his ear again, but he blocked her attempt. "The *first* of the month, actually, in case you lost track of that."

"I'd have lost track of my dick if it weren't attached to my body."

"You used to lose track of what you stuck it in even though it *was* attached."

"Ha-ha." He climbed to his feet, swaying. "Where's my other shoe?"

Rolling her eyes, Genna grabbed his discarded shoe from the doorway. He slipped it on, not bothering to tie the laces, and wandered out of the office.

Genna trailed him, watching him stagger. "Are you still drunk?"

"Probably."

Laughing, Genna followed Dante outside, damn near running right into his back when he stopped in front of the house. "A Lincoln Continental?"

Genna slipped past him as he stared at the car. "You like it?"

His gaze shifted her way. "It's yours?"

Grinning, she pulled out the key, dangling it in front of his face. "It wasn't even running when I found it. I spent the past few months working on it. Impressed?"

"Absolutely," Dante said, approaching it. "Not really surprised, though. You gonna let me drive it?"

"Nope."

"Then I'm not impressed anymore."

Genna rolled her eyes, looking around. "Where's the Mercedes?"

"Got rid of it."

"How are you getting around?"

"I got a new car. It's parked somewhere. *Hopefully*."

"And that is precisely why you're not driving my Lincoln," she said. "Another thing you'll lose track of. But anyway, I'm guessing Matty's still at your apartment. Ugh, it's weird that you have an apartment. You have a *girlfriend*."

"Says the girl who's having a baby soon."

"Okay, *this*?" She waved at her swollen stomach. "This was a happy accident. But *that*?" She waved toward him. "That is you being a mature adult."

"A mature adult."

"Yes."

"Did you know she was my nurse? That I met her at the hospital? That I showed up at her apartment one night, bleeding, and asked her to fix me, and then I kind of just kept going back, because I had nowhere else to go by then? That's not a mature adult. That's a fortunate degenerate."

Genna laughed. "She actually put up with that?"

"She almost shot me once when I broke in, but otherwise, yeah."

"You know, the more I hear about this girl, the more I like her. I need you to get your shit together and work that out."

"I hear you."

Genna grabbed her brother, pulling him into a quick hug. "I'll see you in a bit, don't worry. Just, like, take a shower or something. You *reek* of alcohol."

"Yeah, yeah, get out of here," he grumbled. "Go see your precious Matteo."

Genna scowled, sticking her tongue out at him before getting in the car and driving away. She headed back to Little Italy, approaching the building just as someone opened the door. She slipped around them and trekked upstairs, drained by the time she reached the top floor. Her stomach cramped, tightening, and she clutched hold of it, grimacing. "Not yet, kid. *Not yet.*"

Genna knocked, hearing movement inside, the sound of high heels approaching before locks shifted, the door opening. Gabriella stood in front of her, wearing a long sleeved black dress and heels.

"Hey, come in," she said, stepping out of the way. "Matty *just* fell asleep."

Genna glanced toward the couch, seeing Matty curled up. "I'm guessing he was up all night."

"You guessed right."

"Figures." She looked back at Gabriella. "Nice dress. You got plans or something? If so, you know, we can get out of your hair."

"Oh, no, I've just got a meeting this afternoon. By all means, stay. I know the apartment is small, but you're welcome here for as long as you want."

"I appreciate that," Genna said.

Gabriella ran her fingers through her curled hair. "So you saw Dante?"

"Yeah."

"And he's okay?"

"He was drunk as a skunk and about to fall off the balcony railing when I got there, but he seems better today. Hungover, but okay."

Gabriella nodded but said nothing, heading into her bathroom.

Genna strolled over to the couch and whispered, "Matty?"

The second his name came from her lips, he shot straight up. "Genna."

She plopped down beside him, shoving into his arms as he relaxed again. He pressed a kiss to the side of her head, his hands caressing her stomach as he held her.

"Did you save me some pizza?" she asked.

"Of course."

"Does it have pickles on it?"

"You know it does."

Smiling, she closed her eyes. "You're too good to me, Matty-B"

He nuzzled against her, humming in her ear, "Never good enough, Princess."

CHAPTER 24

Fresh out of college with a bachelor's degree in nursing, the first place Gabriella applied for a job was Presbyterian. She figured it a long shot, being as she was inexperienced, but they took a chance on her, offering her a position.

It took a few years to secure the job in the ICU, and she floated for a while before the fateful day Dante Galante appeared. Years of hard work, long shifts, and concealed heartbreak; years full of losses with not so many happy endings. She imagined working there for the rest of her life.

Guess plans change sometimes.

Because one thing she never imagined, one thing she couldn't have planned for, was that she'd end up in the stifling boardroom, surrounded by staff with the power to discipline, listening as the Chief Nursing Officer laid out infraction after infraction. The unwritten rule was a six-month minimum: after seeing a patient professionally, six months had to pass before you could see them personally.

Gabriella had barely waited six *hours.*

"Now's your chance," the woman said, motioning for Gabriella to speak. "You have the opportunity to defend yourself."

Lie, Dante had told her.

But she was sick of lying. Lying meant denying him. It meant discrediting everything that happened, like there was something shameful about it.

And heck, maybe there was.

Maybe she was supposed to be ashamed… ashamed of herself, ashamed of *him*… but she felt nothing of the sort. Despite the hot water it had her in, despite the chaos loving him caused, he'd been one of the greatest things to happen to her. She saw in him something she didn't see in many others. *Civility.* Ironic, maybe, considering the life he'd been living, considering the family he'd been given, but that just made it all the more powerful. Despite the odds stacked against him, Dante tried to live with honor. And maybe he failed sometimes, but oh how he tried...

"It's true," Gabriella said, looking around at the stern faces as shock set in. Everyone seemed stunned by her words except for Crabtree. He wasn't surprised in the least. "Although, I guess we see it differently. I know it's a morally gray area, being with Dante Galante... I was aware of that from the beginning. I took care of him when nobody else wanted to. The nurses gossiped, and the doctors sneered, and they all avoided him, writing him off, breaking every rule in the book. His medical information was shared in the halls. His wishes were disregarded like what he wanted didn't matter. He was treated more like a prisoner than a patient, but I gave him a chance. When nobody else was around, I was there. And maybe it's wrong, that something grew out of that, but I'm not the only one in the wrong."

"Maybe so," Crabtree said, "but *your* actions are the ones being discussed today, not any conceived slights you believe occurred."

"And fraternizing with patients isn't just a gray area," the CNO chimed in. "It's also a dangerous one. It's taking advantage."

Gabriella tried to keep a straight face, but she laughed at that.

Crabtree's eyes narrowed. "Something funny, Nurse Russo?"

"No... well, yeah, it is kind of funny, because if you think Dante Galante is the kind of man that someone can take *advantage* of, you've clearly not spent enough time with him. Which is sad, considering you were his doctor. The fact that you think *I* had the power to persuade him is laughable. Flattering that you think so highly of my abilities, but still... *wow.*"

The doctor glared at her.

Gabriella knew she had not a chance in the world of walking away from this. It was the beginning of the end. Even if it weren't a terminable offense, which it *was*, they'd fire her out of spite.

"We have no choice but to take action against you, Nurse Russo," the CNO said. "And due to the seriousness, the nursing board will have to be notified, so they can assess the impact this will have on your license, if any."

It would, without a doubt. Gabriella was certain. "So, you're firing me?"

"We're willing to give you an opportunity to resign," Crabtree said. "If you turn in your resignation letter, clearing the hospital—"

"Of any wrongdoing," Gabriella said, interrupting. "Save you from shouldering the blame for *anything* and you'll let me save face."

Crabtree nodded. "You know how it goes."

"I do." Everybody's always worried about their own behinds, not caring what happens to anyone else. "But I'm sorry, you're going to have to fire me, because I refuse to do that."

Gabriella didn't give them time to respond, not wanting to be there when it played out. They'd take a vote, one that would be unanimous, and terminate her on the spot, declaring her services no longer needed. She'd heard of it happening to others, fired for stealing medication or neglecting patients, but she might've been the first to be fired for loving a patient they all hated.

At least Grey's Anatomy got something right, she thought as she strolled out of the hospital, her head down, arms wrapped around her chest to ward off the cold that even the sunshine couldn't suppress. *The future keeps changing, and when you finally catch up to it, it's never how you expected it to be.*

"How'd it go?"

The quiet voice made Gabriella stop short, her high heels planting in a pile of slush on the sidewalk. Looking to the metal bench along the building, her eyes met Dante's inquisitive gaze. She took in his unruly appearance, his messy bed-head and wrinkled clothes, fixating on his untied shoes. "Well… it seems I'll have a lot more time on my hands in the future."

"Sorry to hear that," he said, standing up. "They'll never find another like you. You're one of a kind, Nurse Russo."

"Thank you," she whispered as he paused in front of her. "I always had the best of intentions."

"I know you did."

"Too bad that's not what pays the bills," she said. "I'll have to find a different job. I don't foresee another hospital hiring me after this."

"Someone will," he said. "They'll take one look at you and instantly know your worth."

"You think so?"

"I do," he said. "If *I* could find someone to believe in me, you've got it made. And besides, you know, you've got me. I can cover the rent and whatever else you need."

"Ah, do you have a job now?"

"No, but I can find something," he said. "I hear there's a diner across the country with a recent job opening."

"Sounds like a long commute."

He shrugged. "We do what we have to do."

Gabriella looked him over, smiling sadly when he wrapped his arms around her. Closing her eyes, she breathed him in. "You smell like a bar again."

"You smell like Heaven."

Gabriella tolerated it for a moment before her nose started to twitch. "Seriously, you stink."

"I was supposed to take a shower, but then I realized what day it was and what was happening. I wanted to be here for you. It was more important than showering."

"My nose disagrees," she said as he pressed a kiss to her temple, "but the rest of me is grateful."

Dante pulled away from her, taking a step back. "I also have something to give you. I've had it for a few days, but well, shit happened, and everything went crazy, and I kind of haven't found the right moment to give it to you yet. But when it's the right person, when you've found the right one, I don't think any moment is *wrong*."

Dante reached into his pocket for something, and a swell of intense dread washed through Gabriella, strong enough to make her knees weak and hands shake. *Oh God. No. No. No.* She grabbed his arm, pinning his hand in his pocket, drowning in irrational panic. "Don't do it."

Dante's eyes widened. "What?"

"Look, I love you," she said, shaking her head. *Ugh, how to explain this?* "I love you with everything inside of me, Dante. I do. When I look at you, I feel it, and I know there's nobody else in the world for me. But I just... I've never been that kind of girl, and *ugh*, I seriously hate weddings, and I would say yes, if you asked, but I need time to *prepare,* so I don't think proposing—"

A sharp bark of laughter cut off her flustered rambling. "Whoa, whoa, whoa… you think I'm *proposing?*"

"You're not?"

"Hell no." He made a face, which he quickly straightened back out, looking apologetic. "No offense. I love the fuck out of you, Gabriella, but marriage? Right now?"

She exhaled sharply. "Oh, thank God."

She let go of his arm, motioning for him to proceed with whatever he was doing.

"Anyway," he continued, "the other day, you know, I went to Michaels."

"I remember," she said. "Still have no idea who Michael is, though."

"*Michaels*, Gabriella. The shop."

"What?"

"That place with all the crafts."

Her brow furrowed. "Why would you go there?"

"I saw this flyer in the newspaper, this thing they were having, you know… this class… so I figured *fuck it,* why not?" Pulling his hand from his pocket, he opened his fist. "So I went."

Diagonally across his palm, blue, white, and purple string weaved together in a v-shaped pattern, the ends hanging loose. Her jaw dropped open as she stared at it.

A friendship bracelet.

"You made that?"

"Yeah."

"For *me?*"

"Yeah."

Tears filled Gabriella's eyes, ones she couldn't hold back. She covered her mouth with her hands, concealing her goofy grin, stifling the sob that threatened to escape, as emotion flooded her. He'd made her a friendship bracelet, a real one, with string he'd braided together by hand, the pattern all messed up in the middle like he'd lost his place and forgot how to do it, but yet he forged on. He went out of his way and had gone to a class, a class that was probably full of excited children, making presents for their friends.

"I bet it was nothing but kids, wasn't it?" she asked, her voice strained as she tried not to cry. "A bunch of little girls?"

"Yeah," he mumbled. "I'm probably on a watch list somewhere now. You should've seen the way they looked at me, grown ass man taking a kid's workshop. Not my finest moment. I told them it was for my girlfriend, but I don't think they bought that shit."

Gabriella couldn't hold it back anymore, tears streaming down her cheeks as laughter burst from her. She threw herself at him, clinging to him, hysterical. "You're such a friggin *idiot*."

He sighed. "I know I am."

"Never change," she whispered. "I swear to God, I don't know what I would do if you ever changed your stupid ways."

"Yeah, well, I can pretty much promise that won't happen. If I haven't learned my lesson yet, I doubt I ever will."

"Good." She pulled back, grasping his face, staring into his eyes. "I'll happily drink your poison."

"I'll never ask you to." He grabbed her hand and pulled it away from his face to loosely knot the bracelet around her wrist. "Although, someday I will ask you to marry me. *Someday*. Because your family will kill me if I don't, so prepare yourself."

She ran her fingertips along the bracelet, swallowing thickly. "What kind of benefits does that come with?"

"Benefits?"

"Yeah, I've already got rides from work and orgasms and macaroni and foot rubs. What do I get if I marry you?"

"Jewelry?"

"You just gave me a bracelet."

"My last name?"

"I prefer Russo."

"Half of everything I've got?"

"I think I've got more than *you*."

"Conjugal visits?"

That one made her pause. *Huh.*

"Come on," Dante said, pulling out his keys before draping his arm over her shoulder. "Let me drive you home from work one last time, you know, for old time's sake, while you consider if marrying me is worth it if it means I'll still get to fuck you when I inevitably land my ass in prison someday."

Traffic was light on the drive to Little Italy. They encountered more green lights than red. Not a single police car trailed them. No one cut them off or got in their way. When they arrived at the apartment, a car parked in front of the building pulled away. Dante swung right into the spot, parallel parking to perfection.

He'd never been a big believer in luck. If it existed, he'd been dealt the shittiest hand around. But as everything seemed to fall into place, things turning around, he had to wonder if maybe it was his time.

Maybe he'd just been stockpiling luck over the years, hoarding it like a crazy cat lady with a house full of shit, and time had come for him to cash in his chips.

"I'm really sorry, you know," Gabriella said, taking his hand as he stepped onto the curb, pulling him to a stop beside the car. People moved past them, going about their business. "It wasn't right that I kept the truth from you."

"I get it," Dante said. "It wasn't your secret to tell. Besides, there's something I should've told you. Something I did last year… something you deserve to know."

Gabriella's expression softened. "Something like… Enzo?"

Dante nodded.

"I heard rumors," she said. "Matty confirmed it."

Matteo. Dante's lips twitched as he tried not to sneer at the mention of that guy. "I just figured, in the name of full disclosure, you should know in case that changes things."

"Pfft, please, you're *stuck* with me."

"Sounds nice." Dante leaned over to kiss her. "Stuck with you. Sticking it *in* you. Same thing, right?"

"Pretty much."

"You want to go do that now?"

"I want you to go shower, honestly."

Dante laughed, about to suggest they multi-task, when an excited voice cut through their conversation. "Holy shit!"

Genna burst out of the building, eyes wide, her expression lit up like a kid on Christmas morning. She barged over, pushing past him, purposely knocking him out of the way on her quest to reach his car.

"A McLaren?" she asked, hand glossing over the slick blue paint. "You bought a supercar and didn't even tell me? What kind of shit is *that*?"

Dante shrugged as she spread out across the hood, hugging the damn thing, squishing her stomach against it. "You didn't ask."

"*He's driving that sport's car*," Genna said, making a face as her voice dropped into a low, mocking tone. "*Flashy fucker. How stupid can he get?*"

Dante's brow furrowed. "What?"

"That's what you said about Matty," Genna said. "Those were pretty much your exact words. So excuse me for never in a million years imagining when you bought a new car, it would be *this*."

"My father's a good salesman," Gabriella chimed in, slipping around in front of Dante, her back pressed to his chest as she leaned into him. He wrapped his arms around her, holding her from behind. "He can talk anyone into anything."

"He can sell *me* one of these babies," Genna said, standing up straight as someone exited the building, a smile lighting up her face. Dante didn't have to look to know it would be Matteo. Hell, he didn't *want* to look, so he didn't. He stared straight ahead at his sister, trying damn hard to ignore the guy's presence. "Matty, how much money do we have?"

"Not enough for one of those," Matteo said, his voice quiet, marked with a light laugh. "Besides, no place in there for a car seat."

"Uh, yeah there is." Genna motioned toward the passenger side. "You can take the subway. Me and little sugar cube here are riding in *style*."

"Anything for you," Matteo mumbled as a phone rang, the generic brand of chirping causing Dante's eyes to unwittingly drift right to it. Matteo pulled out a phone. A *burner* phone, Dante knew right away. Matteo answered the call, turning so his back faced Dante. "Hey, we're over by Gabby's apartment. You know where she's living? See you in a second."

Dante's back stiffened, his grip on Gabriella tightening enough for her to take notice. Brow furrowing, she glanced back at him but said nothing. Dante was grateful for it, considering he had no explanation. Despite everything he knew *logically*, the Barsanti skepticism still rooted deep within him.

Matteo's gaze swept around them before settling across the street. Dante cautiously looked that way, groaning. *Gavin.*

Gavin jogged over, flashing a smile at Matteo before looking at Dante. He approached, staring at him like he had something to say, but he averted his gaze at the last second, his attention going to Genna instead. "Well, if it isn't Genna with a G, my favorite person."

Genna tensed as she grumbled, "Son of a bitch."

"My mother isn't a bitch," Gavin said, standing beside her. "She's the nicest of the Brazzi sisters."

"I like to think that title went to *my* mom," Matteo chimed in. "Aunt Lena is nice, but come on..."

Gavin scowled, his gaze going to Gabriella. "Gabby, back me up here."

"Uh-uh, don't even drag me into that," Gabriella said. "All I know is it's not *my* mom."

"I have to give it to Savina," Genna said. "She's probably the nicest person I've ever met."

"Only because you don't know my mom," Gavin said.

"I've met her."

"So? You don't *know* her."

"That's because she never talked to me," Genna pointed out. "She didn't look at me, either. She wasn't even very *nice* to me, now that I think about it."

Gavin waved that off. "You're a Galante. You guys are like the Mets around here... nobody cheers for them, but you've gotta assume, since they're here, someone out there gives a shit, right?"

"Hey!" Gabriella said. "I like the Mets."

"Yeah, and you like Galante there, too, which *seriously* calls into question your judgment." Gavin looked around at all of them. "Actually, you know, I'm not sure about any of you. You're all crazy, driving flashy ass cars around like you're invincible."

"Hey now," Genna said, leaning against the McLaren again. "You talk all the shit you want about us but leave the cars out of it. They're *innocent.*"

Matteo strolled over to her, pressing his hand to her back as his gaze traveled the length of the car. "It's a beauty. Zero to sixty in what, four seconds?"

"Two-point-eight," Genna chimed in.

"And I'm guessing top speed is about 200."

"More like 218." Genna glowered at him. "Jesus Christ, Matty, you graduated from *Princeton*. You should know things."

Matteo laughed. "I must've slept through that class."

"Well, wake up and smell the motor oil," she said, "because this pretty blue baby is coming home with us, whether my brother knows it or not."

Matteo shook his head. "I'm not so sure he's going to hand over the key."

"Whatever, I can hotwire it," she said, glancing in the driver's side window. "Go get me a screwdriver and some bubble gum. I'll MacGyver this shit in about five minutes."

"Please don't." Dante reached into his pocket and pulled out the key. "Take it for a drive, if you want, but don't defile it."

Genna swung his way so fast she nearly knocked herself off balance. "Seriously?"

"Take it," he said, dangling the key. "Just bring yourself back in one piece."

Genna squealed, snatching the key from him. "You're still not driving my Lincoln."

"I'm not surprised."

She skipped over to the McLaren. "Come on, Matty, let's go for a joyride."

Dante scowled. "I didn't say *he*—"

Before he could finish, Gabriella swung around in his arms and clamped her hand down over his mouth. Her expression was stern, that 'say another word and I'll cut you' kind of glare that silenced him.

Matteo walked around to the passenger side of the car as Genna unlocked the doors. Dante glanced over at them, still scowling, not saying a word about it, before he looked back at Gabriella.

"Good boy," she whispered, removing her hand from his mouth to kiss him.

"You're lucky I love you," he said, "because I would've bit your hand off if I didn't."

Gabriella laughed, her gaze flickering past him, over his shoulder. There was a glint in her eye as her expression slowly fell. It happened in slow motion, the melting of ice, washing away the elation, the drip-drop of fear settling in, trickling through her. Mere seconds passed, but to Dante, the moment was a lifetime. A lifetime, because he'd seen that look before. He'd seen that look before *many* times, but he'd only caused it once. The spinning of a film reel, a lifetime of memories playing through someone's mind, a life that could be gone in the blink of an eye.

Terror took over every bit of Gabriella, her mouth dropping open and a lone word slipping out. "Fuck."

Fuck.

Heart hammering hard against his rib cage, Dante turned, every inch of him rigid as fear coated his insides, the blood in his veins ice cold. Ten feet separated him from a gun. It aimed right at his chest, clutched in the unsteady hand of a livid man. *Civello.* A finger touched the trigger, eager to shoot, as a set of unnerved eyes darted around at the group, like maybe he was thinking twice about doing it, second-guessing this decision. The guy was alone and severely outnumbered. Dante was unarmed, but the guy had to know he wouldn't get far. *Tweedle-Whatever* wasn't a genius, but he couldn't be that stupid.

Could he?

Don't do it. Dante stared at him. *Don't fucking do it.*

Seconds passed, strained seconds. Nobody else seemed to notice, and Dante couldn't get his goddamn voice to work to warn anyone. He was a deer frozen in a blinding beam of light until Civello shifted, making his decision. *Shit.*

The guy frantically bounced from person to person before his gaze settled on Dante's car. Genna opened the driver's side door, oblivious, still laughing. *Ding ding.* Anger turned to shock before succumbing to intense rage. The man's nostril's flared, the gun aiming past Dante at the noticeably pregnant Genevieve Galante.

Grabbing Gabriella, Dante yanked her out of the line of fire, dragging her away from the curb, hoping she was smart enough to get out of there. "Go!"

Gabriella *ran.*

"Gun!" someone screamed, chaos ensuing, the neighborhood erupting in mayhem. Dante sprinted for the car, grabbing Genna just as gunfire cut through the air, a stream of bullets raining down on them. Pain and panic; fear and fury. It swarmed him, burning him from the inside, as he dragged his sister to the sidewalk, shielding her body with his own.

Dante watched, his vision blurry, as Gavin pulled out a gun and started unloading on the son of a bitch.

"It's okay," Dante said. "Just stay down."

"Matty," Genna cried, trying to wiggle free. "Where's Matty?"

"Jesus Christ, Genna, *stop*," Dante growled. "Wait a goddamn second."

A second was all she gave him. The gunfire came to an abrupt stop and Genna shoved against him. Dante loosened his hold, giving her enough room to slip away, hauling herself to her feet. "Matty?"

"I'm fine," Matteo said, standing up from beside the car. Genna threw herself at him, crying, knocking him back down.

Dante climbed to his feet, dazed, trying to assess the situation but everything was a blur. Adrenaline rushed through him, so furious his stomach churned, his chest burning with every breath forced into his lungs. People still ran. Others still screamed. His head grew fuzzy. He couldn't think.

He needed to *think*.

Civello lay on the sidewalk in a pool of blood. Gavin paced around, fidgeting, his gun tucked back away, his skin ashen.

"Genna?" Matteo's voice was frantic. "Genna, baby, there's blood on you."

"What?" Genna asked. "I'm not, I mean..."

Dante blinked rapidly, bile burning his throat, engulfing his chest. He saw it, the smear of blood on her arm, transferred from her black shirt. Matteo tugged at her clothes, searching for injuries.

"I'm fine," Genna insisted, looking down. "I, uh... oh shit, I think my water might've broke."

"The *blood*," Matteo said, stressing the word. "Where's the blood coming from?"

"I don't know." She raised her hands. "I don't think it's *mine*."

"Dante..." Gabriella's calm voice cut through as she carefully approached, grasping his arm. "Dante, I need you to sit down."

Dante turned, holding her gaze for a moment, seeing a familiar concern that greeted him every day for weeks. *Nurse Russo*. He blinked a few times before looking down, noticing the dark spot spreading over the blue shirt along the side of his chest. He didn't feel it so much yet, the flood of adrenaline diluting the pain, but knowledge clicked in a hell of a lot quicker. Reaching up, he pressed his hand to the spot, grimacing, blood streaking his fingertips. "I think it's mine."

Gabriella tugged on him, trying to lead him to the building, but the first step he took made his head swim. *Woozy*. He swayed, vision fading, and grabbed ahold of the car to steady himself.

"I..." Dante hesitated. "I need to sit down."

He leaned back against the car and slid down to the sidewalk, blood gushing from the wound when he moved, stabbing pain raiding from it.

He grasped the spot, wincing.

"I need something!" Gabriella shouted. "A towel or a rag or a shirt, *something*."

Gavin stepped over, still sickeningly pale, pulling off his suit coat. Gabriella snatched it from him, tearing Dante's hands away from the wound to press the fabric against it.

"Hold this right here," Gabriella ordered, looking at Gavin. "Press *hard*. I need to run up to the apartment and grab some stuff."

Gavin obliged, and Gabriella started to leave, but Dante grabbed her arm, stopping her. "Wait..."

"We don't have time to wait," she said. "The quicker we get your bleeding stopped, the better."

"His gun." Dante motioned to the pistol tucked in Gavin's waistband. "Get rid of it."

"That's not important right now," Gavin muttered.

"The hell it isn't," Dante said. "It needs gone before the police come."

Gavin started to argue when Gabriella snatched it out of his waistband, concealing it in her coat as she ran inside. Once she was gone, Gavin shook his head. "Your dumb ass is sitting here bleeding and you're more worried about me going to jail? Who's the sentimental bitch now?"

Dante laughed, wincing as it caused pain to tear through him. "Mandatory minimums. Having that gun when they show up will get you an automatic three and a half years at Rikers."

"Ouch."

"Tell me about it," Dante muttered, looking down at his chest. "I can't believe this happened. Someone *shot* me."

"Yeah, well, we knew it was inevitable."

"You aren't laughing, though."

"Of course I'm not laughing."

"You said you would. You said you'd stand back and laugh when it finally happened."

"You know I didn't mean that."

Gabriella ran back out of the building, carrying an armful of supplies, and dropped them on the sidewalk beside Dante, shoving Gavin away so she could get to work.

"I love you," Dante said quietly.

Her eyes flickered to him with surprise. "I love you, too."

He smiled slightly, his vision blurry. "Don't let me die alone in the dark, Gabby."

Gabby. He'd never called her that before, even though she'd asked him to.

"You're not dying, Dante," she said, "nor are you alone. Nor is it even *dark* right now. You're going to be just fine."

"Good," Dante said, closing his eyes and grimacing as she poked and prodded. "Because if I die, I really think Gavin might cry."

"Fuck you," Gavin muttered, standing close enough to hear.

Sirens blared in the distance. EMS, maybe. Police, most likely. A shooting in broad daylight tended to ignite a full response. Medics surrounded Dante within minutes, putting him on a stretcher while officers fired questions his way that he had no desire to answer.

As Dante was loaded into the back of an ambulance, he heard his sister's voice. His eyes drifted to where she stood along the curb, flanked by Matteo and Gavin, police surrounding them, asking the same questions they'd asked Dante.

"Wait, it wasn't *you*?" Genna asked, her voice high-pitched, forced, as she addressed a uniformed officer. "I swear I thought it was. You didn't kill that guy? You sure?"

Man, she was a terrible liar.

She smiled at Dante, but it didn't last long. Her expression shifted as she clutched her stomach, doubling over in pain. She tried to straighten back up, but the second she did, her eyes rolled back and she dropped.

Matteo caught her before she hit the sidewalk.

"Genna?" Dante tried to climb off of the stretcher, but the IVs in his arms tethered him in place, tugging when he moved. Before he could yank them out, medics restrained him, pinning him against the stretcher. "You can't *hold* me. I know my rights!"

"*Go*, Dante," Gabriella begged from outside the ambulance. Not allowed to ride along, officers said, not until she'd answered their questions. *Bullshit.* Matteo knelt beside Genna as medics rushed to her side. "I'll meet you at the hospital."

"But—"

"I swear to God, Dante Galante, if you don't go to the hospital this time, I will end you *myself.* If the blood loss doesn't do it, *I* will."

He intended to keep arguing, but his chest burned, his head pounded, and he wanted more than anything to actually *survive,* so he let them take him to the hospital.

He let them *triage* him.

He let them assess his wound before stitching him up and pumping him full of somebody else's blood and sending him to a recovery room. No surgery needed. Fractured a rib, but hell, he'd fractured a few of those before. That was nothing new.

Give them a day, they told him, so he gave them an hour... an hour before he was sure he wasn't going to die if he skipped out.

He refused further treatment, signing their 'I'm a dumbass but promise not to sue you for it' release form before roaming the hospital, searching for Gabriella. She'd promised to meet him there, so he had no doubt she'd be around *somewhere.*

He spotted her after a few minutes down in the cafeteria, ordering coffee, and staggered up to her. "Can I get one of those, too?"

Gabriella looked at him with shock. "What are you doing?"

"Looking for you."

"I'm right here," she said. "Why aren't you in a *bed?*"

"I got released."

"Against medical advice?"

"Maybe."

She rolled her eyes, muttering under her breath as she gathered the coffees—three of them. "*Idiot*, I swear to God. You're seriously going to die one of these times, and what am I supposed to do then?"

Dante pulled her into his arms, damn near knocking the coffee cups out of her hands. He held her, breathing her in. Vanilla. The hospital stench surrounded them, but she smelled nothing like it. She was the calm in his storm. "Can we just get out of here?"

"Not yet. Your sister..."

"What about her?"

"She's having the baby."

CHAPTER 25

You are who you choose to be.

Johnny Amaro had told Matty that once. He never forgot it. He'd been living in New Jersey, going by the last name Brazzi, when his father asked him to move back to New York. For a decade, Matty had waited for that moment, had agonized over if his father would ever welcome him back home. But Matty had just turned eighteen at the time and had been accepted to Princeton, and he'd already given up on them being a family.

And if he were being honest, he didn't *feel* like a Barsanti anymore.

Matty had confessed that to Johnny Amaro, expecting his uncle to lecture him about family loyalty, but that had been the man's response: *you are who you choose to be.* Guilt nagged at Matty for years afterward, and he eventually tried to be that person, but it wasn't *him.*

He'd chosen differently.

And as Matty sat beneath the blinding fluorescents in that busy hospital waiting room, he just kept wondering... who *was* he? If he wasn't a Barsanti, what did that make him? The name was inked on his chest, a permanent part of his body, but what the hell did being a Barsanti mean for somebody?

Sighing, Matty dropped his head down low, running his hands through his hair. The clock ticked away, torturous minutes passing where everything he knew remained in limbo. Every time a door opened, every time someone walked in, his head darted up, eyes seeking *somebody*, desperate for information.

Emergency C-Section. Full placental abruption.

That was all they'd told him as they'd hauled her away.

Genna was having their baby.

He couldn't be there for her.

They told him to wait.

Wait...

Wait...

Wait...

Please, God, let them be okay.

"She's going to be fine, you know," Gavin said, sitting to Matty's left. "We're talking about Genna with a G here. That girl is damn near as tenacious as her brother. They're like cockroaches."

"Gavin..."

"I'm just saying, it'll take a nuclear bomb to wipe those two out. I'm not worried about either one. Dante's like the Hulk. He probably couldn't kill himself if he wanted. It's that Galante blood. Hell, it wouldn't even surprise me if *Primo* walked through that door right now, still kickin'."

Someone entered then, and Matty glanced up. Not Primo, no, but close enough to be concerning. *Dante.* He stood across the waiting room, his expression stoic, nothing sympathetic about his eyes as they pierced right through Matty.

The guy hated him, no question about it.

He probably always would.

And that feeling was mutual.

Dante wandered over, still wearing a bloody shirt, earning him concerned looks from everyone he passed. A deranged look swaddled him, everything disheveled, his bloodshot eyes lined with dark bags, like sleep was just a fleeting memory. He dropped into the empty chair to the right of Matty, slouching and stretching his legs out, tilting his head back to stare up at the bright ceiling.

"I fucking hate this place," Dante muttered.

He was talking to himself, but Matty still responded. "So do I."

"Can I third that?" Gavin asked. "Thank God my father's being released this week so I never have to come back here."

Dante laughed dryly. "I said that after they released me and I've been back twice since. It's a fucking curse."

"Just when I thought I was out," Matty muttered, "they pull me back in again."

Gavin laughed at the *Godfather III* quote, while Dante closed his eyes and pinched the bridge of his nose. "It's like summoning fucking Satan."

A grin touched Matty's lips. "You sound like your sister."

"You mean my sister sounds like *me*," Dante said. "I taught that girl everything she knows."

"Hence why she's so aggravating," Gavin pointed out. "Got that from him."

"Oh, *fuck off.*" Dante stood to pace around, his gaze scanning the room, settling on the clock on a far wall. "How long has she been wherever the fuck she is? How long is this supposed to *take?*"

"Relax," Gabriella said as she approached, handing coffees to both Matty and Gavin before shoving Dante back into the chair. She dropped two white pills into his palm and offered a bottle of water. "Take this."

Dante looked at her. "Vicodin?"

"Tylenol."

"You couldn't find anything stronger?"

"Yes," she said, "it's called a morphine drip, which they would've been happy to give you had you not checked yourself out like this is just some motel instead of a friggin hospital."

Dante popped the pills in his mouth and took the water from her. He drank damn near half of it in one guzzle before grabbing Gabriella and drawing her to him. Instead of pulling her into his lap, he stood up, slipping around her, shoving her into the chair so he could pace again.

"True or false," Dante said, "the security guards are armed."

Gabriella glared at him. "I swear to *God*..."

"I'm not going to do anything," he said, shooting her a look. "I'm just wondering, if I burst into an operating room, what my chances of getting killed for it are."

"Some of them carry guns," she said. "So I'd say you've got a pretty good chance of being shot."

"Noted."

He paced a few more seconds before Gabriella jumped up, grabbing ahold of him, shoving him back into the chair so hard he winced. She dropped the bottle of water into his lap, pointing right at his face, close enough the tip of her finger jabbed the end of his nose. "You stay right here. I'm going to go see what I can find out.

Ugh, if anyone around here is even still talking to me since I got *fired*."

Matty expected an argument from Dante, tensing as he waited for that famed Galante temper, but Dante just sat there, stretching his legs out and leaning his head back, staring up at the ceiling again.

"She got fired?" Confusion laced Gavin's voice. "When?"

"This morning," Dante muttered.

"Why?" Gavin asked. "What did she do?"

"Me," Dante said.

"Oh." A moment of silence passed before Gavin broke out into laughter. "Ah man, really? She lost her job for fucking around with you?"

"I don't see why that's so funny."

"Because," Gavin said, "you're the *worst* consolation prize ever."

Dante shot right back up, and Matty barely had enough time to move out of the way before the bottle of water hurled by him, hitting Gavin in the chest. Dante paced around, eyes continually flickering between the clock and the exit, before he turned his gaze on Matty. "How can you just sit there? Are you not bothered *at all* by this? Do you just not give a shit about my sister?"

"Of course I'm bothered," Matty ground out, "but making a scene doesn't help anybody."

"Helps me," Dante argued. "I feel a hell of a lot better when I'm *doing* something."

"I bet you do," Matty said. "Doesn't matter who gets hurt as long as the great and powerful Dante Galante feels better about himself. My brother can attest to that."

"Oh, whoa, whoa, *whoa*!" Gavin jumped up, sliding in front of Matty's chair when Dante came at him, hands clenched. "You start fighting and you'll *both* get thrown out of here, and then I'll be the only one who gets to see the baby, and while I'm not going to lose any sleep over that fact, I'm pretty sure Genna wouldn't forgive *either* of you assholes for it."

"Is there a problem here?" a stern voice asked, approaching them. Matty looked around Gavin, seeing an older man in a blue uniform behind Dante. *Security.* No gun on him, just pepper spray clipped to his belt, not enough force to stop someone like Dante but certainly enough to piss him off *more.*

"No problem," Dante said, his tone clipped. "Except that this hospital is *bullshit.*"

"Everything's fine," Gavin said, smiling as he addressed the security guard. "This one's just getting a little impatient. He's going to take a seat and shut up now, though... isn't he?"

Gavin glared at Dante, who just shrugged as he sat back down. Security eyed him warily before strolling over to the side of the room, leaning against the wall to keep an eye on them.

"We're going to have to find some constructive way for you two to work this shit out," Gavin said, retaking his seat. "A boxing ring. Paintball. Couple's therapy. *Something.*"

"There's nothing to work out," Matty said.

Dante motioned to Matty. "What he said."

"Well, that's a start," Gavin said. "You're agreeing on something. I mean, you're agreeing that you hate each other, but that's something, so... keep up the good work."

It took a minute at most before Dante was back out of his seat, and a minute after that Gabriella resurfaced. Matty stared at her as his heart hammered in his chest. He'd tried damn hard to keep calm the hour or so they sat there, waiting, but every second that passed without news was more opportunity for *complications.*

Dante stopped pacing as Gabriella approached him.

"You just don't listen, do you?" she asked, shaking her head.

"You wouldn't love me if I did," he responded. "Did you find out anything?"

"She's in recovery," Gabriella said. "They're moving her to a room."

"And she's okay?" Dante asked.

"She's fine," Gabriella confirmed. "The baby, too."

Matty closed his eyes, exhaling at those words. He felt like he'd been holding his breath for an entire goddamn hour.

"Nobody would give me more than that," Gabriella said, turning to Matty with a frown. "They wouldn't even tell me what she had."

"It's a boy," Gavin chimed in, slapping Matty on the back. "Baby boy Barsanti."

Dante groaned, running his hands down his face as he dropped back into the chair. Up and down, up and down, like a damn teeter-totter.

"How do you know?" Gabriella asked suspiciously, looking at Gavin.

"Matty-B told me," Gavin said. "He knew what they were having."

Gabriella shot Matty a look before turning to Dante.

"Don't look at me," Dante muttered. "Nobody tells me shit."

Gabriella scowled, kicking his shin, before turning back to Matty. "So, a son, huh?"

"Yeah," he whispered. "A son."

He had a son.

Twenty minutes. Twenty more agonizing minutes before someone appeared in the waiting room to address Matty, to tell him Genna and the baby were both safe and sound in a room down the hall. *212.* The second those words came from someone's lips, Matty was out of his chair.

"About fucking time," Dante grumbled, trying to stand up, but Gabriella blocked him.

"We should let Matty go first, you know, to see them," she said. "Give him a minute."

"He's got *one* minute."

"Thirty minutes," Gabriella argued, "at least."

"Fifteen," Dante countered, "at *most*."

Matty didn't hang around to hear the rest of that conversation, wasting not a second longer. Room 212. The number rang through his mind as he raced down the hallway, breaking out into a sprint. *212. 212. 212.* He skidded to a stop when he saw it etched on a panel outside a closed tan door. 212. He didn't bother knocking, his leftover patience still somewhere back in that waiting room. He thrust the door open, bursting inside, and came to a dead stop as soon as he did.

Genna sat in the propped-up hospital bed, hair an utter mess, hospital gown askew. Her face was ashen, but the smile on her lips... the smile made her *glow*. Her eyes were fixed downward, to the small bundle cradled in her arms, wrapped up in a white blanket trimmed with pink and blue. So much warmth radiated from her, so much *love*, that it lit up the entire room. Nurses moved around her, checking vitals and tinkering with machines, but Matty paid them no attention.

His eyes were only for *her*.

Growing up, Matty never wanted children of his own. He never even imagined a reality where he'd bring one into existence. His world had been destroyed when he was just a kid, ripped to pieces by the life he'd been born into, a life he never asked for. But in that life, the one his father had brought children into... the life Genna, too, had been given... you didn't get a choice in the matter. The moment you took your first breath, you became a part of it, and nothing short of death would help you escape. He'd tried, so many times, and each time, something drew him right back in. Because the life didn't give up on you, and it wouldn't let you give up on it, either. There was no *live and let live* in their world... it had been *kill or be killed*. His best friend lost his life, and so many times... so many fucking times... Matty wished *he'd* been the one to die instead.

And that, he knew, was no kind of life for a child. He wouldn't have wished those feelings on his worst enemy. He *hadn't* wished them on his worst enemy. Because according to the life, the one he'd been forced into, his worst enemy sat in front of him, cradling a baby he never knew he wanted until it became his reality.

Now, standing there, he couldn't imagine a world without them.

"Daddy's here," Genna whispered, barely loud enough for him to hear, before her gaze lifted, meeting his across the room. "He looks like he's three seconds away from a trip to the psych ward, but he's here."

Matty stood frozen, in utter silence, until the nurses walked out and left them alone. Slowly, he approached, stepping closer to the bed, as he glanced down into Genna's arms, at the little boy he knew he couldn't live without now. A little boy he'd protect for the rest of his life, a little boy he'd fight to save from the world he'd grown up in.

Dark, thick hair and tanned skin, soft, round cheeks with just a hint of pink. He looked nothing like his mother and everything like Matty. It was like staring at a baby picture of himself. *Surreal.* The baby was fast asleep, his mouth open just a bit as he breathed through it.

"My brother?" Genna asked.

"He's in the waiting room, blessing everyone with his charming personality."

Genna sighed. "Thank God he's okay."

Choosing to keep his opinion to himself, Matty reached down, running his fingertips along a warm, flushed cheek, the touch making the baby stir a bit. "Can I hold him?"

"Of course, you big dolt. He's *yours*. He looks *just* like you."

Matty picked him up, careful not to wake him, and gazed into his face as he cradled him in his arms. "Strong genes."

"*Annoying* genes," Genna remarked.

Matty laughed lightly as he sat down on the edge of the hospital bed beside her, not wanting to move from her side. "Hey, you chose to breed with me."

"Breed with you," she said. "Is that what we did? *Breeded*?"

"The word you want is actually 'bred'."

"Ah, *there's* that Ivy League education kicking back in. Did you learn how to change diapers at Princeton, by chance?"

"I'm afraid not. Must've missed the day they taught us that in my *Behavioral Economics Workshop*."

"Ugh, just hearing those words almost put me to sleep." Genna laid her head back against the pillow and closed her eyes. "Most boring degree ever, Matty."

"It's not meant to be exciting," he said. "It's lucrative."

"Yeah, it certainly came in handy at the diner when you were whipping up omelets, huh? Oh, you want those eggs with a side of behavioral economics? Coming right up!"

He grinned at her sleepy tone. She could've told him she hated him and he would've smiled right through it, knowing she was so far out of it she might not remember a single word, much less mean it. "It came in handy when figuring out why you were blowing so much money fixing a car that wasn't yours."

"Oh, yeah? And why did I?"

"Because you needed to prove to yourself that you could," he said. "You were pregnant, and scared, and your life had been ripped away from you. You needed to know that you could fix something, that you could make something whole again, that you could make it beautiful, because you were going to be a mother and you needed to know that you were capable of taking care of something."

Complete silence surround them as Matty gazed only at the baby before Genna's soft voice responded, "Score one for Matty-B."

Shifting around, he looked at her... *really* looked at her. "You're going to be a great mother, Genevieve. Don't even worry. You're ready."

She smiled softly, watching him. "I'm only ready because of you, Daddy Matty."

Time passed, minutes melting away as they sat there, savoring the moment.

After exactly thirty minutes, there was a soft knock on the door and the others filtered in. Gavin grinned as he approached, his eyes on Genna. "Looking beautiful as ever, Genna with a G. You're *glowing*."

"Screw you."

Gavin laughed. "That was a compliment."

"I know," she said. "Screw you for being *nice* to me again. I don't like it."

Gavin stopped beside Matty, looking down at the baby. "Would you look at that? He's a mini Matty-B."

"My fault," Genna said, lazily lifting her hand, tugging on the IVs connected to it. "I bred with him, apparently. Should've figured those selfish Barsanti people had greedy DNA."

Matty laughed, offering the baby to his cousin. "You want to hold him?"

"Oh, hell no," Gavin said, backing away quickly. "I'm not touching that thing. If I break it, the Ice Princess will *kill* me."

Gabriella approached, shoving Gavin out of the way to take a peak, her expression lighting up. "Oh my goodness, look how precious he is!"

"Do you want to hold him? Or are you afraid of breaking him, too?"

"Oh, pfft, *please*." Gabriella took the baby from him, no hesitation. "I'm afraid of *no* human, not even the tiniest ones. I did a stint in Labor & Delivery once."

"Oh God, does that mean *you* know how to change a diaper?" Genna asked. "Because Matty's professor forgot to show him and my parents forgot I was human so I kind of lack most domestic skills."

"Of course," Gabriella said, laughing as she turned to Genna. "I'm also certified in infant CPR, so if you ever need a babysitter, I'm your gal."

"You, lady, are a fucking *Saint*." Genna's gaze scanned the room before settling over to the doorway, where Dante lurked. He just stood there, in silence, watching Gabriella. "What did I tell you, brother? Call the Pope. We've got us a winner here. You need to wife that up."

Dante turned to Genna, eyes narrowing. "Are you *high*?"

Everyone laughed, including Genna, who pointed at a bag of fluid connected to her IV. "Morphine."

Dante blinked a few times before turning back to Gabriella.

"I told you," Gabriella said, grinning as she approached him, like she knew he hadn't planned to come any closer. "That's what you get for being so stubborn."

"Family trait," Genna said, slapping Matty's back. "Isn't that right?"

"Definitely one of your *many* fine qualities," Matty said, leaning in to kiss her, but she covered her mouth.

"Ugh, gross, my mouth is all fuzzy."

Matty pulled her hand away, kissing her regardless.

"Side effect of the anesthesia," Gabriella said. "Maybe the morphine, too."

"I like the morphine," Genna said. "It makes me all floaty."

Her eyes closed, a grin still on her lips.

"So precious," Gabriella murmured, stopping in front of Dante, standing toe-to-toe. "Look at your sweet nephew, Uncle Dante."

Dante stared down at him in total silence.

"Did you want to hold him?" Gabriella asked quietly.

Dante shook his head.

"Hold my baby, Dante," Genna ordered without opening her eyes. "Don't make me get out of this bed and force him on you."

"Don't go getting your panties all twisted," Dante muttered, carefully taking the baby from Gabriella. "I'm holding him."

"*Him*," Gavin said. "Does he have a name?"

"We haven't really talked about it," Matty said. "We know what we're *not* calling him."

"Primo?" Gavin guessed. "Roberto?"

Genna waved his direction. "Ding ding."

"Gavin's a great name," Gavin said. "Means *white hawk,* which is perfect, you know. I'm white, kind of... Italian is white, right?"

"Italians are *Italian,* dipshit," Genna said. "White is a color, and you're looking more like a latte than a carton of milk over there."

"I'm a hawk, though."

"I'm not naming my son Gavin."

"Why not?"

"Because I know a Gavin and he's a pain in the ass."

"Whatever," Gavin said. "Go ahead and name him something sissy, like *Dante.* I'm sure he'll grow up to be a real winner."

"I'm not taking that bait," Dante said. "Not worth it."

"I like a couple names," Genna said. "I've kind of been digging the name Corrado."

Gavin paled. "Like in *Moretti?*"

"Yeah, why not?" Genna shrugged. "Makes me think of a sweet little boy who likes Batman and reading."

"*Or,*" Gavin said, "a not-so-sweet grown guy who likes shooting people and scaring the day lights out of everyone."

"Yeah, I don't think that's a good idea," Dante said. "Just... trust me on that. You'd be better off naming the kid Enzo."

Matty's back stiffened at the sound of that name on those lips. *Enzo.*

"Not that I'm suggesting it," Dante continued, handing the baby back to Gabriella. "I'm just saying, if you name him after someone, make it someone a *bit* more innocent."

Matty looked at Genna. They stared at each other in silence for a moment before a name seemed to click in his head. He saw it, too, as Genna's eyes widened.

"Joseph?" he suggested.

Genna smiled. "Joey."

Joey.

"Nice," Gavin said. "Now hit us with the *last* name."

Gabriella passed the still sleeping baby back to his mother.

"Do we *have* to give him a last name?" Genna asked. "Can't we Sonny & Cher that shit?"

"Why don't you hyphenate it?" Gabriella suggested. "Galante-Barsanti. He's both of you, both of those families. And separate, okay, you guys were kind of despicable, but maybe put together something good can come out of it."

"Joseph Galante-Barsanti," Genna mused, smiling down at the baby. "I can tolerate that."

Matty stared at them, feeling every inch of him warming, as he smiled. "So can I."

EPILOGUE

The air was comfortable, not a cloud in sight, as the vibrant sun lit up the bright blue sky. Peculiarly warm for a March afternoon, spring still a few days away, yet everything seemed to already want to bloom. The first inkling of it shone on the branches of the trees scattered all around, the subtle pops of green brewing as leaves started to grow. It had been a harsh winter, a fact that had nothing to do with snow. Harsh, because of the bitterness that had seized the city, because of the hurt it had caused, because of the blood that had been spilled.

A *do-over*, Gavin had once asked for. To Dante Galante, it almost felt like a *rebirth*—an ironic sensation, he thought, to feel at a funeral.

"Dad's going to haunt us for this, isn't he?" Genna asked, her incredulous voice low so not to interrupt the priest. "Like, he's seriously going to go all *Poltergeist* on our asses."

"Probably," Dante said, shrugging it off, because as far as he was concerned, his father's *final wishes* were irrelevant. They'd spent their entire lives doing the man's bidding, following his orders, putting their own needs second, and Dante refused to spend another moment of his life bowing down to Primo Galante.

The son of a bitch could haunt him if he wanted.

A joint funeral for former friends turned mortal enemies, men dead set on destroying each other facing the end together. Johnny Amaro had suggested it, a symbolic gesture putting the feud to rest once and for all.

Hundreds amassed together, a lot more than Dante had expected to come, although he suspected most weren't there to pay their respects. No, they just wanted to see the bastards put in the ground. He didn't blame them for it, but no one would get to see that part. The services were taking place on a grassy knoll along the edge of the cemetery, away from both of the families' plots, away from the wives and the sons who had lost their lives, allowing them the peace in death that life hadn't offered.

Two identical gold-toned caskets, indistinguishable, were set up in front of them, both sealed, so nobody standing there knew who was in which one, and Dante was grateful for it, because he didn't want to know. Afterward, after the crowd had gone home, they would be moved to their proper place, quietly buried with their families, but until then, it wasn't about them. No, it was about the ones they'd left behind, the ones who had survived, the ones who had suffered most at their hands.

Their children.

Dante and Matteo stood front and center of the crowd with Genna between them, a human barrier separating the two of them, as she rocked baby Joey in her arms, trying to get him to stay calm. He whimpered and whined, letting out loud cries, but Dante didn't mind. He didn't blame the kid. Hell, he'd rather have not been there, either.

"Eternal rest grant unto them, O Lord, and let perpetual light shine upon them," the priest said, making the sign of the cross over each casket. "May they rest in peace."

A chorus of "Amen" flowed through the crowd before people started to disperse, a hoard heading right for the three of them. Dante sensed it, felt it coming on like a suffocating storm, and maybe it was wrong, leaving them to fend for themselves, but he couldn't stand there another moment and pretend.

Ducking his head, Dante slipped away, passing familiar faces as he made his way through the crowd. He spotted Gabriella off to the back, surrounded by Brazzis, her parents by her side. She'd offered to be with him, to be there for him, but he hadn't wanted to draw that kind of attention to her, hadn't wanted to put that kind of pressure on her. Because as proud as he would've been to have her by his side, this was *his* burden to carry, a road he needed to cross. There were amends he needed to make for problems he had caused, and the last thing he wanted was the woman he loved having to pay for *his* mistakes.

Dante wandered away, past headstones and gravesites, through the vast cemetery, toward the road along the left side. He knew where he was going, although he'd never been there before... knew it, because he'd thought of going there a few times, but he'd never really had the courage.

He approached the area carefully, stopping short, but he stood close enough to read the headstone. *Enzo Barsanti*. He stared at it in silence for a moment before hearing noise behind him, someone's quiet approach, tiptoeing. His back stiffened before a hand ran up his spine, slipping beneath his suit coat. He closed his eyes as nails gently scratched his back.

"How do you fix something like this?" he asked.

Gabriella sighed, standing beside him, leaning her head against his shoulder. "I don't think you can. You fix what's broken, not what's lost. He's gone. You can't fix that. You can't bring him back. But you can fix yourself; you can put yourself back together and not be the person who did that anymore. And I think that's maybe the key, because you can say *sorry* until you're blue in the face, but it doesn't count until they *see* repentance."

Dante frowned. "You sure I can't just send a Hallmark card?"

Laughing, Gabriella jabbed him in the side. "Pretty friggin sure."

Dante took her hand, pulling her around in front of him. She wrapped her arms around his neck, gazing up at him with a twinkle in her soft brown eyes. Dante's hands settled on her hips as he leaned in to kiss her, barely getting a soft peck before a voice cut through the area, loud, disrupting the moment.

"Oh, come *on*! Really? You two are going to do that *here?*"

Dante cut his eyes to the right, glaring as Gavin approached.

"We weren't doing anything," Gabriella said, slipping around in front of Dante, pulling his arms around her and holding on to him.

"You were practically humping his leg on top of a grave."

"Was not."

"Was so."

A throat cleared, and Dante turned his head, tensing when he saw Matteo and Genna appear.

"It's actually 'were'," Matteo said. "Not 'was'."

"And gross," Genna said, making a face as she walked over to them. "Keep it in your pants, bro. We're at a funeral here."

"Just one minute," Dante grumbled. "*One* goddamn minute. That's all I wanted. One minute to catch my breath and be alone, and I can't even get that."

"Nope," Genna said. "And seriously, *foul*, by the way, leaving me to deal with all of those people alone."

"You weren't alone," Dante said. "You had Matteo."

As soon as he said that, every eye in the area settled on him, shocked expressions crossing faces. He looked around at all of them, brow furrowing. *What the fuck?*

"Did you just...?" Gabriella asked, looking back at him.

"Did I *what*?" he asked.

"Bequeath Genna with a G to Matty-B," Gavin chimed in.

Dante scoffed but didn't have a chance to respond before Genna groaned. "*Bequeath*, Gavin? What am I, an inheritance?"

"I like to think of you more like a debt, personally," Gavin said. "Like that hospital bill we all know we have somewhere but nobody ever wants to pay, because it's a lot of damn money for something that ought to be free."

Those two bickered back and forth for a moment as Matteo stood silently, gazing past Dante, his eyes fixed to the graves nearby, to where his mother and brother were buried, to where his father would, not long from then, come to rest. Guilt festered inside of Dante, nearly spilling from his lips, but he swallowed it back, knowing if the roles were reversed, Dante wouldn't want to hear it. Not then. Not there. Maybe someday, some other place, but not in that moment. A bullshit word like *'sorry'* wouldn't be enough. Gabriella had been right about that.

Someday, he'd find a way to make amends, but until then...

"Well, this was fun and all, but this beautiful woman and I are going to take our leave now," Dante said, tugging Gabriella with him as he took a few steps away.

"What?" Gavin asked. "Where are you going?"

"Somewhere you're not," Dante answered, looking back at him. "Look, G... it's not you, it's me. I need some space. But don't give up hope, you know, because I'm sure there's somebody out there for you, but that somebody's not me. I need a break from these fucked up *family reunions* we keep having."

Although he flipped him off, Gavin cracked a smile at that.

Dante turned, his arm around Gabriella, pulling her closer to him as they walked away, hearing Gavin's voice call out behind them: "Dear Diary, today I learned that Dante Galante wasn't just my friend, he was a part of my family, too. And I've gotta tell you... I think I might be better off for it."

Acknowledgements

First and foremost, I need to thank everyone who emailed me, tracked me down on social media, or approached me at book signings to ask where the f*%k the sequel I promised you was. Honestly, this book wouldn't exist without your persistence. I started and stopped this story probably a dozen times. I scrapped tens of thousands of words more than once to start over with a blank page. Something just didn't feel 'right' to me, and I couldn't put out a story that in my gut I knew was 'wrong' in some way. It took over a year, but here it finally is, and I owe that to you. Thank you for never giving up on Matty-B.

To Sarah Anderson, who never once doubted I'd finish this thing, even though I repeatedly said it just wasn't happening. Thank you for letting me borrow Doris at the diner! To Nicki Bullard, my best friend, who (more than once) cleaned my house because I got lost in a writing haze and things went to hell all around me. Seriously, I don't know what I'd do without you.

To my family (especially my dad, who reads all my books, even if he probably wishes he could *unread* some of those crazy things I've written). I love you.

Cynthia Rodriguez, my fellow Marvel-loving friend, thank you for being such a genuinely amazing person (and for texting me to remind me when I was supposed to be writing). I really wish I could insert a bitmoji here.

Special thanks to Nikki Cook, who was kind enough to let me pick her brain with my nursing questions. I likely screwed it all up, but your explanations helped immensely!

So much love and gratitude to the super talented Shauna Kruse for the amazing cover photo, and to the stunning Michael Fagone for lending that gorgeous smile! I couldn't have imagined a more perfect "Dante".

Made in the USA
Middletown, DE
14 September 2016